GIDON

THE LEGEND BEGINS

A SAGA OF PARALLEL EARTH

DR. MICHAEL L. FORD

ISBN 978-1-63874-947-9 (paperback)
ISBN 978-1-63874-948-6 (digital)

Christian Faith Publishing
832 Park Avenue
Meadville, PA 16335
www.christianfaithpublishing.com

Printed in the United States of America

Dr. Warren's Recommendation for Dr. Ford's novel.

I have known Dr. Ford for over 25 years. I have always respected him as a military veteran and as a scholar of the Bible, especially Bible Prophecy and as a teacher and counselor. I consider him to be a special friend.

The book demonstrates Dr. Ford's vast knowledge and creativity as he develops the characters, especially the wise women such as Brunhild (The mistress of Gid-visu), Oma the wife of Fat Max, and Lady Dolores the chaperone of Princess Loretta. Further the development of the fictional kings of that day and time and the prophet of the time shows Dr. Ford's skill to hold the attention of the reader.

I highly recommend this book as an illustration of the ongoing battle between good and evil. This book is a fantastic read for anyone interested in both the Old Testament times and a good fantasy mystery.

Rev. Prof. Ray Warren, Ph.D.
Senior Faculty Adviser
Covington Theological Seminary

Dedication

To the Invisible yet Triune GOD

In whom I live and move and have my being, who has preserved me for the writing of this work, for purposes I do not know.

And to my faithful wife of fifty-one years

Beverly Kaye Dukes Ford

Who through the years I have known her, has contributed greatly to my ideas on women of wisdom.

Also, I must mention

Abby Myers

She is the one who gave me the character of Brigitta and patiently repeated hand gestures and other actions that brought concepts of feminine movement into my mind.

No page dedicatory would be complete

without mentioning my mother

Mary Ella Pate Ford

First among women, now with the LORD, and my first ideal of womanhood.

And in conclusion, I mention by name my father

Harest Lendon Ford

Though I have lived my life among heroes of our Age, he remains the bravest man I have ever known. He is the person from which the main of my heroes in the book are modeled.

Finally remain the unnamed persons

Some whose names I never learned

Who contributed by the experiences of life they gave me.

Preface

This book has a premise rooted in both scientific speculation and the Holy Bible.

A little explanation is in order to explain what I mean.

The Hebrew scholar Nachmonides (1194-1270) whose actual name was Moses ben Nahman, though he was also known as the Rambam, can number among his multitude of accomplishments the formulating of the idea we live in ten dimensions, which put him about seven hundred years ahead of Particle Physicists. He derived his idea of ten dimensions from the study of Genesis.

It could be said that Nachmonides was only partially correct in his ideas on the ten dimensions because he said that for us only four dimensions are knowable and six are unknowable. But that really depends on what you mean by knowable. We are continually aware of the three spatial dimensions and time. The remaining six are referred to as "curled" into a very small area called a Planck length. As such it is outside the normal human senses and only inferable by indirect means.

One of the realizations I came to in high school science was that when we look out beyond our own galaxy, we discover from our privileged position in The Creation a multitude of galaxies outside of our own. And when we take our microscopes and look inward, we find very much the same thing. Neither looking outward or inward do we find an infinite Creation. Both are finite. But what we see and understand as finite is still filled with wonder God intended for us to discover.

One of the interesting ideas to come along is that, even as we have dimensions beyond the range of our senses, we also live in a multiverse. In short, some physicists have developed theories about parallel universes that exist just outside the realm of our senses. Some have developed models that make this idea more likely than not. I do not know if they are right or not, but it makes an interesting idea to play with. Which thing I have done in conceiving this series of books with a higher purpose in mind.

The whole idea of parallel universes, the big, is dependent on Quanta Theory, the little.

It is the world of subatomic particles that suggests the existence of parallel universes. Unlike many who play with this idea, I think that if parallel universes do exist, they would not be infinite, but rather finite, for the reason Creation has both a beginning and an ending.

As the galaxies, including our own, are relatively flat, so are our concepts of reality. It is my idea that parallel universes would be rather flat copies of our own with but a little variation, yet still bound by laws of physics we do not entirely understand. Therefore, in any world like our world in a parallel universe, there would essentially exist the same thing with minor deviations that would make that world and those within it unique. You would not find a carbon copy of yourself but someone very much like you.

This minor variation between theoretical parallel universes is why I can play with geography and topography, as well as some language and custom in the parallel world of my invention, and still speak to moral and ethical (biblical) issues pertinent to the world we live in.

Perhaps in coming books in this saga I shall be able to expand on the subject covered in this preface. It is my hope you will find it interesting enough to want to read farther.

Introduction

In 1884, Edwin Abbott (1838-1926) wrote *Flatland: A Romance of Many Dimensions*, which has been characterized as science fiction though some sources did acknowledge it as being more accurately mathematical fiction. Though this work regained popularity among science fiction buffs in the 1950's it was not until near the end of the twentieth century theologians began to pick up on his description of two dimensional creatures and how they might perceive people who are at time called three dimensional and relate that to how we might perceive God who exists in more dimensions than we are even now presently aware of.

Newborn babies are aware of three dimensions, the length, width, and depth of their existence. This knowledge comes from their struggles in the womb. It takes further development of the brain during childhood development to make them cognizant in some degree of a fourth dimension we call time. It took a Greek philosopher named Euclid (330-275 B.C.) to put the fact of our physical existence into a mathematical expression we call plane geometry. And as is far too often the case, Aristotle and Ptolemy came along to prove that any more than three dimensions was impossible, another of those erroneous ideas that went unchallenged because of the reputation of the sources. In this case the idea stood for well over a millennium.

Nachmanides (A.D. 1194-1270) also known as "the Ramban" believed "in the Torah (first five books of the Bible) are hidden every wonder and every mystery, and in her treasures is sealed every beauty of wisdom." To him, after years of study in the Book of Genesis, he discovered in Scripture's hidden messages information that our universe had not less than ten dimensions. People have a tendency to denigrate the workings of the minds and research of theologians, but the truth is today it is quite easy to demonstrate mathematically ten possible dimensions even though our awareness of them with our physical senses is quite limited just as the newborn baby has little conception of time even though his very first lesson in time was when he got hungry.

There are a lot of things we do not understand. Not only are we ignorant about the world we live in but about the entire relationship of Creation itself. For instance, our natural senses perceive time as a straight line beginning at birth and ending in death. But we know time existed before our births and in all likelihood will continue after we have long returned to dust. Yet the Bible tells us of an eternity before time as well as continuance when time shall be no more, so time itself is like a comma in eternity. We get some perception of this in the writings of people, inspired by the Creator, who exists outside of time, when He allows these men to see the future. In short, while Euclid's plane geometry leads us to suppose the shortest distance between two points is a straight line, the very action of inspired seers seeing the future and correctly foretelling it proves the shortest distance between two points in certain dimensions, like time, is not necessarily a straight line. A hundred years before Einstein the son of a Lutheran pastor, who happened to be a theologian and mathematician, figured that out.

It would be possible to continue in this vein to demonstrate some very interesting things that have come into the world of hypothetical possibilities concerning reality in the last century especially with the development of quantum theory. Every time I learn a bit more on the subject my amazement grows. There are people of science who now not only talk in terms of dimensions but even parallel universes that in terms of dimension we might explain by saying they exist alongside one another. It is in the spirit of such possibilities this book about people in a parallel earth is written.

In this parallel earth things are very similar to our earth. However sometimes slight differences do exist in geography, geology, and even historical progression. In this parallel world the time period encompasses many things related to our own world between 300 and 1500 A.D. and that is a lot of time. The people you will find are very similar to people we find in our own world in any generation. The principle character around which our observation of this earth is focused is a young man named Gidon. He experiences the end of boyhood and the entrance into full manhood at the age of sixteen as we observe what he does.

Each of the persons you will learn about in the book has free will. They choose how they act and react, each consistent with background and the values they place upon the things in their lives. I have learned a lot from watching them and considering the reasons for their actions. Most of them are quite likable and you can have good emotional feelings toward them even when you do not necessarily approve of their actions or decisions.

Because this is a parallel world the people are composites of persons you might find in our world. It is just possible as you experience these people and watch their lives progress, you might even find someone very much like yourself.

Chapter 1

The King's Rider

It was not yet evening, but Gidon was certain the men breaking ground for spring planting would competently continue going about their day's business. So he decided to do other things. Land was something his father Gid-visu had added to his interests as Gidon's sixteenth birthday approached. Gidon knew his father had the objective of building security for his son. That is, however much it was possible in this troubled world. Gidon thought of himself as his father's only son, but these were words never to be uttered openly. They would bring up very painful memories of loss for Gid-visu. And Gidon loved his father deeply.

Gidon was always glad to get to the tavern early. Ever since he was able to walk it was one of his favorite haunts. It was fun to watch and listen when the occasional traveler passed through. But the best thing of all was Fat Max, the tavern keeper. When no one else was around Fat Max would tell him stories about his father; about the history of the village, and sometimes he would gossip in all confidence about people now living in Eastwatch. But Fat Max usually did not have anything bad to say about people even in his gossip. Now, since Gidon's mother had died, his father had bought half the tavern. They took the bulk of their meals there, lingering especially during the winter to talk and listen to people.

Last fall, Gid-visu decided not to take to the forests anymore when the days were coldest and furs prime. Age catches up with all and it was said he was over three hundred years old.

The tavern sign, featuring a stag and beer tankard, was just coming in view when he saw Herman the Schmeid had seen him and was heading his way. Gidon groaned inwardly. He really did not want to talk to him. When the village smith had died suddenly, Gid-visu had sent out a call looking for young apprentices that might be elevated to take his place. Herman the Hammer, whose business was in a nearby hamlet with the unremarkable name of Kleines Dorf, had offered to sell one of his apprentices, also named Herman.

Both were named after that great chieftain, Herman the Cheruscan Prince. Herman was the son of Segimerus, a leader of the Cheruscans, part of the southern tribes of Gomer. Perhaps Segimerus had named his son Herman because it meant "man of war" and men of war were needed. People often named one of their children Herman because Prince Herman had led the united tribes against invaders from the distant South giving them their greatest defeat. These southern invaders were the product of their first chieftains Remus and Romulus who were said to have been raised by wolves.

Gidon resolved he would never name one of his children Herman because he had not seen a Herman yet he liked. And now he had to stop and talk to this one. It was not that Herman the Schmeid was not competent enough to make nails or hinges and other stuff. He could set a horseshoe as well as anyone. But at the finer skills of the blacksmith trade he seemed unable to do anything well. No wonder Herman the Hammer was willing to sell the indenture to his father. Oh, this schmeid kept the stables and did other small things as well, but Gidon thought him really stupid and boring.

"Gidon, I need you to tell me what to do," were the first words out of Herman the Schmeid's mouth.

"What is the problem?" Gidon said in a tone letting him know he did not wish to linger.

"A King's Rider has come to town with his warhorse and a huge pack horse."

Gidon loved the big warhorses that could be so gentle to be around, yet he had heard how their character was transformed in battle. "How big was his schlachtross?"

"More than eighteen hands and a chest like a barrel!" said Herman.

The conversation had just gotten interesting but Gidon was not going to let on too much that Herman had piqued his interest. "So what is the problem?"

"The Rider said, 'Take care of my horses', but he did not tell me what to do."

Once again Herman the Schmeid had lived up to Gidon's opinion of him. "You give them both the finest feed you have and put them in clean stalls. Then you curry and brush them both till they gleam. You make sure that all their shoes are in good shape and clean their hooves. Then you will clean the bridle, saddle, and halter of the animals making sure nothing needs mending."

Herman complained, "That may take all night."

"Well then, you better get back to the stable and get on with it,' Gidon said with just a hint of cool unconcern in his voice.

When Herman walked away like someone overwhelmed, it was all Gidon could do to keep from laughing out loud. But he would like to see the horses. One of the kings, and he was not sure how long ago, had fought with wild men called Symmachians. They believed the devil had created the flesh of men so there was no atrocity they could not do to others. But they bred very fine horses. The story was that while that ancient king had not fully defeated those people in battle, he had caused them so much damage they were convinced not to come eastward into this kingdom again. And he had captured some magnificent horses whose bloodlines still flowed through the horseflesh of Alemanni steeds. Yes, he would like to see the horses but he wanted to see the Rider more.

The little village square with its central well stood alone this time of day. It marked the central point from which the village began centuries earlier. Women still came early and late to draw water from the old well. It was easy to cross with no one to strike up conversation at this time of day. He entered the tavern with no further delays.

Even with the windows thrown open to allow in the fresh spring air it was almost possible for the casual patron to miss the dark figure positioned at a table in the farthest corner. Even the chainmail which covered the woolen inner garment appeared dark as he sat with the metal rings partially hidden by a long dark cloak. While the corner had a slight shadow anyway it seemed the man at the table with his back in the corner somehow made it darker.

Gidon made his way to the left and the counter behind which Fat Max stood, all the time trying to take in all he could about the Rider. He leaned his staff against the wall where he would stand. He tried to make it look like he was looking at Fat Max, but was all the time watching the Rider. Gidon wanted to learn all he could about his visitor. It was also clear to Gidon the man was taking in everything about his surroundings, Gidon in particular.

What Gidon saw was a man who, when he stood up, would nearly touch the ceiling. It was probably seven feet from floor to ceiling and that was quite a respectable height in a world where many were barely five feet or perhaps a little more. This man had to be well over six feet. He was lean and strong. Gidon imagined he could swing the double-edged long sword he had leaned against the wall within comfortable reach quite handily. The expressionless way he set his face and the steeliness of his eyes was a look he had seen before in men who made a living of warfare. It was the look of the professional soldier, and Gidon knew from the many stories he had heard about King's Riders they were very capable for battle, be it single combat or an overwhelming gang of ruffians.

Gidon knew there were two kinds of Riders for the king. The first were simply called King's Riders. The second were called Long Riders. Like every boy in the kingdom he had grown up with stories about King's Riders and pretended to be one with his friends. The King's Riders usually traveled alone within the kingdom carrying messages from the king to the elders of the towns and villages. But they were not mere messengers. King's Riders would be the ones who would hunt down malefactors and dispense the king's justice when local authority failed. They had their fingers on the pulse of the kingdom and they spoke in the name of the king.

The Long Riders often traveled into other kingdoms, sometimes escorting dignitaries representing the king. When traveling without an obvious mission they often gave it out they were involved in quests as they observed what other kingdoms were about. It was of these men you often heard stories of the slaying of dragons and rescuing maidens who were always of great beauty. They usually traveled more heavily armored than the King's Riders with a squire and other attendees such as men at arms. They were usually more ostentatious in their display of wealth, while King's Riders appeared to live quite simply. King's Riders did not usually live to grow old and retire from the work. Yet, every child dreamed of being one. Most people did not travel far from their own village, if not called to war. Gidon had seldom seen a Long Rider since his village was away from most travel routes. The times he had seen a King's Rider he could probably count on one hand. He had seen warhorses because his father had a friend, Herr Tweitman, who raised and trained them. But his lands were three days travel and such a trip was rare.

"Hi Gidon, I was not expecting you so early," Fat Max said.

Gidon was aware the King's Rider was watching him intently. Gidon believed he probably thought a person so young being at a tavern this early was on his way to being a lush and ne'er do well. Gidon had forgotten it was not the average lush that would be carrying a fighting staff with a carved fist at its top or wearing so fine a knife in his belt. He explained his purpose more loudly than necessary, "I thought I would come by and see if you needed any help with accounts." The reason Fat Max had agreed to make his father a partner was, even though he operated a great tavern, he sometimes had problems paying the people who sold him his supplies. As Max had gotten older, he had lost interest in that part of his business. And Gid-visu had made Gidon responsible for making sure that, while most creditors were paid on delivery, all were paid as agreed.

Fat Max lowered his voice. "You see our guest." It was more a statement than a question.

Gidon gave a slight nod.

"I wonder what is wrong?"

Gidon gave a slighter shrug intending the communication not to be perceptible to the King's Rider.

"He asked about your father as soon as he came in. Gidon felt a slight tremor run through his body. "I think we are going to war again," Fat Max opined.

Both Gidon and Fat Max were looking at the Rider who was looking back with no expression on his face.

"Father and the king are friends." Gidon wondered on the strange relationship of these two men of different stations in life. While Gid-visu had been to war three times in Gidon's lifetime, just fighting in a king's wars did not automatically make you the friend of a king. Granted Gid-visu was renowned as a bowmaker, a skill valuable to a king, but even that would not draw the friendship of a king, so it was another layer of mystery surrounding a father who seemed filled with mysteries.

Both Gidon and Fat Max knew the bows and arrows Gid-visu had been manufacturing during the last three winters were not being made for hunting. This very day, the man had spent much of his workday producing well balanced arrow tips designed to penetrate chainmail and armor, one of those jobs not trusted to Herman the Schmeid. The balance of the points on the end of an arrow shaft may determine whether an arrow flies true to its intended target or not.

Gid-visu had the reputation as the finest bowman and bow maker in all of Aleman. Men traveled great distances to get one of his bows. From start to finish the finest of his products took a full year to make. And Gid-visu had been known to burn any that did not meet his standard. When bows were made to order, they were custom designed for the individual. And even those made without an order were each a unique product that conformed to the best attributes of the wood and other materials he used to make them. On his own, fifty bows were all Gid-visu could make in a year not counting special orders. As Gidon became old enough to learn and help in the shop he had been able to make a few more. For one of Gid-visu's custom made bows it was not uncommon for a man to pay a year's income. For the last three years all the bows Gid-visu had made he had refused to sell. That is, except for special orders. It was the special orders that helped finance his other interests in life, or so everyone thought.

Bring me another mead," the Rider ordered. He was a man used to being obeyed.

Fat Max was well known for his mead made from aged rainwater mixed with honey and beer yeast. Many had spied on him trying to learn the secret of his mead, the secret that made his better than that in any town near and far. Discovering he let it stay in the sun forty days was easy. But the secret ingredient he added was something they all had failed to uncover. None knew he added the residue from wine made by nearby monks. That was what made his mead different and more satisfying than others produced round about.

Fat Max called for a red-hot poker from the kitchen and thrust it into the tankard of mead, heating it. He then delivered it to the Rider's table. The soothing warmth would work its magic on the weariest of travelers and workmen. Even so the King's Rider only allowed himself to go so far in relaxing his state of vigilance.

He looked at Gidon with that cold stare that seemed to see through a person. "Your name would be Gidon."

Gidon looked back and said, "How did you know?"

The Rider pointed at the knife at his side, not mentioning he had heard Fat Max greet him.

"It is a good knife but how did that tell you who I am?" Gidon was confused at how he could tell his name from a knife.

"We heard of the incident with the supposed robbers last Fall. I see you have the knife of a man we had been interested in. The question is if what we heard about how you got it true or not?"

Gidon's discomfort and confusion exposed itself in a return that was a bit testy. "I don't know what you have heard. But what is it to you?"

"I am Chief of the Long Knives, and the truth about that encounter as well as what you know and do not know is important to us."

The Rider stated the situation so matter of factly and coldly it almost made Gidon's blood run cold. The Long Knives were an order of master fighters who excelled in all weapons, and even unarmed combat against armed opponents. It was the first time he ever considered such men would be among the King's Riders but now the reality was staring him in the face. The really bothersome thing was the Long Knives believed the knowledge of weapons and fighting techniques should be very limited outside those who were professional fighters. It was troublesome that these men would be concerned with him. And now here he was talking with the man who said he was their chief.

"Why did you come for me?"

"I did not come for you. I have king's business with your father and the other village elders. You need to have a little humility. The king's business gave me an opportunity to look you over and find out if the story was real or not. If we were concerned about you, we would have been here long before now."

Gidon felt a strong sense of relief. He would not care to be on the bad side of the Long Knives or with the King's Riders either for that matter. And this man was both.

They had scarcely finished the conversation when Fat Max's wife entered the room. She was carrying a fragrant hot bun fresh from the oven and a huge slab of venison and cheese. The odor filled the room and made palates water. Though she was much shorter than Fat Max she was just as wide and moved with a grace only seldom seen in large women. As she sat the plate in front of the King's Rider she hollered "Haki! Poppa, our little Haki has come home!"

Before anyone could say a word or make a move, she had grabbed the Rider's head and buried it in her ample bosom. Gidon expected a violent reaction from the man, but instead he stood up towering over the woman. He wrapped his long powerful arms about her and squeezed her to him, kissing her on the head. "Oma, how I have missed you! It has been more than twenty years. Tell me how did you recognize me?"

"Haki, I love you like I loved my own children. How could I not recognize you?"

Fat Max explained to Gidon that Haki was one of the children born to the garrison that was once stationed outside the village for protection against invaders back in the days when danger would come from beyond the mountains and through the Giant's Gap to their East. His children had played with the soldier's children before the troops reposted to another location. It did not seem to bother him at all that his wife had recognized the boy grown up and he did not.

"How is your momma and poppa Haki?" It was a typical thing for a woman to ask about missing acquaintances.

"My father is dead. He fell in battle against the false king Goraleck ten years ago. Mother lives outside the king's castle in Almanya where fallen officer's wives now go. The king has provided they should be cared for and protected from any who might seek retribution because of their husbands." Gidon thought that might have been the longest conversation the King's Rider had carried on with anyone for some time. He was sure that personal information was not something he ordinarily gave out. But he addressed Fat Max's wife as if she were his own grandmother and had every right to make demands of him. She had treated him with that same sense of loving authority also.

Gidon did not know much about the business of the king, but he did know kings providing for the widows of their officers was a very uncommon thing. When the present king's father had become a follower of the One God, who is invisible, the atmosphere of the kingdom had changed. It probably seemed strange to many peoples round about who still worshipped the old gods but many often remarked how much better it was to be an Alemanni than a resident of one of the surrounding nations.

It was also strange for a father to put his son on the throne while he still lived and was not infirm. But the old king now spent much of his time studying with the priests of the new God, who while invisible had a Son, but one who promoted love without debauchery. Gidon thought it very strange compared to the old religions. He had learned much about it from the chief priest, called Bishop Elisha, who was in charge of the other priests occupying the old military fort outside the village. They had turned it into a monastery within months of the soldiers departing many years ago. It was, Gidon thought, turning into a very interesting afternoon.

The chief priest at the fort was the same one his father paid to teach Gidon to read and write as well as work with numbers. This made him more accomplished than many nobles of the day. But his tutor had not been satisfied with just the basics. He had drilled much more into his head from the time Gidon was very small. The lessons would go on for hours, and especially on the days when the land was blanketed with so many feet of snow even short trips were impossible. One of the things the priest taught him was about the conversion of the old king, named Gregor the First.

When that king was still a young man, but already getting a reputation, not only for fierceness in battle, but also the skill with which he planned military operations and carried them out, an event occurred that changed his life. During a patrol along part of the southern border, his troops had captured a priest from very far away who claimed his God had sent him specifically to the land of the Alemanni. This priest had told Gregor that one day he would be king, and that if he worshipped his God and no other, he and the kingdom would be blessed. This news had not been well received at all by Gregor for he had two brothers older than he. They had always been close and news of such a prophecy could create dangerous divisions in the family. It could even cause the older to try and kill the younger out of fear.

The threat of brothers trying to overthrow brothers had been the cause of much fratricide in ruling families down through history. But when Gregor's oldest brother died in battle and the second brother succumbed to an infection, he suddenly found himself King of the Alemanni. This and notable adventures that seemed to have miraculous outcomes caused King Gregor to not only profess his allegiance to The Invisible God but to desire to study the principles of the faith.

One of the teachings of this first missionary priest concerned King Gregor's name. His name had the double meaning of "watchful" and "vigilant." The priest told him that the Invisible God gave men He favored their names. The name Gregor, he was told, occurred in various forms in many lands and tongues because his God wanted all men to be watchful and vigilant according to the station in life they were destined to. In the king's case, he was to be watchful and vigilant so the land was protected against enemies and the wellbeing of his subjects pursued. To the king's crest, Gregor the First was inspired to add the three-word motto "Watchful, Vigilant, Faithful." Gidon's tutor used his teaching on the king's name to inform him his own name had a meaning which was "he who cuts down." When Gidon had questioned what that portended for his own life's purpose the priest told him he would have to wait and one day he would understand.

Gregor the Second was literally schooled in the new religion from the time he could talk. He was also sincere in the faith like his father but at times seemed to compromise his beliefs. Many attributed his wavering to the influences of people such as a wizard brought into his council to serve the king. Wizards, once common place among the Alemanni, were so rare since the coming of the Invisible God that the only one who showed himself was Zauberer the Wise, who it was said had gone by many names as he traveled both through the world and time. Gidon had no idea how much of a role the wizard would one day play in his own life.

Gidon realized he had become lost in thought when his father Gid-visu entered the room and Fat Max called out a welcome. Several patrons had come in and two of the elders were now seated at the special table reserved for them. The table was distinguished because it was partitioned by a single half wall separating it from people entering the tavern. The table was near the fireplace centrally located next to the far wall opposite from Fat Max's counter. The partition allowed light from the front windows while at the same time making a barrier against other people first entering the room. In harsher days this arrangement was sometimes a means of defense against enemies.

The wall where the notables seated themselves was decorated, almost cluttered, with the relics of past accomplishments that brought prestige not only to them and those long dead, but by extension the very village itself. Gid-visu had a welcome seat at that table but on this evening, he walked all the way across the room to where the King's Rider was positioned.

Once again Gidon was embarrassed by the very thing his father was constantly cautioning against. He often got so deep into his own thoughts he lost awareness of what was going on about him. It was a dangerous thing to do, Gid-visu constantly warned. He hoped that his distraction had not been noted, but deep inside he knew his father had not missed a thing.

It had been a surprise when Gidon's father walked across the room straight to the King's Rider. It was doubly so for they greeted one another with the warmth and friendship of brothers in arms long separated. And when they seated themselves, it was side by side as men who would talk confidentially and still watch the room together. How did his father know this man?

Watching his father, Gid-visu, and the King's Rider, the legendary Chief of the Long Knives, as they talked intently, was a new and interesting experience. At one point the Rider pulled a parchment almost magically from his garment. It appeared some kind of document from across the room. Then he pulled another item which appeared to be a map on a fine skin called vellum. Gidon could not tell what it was a map of. He did suspect it was an area he did not know since the forests eastward of his home were the only places his father had ever taken him. It was one more thing he had to wonder about. Then there was also the question of why the King's Rider and his father both looked up at him occasionally while they were talking about whatever it was?

By the time his father gestured to Gidon to join the two of them the materials were safely hidden away and he correctly supposed that though they had looked at him while pondering over the map the subject of what was on it was not going to be shared with him, at least not now.

"Gidon, this is Baron von Krieg." This introduction told Gidon a lot more about the man he had spent two hours studying and thinking about. The title Baron was not given an Alemanni unless it was earned by being distinguished in war. Krieg was not a place but the subject of war itself. Here was a fearsome man indeed. A man, who at present had no permanent home. Everything he learned about him bespoke a man whose entire purpose in life was focused around the subject of warfare and conflict.

Gid-visu continued, "He wishes to ask you some questions about the two robbers you surprised in our camp last fall."

"First tell me your story in your own words." Baron von Krieg said. When such words came out of this man's lips it was as much a command as an instruction.

Gidon chose his words carefully: "Father had sent me looking for stones of value in a secret place he knew while he searched for seasonal herbs needed by the apothecary. I found some Sorcerer's Stone prized by alchemists and others and was bringing it back to camp when I caught the movement of two men. I thought they were looking to steal our furs but, after watching them a few minutes, I thought they were trying to see the best places they could position themselves to watch us when we were in the camp.

"I supposed they planned to wait to steal all they could after we had completed our work. I stepped into the campsite, thinking to run them off. After all, I am bigger than most men. I thought it would be easy, but they did not run. The larger man came at me with the knife I now wear on my side in his right hand. He tried to thrust upwards into my heart but I sidestepped him and caught his upper arm with my left hand and pinned his lower arm with my arm while I thrust my knife into him with the same move he had tried to use on me. The other man ran, instead of attacking for some reason, and that is about it."

"That is a pretty good report," said the Baron. "But your assumptions were all wrong."

Gidon saw a hint of a prideful smile on his father's face and could have sworn that just for a moment a wry grin passed across the face of the man whose business was so consumed with death. Gidon said nothing, waiting for an explanation.

"The first question you should ask yourself is what a common robber would be doing with a knife so fine as the one you now have on your belt? I am surprised my friend did not tell you a little of the situation."

Gid-visu now responded, "I did not think my son would be in any danger in time to come since I was obviously the target. So I saw no purpose in causing him to be obsessed about this."

Gidon wondered how his father knew this and had kept it to himself for so many months? But he knew the best thing he could do if he did not wish to seem foolish was to be quiet and wait on these men to speak. He was again the attention of the Baron.

"Did the man also have a sword made of the same quality steel, perhaps with a matching grip and pommel of one piece like your knife? Does the blade have the inside of the curve sharpened instead of the outside?"

Gidon nodded, afraid to speak in his confusion.

"Where is it?"

"It is in my room at home, Baron Long Knife." Gidon immediately grimaced in embarrassment at his error in addressing the man. But both his father and the Baron seemed to find it immensely funny.

"Why are you not carrying it? I would think a young man such as yourself would want to show it off."

"My father taught me long ago that no man should carry a weapon he is not adept at using. It is likely to get him killed." Gidon said, grateful he had not succumbed to the temptation.

Gid-visu then said, "I cleansed the blade lest it had been treated with poison."

The Baron nodded appreciatively and again turned his attention to Gidon. "You did notice the blade is sharpened on the reverse of the curve? This blade was developed from a harvesting tool. It is called a Yataghan and is now favored among a secret society of assassins far to the East. If you want to get a feel for the blade use it to cut grain sheaves at harvest time. That is, if you are home for harvest."

Gidon asked, "What was your second question?"

"The second man who ran; how was he dressed?"

"He was dressed in Woodland Green like myself. I had expected him to attack, but when he ran instead my first impulse was to follow. But my knife was caught in the man I had just killed. So by the time I had tried to get it out; then picked up the other man's knife, he had already put some distance between me and him. It had not occurred to me he was an assassin."

The Long Rider said, "He was not an assassin. Only the first man was. He was probably a hunter who had been hired as a spy, then used as a guide to take the assassin to your camp.

Without waiting for Gidon to ask the Baron continued, "Now my third question. Since you have the assassin's knife at your side, where is your old knife?"

Gidon replied, "I made a new scabbard for the knife so it attached behind my back on my belt. That way I can reach behind me and pull it out should I ever need a second knife again."

Baron von Krieg spoke to Gid-visu, "Your son has the makings of a fine man at arms. He will be my squire on the way to the king's palace and I will begin his education."

That declaration was not how Gidon had intended to spend his summer for he thought this would be the year his father would select a wife for him to marry in the fall. But he knew the inevitability and honor involved in what the Baron was doing. It could scarcely be a better situation for him under the circumstances.

Baron von Krieg reached down and picked up a leather pouch at his feet. He pulled from it a green tunic with the Alemanni king's crest over the heart area. It was made to simply put on over the head and be open at the sides so not to restrict movement. The tunic was designed to be held together by an equipment belt such as what currently held Gidon's knives in place. The crest had a black eagle with two heads looking in opposite directions indicating the king was over both the religion and the state. The background was a deep red signifying the blood of those who gave all for their country and religion. The crest was in the shape of a shield formed by a golden outline signifying the kingdom itself. A banner went across the shield below the eagle with the words "Watchful, Vigilant, Faithful." Over the abdominal area of the tunic was a silver long sword with the point down so it was like a sword used as a crucifix and to either side there was a dagger with their points up. This was the symbol of the Baron himself, and testified to his mission to defend the kingdom. He handed the tunic to Gidon.

"When we meet with the elders shortly it will be your job to stand behind the chairs of your father and myself. You should watch the room constantly to be ready to warn us of danger while at the same time listening to all that is said without uttering a word. You will find this is not as easy as it sounds but you can do it. It is your first assignment as the squire of Baron von Krieg! Now put your tunic on."

As Gidon stood before them and loosed his belt, laying it on the table, he was aware one of the widowed daughters-in-law of Fat Max, Brunhild, was standing in the doorway to the kitchen passage. She called the other widowed daughter in law, Gwynedd, to come and watch. He was often aware of them watching his father since their husbands had died in the last war. No doubt both had set their eye on becoming Gid-visu's wife even though they appeared a third his age. Yet tonight, they had taken occasion to watch both him and the King's Rider as well. Now he, Gidon, had become the object of attention even though the youngest of them was at least four years older than he was. He felt both a mixture of pride and embarrassment as he slid the tunic over his head and buckled his belt around this symbol of his rise in status.

The Baron then said, "You and I will be traveling with your father to Almanya the city of King Gregor. As we go, I will be training you, and then after we arrive you will continue your training with many teachers. We can never say what may occur in our time in this world, but if you live, I promise you will have an interesting life."

Chapter 2

Gidon the Squire

Morning came early for Gidon. The meeting of the elders lasted far into the night. As Baron von Krieg explained to the elders of Eastwatch by the Rising of Little Dan, King Gregor II was merely calling in his army, both those who had been to war and those who had come of age since the last war. A mustering without war was something never before done. Each man was going to spend a month of intensive training. No men of an age to fight would be excluded in the hope the next war would result in fewer men dying in battle.

The elders had been hearing from the few travelers that came through Eastwatch Goraleck was causing trouble in the West once more. They of course had presumed they were going to be called on to defend the country once again. The Baron did not tell them King Gregor hoped to hold Goraleck in check with larger, more powerful, and better trained forces. Such ideas would not have meant much to men whose daily concerns were on more mundane things. But the idea of fewer dying in the wars was a welcome thing for the sorrows of war tended to reach into every family.

Goraleck held more land than all the other lords who had once considered themselves kings before the Alemanni had become nominally united. Not only that, he had very rich lands with many waterways. That was Goraleck's problem and also his strength. The Northmen were not at all opposed to bringing their shallow draft dragon ships up the same streams and rivers for their ravaging and raping. This meant Goraleck had to keep fighting forces at the alert. And it assured his standing army was accustomed to combat against the fiercest of fighters. Most of the Alemanni who were faithful to King Gregor believed it was not a matter of *if* they would go to war, only *when* they would go to war.

Gidon had found it truly was difficult and exhausting to keep a watch on the room noting who came in and went out, and also pay attention to the conversation at the elders' table. It did not help that they spoke in low tones, so others moving about could not easily hear. He almost missed that he was volunteered when it came down to dividing among them whose sons would be sent to which outlying farms and hovels. It had quickly emerged no one wanted to send their son out to call Herman One Eye and six of his sons to come to the registration. There were also the decisions about which men of reputation should be chosen to travel to communities within a day's ride or more to start the chain of sign ups and call ups round about.

Gidon had not been thrilled when Baron von Krieg said, "With Gid-visu's permission, we should send my squire to Herman One Eye" Had he not been so unhappy at the prospect of going to talk to Herman One Eye he would have been surprised Baron von Krieg, Chief of the Long Knives actually asked his father's permission.

The bishop had looked at Gidon when he got the assignment and said, "Remember Gidon, a soft answer turns away wrath." Everyone was aware of Herman One Eye's churlish nature. He was surly and vulgar and there was no reasoning with him. But added to that he was so big and strong it was often said he must have the blood of the ancient giants in him. On top of it all he once came into the tavern already drunk on beer and caused such a disturbance Gid-visu knocked him out with a fire poker. And Herman One Eye was the sort to carry a grudge, and focus his ill will on a son.

Gidon had finished the past day much more humbly than he began it in spite of being elevated to the position of Baron von Krieg's squire. He even had pity on poor old Herman the Schmeid. The last thing he had done was go by the stables and tell him he could quit working and go to bed. The King's Rider would be at the village for a few days. The one consolation was how wide the Schmeid's eyes became when he got a look at Gidon's new tunic.

There had been some pleasure in being woken in his cot by Fat Max's eldest daughter-in-law Brunhild. After all she was quite pretty and smelled wonderfully. He had gone through the period of infatuation a young boy might have for an older woman. Now normally he did not think much of it for she had cared for Gidon's mother in the illness that took her life. Then she kept the house up in addition to her work at the tavern. This was so the house would not go to ruin or be looted as often happens with abandoned homes. After his wife's death all the staff of his home had been dismissed leaving his house empty most of the time.

Gidon had spent much of his time in the days after his mother's death with the Bishop Elisha being drilled in his studies. He had been worked so hard living in the disciplined life of the monastery he scarcely had time for grieving his mother's death. When the war was over Gid-visu came home but Brunhild's husband had not. It seemed the most normal thing she continue her labor in their home. But today he felt her looking at him differently, and the porridge she had waiting for him was a wonderful way to start out fortified for the day.

Baron von Krieg joined him at the table. While they were eating the Baron asked if he could ride. Normally he would have answered in the affirmative but he had already learned it was necessary to answer questions specifically. Gidon told the Baron his experience of riding was only on the small sturdy half wild ponies used for farm work like pulling cart and plough. He told him he had one of the mountain ponies that could make thirty-five miles in a little over three hours. This seemed to satisfy the Baron for the moment. But when Gidon got to the stable he found the Baron had gotten there before him. He had an old saddle, which the Schmeid had kept in good condition, saddled on his pack horse.

"Gidon, this animal is not like the wild ponies you are used to. You do not have to pull his head like on a plow with long reins. You just lay the reins against his neck and he will turn away from the rein to where it is held slack. This horse will respond to the movement of your feet and the shifting of your body. I want you to take time to get to know him as you go out to see Herman One Eye. Do not be in a hurry to get there. If you get to know this horse, he will surprise you with what he can do. His name is Begleiter and he will respond to it." And with those parting instructions the King's Rider left so Gidon would not be embarrassed the first time he went to mount so tall a horse.

It was only after he was mounted and settled on the horse that Gidon noticed Herman the Schmeid looked worried. "What is bothering you now?"

"That horse is well named," the Schmeid said. "When I tried to separate the King's Rider's horses into separate stalls, they nearly knocked the partition down. He is well named as a companion, and it is strange to see stallions who do not like being separated. I hope the war horse will not tear the place apart while you're gone."

Gidon tried to reassure him, "I do not think it will be a problem because these are working horses. Last night they were bedding down." But his voice lacked true conviction. After all he did not know the horses and he had seen some ponies act strangely when separated from another animal they were attached to. He had even heard once of a duck who had gotten attached to a pony and followed him all about the stable, sleeping in his stall at night. Animals were sometimes funny about how they would go about their lives.

Once Gidon was clear the stable he made a decision. Since the Baron had told him to take his time and get to know the horse whose name meant "companion", it seemed a fine excuse to delay what he feared would be a confrontation with Herman One Eye. He decided to take a longer route past the old fort/monastery. After all, the bishop said that in these days of unrest it would be a good time to clean the moat and get it back into service as a defensive position. And Gidon had never seen a moat cleaned.

The moat at the monastery was different from most moats because water from the river could flow through it until it came time to dam it and clean it up. It was also not the receptacle for the human waste of the monastery. One of the apprentices in training to be an acolyte would be given the onerous chore of removing the waste daily. Gidon had never seen the gates lowered to block the river. The way the moat was constructed meant the walls of the old fortress were surrounded on all sides with a small island between fortress and river on the south side. By means of a bridge that could be raised and lowered this area could be tended for the raising of plants more water loving than the average. The main drawbridge was on the northward facing side. Gidon could not remember either of these bridges being raised just as he could not remember the dam gates being lowered. But he had been but a child when the last war occurred. Gidon expected to learn a lot when he visited and saw how they managed things.

On the ride there he was absolutely thrilled with Begleiter, for he was a true companion. Gidon watched his ears always cocking themselves back toward Gidon to tell him he was paying attention. And Gidon was happy, forgetting the chore ahead for a bit. He sang and it seemed the horse matched the rhythm of his song with his gait. The warhorse rode so smoothly. It was nothing like riding the tough little ponies whose business was getting you there and jangling every bone in your body in the process. Gidon began noticing that the horse was not only paying attention to him but watching the area around him as well. No doubt about it. This was quite a horse!

As Gidon approached the monastery he had moved to the road that led to the front drawbridge. He could see the six little huts on the western side where Hearth Women, many who had children of the priests, lived. These women were not formalized as wives but had a status more like concubines. He could see they were working on the same side as their huts harvesting something from the moat. He would have to get closer to see exactly what they were about but he did have a suspicion they were harvesting elvers.

He saw there were priests doing the same thing on the east side, placing their catches into baskets with lids. It would take two of the apprentices to carry the baskets into the monastery when the baskets were full. But there was one thing on the priest's side he found very unsettling. At this distance it appeared like a huge tabby cat that was catching eels. The priests were tossing them to it as they worked. If that was a tabby cat, he thought, it had to be the biggest one he had ever seen.

As he got closer, he became more certain that was no tabby cat, even though his coat was a mix of tawny orange and tan just like a tabby's. He could make out the long tusk on the right side of his mouth and Gidon knew these priests were feeding and playing with an old sabretooth tiger. That was both an awesome and a fearsome sight no matter how you looked at it. They would toss him an eel and he would catch it, tossing it again into the air and catching it in his massive jaws. After he was done playing just like a house cat might play with a mouse, he made it a meal and waited for his next treat. The little children, too small to work at preserving the bounty of elvers for the next winter, were quite delighted with the whole thing. Some of the braver even ventured to pet the sabretooth as they would a familiar house cat.

The bishop saw Gidon and began coming toward him with one hand up in greeting. In the other he used his shepherd's staff for balance. Watching him cross the land it suddenly occurred to Gidon just how old the man must truly be. It seemed as though he had always looked the same as he did right now. "Hi Gidon, I did not expect you to come my way today."

"Baron von Krieg had wanted me to take time to know how to work with his pack horse Begleiter on the way to Herman One Eye's hovel. I thought I would come by and see how you drain the moat." Gidon explained.

"Well, if I were you, I would be in no hurry either," the bishop said. Gidon was about to explain the Baron had really told him to take his time and get to know the horse when Begleiter began to snort and paw the ground. Looking beyond the bishop, he now saw the great cat sauntering toward the bishop in the manner that had always been common to the feline kind.

"My horse does not care for your cat," he said in a way that told the bishop he was not all that comfortable with him either. The bishop smiled and walked toward the tiger saying, "Come hear Snaggle Tooth." He motioned to a young apprentice who literally came running. "Take Squire Gidon's horse and give him some water and cut up an apple from last year for him. He has a way to go before he will rest this day." Gidon felt a little embarrassed that he had not brought something for Begleiter to have when he stopped for lunch. It seemed to him he had been making one mistake after another since the King's Rider arrived.

The bishop began to explain that he had begun to set things in order as soon as he arrived back home in the early hours. By first light they began to rake the silt and mud out of the seats the gates lowered into. They had put special handles on hoes so they could scrape the material out of the way without getting wet. But even so, several of the young men fell into the water anyway. The bishop chuckled as if he had a private joke over the new found clumsiness of the young men. But all the while as he was talking to Gidon it seemed the tiger was maneuvering the two men closer and closer together.

The cat gently bumped the bishop and he laughed. "Snaggle Tooth does not like being left out of the conversation. He is very smart and knows when you are talking about him and when you are not."

"That is hard to believe." Gidon said wonderingly. He had long ago learned when the bishop said a thing, he had a firm basis for it.

"Why do you find that so surprising? I taught you how it was a serpent who spoke to the first woman and deceived her. I also taught you about the donkey that spoke to a prophet. It used to be all the animals could speak to men before they sinned. And the animals that serve us now understand far more about what we say than we do about what they say." The bishop continued, "There are many kinds of sabretooth cats in the world. There is one who lives a little south of the land I come from who is marked orange with black stripes. He is a killer. Why he will even attack rhinoceros and elephants."

Gidon was befuddled now. "What are rhinoceros and elephants?

The bishop said, "How am I going to explain this? You know about the great beasts to the North called Mammuts, or in the common tongue mammoths. While an elephant is like a mammut it does not have wooly hair and its tusks are not as huge as on a mature mammut. People sometimes train them and they are used to lift great loads and even to fight in war. The elephant does not smell as badly as the mammut either.

Gidon said, "I do not know how they smell; I have only seen drawings of them. But what about this rhinoceros?"

"The rhinoceros is a ponderous beast with a horn in the middle of its head, not unlike a unicorn, whose horn is higher up on his head. He cannot see very well and so he has a very bad temper. Its legs are very short and heavy and he weighs a great deal."

The bishop continued, "Now Snaggle Tooth is different from all his kind. It seems when God put the fear of man into the beasts, he left Snaggle Tooth's variety with an attitude toward men not unlike a house cat, only smarter. Do you suppose God marked him like a house cat so men could see his coat and recognize his nature?"

"I don't know," Gidon said. "Even with one fang missing he is very intimidating."

"That is why I call him Snaggle Tooth. I am not sure how he lost it but he is very old and anything might have happened. His kind only uses those fangs defending their mate and pride. That is different from the other varieties of sabretooth, who use them for killing prey. His kind mate for life and will not take another unless their mate is killed. Snaggle Tooth and his kind prefer fish and other creatures from the water like eels. They will use their fangs to tear apart rotted tree trunks and insect mounds to get larvae and grubs, That could be how he lost his fang. And he is so old it will not grow back. One thing this animal will do just like a housecat. If he is very hungry he will eat dead things newly killed, including people, even though he will not normally kill them."

"How did you learn all these things?" asked Gidon.

"Many things I learned from books. Some of those books were so old no one seemed to care about them anymore. Other things I learned from experience when God gave me the opportunity. I had prayed for wisdom." Now the tiger was between the two men and pushing against both. "Scratch him behind the ears and speak to him boy," the bishop instructed.

Gidon was rewarded with the wonderful experience of hearing a sabretooth purr. It was a great rumbling sound.

"Now get on one knee before him and scratch him behind both jowls." As Gidon complied, the sabretooth picked up his right paw and pushing past Gidon's arm laid the massive paw across his shoulder. "It is done. This cat has just told you he will be your friend for life."

It had been a remarkable morning but the demands of his mission now reasserted itself in his mind. With the sun beginning to get very high in the sky he resumed his journey to give Herman One Eye the message to come to the mustering. Truly Herman One Eye was one of the big reasons Gidon had a prejudice against people named Herman.

By the time he arrived the sun was still high but well past noon in the western sky. Gidon looked over the ridge line and saw Herman One Eye and his older sons loitering about. He decided to circle the hovel and approach from the north so he would not have the sun directly in his eyes, nor would he have the outbuildings blocking the view of the yard. His father had taught him about being on guard against surprises.

When he came over the hill crest and began riding down into the yard, he saw Herman One Eye was already on his feet. As soon as he came near, the man was almost leaning backwards in his attempt to stand even taller.

"Well, if it is not Gid-visu's whelp…or should I say kit?" Herman boomed. The statement was obviously a slur on the fox symbol his father had adopted after following one to his folly. It had been a rare silver fox and he had followed it farther and farther into the forest till by some strange happenstance he arrived in another land. "Look at the pretty tunic he has. I bet he thinks he really is something now."

Gidon felt the blood rush into his face and Begleiter, sensing his rider's emotions, signaled his displeasure with nostrils flaring, neck arching, and hooves stamping angrily. He could see that affected Herman One Eye's sons even if it did not stir their father.

"Maybe I will just spank your ass and send you home crying to your poppa," he said.

At this point Gidon knew he was going to have a fight. Herman's real problem was probably his antagonism toward his father for knocking him out with a fire poker as well as his normal surliness. He was always a bully and would pick on anyone, especially when he was drinking. But he would harangue anyone when he thought he could do it. Gidon was determined he would not spend his life enduring this man.

"How about I take my staff and put a knot on your dumb head!" Gidon spoke aggressively as he dismounted. "I was going to tell you that you could come in tomorrow to register you and your sons for king's muster, but you will be going in tonight. Both you and your sons will come now because you are too big a Scheiße Kopf to be trusted to behave like men."

Gidon knew immediately he had said the wrong thing when Herman One Eye signaled to his wife, a gaunt slatternly woman who was standing in the doorway. She came to him carrying a short pike of about ten feet. This was four feet longer than the fighting staff he was holding. Gidon then remembered stories about how Herman One Eye had handled the pike in combat. It was truly a dangerous weapon in the hands of a man who knew what he was doing. And there was no doubt this man knew what he was doing and had the power to use it effectively.

Gidon groaned inwardly. He was really messing up and this one could prove fatal. Yesterday he had learned he had defeated an assassin only because the man had underestimated him. And now he could die because he had underestimated the situation in his prideful moment. It was plain he could not be more powerful than Herman One Eye so he would have to call on the speed of youth and outthink him if he was to have any chance at all.

Since Herman was using a pike and had the reach, he would have to have quickness and work in some surprises. But he had an idea. "Okay Herman, since you want to use a spear point and draw blood, we will have some blood."

Gidon reached up to the top of his fighting staff and grabbed the carved fist on its top. He gave it a quarter turn and lifted the carved fist off the pole revealing a short blade hidden in it. "I tell you what Herman, since you like being a braggart and a bully, why don't I just relieve you of your remaining eye so you can learn humility?"

Herman answered with a growl, but when Gidon fell into a pike fencing position that allowed for block and counter thrust to the head he began to think about the situation. He realized that harming the son of Gid-visu, a young man who now wore a squire's tunic, could either get him hung, beheaded, or incarcerated in a dungeon for the rest of his life. These thoughts made him hesitate just a little in spite of the fact his sons were urging him on.

As Herman One Eye made his move, Gidon stepped to his left making it harder for him to focus on Gidon. There are limitations for a man with a blinded eye, and Gidon had instinctively taken advantage of the fact. Gidon then moved his staff under the pike deflecting it away and dropping the blade down to make a rather thorough wound in Herman's left leg. The shock when the blade hit the bone caused the leg to collapse under him and Gidon then put his blade right over Herman One Eye's heart.

"I yield, I yield," was all Herman could say.

Gidon noted with relief that the leg wound was bleeding quite a bit but was not pulsing with his heart. He turned to the boys who were standing dumbfounded and said, "One of you idiots get a piece of cord right now." Only three of the six responded. The other three were like people who had lost their senses and become transfixed.

Gidon spoke to the man's wife who was keening sorrowfully and loudly. "Hush woman, he is neither dead nor dying. That is, if you do what I say. Do you have a clean piece of cloth in the house?" She nodded. "Well get it."

"He turned to the three boys still standing doing nothing. "You idiots close your flytraps and go hitch up your goat cart."

By this time one of the first three had returned with a piece of cord and Gidon showed him how to take a stick and cut off the blood flow. The woman came with a piece of cloth she called clean, but Gidon was not at all happy using it to cover the wound tightly. It took some effort to get Herman One Eye into the cart. But it did not keep him from complaining about Gidon taking him in even though he was hurt.

Gidon asked Herman One Eye's wife to make them up a bit of water for the trip. She did it grudgingly but she made them not one bit of food to eat on the way. Gidon thought to say something but decided she was really just discouraged with her life and this was the one way she could register her protest. In any case they would not starve to death on the journey. He was actually concerned that Herman One Eye had enough to drink to make up for all the blood he had left on the ground. That blood was already drawing flies and chickens.

Gidon noticed at one point a son of Herman, one of the older boys, seemed to be trying to slip around behind him. He started putting the carved fist back on the top of his fighting staff. Without even seeming to look at him he said, "If I just beat your father what do you think I am going to do to you if you try to jump me from behind?" The fellow moved over to the cart and stood beside it. Then Gidon spoke to the group. "If you behave, I will let you walk along with the cart. But if you give me trouble, I will tie your hands behind you and put nooses around your necks. That way if any of you stumble, then I will just have hanged you as we go." After that it looked as if the fight had gone out of them. But he made them lead out so the whole group would never be behind him.

Only once did Gidon look back at the place where they were leaving. It seemed to him the hovels the animals lived in were as good, or better, than the hut Herman's family inhabited. He shook his head. Why would people be satisfied to live like this? He considered the campsites he lived at when in the woods better than where they lived all the year.

It was just about an hour since they had gotten underway to get back to the village when he spotted an orange and tan newly made friend sitting on a hillock. He decided to have some fun out of these people who had to this point just been a worry on the road. He took the meal of bread and cheese that had been packed for him this morning by Fat Max's daughter in law and leaving his horse at the cart he said, "If any of these try to run Begleiter, you have my permission to bite and kick them a little." The horse neighed and shook his head so they had little doubt the animal understood him perfectly. In fact, Gidon began to wonder if this was not so as well.

Gidon walked up the slope and Snaggle Tooth rose, stretched himself, and began walking toward him. He sat down looking back at the men who were watching what was taking place with wide eyed wonder. The sabretooth came and set down beside him. He broke the bread and cheese into two pieces and then further divided the portion for Snaggle Tooth so it would not get stuck in his throat as the bread got mushy. Then he and the cat set side by side and enjoyed a time of fellowship. Gidon wondered if the old cat was as amused as he was at the men's consternation?

When he walked back down to the horse, he asked Begleiter if his captives had been good? Again the horse snorted and bobbed his head. So Gidon mounted and they continued on their way. He pretended not to hear the sons of Herman One Eye talking among themselves. But the gist of the conversation was wonderment over his power with animals. Could he be a wizard?

Gidon began to realize he was using up too much time having to haul Herman One Eye on the goat cart and tonight was supposed to be a nearly moonless night. So Gidon said, "Don't you fellows get any ideas about running off in the night. I told my cat he could go ahead and eat anyone who tried to run away." A moan went up, but Gidon knew no one would even get a little way from the goat cart, even to urinate, for fear of the sabretooth.

Indeed, by the time they entered the village it was quite late, but the tavern was still filled with people. Herman One Eye's sons helped him into the tavern but the leg had gotten so stiff he could only lay in front of the fire.

Gid-visu said, "What happened?"

"Do you know what your boy did? He stabbed me with the little spear in his fighting staff." Herman One Eye tried his best to look like an innocent man who had been badly and unfairly treated.

Gidon said, "You are lucky I did not take your last good eye like I said. Every time you look at anything anymore you need to remember you only see by my grace."

Herman's sons, encouraged by their father's complaining chimed in. "Gidon threatened to let his horse bite and kick us and then he said he would let his tiger eat us."

Gid-visu was looking at his son with a good deal of amusement. But the villagers taking it all in did not know what to make of it. Gid-visu looked at Herman One Eye and said, "The next time you try to fight a man with a pike you better first find out if he is able to fight or not."

Now it was Gidon's turn to be surprised. The only way he could have known about the pike was to have been there, for the subject of what had actually happened had not yet been told. He could just picture Gid-visu, concealed with his bow, prepared to take Herman down had things gone badly. It was great to know his father had cared so much, but he also knew his father would not always be there when trouble threatened.

Gidon lost no time getting out of the tavern even though many of the patrons wanted him to stay. He had an appointment at the stables with Begleiter. Herman the Schmeid could have the goats and their cart to care for but that great horse deserved personal attention from the one he had served so well.

It had been an amusing thing to watch the Baron's horses reunited. The way they had bugled and neighed back and forth you would have thought they were going over the adventures of the day together. And he got a great greeting from Begleiter when he came back in as well. Gidon and Herman fed and curried the horses together and Gidon tried to explain the truth of what had happened in spite of all the Schmeid had already heard from a friend who had been at the tavern, No doubt it would be one of those tales told and retold, so people who had actually lived it would not recognize it as their story one day. And Herman One Eye and his sons would not help matters. They would have to build up the story of how they were handled by a sixteen-year old so it would not seem so embarrassing to them in time to come.

Gidon's bed felt very good when he finally made his way to it. But sleep did not come so quickly as he thought it would. His mind replayed and analyzed the events of the day.

One of the surprising things was a new appreciation for Herman the Schmeid. He was a young man, though considerably older than himself, so perhaps he should give him some slack on his deficiencies as a blacksmith. He certainly made up for it in the ways he cared for the stables. And finding out he had been caring for old equipment, not in use and abandoned in the tack room, had certainly been a surprise. It showed him more conscientious than Gidon had thought.

Meeting a sabretooth tiger had really been an amazing thing. He was looking forward to the coming adventure of being the squire of Baron von Krieg and learning more about taking care of himself. But part of him would really like the opportunity to get back to the forests and have some adventures with the great cat. A sabretooth would not find a welcome where he was going.

And then there was Begleiter. How he was going to miss him since he would be giving him back to the Baron. He would love to have some more time for riding the great horse instead of seeing him carrying the packs of stuff a King's Rider needs. He loved the way the horse responded to him and seemed to be always listening and part of the adventure. Yes, the day's adventure with him carried with it the sorrow of having now to give him up.

Thinking on critters, the eels had presented a mystery. The Little Dan had no known route to the ocean. The bishop had told him the elvers migrated to the oceans to have their young and that was where the newborns stayed eating very small life before they migrated back into the streams and rivers of fresh water their ancestors knew. How did they manage that? He wondered if he would ever know the answer.

But one thing had troubled him all afternoon. He had called Herman One Eye a Scheiße Kopf and his sons he had called idiots. His father had told him for years that you could make peace with a man you have a fight with but the man you insult or demean would hate you and be bitter toward you always. He knew that to be at peace with himself something would have to be done to make peace with Herman One Eye, a man he really did not like. He considered telling him he was sorry for calling him a name, but he suspected a man like him would only view it as a sign of weakness. But he really needed to do something about it.

And speaking of weaknesses he had seen he had a big one this day in not being circumspect in his words. Acting presumptuously was a bad trait he was going to have to bring under control lest he die for being stupid. If circumstance came to the place where he had to die, he did not want to die stupid!

Then with all this in his mind he finally fell asleep and spent the night dreaming of riding Begleiter and running through the forest with a sabretooth tiger.

Chapter 3

Duty and Honor

It seemed as if Gidon just closed his eyes and he already smelled the fresh morning scent of Brunhild, eldest daughter in law of Fat Max. Her alluring woman scent mixed with the odor of freshly baked bread seemed particularly strong this morning. He slowly opened his eyes trying to make the wonderful smell of her last as long as possible. But what he saw first, was not her pretty face with its enticing smile, but her breasts almost against his face straining to be set free from her partially unbuttoned bodice. No wonder her scent seemed so strong. His face was almost buried in her breasts!

He had to actually tilt his head up to see her face. But the smile, pretty as always had just a hint of some secretive design he had not seen before. "Why Gidon," she said, "what are you doing?"

He felt momentarily confused, flustered, and embarrassed. Deep inside he knew he had been the instigator of nothing. And he watched as she slowly raised herself to her full height and stood there like the female warrior of myth and legend for which she was named. He knew from the heat in his face that he was blushing and the impulses she aroused were laid out in plain view. His mind wanted to picture her naked. But while he had seen many women's breasts, for it was the custom to nurse babies whenever and wherever they were hungry, he had never seen a grown woman unclothed. Children of both sexes might run around and even play unclothed but by the age of five, simple nudity for the sake of being naked was taboo.

For the first time in his life he addressed her sternly and without any formality. "Why Brunhild, what do you think you are doing?"

Her face and body seemed to collapse together but she still managed to find the spot where she could hide her face into her arms with a bit of grace as she wept. "I thought you wanted me to let you see a little of me. I was just trying to please you."

Gidon had really wanted to see more of her and that caused him more discomfort. He was red in the face again and he dared not stand up for his manhood was very erect under his nightshirt. "What made you think that?"

"I see how you watch me, and every morning you take a whiff of me before you ever open your eyes."

What she said was true, there was no denying it. He had thought it was a secret pleasure. He remembered his poppa had once said there was no use trying to hide a thing from a woman. She has senses that men know nothing of.

Gidon really knew nothing of the ways of a woman but he thought at least part of her crying was the attempt to continue to work her wiles on him, so he tried a little ploy of his own. "Why don't you stop your tears and tell me what is really on your mind."

Brunhild's tears seemed to disappear almost as quickly as they had come. They were replaced with words that just gushed out. "Oh Gidon, you and your father are going away. And who knows whether you will ever come back. I do not mind caring for your home. In fact, I enjoy it. But I am a widow and not getting any younger. I need to marry and have children. Nobody comes around trying to court me except people like Herman One Eye's sons and I would rather die than bed one of them. All the good men about assume Gid-visu has been bedding me since your mother died, but even though he has been very good to me he has never taken advantage of our situation. Truly he has always been most kind. I thought you might want me even though I am a little older than you. I am still young enough to make you a good wife. And I would try very hard to please you."

The revelation had the necessary effect of causing his body to relax. He had even shuddered with the thought of either of Fat Max's daughter in laws being married to one of Herman One Eye's sons, remembering how worn and sad his wife looked. He thought it now safe to get out of his cot and picked her up gently getting Brunhild properly seated in his chair while all the time trying to think. It was then he became aware the early emotion had stained his nightshirt and the smell was apparent. He could see Brunhild knew it too but was not going to show her awareness to him. *She is a very smart woman*, he thought.

"Listen." Gidon said. "It is true my father had intended to make me a match this year since I am now sixteen. But we had planned, not knowing about the muster; or that Baron von Krieg would make me his squire. It is very likely that I will be gone some time, and since there is some danger this is no longer a good time for me to marry."

"What shall I do? What shall become of me?" Brunhild mourned at her plight.

"Normally I would not tell anyone about this but you already know most of it. You have heard how it was when Gid-visu came back from his adventure and found he had been gone three hundred years. He was in a terrible state of mourning for his lost wife and children and even though he came back with great riches, for a time he was not able to do anything for his sorrow. Part of what saved him was my mother and the happiness she brought back into his life. So, when he returned from war and found she was dead can you not just imagine how much sorrow he felt?"

All this time Brunhild was nodding. "I saw the pain of her loss hit on him hard. I thought for a time we might comfort one another in shared sorrow but he withdrew into himself."

This time it was Gidon's turn to nod for he had felt keenly being shut off from his father just when he hoped, even needed, to be with him in the shared loss of his mother. He said, "Well I think that is why he did not turn to you and seek you out. Perhaps he has been reluctant to know love with a wife again. But maybe now if I talk to him, he might change his mind."

"Would you do that for me after I have made a fool of myself?" she asked.

"Of course. You know I am quite fond of you and you have made yourself a part of our lives all these years. We need to do something. After all, Fox Home does need a lady."

Gidon took his time getting ready after she left the room. One of the reasons was he wanted to think. The other was he was very self-conscious about what had happened with his body and did not want anyone to make wrong assumptions at the breakfast table. But when he entered the dining room and saw the Baron, he knew his wait had been in vain. He had seen Brunhild come out of his room with her bodice still open and the natural assumptions were made.

Gidon sat down to find his favorite farmer's breakfast had been prepared and thought to himself Brunhild had really planned this morning thoroughly. Instead of being angry he felt admiration for her forethought. Truly she would make a formidable wife.

"Where is my father?" Gidon asked the Baron.

"He grabbed some fresh bread and put honey butter and a piece of schnitzel in it and headed out. He said something about having a son who was going to waste the morning so he had to go check his laborers to make sure they were finishing the laying by of the fields."

It seemed it was Gidon's morning to blush, but he did see it had all been said in humor and he really was not in trouble with his father, who was well aware of his industry. The one thing he had wanted to do before the whole issue with Brunhild had come up was discuss with him what to do about Herman One Eye. He still had a keen sense of guilt over cursing the man.

"It is necessary I go out for a bit even though Father is taking care of the workmen." Gidon said this aware of the fact he no doubt had responsibilities to the Baron.

"Going to see Begleiter is hardly something that is necessary," the Baron replied.

Gidon thought it must be his day to be caught off guard, but he had learned to be honest. "That is part of what I want to do, but the truth is I need to see Herman One Eye."

"Ah yes, the man who insulted my squire…I had thought to punish him, which is my right. But on reflection I am going to leave it up to you what his punishment shall be. Do you want to flog or hang him, or maybe just cut off his head?"

"No my lord. If I were to kill him, King Gregor would lose a good fighter with the pike, and I would make enemies of all his sons. That is, if I have not done that already. I think he was punished enough because I wounded his body and his pride. Now I would like to try and win him to my side so that he will always be dependable and we will not have to kill him," Gidon said.

"Gidon, I am beginning to think I made a wiser choice than I first realized when I made you my squire. I had no plan to punish him too much, for men often make other men enemies or unwilling servants when they misuse their power over them. The Burgomeister took him from the tavern and put him in the dungeon below his house."

Gidon groaned, for the Burgomeister in his opinion had been in the post too long. His father had been Burgomeister before him and when he had built the new home, much bigger and grander than the old, he had added a dungeon, something the town had never had before. Not even when there was conflict coming from the East. He felt this man sometimes wanted to act as if he ruled the people whose welfare he was supposed to be concerned for.

When Gidon made some expression of that sentiment Baron von Krieg gave one of his cold smiles and said, "Since you are my squire, and I think you worthy, I will let you in on a secret. After your father sees King Gregor, may his house continue, I think you will see him become among other titles the Over Burgomeister of the whole region. But that is something we will keep to ourselves for a time."

Once again Gidon found himself wondering about the strange friendship between his father and the king. Since no one saw fit to tell him and he knew better than to ask, he would wait for the day it became clear.

"One thing you can do while visiting Begleiter is to tell the stableman to have our horses saddled to ride, without armor, at sundown. This is Samstag and since the bishop is an Ebiru we will not ride to the monastery till sundown. There we will keep watch in the chapel overnight and have sunrise worship there on the Son's Day. Then we will travel back here to attend meeting in the church before we break our fast and rest."

Gidon thought to himself, *Now that is some of what we do not think about when we start out to be a squire!*

The King's Rider had one more parting instruction. "Tell your woman to prepare us baths this evening. We will go to the chapel clean in body if not in mind. And, make sure you are back in time to get it done." Gidon started to say she was not his woman but decided to just leave that to sort itself out later.

Gidon stopped only long enough to tell Brunhild what Baron von Krieg planned concerning baths and gave her a few coins to hire some labor to heat and fill the tub, and that she should get the serving wench from Fat Max, whose job it was to help gentlemen with their baths. He was determined that Brunhild should not do the chore considering his plans for her. Then he made straight away for the stable.

Herman the Schmeid put a clandestine interpretation on the night ride Gidon told him to prepare for. He expressed some concern that the Kings Rider's warhorse would be wearing no armor, but he decided they must be intending to move speedily and not going to the monastery at all. Needless to say, once Gidon saw the Schmeid had his imagination going full tilt it amused him to not try too hard to dissuade him. He even went so far as to tell him not to let anyone know they were going. Of course this confirmed in the Schmeid's mind all he supposed.

Next, he set out to find Gid-visu. As expected, he found him sitting on a rail by the side of the field watching the men plow while he enjoyed a cool drink of water.

His father acknowledged his presence by saying, "I have been thinking of going out there and taking a plow over. It would feel good to stretch my muscles reaching out to the plow handle."

"Do not do that. I have something very important to talk to you about."

"What is on your mind my son? I have been very pleased with how you have conducted yourself these past days. But then I am always proud of you."

This rare praise momentarily took Gidon's words from him. But he thought the praise all the more meaningful because it was rare.

"Poppa, I wanted to talk to you about Brunhild."

Gid-visu looked at his son seriously. "Son, I know you are feeling the urges of a man but I want you and the woman you marry to have the experience of being each other's first in bed and in love. I remember that experience well when I first married. And I was the first man your mother ever knew as well."

"No, no, I am not talking about me. I am talking about you. Brunhild has been taking care of us since Mother died over three years ago, and she is paying a price for it."

"What do you mean?" Gid-visu looked seriously concerned. "I have given her small gifts and made sure she had no lack for her kindness. And she has seemed to be enjoying being in our house. I do not think I have treated her unfairly."

"Father, have you ever wondered why men of standing do not come seeking her in marriage? She is a fine-looking woman of good disposition, but still they do not come." Before Gid-visu could answer he told him, "They do not court her even though she was married only months and have no children because they think you are bedding her!"

Gid-visu said, "Then I will have the town crier announce through several nights that is not the case and she may be wooed."

Gidon then spoke to him with intimacy as a father speaking to his child, "Don't you know that if you did such a thing you would only confirm what they believe?"

Gid-visu began to rock back and forth as he considered the situation. "I cannot marry her. Granted there have been times when her very presence stirred me strongly. But I cannot marry her!"

"Why not pray tell, for I know you are lonely. I have heard you some nights in your room when sleep would not find you. She needs you and you need her. Right now, when we leave, she will be like the unrecognized mistress whose master did not think enough of to acknowledge or take with him." To Gidon it seemed so simple, but he could see that to his father, it was not simple at all.

But suddenly his face broke into a smile. He had the solution. "Gidon, I cannot marry her because I know King Gregor plans to elevate my status. This will probably include betrothal to some lady of the realm. What I can do is make Brunhild my mistress of Fox

Home, and then she will have the status in the region as the lady of Fox Home. What do you think about that?"

Gidon thought a minute and answered slowly. "It would probably be good if you do so formally and make sure you plant a baby in her before we leave to see the king."

"Yes, I will see Fat Max and Herman Candlemaker today. And I will speak with the bishop before he conducts services tomorrow."

Gidon had forgotten Brunhild had a living father who was in his late forties. She had become part of the tavern when she married and he did not remember her ever making reference to him. It was the first time he had ever wondered about their relationship.

Once again Gidon spoke, and it was like he was advising his father instead of the other way around. Once Gid-visu had gotten hold of the idea it was like he was all in. "Don't you think you should talk to the woman first? She is not a young girl without an opinion in the matter."

"Of course. Thank you son, I am going to do that right now. Don't you want to go with me?" Gid-visu seemed to be making the idea of making Brunhild his mistress more and more his own. But in some ways as he planted the idea deeper inside himself, he seemed to have all the uncertainties of a young man and not the forwardness of the seasoned adventurer he was.

"Perhaps I will get home before you finish talking things over with her. But right now I need to go and tend to Herman One Eye." Gidon set his face grimly back toward town and, as he walked, he prayed. He was not sure if he was talking to the Invisible God; His Son who died and rose from the dead, or some one of the pagan gods his ancestors worshipped. But he knew he was going to need even more wisdom than he had used trying to solve Brunhild's problems.

The trip over to the Burgomeister's house was the longest of the day, or so it seemed. Gidon was beginning to discover an awful truth about being a man, and especially a man of responsibility. Too often you find yourself doing things you would just as soon put off—indefinitely. But as with all dreaded things you sooner rather than later would arrive at them. And Gidon was not any more certain of how to handle the situation with Herman One Eye than when he started out this morning. He realized in retrospect he should have approached the problem of this surly giant of a man and his sons before he talked with his father about Brunhild because afterward it would have been useless to seek his counsel on the matter.

At the front door of the Burgomeister's home Gidon saw they had finished installing a cord that went to a little bell inside. This was an affectation recently added because his wife had heard that was the way more genteel people announced themselves these days. But Gidon decided he did not want to play the game with them so he grabbed the door clapper and gave three knocks of sufficient force to make the sound echo inside the hall.

A local man, hired to serve, opened the door. He looked behind him carefully and then said, "Hello Gidon. What are you doing here?"

"Good day to you, Herr Brauner. Why are you stuck in here on such a nice day?"

"I owe Herr Burgomeister money, so I have to work it out."

"I would think if you were free to work at your trade the debt would be paid more quickly," Gidon said sympathetically.

"I do not think he wants it paid quickly." The man sighed.

"Herr Brauner I need to go see my prisoners, Herman One Eye and his sons," Gidon said switching back to business as he heard someone approaching.

"Why Gidon, it is a very early hour to come calling." It was Brigitta, the spoiled daughter. The bishop had once told him that her name meant exalted one, and in her house she was. He said that was why she always thought everything was all about her. He warned Gidon several years ago this girl would make a terrible wife for some man. But Gidon knew a farmer's daughter by the same name who was always busy with needle and thread, when she was not helping with the farm work. She would probably make some happy man a fine wife. Maybe you cannot always believe in what names mean!

"Brigitta, it is not for calling on a young lady I am come. I am on king's business and must speak with your father.

Her lips formed a little pout she no doubt thought attractive. How much more he preferred the expression on Brunhild's face when she was genuinely disappointed. *In sorrow or joy she is attractive,* he thought. He started to envy his father just a bit.

When the Burgomeister came and asked Gidon's business he said, "I am come to check on my prisoners."

The Burgomeister replied, "You mean my prisoners for they are in my dungeon. I plan to have a council hearing tonight where we will decide their punishment." It pleased the Burgomeister to have such control over Herman One Eye for he did not like him at all.

"Herr Burgomeister, you are mistaken. I took them prisoner while on the king's business in my duties as squire to the King's Rider, Baron von Krieg. They are my prisoners and I will decide their fates. Perhaps you would like to answer the matter to my lord or perhaps even King Gregor himself?" Gidon was enjoying using his position this time and making him think he might even have influence with the king.

The fat old man licked his lips. "No, no, Squire Gidon, I did not understand. Please excuse me. I thought they had been brought to me for justice."

Gidon knew this was a lie, for he had them scooped up in the tavern where Gidon left Herman One Eye laying before the fire. He never had the men put in his charge but rather he took advantage of the situation. As Gidon stared at him the old man got more and more pitiable in his sight.

"Well, since it is all just a misunderstanding let us waste no more time, and we will go to see them together." As he spoke, he could see that the old man did not relish dragging his corpulent frame up and down the stairs. "But perhaps you are busy with more weighty matters and would prefer to send Brauner to assist me?" The immediate relief was apparent on his face.

Brauner came immediately. Gidon knew he had been listening without ever reading the delight on his face. As they descended into the dungeon it seemed the light of the lantern Brauner carried was being consumed by the darkness. And when Gidon saw Herman One Eye and his sons, he was moved by compassion. They had spent all the time since brought to this place in deep darkness and a couple of the boys looked utterly wild eyed. And this in less than the hours of a day and a night!

"Herman, this is Gidon. How are you doing?

Herman groaned, "I am in pain in this dark and damp. I fear my leg will become infected and have to be cut off."

"Do not worry. I am going to take care of it. But first we must talk. Do you remember when we had the fight at your home? I wanted to tell you I am sorry for cursing you. But why did you threaten me? I have never done you harm." At that Gidon waited.

Herman groaned again. Then he began to think. "Maybe it was because I was mad at your poppa. Or maybe because I do not want to go to war again or see my sons go to war. I don't know. It is just sometimes I do and say more than I mean or should say. I am sorry."

Gidon said, "That is good Herman. I do not have to flog you or hang you, or even chop off your head. If you forgive me and I forgive you then we could be friends."

For the first time Herman looked at Gidon with his single glaring eye. "You mean that? You want to be my friend?"

"Of course, Herman. If we can trust each other and treat each other the way we should, we can become great friends. I think you need some friends." Gidon started to feel good about the whole thing. "Tell your sons to pick you up and take you to the tavern. I will see you get a little room, food, and treatment for your wound. You are going to be good and try to be nice to everyone who tries to help you. Is that a deal?"

Gidon was very surprised when Herman One Eye caught Gidon's hand and kissed it.

Later, when Gidon had everything set up, even though Fat Max was not particularly pleased with the deal, it became necessary to do something about the sons. So Gidon told the oldest five to return to the farm and get the land plowed and planted. He promised he would be there in three to four days to inspect the work. And then he warned them not to be laggards. If it was not right, he promised he would give them what their poppa should. The youngest he left with Herman in the hope this would reduce the load on Fat Max and his workers.

In just the short distance home his imagination began to run wild. What if after all this persuading Brunhild was discouraged by

Gid-visu's new enthusiasm and she turned him down flat? What if she was so determined to be a wife, she refused to be his mistress? What if she decided that she would rather have him and told his father so? He tried to push the last idea out of his head knowing it was illogical and his thinking was still distorted by the breasts that were in his face when he had first opened his eyes. *Gidon, you really need to grow up!* And then he looked around. The idea had been so strong he was not quite sure he had not said it out loud.

When he entered the door at Fox Home, he was surprised to see one of the oldest priests from the monastery guarding the door. He had known he was of the order of fighting priests, men who seldom live to grow old. He was sworn to his order, his bishop, and his monastery, to protect the people in that order. These men frequently went to war alongside the king who ruled the land where their monastery was situated as part of keeping those vows.

Gidon apologized, "In all the time I have been seeing you I have never known your name."

The priest said, "I am Brother Jonathan, the Sword. My brother guarding the back door is Brother Judah, the Hammer. We are both brothers in faith and brothers in flesh. Our mother was called Solomonia. And we will defend this house and its lady while you and your father are away.

"Oh, I see," said Gidon.

"No, you do not. But one day you may, if it be God's will. If you fulfill your name—'"he who cuts down,"' as is your destiny in God's plan from before the foundation of the world. Then you may understand. That is, if you live long enough."

Gidon knew it was time to break his conversation with this unsettling priest who seemed to see beyond the present reality. He was told he could find his father and Baron von Krieg in the receiving room. It was the place where all important visitors were brought.

When Gidon entered the room, he caught the look he did get as well as the look he did not get. The look he did get came from Baron von Krieg and it told him plainly he now knew Gidon had a secret and had kept it from him so he had misjudged the situation. And he was still not sure how much of a secret he was keeping. The look he did not get, did not come from Brunhild, for she had eyes only for Gid-visu. He had already seated her on an ornate footstool by his left side befitting her new position as mistress. From that point she held his armrest with her right hand and he placed his left hand over hers holding it gently. Gidon thought to himself once again what a very smart woman she was, and felt just a tinge of regret that he had not taken her offer himself. But that was an emotion he pushed away and buried deeply as he prepared to love her almost as a second mother. Thus he would honor his father.

He addressed Gid-visu directly. "Father, don't you need to make contact with Fat Max and Herman Candlemaker?"

"No," Gid-visu replied. "Brunhild and I have so little time left together before you and I must leave. I am determined to spend every possible moment with her. I sent for them!"

As if on cue Fat Max and Herman Candlemaker were escorted in by Brother Jonathan but the scene was darkened because the Burgomeister was with them. Evidently he was still a little fearful because of what Gidon said to him in the morning. He went directly to Baron von Krieg making apologies and begging forgiveness for usurping authority. Once again he fell back on the lie he thought Herman One Eye and his sons had been delivered for his judgment. It was so blatantly obvious that it was a lie, yet it escaped him entirely everyone knew he was lying. Gidon was beginning to be able to read the Baron's looks, and if he understood the one he gave the Burgomeister right then, Baron was thinking something along the lines of "You insufferable fat maggot!"

One of the reasons for contempt for the Burgomeister was apparent in the situation. He thought his business more important than anyone else's. Gidon could see how his daughter Brigitta came by her attitude. She got it from her father. He seemed to be oblivious to the fact the meeting between Gid-visu and Fat Max and Herman Candlemaker was arranged and he had not been invited. He had just butted in like a brash goat.

It was Fat Max who managed to swing the flow of events back to the purpose for the meeting. You could always leave it to Max to handle social situations well. But then a man who runs a tavern should be able to do so. "Gid-visu you realize you are taking from me my very best little helper."

It was then Brunhild seemed to come aware of other people in the room and she took her gaze away from Gid-visu to look at them. "Darling Max, you know I will not be able to stay away from you and Oma, so I will be with you quite a bit once my lord has gone to the king's castle."

As she turned Gidon saw she was wearing around her neck a ruby held by a golden chain. He remembered well when they discovered that stone in a gravel pit at the opening of a cave way deep in the forest. It was one stone Gid-visu said he would never part with. He had it polished and set in a gold and silver setting and kept it for years. It was one of those rare stones that people said had a captured star in it, while the more religious said it showed the cross of the Son of the Invisible God. Even across the room it was a thing of great beauty.

Its beauty had not been lost on Herman Candlemaker either and as he reached out toward the stone to look at it Gidon saw Brunhild pull back. It was the first clue he had ever had about why she never mentioned her father. She was afraid of him. Gidon stored that information away in his mind. Someday he might have to do something about that. He resolved to tell Brother Jonathan to be on guard against her father while they were gone.

The meeting proved to be rather friendly with wine and sweet breads served to the guests. Gid-visu did not explain why he could not take Brunhild to wife. And even though Herman Candlemaker hinted a few times about some business or financial arrangements he and Gid-visu might get into, things went rather well. Brunhild rose to serve the guests with the sweets herself and at one point seemed to lose her balance as she came around Gidon's chair. She stabilized herself by grasping Gidon's shoulder and giving it a secret friendly squeeze. So much communicated in so little! She had made him aware of her gratitude and friendship without saying a word. What a very smart woman!

It was agreed the announcement of Brunhild's status would be made at the church on the morrow and Gid-visu and the bishop would draw up a formal written agreement and then have pledges made in the evening.

When the visitors finally left, Brunhild told the men she had set everything in readiness for their baths. Gid-visu said that since he heard Baron von Krieg had wanted to bathe, he had ordered his sauna heated and would like to join them in a good sweat to rid the body of impurities before going to the tub.

Gidon used to enjoy the times he had spent with his father getting a steaming cleansing and scraping the body to get rid of dead skin and so forth. But this time that pleasure was going to be denied him. The Baron said Gidon would have to stand guard outside the sauna while they were inside in a vulnerable state.

Gidon sighed. There were some drawbacks to being a squire to say the least. He only hoped he could last through the night after they got to the monastery chapel and began their vigil. It had been quite a day with three major situations having to be dealt with. Gidon felt he had prayers answered beyond all he knew to ask. Perhaps the Invisible God really did like him.

Chapter 4

Keeping Vigil

Gidon hoped he would get a turn in the tub this evening with sufficient time to doze in its warmth. He was not relishing standing outside the sauna on guard while his father and the Baron enjoyed its cleansing powers.

Brunhild had shown foresight for everything needful for the baths and when Gid-visu had informed her he planned to use the steam sauna in back she took care of that as well making arrangements not only for Fat Max's tub and wash-girl to be brought over but hiring a young boy to tend the sauna fire. It burned from the outside to heat the rocks on the inside. Even the water buckets on the inside had been refilled in the sauna and were waiting.

Fox Home was one of the few homes in the Eastwatch village that had its own bath tub. Gidon's mother had seen to that when Gid-visu put in the sauna. Gidon had vague memories of the family enjoying the sauna together and running out to jump in the snow. But other than the comforts of her breasts he had no other memory of her body except for her face which always looked at him lovingly with large blue eyes.

Brunhild had specifically chosen Getrudis as the wash girl to come over from the tavern. She would have two men to assist in bathing this evening since Brunhild made it very plain she would care for Gid-visu personally. Ever since Getrudis' father had sold the girl to Fat Max as an indentured servant one of her duties had been to aid travelers in bathing, if they so desired. Many thought such niceties more than once a year unhealthy. Sometimes it had been difficult persuading more obstinate travelers her duties ended with helping them get clean. One would wish the girl's father had acted in the hope she would have a better future than he might offer. In any case, in spite of her small stature and delicate frame, she did indeed have the kind of strength her name implied.

When the men gathered in the back of the home, which was surrounded by a high wall, they began stripping the inner garments they had come out wearing and hanging them over a line beside the sauna. Baron von Krieg looked around and said rather loudly, "Where is my wash girl? I need to give her instruction before we go into the sauna."

Brunhild said, "She is in the room with the tubs. She has some fragrance to put into your baths."

The Baron replied, "If she has already put it into my tub it will have to be poured out and cleaned. My back often gets inflamed when such things are used and it is hard to cure the swelling once it has started. Besides that, she needs to know what I require of her while we are in the sauna."

Someone had told Getrudis the Baron was calling for her very loudly, implying he might be angry. It seems some people always seem to get pleasure from unnecessarily alarming the weak and helpless. She came running wearing only the sleeveless tight shift regularly used for wear when giving baths. She was in such a rush her young breasts moved under the garment in a way that was arousing to men even though she was unaware of it. She stood before the Baron chest heaving and shaking in fear, for she was overawed by so great a lord.

The Baron looked at her and said, "Calm yourself girl. I am not going to eat you."

"Yes, my lord," she said automatically even though his words had not done one thing to calm her.

"After we have been in the sauna long enough to have a good sweat and our calluses and scars have become softened, I want you to come into the sauna, clean my back, and then use this on the scars on my back." He handed her an alabaster bottle. "This bottle of potion

Zauberer the Wise made for me. You must rub it in very thoroughly and firmly."

"My lord, I do not understand. I have never done such a thing." Getrudis said.

The Baron turned his back to her so she could see what he was speaking of. It was a mess of scars that looked as if someone had tried to flay the Baron with a particularly nasty whip. His broken and torn skin seemed to have been stitched and pulled together by some coarser string than any designed for the purpose. The holes where the skin had been pulled together and stitched were scars in themselves—scars that became oil pockets and looked most unbecoming and unhealthy.

"When the skin is softened and you have cleaned the pores this potion will keep it from being inflamed and help soften and diminish the scars so they are not so uncomfortable. They will never completely go away." The Baron was so matter-of-fact about something that looked so ugly and was obviously the evidence of terrible torture that Gidon was amazed.

"And by the way, girl, do not wear that shift into the sauna. If you do, it will get all wet, and you will chill when you come out. Not only that when we get to the bath you will get droplets of your sweat on me while you work. I will not like that."

Getrudis seemed to be blushing all over. "My lord, I have never stood before men naked."

"Do not worry about it. You are not going to stand before us; you are going to stand behind us. Wrap a towel around your waist as we do."

The Baron acted as if the matter was entirely settled and Getrudis saw she had no recourse and no champion as Brunhild had already departed to correct the bath water problem. The poor girl turned toward the line and took her shift off, hanging it beside the men's clothes. Gidon had to this point just been watching the conversation, but now as her shift came over her head, he saw a woman's body from the back for the first time in his life. He was transfixed!

It was then Judah the Hammer spoke to the Baron. "It is not necessary Gidon should miss getting in the sauna. I am at watch at this door, so I can see the entrance to the sauna and stand guard for that as well."

The Baron looked at Judah the Hammer and a light seemed to come into his eyes. "I know you. You and your brother stood with me holding a breach for an entire day of unending fighting. I have never seen two men swing their weapons so continuously and tirelessly. I thought my own arms would fall off!"

Judah the Hammer smiled grimly and returned the compliment. "That day I saw the finest swordsman and the bravest warrior I have ever beheld in my life. I consider that day of fighting by your side a great privilege. We received strength and cunning from on high. Truly God was with us that day as we fought back men who served the Evil One."

The Baron then said, "I would consider it a great honor if you would watch and let my squire be cleansed. For tonight we must keep vigil at the chapel."

"I know," said Judah, "for the bishop said you were coming."

Baron von Krieg looked surprised because his plans for this night had not been noised about. Judah said, "We do not call him Bishop Elisha for nothing. God whispers in his ear even what the king plans in his private chambers."

The trip to the sauna began rather pleasantly as the men sat together in quiet comradeship. Finally Gid-visu told the Baron that in all the time he had known him, he never knew about the cause of the damage to his back. The Baron said that being taken captive because he made a mistake in judgment was not a thing he liked to talk about. It had happened when he was very young, almost as young as Gidon, and had his first squad of men to command. One thing he had learned from the experience was that he would die fighting before he ever again surrendered. And at that point talk about the subject ended. Gidon knew if he wanted to know more it would have to wait for another day.

Shortly later Getrudis entered the sauna and moved quickly to a place behind the men. Try as he might Gidon could not resist the temptation to peek at her. It seemed the towel around her waist only made her body more appealing. As the men scraped their bodies she worked on the Baron's back. Her sensitive spirit showed through, and a few times she sobbed as she worked, so closely she identified with the testimony of suffering in his back. But she worked thoroughly, and it took a long time. Gidon thought he was going to have to head for the door. The heat was getting to him. But just at that moment she opened the potion and began massaging it into the Baron's back. The odor, both heavy and pleasant at the same time, revitalized his stamina.

Gidon said, "I have not ever smelled anything like that."

"Zauberer said the potion comes from spices and unguents to be found in the land of the Hebrews. Part of it was among those gifts seers brought to the Son of God when he was a baby of about two years of age. It is a thing of great expense but worth all it costs for the healing it brings." The Baron said Zauberer only gave him enough of the potion to last through the time each trip should take if he did not waste it. There was a temptation to use it too often.

When they entered the tub room, which now was a little crowded with two tubs, Gidon noticed Brunhild had on the same sort of shift that Getrudis had once again donned. It had never occurred to him till that moment that she had, at times, had to be a wash girl at the tavern. There was a great difference in how Brunhild filled out the apparel than Getrudis did even though he now knew her body was all woman. Brunhild was simply more fully matured. Gidon wondered at what age a woman's body ceased maturing and began aging? Life was so full of mysteries it seemed, and as he thought on the matter, he realized the more he knew about life the more questions he then had to seek answers to. But when it came to things like the mysteries of a woman, he simply had no one he could comfortably ask.

Baron von Krieg rose in his estimation when he saw him slip Getrudis a silver coin whose worth was far more than most people of the Alemanni might earn in a year or even several years. With such a coin she might even be able to pay out her indenture if a circumstance developed that made it worthwhile.

The timing seemed almost perfect, for the sun was down just before they took their leave of everyone, and headed to the stable for the horses. Gidon did look forward to riding Begleiter again. A moonlight ride, except this time of the month there was little moonlight.

Even before they departed, Gidon received a lesson from the King's Rider concerning how he should distribute his weapons on the horse to readily access them. It was explained that a man whose duties required continual readiness for combat was different to that of an anointed knight who might travel with minimal weapons at hand. The knight errant usually vied with others of his status following chivalric rules. What many a King's Rider would encounter were situations where there were no rules, except the rule of survival. That generally meant the best prepared won.

By the time they had finished the lesson, and both men had their weapons distributed, the horses were stamping their front feet with impatience to be outside on a new adventure. But as soon as they were out of the stable and on the way Gidon was amazed at how these horses settled down and moved quietly using their own senses to keep watch as they went. Gidon remembered how Begleiter had done that on the trip to Herman One Eye's sad excuse for a farm. The Baron said a lot of the horses' alertness had to do with its attachment to its rider. And it was also a great advantage when a man must travel and he was already worn from the day's activities. In time to come, Gidon would come to appreciate that advantage.

On the way the Baron began a game of reading the areas they were traveling through. Which sections of wood were close enough to the roadway to make it easier for someone to position themselves to do them mischief? At one point he got Gidon to watching a clump of brush ahead that was about forty feet from the roadway and twenty feet from the tree line. As they approached and Gidon was fixated on it he got the impression it was moving.

He told the Baron and he laughed. "That is a common nighttime illusion, and I wanted you to see it. When you see something like that, look away and watch it only from the corner of your eye. A brigand is more likely to move if he thinks you are not watching him. A well-trained assassin is unlikely to move no matter what. That is sometimes the thing that gives such men away. They have been so thorough with their disguise it does not respond to the breeze as it should."

Gidon realized that for all his knowledge of the forest, he had much to learn about the way of the warrior. And who was better to teach him than the Chief of the Long Knives? It was beginning to dawn on him more and more how greatly he had been honored when the Baron had chosen him to be his squire.

The thump of horses' hooves on the wooden drawbridge of the monastery, as well as the clatter of those hooves in the courtyard, were a whole new experience for Gidon. Together with the scent of the freshly flooded moat it made for a memory he would recall at special times in years to come. Sure, he had ridden his mountain pony to the monastery many times but the smaller creature could not make the impression on the timber of the drawbridge and cobblestones of the courtyard these huge horses could. And there were other factors. He had often come riding to the monastery when weather threatened to be inclement for a length of time. These were times for study and weather altered the sounds. Also, he usually dismounted and walked his animal into the monastery out of respect for the holiness of the place.

This night, he had first been ill at ease for the safety of the monastery, for not only was the drawbridge down as usual, but also no one seemed to be guarding the access. He knew these priests were men of faith but considering the bishop had been increasing readiness for some threat, he thought to see guards posted. But when he was about to ride onto the bridge, he saw above him on either side two men with crossbows positioned so any unwelcome intruder could be stopped. A sad time when places of worship and needed guarding!

A voice sang out in a melodious baritone "Baron von Krieg and Squire Gidon." And so they were announced and men appeared in the courtyard to help them with the horses and their weapons.

Bishop Elisha arrived as they began the walk to the chapel. "All is in readiness for your vigil. I hope you do not mind but I have two men who need to do their vigil this night in preparation for their ordination into the fighting priests. I hope to send them North with you to the King's muster for further training."

"They will be most welcome." The Baron had lapsed again into his usual compactness of speech in contrast to the lengthy conversations they had enjoyed on the road.

As they came to the massive doors of the chapel already standing open before them Gidon saw two middle aged fighting priests on either side. The Baron addressed them formally. "What be your names O holy warriors?

The one on the Baron's right hand answered. "Though we be two, we are but one in name. In the tongue of the Ebiru we are called Ur Menahem."

"That being interpreted," said the one on the left; "we are the faithful watchers, keepers of the gates. None shall pass these doors to disturb thy holy vigil while we yet live."

Baron von Krieg reached into his bag and pulled out four gold coins, giving two to each. "In that unhappy circumstance, no base coin shall hold so noble eyes."

As Gidon entered the chapel one step behind his knight he saw a sight such he had never seen before. Nearest to the door were two priests standing beside swords held upright in blocks that secured the tip of the blade so each looked like an upright cross. To the right of each sword lay neatly folded the inner padded garment on which chainmail was worn. And newly made chain mail was carefully laid upon it. Upon those two items were clean white tunics with the ensign of a red cross over which was placed a golden crown, which Gidon had observed were worn by all the fighting priests of the monastery.

Baron von Krieg stopped directly between the two priests. "What are your names?"

Again the one on the right answered, "If it pleases, lord we have none, having forsaken our old names and not yet having received our new."

The Baron nodded and walked forward taking his sword out of its sheath and placing it upright between the blocks in his space at the front of the group. Gidon saw no place to go but to the place set slightly behind the Baron and to the right where there was already an unattended sword set upright with the same arrangement of materials as the priests, with the exception the new tunic had King Gregor's and the Baron's ensigns on it, even as the one he had been given only a few days earlier. He did notice this tunic material was white, not the green tunic he now wore. He saw his bow and fighting staff were already in place by the clothing so he knew he was likely in the right position. When the Baron laid his long knife beside his mace already arranged to his left, Gidon did likewise with the knife he had taken from the would-be assassin. He only surmised this was right since he had not been given any instruction.

It was then the Baron began to intone a poem to the sword:

> "Thou art my sword,
> Blessed be Zillah who bore the man who forged thee.
> Thou art my sword,
> Blessed be the God who taught her son to be an artificer in iron.
> Thou art my sword,
> I dedicate thee anew to the purpose of justice in an evil world.
> Thou art my sword,
> Thou wast purified seven times to fulfill thy holy purpose.
> Thou art my sword,
> Thy metal was folded back upon thee so thou might cleave in strength.
> Thou art my sword,
> Thy gift to the blessed is a quick death and to the undeserving maiming..."

At the beginning of his poem Gidon had been catching the aroma coming from the Baron's treated scars which were more potent in the closed room warmed by many candles. He began by thinking upon the meaning of the Baron's words. But as he continued to intone the poem in a sort of monotone, his mind began to drift and his body grew heavy. How long he was in this state he was not sure. For a time, each *Amen* coming from the men behind him with every point made, had kept him alert. Yet slowly his alertness declined. When the Baron stood, he came back fully aware and stood as well, hoping again he had done the right thing.

The Baron went toward the altar of the chapel and bowed, then turned to his right. Gidon did likewise, followed in single line by the priests. In this manner they circled the inside perimeter three times before resuming kneeling positions before their swords. This time Gidon looked at his sword closely. It was then he saw the pommel of his sword was the carved figure of a sabretooth, having only one fang. His blade was as long as the Baron's singlehanded sword but narrower. He longed to pick it up and feel its weight and balance, but he knew this was not the time.

After some minutes, the Baron said, "One of you brothers give a prayer that the Great God will teach our hands to war for His glory." The priest on the right complied.

Afterwards, the Baron again rose and approached the altar, bowing as he drew near. He followed the same procedure as before but this time the chapel was circled seven times before returning to the kneeling position before the swords.

Again the Baron spoke. "Brother pray we should never falter before the enemy or in any other way bring shame unto our God."

This time the priest on the left complied.

Then the Baron arose and approached the altar again, performing the same ritual with the exception he circled the chapel nine times before returning to his position before the sword. From that point he appeared to always be at prayer except for periodically standing and then returning to his prayer position. Gidon was grateful that someone had put hassock pillows on the floor to place the knees upon. He was sure that had they not, he would not have been able to walk by morning.

As the morning sun rose, a procession of priests entered singing songs of praise. Bishop Elisha came in with a cup of anointing oil to bless each man separately:

As he poured oil on the bowed head of the Baron he said, "Blessed art thou, Baron von Krieg. As thou hast chosen to serve

God and king, I anoint thee with the Joy of Gladness. Go forth in thy dedication and the rightness of thy cause."

Then he turned to Gidon and as he poured the oil over Gidon's now-bowed head he said, "Blessed art thou Gidon, son of Gid-visu, I anoint thee in the Name of the Most High, squire to Baron von Krieg and sanctify the weapons of thy warfare to the service of the same."

He then ordered the Baron and Gidon to don the new clothing the priesthood had provided. The old tunics were handed to priests who carefully folded and wrapped them.

Next the Bishop turned to the two young priests. "Have you had a vision of your holy calling and names?"

They answered with one voice, "Nay brother Bishop."

"Then you must fast one more day and tonight sleep dressed in thy new vestments of calling. Then the vision will come."

All four who had stood vigil the night before were served The Holy Warrior's Communion before the priests returned to their fast and vigil. The Baron and Gidon exited the chapel to find a meal prepared in the courtyard for them where they could eat and watch their horses prepared at the same time. Baron von Krieg's fasting plan had been altered by the bishop. And Bishop Elisha always moved with purpose, even when others did not understand the cause.

The two brother priests Ur Menahem joined them. "The bishop has ordered we join brothers Jonathan the Sword and Judah the Hammer in keeping watch at Fox Home till relieved."

"Where is the bishop?" Baron von Krieg asked, apparently expecting him to join them before they departed. Gidon too had wanted to thank him for the sword and chainmail as well as the new tunic.

"He has departed for Eastwatch," Ur Menahem spoke as one.

Gidon opined, "Then we should catch up to him on the road."

This time only one of the priests spoke. "I think not, for he said he was late. And like the holy evangelist Philip he was taken." The man spoke so matter-of-factly it was as though miraculous events were things expected, even daily occurrence to him.

After the meal Gidon was eager to be on the road and to shake off some of the weariness that reasserted itself after eating. He saw the priests had attached his new sword to the side of the saddle in the same manner as the Baron's long sword. He expressed concern that he should have it so ready when he had not yet been trained on it only to be told the bishop had ordered it so.

The Baron spoke thoughtfully, "Apparently the Bishop thinks you will need it. It is a sword made for you and likely will fit more aptly into your hand than any other."

A two-pony cart was brought out for the priests Ur Menahem. "The bishop said we would need this." That was all the explanation they offered. Probably they had no reason to give. Instead of running at a soldier's pace they would ride by order of the bishop. And for now, that was reason enough.

When the men got clear of the monastery walls, and the morning breezes flowed unobstructed, it was plain all were refreshed. The Baron rode quietly at the front showing no interest in beginning anew the game of picking out potential ambush points. But Gidon believed, in spite of his apparent mood of contemplation, long years of habit kept his senses working at surveying his surroundings. He had already come to believe there was never a point of perfect rest for a King's Rider or for one of the Long Knives either. He did not know if he could possibly hold up to the challenge of such work for a lifetime like the Baron.

One of the Ur Menahem called Gidon to ride beside the cart. He asked, "Is there anything you want to know about the vigil you have just kept?"

Gidon mentioned the ritual of bowing to the altar and then turning to the right and circling the inner perimeter of the chapel.

One of the Ur Menahem said, "That is part of the ritual of our order. We bow to the altar as the acknowledgement of the Son's sacrifice to make it possible for us to come to Him. We circle the chapel to the right in reminder the definite order of time and the earth's rotation are as one."

"That is very interesting and makes perfect sense. But what of the numbers of times the circle is made?" Gidon asked.

The priests looked pleased. "The first three circles represent the completion and perfectness of unity. It is the first prime number without separation so it represents the Persons of God. We circle seven times in the remembrance of the fullness of God's divine perfection. All His plans for man and the world will have perfect completeness. And finally, we circle nine times. This is partly a mystery of God, yet we do know that it is the fullness of God's blessing to all things. In the perfect tongue first spoken by men, all letters have numbers and all numbers have meaning. It is by perfect knowledge of these letters and numbers God has but to speak to Create. Do you have more questions?"

Gidon said, "Learned men, I have more questions than my brain can handle. Let me think on these things for the moment."

They had not yet gotten to the place where they had played the game of moving bushes the night before when Gidon noticed a low mound of brush and leaves he did not remember. He thought, *I am being confused by the different vantage point,* and began looking ahead for the brush that fooled him the night before. Suddenly the Baron's war steed gave out a sharp cry and bucked away to the left.

Begleiter with nostrils flaring swung himself to the right straight at the low mound Gidon had looked at before. At that moment the warhorse had a mind of his own. As a man popped up from the ground Gidon realized the brush was a blind from which to kill men. Begleiter and Gidon were nearly on top of the man when he pulled his new sword out and swung it in a long arc, nearly cutting the would-be assassin in two.

Begleiter bobbed his head and pranced, as if he heartily approved of Gidon's actions, as he headed back to the Baron's steed while blowing and neighing most ferociously. The two fighting priests went to inspect the man and survey the perimeter for any more danger. The Baron looked at Gidon approvingly. He almost had his saddle off the war horse. It had to be removed very carefully for the arrow had pierced the saddle before it entered the flesh of the mighty steed and now it could not be pulled straight out. Gidon had wondered what the horse was called for he had never heard the Baron use his name, but now it came.

"Good Schlachtross, you are a fine fellow," the Baron said.

Gidon now knew the horse's name. He had taken the common term and turned it into the war horse's term of endearment. How gently and lovingly he spoke to the animal as a dear friend!

"What are your thoughts Gidon?" The Baron spoke as he had now moved the saddle where it could come off with a minimal amount of pain to the horse.

"I think that if the bowman had been trained by my father one of us might now be dead."

"How is that?" The Baron spoke as he dropped the saddle to the ground with the arrow still in it; not caring for any blood from the horse that got on him.

"My father always told me that when you fire an arrow in battle you do not watch to see where it goes. It will either hit its target or not. Instead, you nock the next arrow and get ready to shoot again. There is enough time to inspect your work after the battle is over! This man paused to inspect his work!"

"Your father is a wise man and I have seen him in the practice of what he teaches. What do you think we should do with this man's equipment?"

"I think we should take it including the arrow you have there to my father. He may very well know who made it and that could lead us to who is behind the ambush."

One of the priests had reached into his bag on the cart and pulled out some salve. He put it on the horse's wound before closing the hide with a couple of stitches. "This horse should not be ridden until the wound heals," he opined. We can put your saddle and gear on the cart."

About this time a man began screaming in the distance. "Get him off me! Don't let him eat me!"

Gidon told the Baron, "With your permission I will check this out. I have an idea what may be going on."

The Baron simply nodded and without any more delay Gidon rode toward the noise. What he saw made him leave Begleiter on the roadway for he had not yet warmed up to Snaggle Tooth. There was the sabretooth sitting calmly on another would be assassin's back.

But to be fair the man was not only face down suffering the weight of the cat but also the pain of the great claws, each with hundreds of pounds of power firmly fixed into his skin.

As Gidon walked up he would have sworn, if great cats could smile, Snaggle Tooth gave him a smile. "Well my man, what do you say? Do you yield?"

"I yield; I yield, please do not let him kill me!" The man was in tears.

"I do not know if I can do that. He really wants to eat you." Gidon was enjoying teasing the villain. "What do you say, Snaggle Tooth, can I have him?"

The cat gave what Gidon knew to be a mew but it sounded for all the world to the varlet like a low growl.

"Please my lord. Save me and I will serve you well," the man said.

Gidon doubted he could trust this man for faithful service. "I am no lord, but I could take you to my lord and if you answer all questions, well, you might yet breathe a little longer."

"You have my word on it," the man answered hopefully.

"Very well. Snaggle Tooth, if you will give me this mouse, I have another I just killed. You may have that one." The cat obediently stepped off the man, but the would-be killer could not rise on his own power. By the time Gidon had him on his feet his new tunic was covered not only with the first man's spatter that came from cleaving him but also the blood from the wounds made in the back and shoulders of Snaggle Tooth's captive. He wryly thought, *Well, it was a nice tunic.*

Gidon made the man walk ahead of him and Snaggle Tooth back toward the place where the first attack occurred. Begleiter kept his distance but kept apace of them on the road. When the man saw the condition of his partner in crime he paled visibly.

The priests recognized Snaggle Tooth immediately and called out to him, but the Baron and his horse were no more thrilled at his presence than Begleiter. Gidon's prisoner seemed to be confused by the whole thing but that did not keep him from accepting the attention to his wounds the fighting priests offered.

Snaggle Tooth and Gidon walked side by side to where the half-severed corpse of the bowman lay. Gidon removed the balance of the accoutrements the priests had not already got and once again, as when they first met, he knelt in front of the great cat reaching out to scratch him on either side of his massive jowls. The sabretooth raised his front right paw and placed it on Gidon's shoulder. It seemed they were renewing the pledge of friendship as on the first occasion of their meeting.

Then the sabretooth grabbed the corpse and began dragging it toward the wood. The prisoner cried out, "Are you really going to let him eat my companion?"

Gidon looked at him, "Of course. You heard me promise him to the cat. I keep my word. Beside your partner does not need that body and my cat is hungry. We cannot just leave him laying around stinking can we?"

This seemed to amuse the Baron greatly but the priests were not quite so sure it was the right thing to do. When Gidon suggested the Baron might like to ride Begleiter he declined choosing to ride on the back of the cart and speak encouraging words to his horse. So Gidon made the prisoner walk at the front of the entourage with a rope around his neck.

Chapter 5

Challenge in Eastwatch

The Baron was disappointed to have missed the service at the church. The rituals would have been memorable in the edifice still in the process of being built after many years of work. Originally it was constructed of giant timbers but now was being built skyward and surrounded by stone. When finished its tower would serve additional duties as a lookout tower and plans were already drawn up so a fire could be kindled at the very top as circumstance warranted. Even when there was no winter vigil, events like someone lost in the forest, would mean a better chance of survival. They would be able to see the fire from a great distance and find their way homeward.

But this night the plans for so fine a structure was secondary to his concern to be with his friend Gid-visu, as the formalities of his arrangement with Brunhild were legalized, and her future made secure. In this way any children she produced would also not be considered bastards. He knew the relationship between him and Gid-visu was something of a mystery to the entire village, including his son, and it pleased Haki, now with the noble title of Baron, to keep it so. It was not that he still had a bit of the youthful enjoyment of perpetuating a mystery. He had once been known for that. No, it is the old story of the man who must walk dangerous paths. It is not wise to give away too much of oneself.

Upon entering the village, the men went first to the Burgomeister's home and banged the clapper. Gidon noticed the

Baron did not like the affectation of ringing the little bell any better than he did. Herr Brauner was soon at the door, faithful to his post. Baron von Krieg was not yet fully aware of Brauner's unhappy situation, "Where is your master?"

"He is at Fox Home where many of the villagers gather to fete Gid-visu and Brunhild."

The Baron spoke: "We need to get this varlet in the deepest part of your dungeon till tomorrow. Shackle him to the wall and lock all doors in between him and the outside."

Gidon spoke and asked, "As an old friend of my father's, why are you not at the party?"

Herr Brauner looked sad. "Herr Burgomeister forbade me to go."

The Baron asked, "Is there a wrong that needs to be set right?" He could see the man was neither serf nor slave.

Gidon felt guilty he had not told the whole story to the Baron earlier. "Yes, Herr Brauner owes the Burgomeister a sum he could best repay working at his trade. But the Burgomeister keeps Herr Brauner working as a servant when he could more readily pay working at the leather trade."

The Baron smiled one of those smiles that had a harsh intent behind them. "Well…I require you to be at Fox Home this evening. If you see the Burgomeister tell him you are there by my order. And, before you leave tonight, we have some business that must be discussed when others have departed." It was plain to Gidon, from the way the Baron said these words, he liked the Burgomeister no better than he did.

From the Burgomeister's home it was but a short distance to the stable where Herman the Schmeid was at his post. Herman had grown quite a bit in Gidon's estimation. The Schmeid's eyes widened at the sight of the amount of blood on Gidon and the lesser amount on the Baron. But he was absolutely in sorrow when he saw the Baron's horse had been wounded. He waited for Gidon to speak but it was the Baron giving out instructions now. "Schmeid cover my horse with a blanket so no flies may get in the wound. Secure our equipment and take care of the priests' ponies and their cart. Give the horses the best feed you have for they have certainly earned it."

It was now time to get to Fox Home and enjoy the night. Gidon hoped they would have his favorite treat called pig's ears, a pastry very delicate. It was called pig's ears because with a little imagination it could be said to look like a pig ear. It was so good and so seldom to be had.

When they arrived at Fox Home the priests Ur Menahem greeted Jonathan the Sword warmly and explained they were to share guard duties with he and Judah the Hammer till relieved. The old man, Jonathan the Sword, was very appreciative of the help. So with one priest staying on duty at the front, Jonathan and the other priest went together to relieve Judah the Hammer. Since the Ur Menahem had already stood watch over twenty-four hours, and made a trip of adventure, it was agreed Jonathan and Judah would only take an eight hour break to sleep before returning to the posts. The plan was to eventually get to a regular watch cycle. To fully recover would take some time because both sets of priests had been sleep and rest deprived. If there had been an abundance of men to stand watch the normal watch cycle would have been four hours. But one must do his best with what he has.

Much of the celebration was confined to the receiving room and the back with its walled yard. All the food and drink had been prepared and brought from other places except for a newly weaned calf being turned on a spit over the fire-pit. As the meat cooked it was trimmed away so all the revelers could help themselves with no meat over or undercooked.

Musicians playing in the two locations were quite different in their choices with those in the receiving room playing more formal pieces. Troubadours would take their turns in both places. Already some songs had been composed by them, singing of the brave Gid-visu and the beautiful Brunhild. If they were to be believed their love story was already one of the epic tales of romance for the ages! Gidon overheard one portion that went this way:

The silver fox, brave and cunning,
Took the fair young maid, whose lips were as the rose,

She swooned with the overwhelming joy,
Of such love no poet can compose.

Gidon heard an unwelcome voice, groaned inwardly, and turned to face Brigitta, the Burgomeister's daughter. She was in the middle of saying that if he had worked things rightly, they could have been celebrating their union as well. Then she became aware of the blood that covered his tunic front and was even in his hair. She had been so full of herself she had totally missed seeing the blood all down the back of his cloak when she came up behind him. She actually seemed to stagger and it was not the affectation most of her actions seemed to be. Gidon thought to himself, *This girl has had a really sheltered life. Such a woman would never be suited to a man of action and determination.*

Oma came up at that time saying, "Haki and Gidon, you boys are such a mess. Step into this side room and take off your tunics. Haki, is your cloak bloody too?" He just shook his head. There simply was no arguing with Oma when she took charge. And so it had been with all the Omas among the descendants of the Alemanni, and ever since.

As Gidon stepped into the little room, where Oma had directed them, he took some satisfaction in the knowledge Brigitta was left standing all alone and ignored. It was not long till Oma was back with Gwynedd, the younger widowed daughter of their fallen sons. "Gwynedd will take your tunics and Gidon's cloak to soak them and get the blood out." Oma gave Gidon the old cloak from his chamber so both men would not be wearing only chainmail when they went out among the guests.

He had not thought about it for a long time but suddenly recalled the story of Gwynedd. It had been told him during the time when his mother was sick and Brunhild was caring for her. Though Brunhild would have been barely twenty at the time, there was a night where in his sorrow, Gidon, who was probably not yet thirteen, had lain in her bed and been cuddled by her. He was sorrowing for his sick mother, so Brunhild told him the story of Gwynedd to get his mind on other things and allow him rest.

Gwynedd's mother had been in the possession of Roma people traveling past her father's farm when he saw her and bought her from them at a great price. He was very captivated by her beauty and learned she was of the wild woods people of an isle across the narrow sea called Eire. Brunhild told of a great hero of her people named Cunedda who included among his mighty deeds the fathering of many warrior sons of renown. It was from this famous hero Gwynedd's mother was descended. It was also said of Cunedda that he once swam the narrow sea. Gidon doubted this was possible. But when Gwynedd was born her father gave her the name in honor of her mother's people so far away.

Baron von Krieg washed his face and hands in a basin Gwynedd brought. But before Gidon could do likewise, Oma grabbed Gidon's arm saying, "Gidon you must be of help this evening and comfort poor Getrudis."

"Why what is the problem Oma?" he asked.

"We have a new lodger and he has frightened the poor girl half out of her mind. Now Gidon, I know you will be a good boy and a fine master to her and do for her what she needs to get peace in her mind." Oma laid a burden squarely on Gidon's shoulder.

Gidon did not think Oma was at all afraid of the man she was talking about, but she did not treat Getrudis' fears as childish or illegitimate. The truth was Oma was not much afraid of anyone.

He was about to tell Oma he would do what he could when Getrudis entered. "Gidon, you did not get all the blood out of your hair. I will have the servants to heat you a tub for a good bath. You are not wounded, are you?"

In spite of the words of concern that should have seemed natural there was jerkiness in both her speech and movements so unlike her usual gracefulness.

Gidon looked at her and realized his experience was insufficient to understand all that was going on inside her. He shook his head indicating he was not hurt. "We will do that, but first I want you to walk with me as I speak with the guests and get a bit to eat." He just realized that he had not eaten at all since the morning and with all the action this day he now felt ravenous. Beside this, it gave him some satisfaction to know Brigitta would see him with Getrudis, a girl she considered beneath her station. She would then know, or he hoped she would realize anyway, he preferred the wash girl's company over hers. But then, he thought, *She probably is too dense and vain. It is just as likely she will only be jealous of Getrudis.*

As Gidon walked out among his friends of the village he suddenly discovered he was enjoying himself and the tiredness of two days without sleep faded. In the receiving room Gid-visu and Brunhild were positioned much as they had been the day before. However, there were a number of gifts now arrayed in front of them. Gifts of a kind that might be expected in a poor village where almost all things were made by the inhabitants. But the handiwork was beautiful.

As he approached his father and Brunhild, Getrudis was still holding his arm; even so she managed a curtsy before the happy couple, without ever releasing him. Gidon heard a snigger from the corner and knew it had to be Brigitta, ever the critic of others.

Brunhild was first to notice the blood remaining in his hair. "Gidon, were you wounded?"

"No dear lady," he answered, reflecting her new position in relation to him. "I did a hurried job of cleanup but Getrudis has promised to get me spotless before I sleep tonight."

The Baron interjected from his seat to the right of Gid-visu; "To be fair to my squire, he was fairly drenched with blood this day. Had it not been for his quick response it might have been that not only my horse but myself might also have been wounded."

"I think my lord the credit ought to go more to Begleiter. He was doing the thinking for both of us. I just went along for the ride." Gidon was unwilling to appear as if the incident had changed him. He wanted to show noble humility regarding heroic action. And it was the truth.

The Baron actually snorted. "You should have seen him swing his new sword." He nodded to the bishop who had it made. "Had it been as heavy as my own sword he would have cut that would be killer in twain. He nearly did it anyway! And between him and his sabretooth pet they caught the other assassin and turned him into the wounded sniveling coward that he is. That is where most of the blood got on Gidon. I did not need to do anything but take care of my wounded horse. He is a very good squire to have!"

After all the Baron had to say, Gidon sensed the people in the room were looking at him in a different light. Not the least of which was the pretty wash girl hanging on ever more tightly, but even more confidently, to his arm.

His father showed no amazement over anything. "Well the day is done for fighting I would think. Let me get a man to carry your weapons to your chambers so you can enjoy the festivities."

When he said this, Gidon noticed the Baron had not divested himself of his weapons. And he was inclined to tell his father he preferred to stay armed but it was Getrudis who spoke presumptuously: "Oh no sir, he makes us feel safe."

Then she realized what she had done and kneeled with head down before Gid-visu. The Baron laughed the most genuine laugh Gidon had yet heard out of the man. Then Gid-visu and Brunhild broke into laughter, quickly followed by the bishop and most in the room. Gidon saw Getrudis had turned very red.

But it was Brigitta who broke up the merriment with her desire to interject herself, upstage Getrudis, and make another play for Gidon. She latched on to Gidon's free arm and said, "Does he not look very dashing in his chainmail and sword?"

Gidon sought to free himself from Brigitta as best he could without being rude. "Father, I am famished. Allow me and Getrudis to go outside and get a bit to eat. I can smell the calf roasting even in here and it makes my mouth water."

Gid-visu nodded. And as Gidon headed for the door he saw the Burgomeister approaching the Baron. He would later learn the man had asked him about Herr Brauner. The Baron told the Burgomeister the man's skills were needed for the war effort. Somehow the subject that this was a training muster was overlooked. Then he went on to say that seeing Brauner was so important to the king's plans, he was quite sure the Burgomeister would want to do his part, by forgiving the balance of the man's debt. Everyone who learned what happened was pleased that the Burgomeister, who could be so unfair to others, should have a bit of a comeuppance to close out the episode of his ill treatment of Herr Brauner.

*****

As they stood near the pit where the calf was being turned so it would cook evenly, many people came up to speak with Gidon. It was different than it had always been previously for now they were talking with him more as they did with his father. He was no longer being looked at as the boy who had grown up among them.

During this time· Getrudis busied herself getting Gidon a nice cut of meat and putting it between two pieces of bread called Landbrot. She knew he loved the plain farm bread freshly baked or not. It was second only to the three seed bread called Dreikornbrot. But to Gidon the three seed bread just had to be freshly baked to be at its best. The bread and meat, with a coating of honey and butter, made for a wonderful treat for a hungry man. Getrudis had never missed an opportunity to watch and learn about Gidon as he came and went at the tavern, and tonight she demonstrated that knowledge in both simple and surprising ways.

Brigitta had taken herself across the yard to stand uninvited among some of the young people while all the while studying the situation between Gidon and Getrudis with not a little bit of jealousy. Gidon was not unaware of her pique. He was enjoying it immensely.

It seemed not long until he realized the evening was far spent. It was much later than his normal time to rest when he was not out in the wild, and he had been two days without rest. He turned to Getrudis and asked, "Will you accompany me to my room and help me out of this mail? I am feeling a bit stiff."

As they went to his chambers, he saw Getrudis motion to the same boy who had kept their fire at the sauna only a short time ago and knew his bath would be in readiness soon.

A surprise was awaiting Gidon when they got to his chambers. The Baron and Gwynedd were in there and she was helping him out of his mail. The Baron explained, "I think we should sleep more closely in these perilous times. I plan to make a pallet on the floor in front of this fire."

When the Baron was rid of his chainmail, he got down on all fours on the pallet Gwynedd had laid out. "Come here girl and sit on my shoulders." Gwynedd looked a bit flustered but did as she was told only to find her outer garment was too padded in the bottom. It threw her off balance. So she got up and removed her outer dress and set back down on the Baron's shoulder blades where her backside could find balance on his broad back. The Baron promptly stretched out his legs so he was perched on his fingers and toes. In that position he lowered himself and Gwynedd to the floor and pushed them both back up ten times.

The Baron said, "I am a bit out of practice. This is the first time I have been able to do this in over a month, and it needs to be done every night. Gidon, you saw what I did, so now you come and try it."

Gidon thought to himself *Gwynedd is heavier than Getrudis and I need some advantage since I have never tried this before.* He said, "Getrudis will you come and sit on my back?" He hoped the shorter lighter woman would help him keep pace with the Baron.

Getrudis did not hesitate shedding her outer dress so she set on Gidon as soon as he got in position. Gidon had a thrill run through him when he felt her hips spread as her weight came down on his shoulders. The Baron was a cunning man he thought, getting a pleasure of the woman as he exercised, and all without her knowledge. But he found doing his ten pushups were harder than it had seemed for the Baron. He would have to get Getrudis and practice daily he thought with not a little anticipation.

When Gwynedd went to leave, the Baron attempted to give her a coin but she refused. Gidon thought to himself, *She likes the old guy and he has not fooled her a bit!*

Getrudis had to put her dress back on to go with Gidon to where the tub was in readiness. Gidon was wearing only the woolen garment on which the chainmail rested and a pair of inner breeches. For a little bit of time Getrudis had managed to relax but now it seemed the fear that had so undone her had returned. When he got to the bath, he took his clothes off and laid them over a holder made for that purpose. He dared not look at Getrudis lest his body betray him as it seemed to always want to do.

He could hear the girl undressing behind him. It was then she began to speak. "I am sorry I do not have my washing shift. I did not know you were going to be coming home bloody. I apologize and am embarrassed that it will have to be as in the sauna."

Gidon momentarily had the vision of when she had entered the sauna with nothing but a towel around her waist but then his mind began to work again. "*Wait a minute! She could have borrowed Brunhild's washing shift if she had wanted to be modest!*" But Gidon thought he was beginning to learn something of womanly manipulation. The quiver in her voice was not as it had been when she was forced to disrobe to go in the sauna. And she was not shaky because of nervousness about Gidon. She had made it plain, standing before his father, she looked upon him as her protector. It was as Oma said and she would be terribly disappointed in him if he acted ignobly. But temptation is strong when you are sixteen and have such opportunity.

He quite forgot the fact he was naked and came out of the water turning to face Getrudis even as she was pulling her inner garment over her head. Because of his move, when her hands came down and she was naked before Gidon, he also was naked before her. But Gidon was not thinking of that for the moment. He knew he would not be able to help the situation if he simply accused her of wanting to be naked before him to use him for protection.

"Getrudis you are scared and you need to tell me what is scaring you if I am to help you." He feigned total ignorance of the situation Oma told him of.

"My lord, I am terrified of the man who came to stay at our tavern this morning. I fear to go back to the tavern and I am afraid this man will murder everyone I hold dear and there is nothing I can do about it."

He thought to himself it was strange how all this evening he had been called Gidon and she had treated him with familiarity, in a way that was more open, yet in keeping with the time they had known one another. And now she addresses him as lord when they are both facing each other naked and alone. *It is strange how a woman's mind works.*

"Getrudis, you know that neither the Baron, my father, nor myself will ever let any harm come to any of you if we can help it." It was the truth and he stated it very matter of factly meaning to be reassuring.

The girl acknowledged his words but in a broken voice said, "But you should have seen him. He came into the tavern and set exactly where the Baron likes to sit. He had a broad sword and a long knife similar to what the Baron wears."

"It sounds like he might be another King's Rider." Gidon opined.

"Oh no Gidon, he wore no insignia. He had a big hat with a wide brim that he always used to keep his face in shadow. But I saw it when I brought him his mead." She shuddered as if a shocking experience was happening all over again.

"Go on," Gidon said, "tell me what it is that makes you so fearful."

"On the right side of his face, he has an awful scar as if someone sliced it open to the bone and it had to be put back together. On the left side of his face, he has a scar such as you might see on someone who has fought duels. His left hand is missing half of the last two fingers and the hands looked like the bones had been broken hitting things. I first thought he might be some kind of highwayman."

"Getrudis," Gidon spoke soothingly, "all these things you are saying might have happened to any man who has gone to war. If I come back scarred, will you be scared of me?"

"I have not told you the worst of the matter. It was first his eyes and then his voice. His eyes seemed to put out a light of their own and the part that should be white was yellow and there was no color in his eyes. The iris was as black as the pupil. Then his voice sounded so eerie when he spoke. I have never heard a voice like that. I am afraid to go back. Even when he smiled at me it seemed like an evil gawp."

It was as if the strength forsook her legs. She closed her eyes and sank to her knees bowing her head and slowly falling forward till her head touched Gidon's bare leg. It was then she opened her eyes only to discover Gidon's body had rediscovered its passion and his male member was reaching out to her. Her eyes widened at the close confrontation.

Gidon felt embarrassed. He reached down and gripped her upper arms firmly bringing her back to her feet. Already at sixteen his strong hands could reach all the way around her upper arm. "Listen to me, you do not have to sacrifice your flower or compromise yourself to get my protection. The matter of fact is that you are indentured to the tavern and my father owns half the tavern. So, in a way you are mine to take care for."

That was very true and Getrudis knew it. Many a tavern wench in other places fared very badly because of the rights of the tavern owner over her.

"But what is more important is I like you. I would not ever let anything bad happen to you or force you into something to demean you. You indicated that you knew that tonight, so why worry? That is my job."

Getrudis went forward and rested in his arms with her head under his chin, and so it was their bodies were touching. It was at that point he felt like cursing his maleness for it seemed that wicked member was trying to reach out and find her flower without him having anything to say in the matter.

Gidon gripped Getrudis arms again firmly, moving her away from his body. Then he swung himself around and got back into the tub. He tried to get his mind away from how his hands had yearned to cup her breasts and comfort her. But in truth he was unsure who would have been comforted in such an action. And what would such a thing cost in terms of trust and future relationship? And what would Oma say?

The memory of this night he thought would stay with him always. But one memory would be especially warming and that was the loving attention Getrudis poured out in getting his body and hair purged of all the blood that was upon him. During the time of their conversation the water had grown cold but it just did not matter. She went to a great deal of trouble combing out his hair and making it clean, fragrant, and soft. It was, all things considered, a wonderful bath. But one thing surprised him as Getrudis put her inner garment back on and then toweled him dry. It was the request she made.

"Can I stay here tonight?"

"I expected you would. I think Oma was expecting you would not go back to the tavern till morning." Gidon thought that maybe he should not have said that since she did not know what Oma had said to him. But Getrudis seemed to overlook what the statement implied.

"No, I have a request to make. Will you be my bed fellow tonight?" Getrudis smiled sweetly. "When it was so cold last winter Gwynedd, Brunhild, and I slept together. I have slept alone the rest of the time. I was raised in a large family." Gidon knew that large families in the farming hovels often had to sleep together because of a lack of space. She was clearly asking to be with him as if he was one of her siblings and nothing more.

"Well okay," he said, "but I must get to bed straight away. It is a long hard day tomorrow and I have not slept in a long time. And you know I must also meet the man who scared my Getrudis."

Most of the house was already quiet as they slipped across the house and into Gidon's chambers. The Baron stirred on his pallet but, other than that, gave no indication he was awake. Gidon, however, did not believe for one minute he was truly hard asleep. The two young people went through the arch to his cot and Getrudis shed her outer garment while Gidon replaced his clothes with his sleep shirt. He noticed it had been cleaned of the stains from the last time he wore it and blessed Brunhild's thoughtfulness.

He slipped under the furs and held them up so Getrudis could come in. He asked, "Would you like me to fold a fur so you could have more separation from me?"

"No!" Getrudis went under the covers facing directly toward his body and confidently laid her head on his shoulder, with the top of her shoulder in his armpit. "Isn't this nice?" she said.

Gidon was not so sure, feeling those stirrings which caused him so much embarrassment. He smiled at her then pretended to go to sleep. Even though he was exhausted it seemed to take forever to actually get to sleep. He had never lain with a woman this way before.

It seemed he had actually been asleep just a little while when Getrudis turned over pushing her backside up against Gidon but not moving much on his arm. He liked the smell of her body and her hair. He laid his arm over her waist similarly to how it had been when she was facing him. Then he dozed off again.

He came awake. Did he move his hand or was his hand moved? He did not know so he lay very still. As far as he could tell Getrudis had not responded but his hand was definitely cupping her breast. He wanted very much to fondle it and more, but now he was the one afraid. He was afraid he would lose this wonderful moment. He was also afraid if he tried to remove it, she would waken and catch him. Not knowing what to do he allowed sleep to overcome him with her breast firmly resting in his hand.

Oh, how his sleep was assailed! It seemed every time he was beginning to be in deep sleep, she would move her hips. Once after he did have a very heavy bout of sleep, he woke, and she was up higher on his arm, and he found both hands inside the fabric. Both breasts were now captive to his hands. He again thought that if Getrudis woke and found what he had done, now more than before, she would never believe it had happened in his sleep.

Later Gidon was again in agony. Surely that spear pressing her legs would waken her but it seemed she but parted them a little so it slid between her legs. *Those pretty legs! Now don't start thinking about them! How had the garments they had worn to bed rose up so high?*

It took great strength of will to force his body and mind back to sleep once more. But at last he did manage to get to sleep. And when he awoke Getrudis was sitting on the side of his cot, stretching her arms toward the ceiling and rearranging her garment.

"Good morning Gidon. Thank you for a wonderful night of rest. I do not know when I have slept so well. You made me forget all about my fears. Can I come back tonight and have you as my bed fellow again? I felt so safe in your arms."

Gidon was at first unsure he had been refreshed at all by the traumatic night that had passed. But little by little he would realize something had happened to either strengthen or change how his body was able to deal with stresses.

When she stood to put on her outer dress Gidon saw the stains of his temptation was on the garment she had been sleeping in. Funny how she did not seem to notice!

"Getrudis, I do not know if I will make it back tonight or not. We are going to have to seek out the gang of would-be assassins. If we are not successful right away, I may be out a few days."

The Baron looked through the archway from the fireplace where he had rolled up his pallet. "Boy, you never cease to amaze me."

Gidon knew that once again it would be impossible to explain to him things were not as he was assuming. So once again he was in a situation with the Baron where he thought it better to just not try right now.

As Gidon was trying to cleanse his body from the stains of the night emissions Gwynedd came in with their clean tunics and Gidon's cape. She looked at Getrudis knowingly. Both men began to dress themselves and it was then Gidon thought he would ask the Baron's advice. "I am wondering whether or not I should wear my new sword since I have not been trained on it. What do you think?"

"Well, you did show some talent with it. But you are right, you do need training. I would suggest you wear it while in the village, for the villager's sake, and then take the tools you normally use with you to the forests."

Gidon nodded, seeing the wisdom in his words. But what was really on his mind was whether Getrudis would get into any trouble, or whether Oma would think less of him. He was afraid Gwynedd might talk and that would not be good.

"The new guest rooming at the tavern needs to be seen about. He really frightens Getrudis." Gidon remarked.

The Baron looked thoughtful. "I would not worry too much about him. In fact, he sounds just like someone I thought might show up. If he is who I think, he is a member of the Long Knives."

Gidon remembered what Getrudis had said about the long knife, not unlike the Baron's, the man who frightened her carried. It could be before this day was over, they would have another lesson in not jumping to conclusions no matter how it turned out.

Chapter 6

Preparation to Search

There was no doubt Gidon was the last to observe that the bottom of Gwynedd's skirt was soaking wet. His mind was troubled by many things, and not the least of these was Getrudis. How aware had she been of things that had transpired during the night?

The Baron, however, never missed much. "Gwynedd it is really coming down outside?"

"Yes, m'lord, some of the streets are fairly awash with the water," Gwynedd said. "What I fear is those who rushed the planting of seed for the sake of the muster might have much washed away by so heavy spring rains." She would think of those things having grown up on a farm.

Getrudis had begun dressing Gidon in his mail as soon as he pulled the woolen garment over his head. It seemed she was taking an inordinate amount of time doing it, having to get things just right. He turned to face her, "I saw you with nothing but a shawl to cover your dress last night. You have no cloak with you, so you shall take my old cloak and wear it to the tavern."

Getrudis nodded meekly, hiding the fact she was thrilled to wear a garment belonging to Gidon. Her smaller stature meant she had to look up to see into Gidon's face. She grasped both his hands, hanging by his sides, and lifted them to her lips kissing each one separately. "One thing you said last night is so very true. You are my master and lord, not because I am bound by law, but because you are dear to me."

Gidon smiled and thought to himself. *Why you sexy little vixen!* While he still did not know how much of what went on last night she had orchestrated, there was now one thing he was sure of. The movements of his hands into her clothing and over her breasts, had been something she was aware of. And he now thought she had perhaps even manipulated at least some of the activity while he was deep in sleep.

He followed Getrudis and Gwynedd to the front door and the last thing he heard was Gwynedd telling Getrudis "You had best get washed off and into clean clothes before Oma sees you."

Gidon's mind was at ease now because he knew Gwynedd would keep secrets.

When the Baron finally indicated it was time for them to be out the door, Gidon was completely willing to be on the move. Once out in the weather he noticed that at least one of the consequences of the heavy rain was most welcome. In the poorer parts of the village, old ways of just throwing out garbage into the street still made for quite a mess even though the serfs were told over and over to carry their waste to a deep ravine set aside for the burning of such matter. They had even given the refuse dump a name calling it Feuer der Hölle, or Fires of Hell in the common tongue. But the rains were moving the trash out of town. That was a real blessing from the heavy downpour.

The first stop was to check on the condition of the war steed. The Baron told Gidon a man should always see to the care of his horse above all else. A horse can be the saving of a man's life or the losing of it. Why it is even possible a single horse in the right circumstance could make the difference in a battle. The one unhappy consequence of the visit was Gidon discovered the stables had developed a leak in one corner. Not serious at the moment but such a problem left unattended would spread and the cost of the thatcher to repair it would also increase.

Herman the Schmeid told Gidon the bishop had taken the monastery ponies and cart early. All their gear was securely stowed in the tack room instead of being covered just by a tarp. He was glad because he had left his bow and arrows in the Schmeid's keeping. He had not wanted to carry it in while the festivities were going on. The

Schmeid whispered confidentially in Gidon's ear, "I did not give the ponies the same feed I gave the Baron's horses. They are so used to living on poorer fare I did not want them to think I was trying to poison them."

Gidon laughed heartily. "I think they would like being spoiled a bit by anything we have here. Even the hay is far superior to what wild ponies eat. But in any case, we will not bill the monastery for anything their ponies have eaten." Aside from blessing the spiritual leadership there was the practicality of four fighting priests doing service at Fox Home.

Gidon asked the Schmeid if he would go to Fox Home and get his protective skins for his bow and arrows making sure no moisture got inside the casing? And of course, he readily agreed. He had thoroughly enjoyed the food Gidon sent over the night before and would be pleased if offered more. Then it was time for them to go to Herr Brauner's home and shop to complete the agreement they had made the night before.

Gidon expected plans would be completed while they were at Herr Brauner's but instead the Baron asked him to join him for lunch at the tavern midday. No one was interested in going out in this rain but it was an honor to be invited to eat with such a man as the Baron. And Gidon suspected Herr Brauner would even go into the black mountains to the South, where it was said all manner of consorters with devils met there with demons and such, if the Baron asked.

When they entered the tavern, the Baron led the way to the spot Gidon normally stood. This time Gidon did not lean his fighting staff against the wall. The dark stranger was already seated in that darkest corner the Baron first chose when he came.

Fat Max did not have the usual exuberant greeting for Gidon, and this raised fears in his mind that perhaps things had not gone well with Getrudis when she returned this morning. But neither was Max extending himself to be more than civil to the Baron. Could he be unhappy with him because of Gwynedd? Gidon did understand that Fat Max had a protective attitude toward both women. That was his way. He had love to be poured out on both his widowed daughters-in-law and the indentured girl as well.

Oma however had none of Fat Max's reserve when she came padding into the room. She walked straight up to Gidon and said, "Thank you for comforting our little Getrudis. When she came home this morning, I could hear her singing as she prepared for work. And she has been humming when she could not sing ever since. It makes me joyous to see our girls happy." And with that she gave a meaningful look at the Baron. He did not miss it even though he seemed to never take his eyes off the man in the corner.

When the man changed position revealing more of his face Baron von Krieg started walking toward the table. "Brute', what do you mean scaring my wash girl half to death? My god but you have gotten not one bit prettier since last I saw you. But maybe you have gotten uglier?"

While all this was going on, Fat Max was whispering heatedly to his wife, but Gidon was close enough to hear some of the conversation. "Why did you get Gidon to pay attention to Getrudis? That is an awful temptation to put upon a lad of sixteen. And nothing can ever come of it!"

Oma was unperturbed, "Now, now, poppa, we will talk later." And with that she walked calmly back into the kitchen.

The man called Brute' had risen to his feet. And if the Baron was close to the ceiling in height, towering over most of the citizens of Eastwatch, Brute' was taller. Gidon could see why this man might cause such fear in Getrudis.

"Your wash girl huh; is that all she is?" He tried to grin at Baron von Krieg but his scarred face did turn it into a leer that seemed to have an evil quality.

The Baron laid out the relationship: "No, she is my wash girl and a very good one. She says she belongs to my squire, but she is indentured to the tavern. Come here Gidon."

Gidon walked over. He had not known the Baron heard what Getrudis said to him before leaving this morning. But Fat Max heard the Baron's words to Brute' too. *It would be interesting to be a fly on the wall in the room where they had the talk Oma had put off till later*, he thought. But the Baron's soldier humor with this man did not make Gidon any happier with the day.

The Baron's introduction of Gidon to Brute' showed both of them what the Baron thought of the other: "Gidon I want you to meet one of the best fighting men I have ever known. He was once a centurion of the Italian Band; Brute' this is my squire Gidon. He is quite a monster killer. When he was but fifteen, he killed a Persian assassin and yesterday he killed a man trying to kill me, almost cutting him in half with his sword. You better watch out for him. He makes friends of sabretooth tigers!"

All the Alemanni knew what the Italian Band was and did not like them. They liked nothing about the generations of the wolf children, who had marched North to invade the lands of Gomer, whether they had been part of the invading forces or not. Still this man, who had once held a high position, was now here as a friend of a King's Rider. There was surely more to the story. At least part of it was about to be answered.

The men set down together, but Gidon stood until he was beckoned to take a seat. It was then Getrudis appeared with a tankard of whipped goat's milk, for it was not yet noon. She set the drink before Gidon with her hip just brushing his shoulder, an act not lost on Brute', he asked, "Are you the wash girl Baron von Krieg says is afraid of me?"

She lowered her head and shook it for no, but her actions told a different story.

"Is it that you do not like my warm smile?" he asked in his weird sounding voice. Without waiting for an answer, he said, "You should like it for your Baron gave me my smile so all the little wash girls would run from me."

Getrudis did not know what to do but stand there with eyes cast down dumbly taking the teasing.

"Leave her alone!" Gidon surprised himself, speaking up to the Baron's awesome friend, but Getrudis quick glance of appreciation was its own reward.

Brute' tried to laugh with what he had for a voice. He spoke to the Baron, "I think your squire might really be a very dangerous man indeed."

Then he spoke to Getrudis, "Do not worry little flower, I only eat big bad people. Now go get me a tankard of what he is drinking."

"You are right my friend, that girl belongs to your squire. She belongs to him if for no other reason she sees him as her protector." Brute' had put his analysis on the situation.

The Baron gave a little laugh and said, "He seems to have an impact on a lot of women. I wish that all such were drawn to me like they are to him."

The Baron began the business at hand. "I am glad you were able to come. I need your help building a company of men able to soldier and serve right here. And I want you to train them. One of our fellow Long Knives lives in the village but he will be appearing before the king shortly. He was the target of the assassin, a Hashshashin, that Gidon killed last Fall. I believe the assassins we encountered yesterday were after me. They were common varlets but probably hired by a Hashshashin. I do not know who hired these Hashshashin but I have my suspicion it was Goraleck. I have reason to believe he will soon challenge our king again."

Now, Gidon knew definitely his father was one of the Long Knives and the Chief of the Long Knives was not planning to send all who registered for the muster to the training up North. What he was so unsure of was the intent behind his plans.

Brute' explained he had lost his horse while traveling at night to get here. "My yellow eyes see better in the dark than did my horse's, though they be not as good as cats. It was a good horse and I was sorry he tripped in a rut worn in the dirt road when I was a little careless and resting as we traveled. As you know there has been precious little moonlight these past few days but it begins to change this night. That is, if we can see through the rain."

"There is other business that takes me where I can also pick up a couple more horses already trained to our needs," said the Baron. "But, even with hard riding I will be gone at least a week and things must continue here. Brute', if you and Gidon will be so kind as to interrogate our prisoner it would be very good. Frankly I do not think the man is familiar enough with the area to give you instruction on how to get to their hidey hole. And I would advise against taking him out as a guide because he is likely to give you away. Promises he made to Gidon are unlikely to mean anything if he gets a chance to escape."

Gidon wished the Baron would take him along but he could see how he would better serve here.

The Baron summoned Fat Max and asked him to pack some provision for three days. He told him to charge Herr Brute's expenses at the tavern to his account. Fat Max said, "Gid-visu told me to charge him for your expenses Baron. Does this mean I also charge him for Herr Brute'?" Gidon nodded.

Brute' mused, "Since my disfigurement many have been fearful of me. They often think I will kill them because of the way I look. But since my arrival at Eastwatch there has only been one person I really wanted to kill. That is the man in the room next to mine. The Baron and Gidon laughed because they knew he was speaking of Herman One Eye.

"We have plans for Herman One Eye," the Baron said. "But you can blame Gidon for him being up there. He is just one of the people my squire has wounded since I got here."

Gidon knew the Baron was teasing in his own way. But at the same time, he was building him up in Brute's eyes. Just as he had been doing with the villagers; making them understand that Gidon was no longer a boy of the village but a warrior worthy of respect.

Brute' started saying it was his opinion both King Gregor I, and now the son, had been too lenient with Goraleck, and should have sent him to the eternity he deserved long ago, when Herr Brauner arrived. As he came in, he noticed Bishop Elisha had entered and seated himself at a table near a front window. The window blind had been adjusted so rain did not come in as long as the wind did not blow hard, but fresh air still managed to come in with its clean rain scent.

Baron von Krieg motioned for both Herr Brauner and the bishop to join them. Gidon wondered if the bishop had been miraculously transported again? After all he had just left for the monastery this morning, and here he was at noon time back in Eastwatch. While they waited for the noon meal to be ready the Baron put Herr Brauner between himself and Brute', telling Gidon to come stand behind him and look over his shoulder. Once again, the Baron was pulling plans from out of the hidden recesses of his clothing as he had done when he met with Gid-visu.

The plan he unfolded before the men was a set of diagrams for some very unique leather-based breast armor that also shielded the groin. Brute' said he had seen a lot of armor but had never seen anything quite like it, and leather armor was very common to the legions. It was a combination of the fabric padded armor and chainmail built under the leather base. And it was designed so one size could be adjusted to fit most men. Herr Brauner said he could do his part but he would also need women skilled with heavy needles and a schmeid capable of making the chainmail portion. He knew Herman the Schmeid well enough to doubt his abilities.

The bishop interjected, "I have a very good smithy, who is wonderfully capable in armaments. He could come to Eastwatch and teach Herman the Schmeid while they prepare so large an order as fifty sets of armor. Also, among our Hearth Women are those skilled with needles and threads of all types. They could surely do some of the work while teaching women of the village already skilled in the finer stitchery how to speedily use needles the size of sail needles."

The Baron said, "All who are recruited will be paid for their work. Brute' will be here to see the project through, and he will keep record of each person's labors."

No doubt the women had been watching the progress of business. As soon after the diagram was delivered to Herr Brauner, they began to bring out the soup and bread that would constitute the noon meal.

It was Gwynedd and Getrudis who handled the bowls and platters of bread. But Oma came out and said, "I have made some of my special Dreikornbrot in honor of my good boys. I hope you all enjoy it." The warm fragrance filled the nostrils of all the men at the table. Nobody could bake like Oma!

As Gwynedd came back around to refill soup bowls Baron von Krieg said to her, "I have to go away for about a week or more so I will not be able to exercise for a little while. But you will not forget me?"

Gwynedd looked at him sweetly and said, "I will anxiously await your return m'lord."

After she had finished her serving and walked away Brute' said, "And you wish you had Gidon's way with the women!"

The men had eaten their fill and the Baron left the group at the table. He was the more anxious to be off and get back since talking to Gwynedd. He thought to himself that he was not as old a dog as he thought, being excited by such a beautiful woman.

Gidon had already figured out the business Baron von Krieg had to attend to, other than acquiring horses, was reporting to the king. He remembered the friend of his father, who raised and trained war steeds also had carrier pigeons by which he stayed in contact with the king's castle.

Bishop Elisha was very quiet since he had informed the men how they could assist in the project. But now, with stomachs filled, the Baron gone, and Herr Brauner leaving shortly after, it was time for him to speak. He now brought Brute' and Gidon's mind back to business. "It is time for us to go to the Burgomeister's house. We will find all is not well there."

Today it was not a stroll but a slog to get to his house in spite of the cobblestones along that street. Gidon imagined the poorer areas could not even move a cart without bogging down. It would have been easy to say that with this hard a rain, with heavy droplets coming almost straight down, things should be put off to the morrow. But none of these three men were of the type inclined to delay. And with the bishop's words that all was not well, Gidon, who had not learned the patience of manhood in more things than hunting and fishing, did not want to follow the bishop's example of systematically putting all things in order.

When they knocked on the door of the Burgomeister's, Gidon was surprised to see him open the door himself with a mace in his hand. Blood had been flowing down the right side of his face in such quantity that it had stained his garment on that side all the way to the navel. In the floor lay an old family retainer, whose forefathers had served for generations. He would have been the one to answer the door when the assailants came since Herr Brauner was freed of his obligation. It was plain to see he was quite dead. The old man's skull had been crushed in on the left side.

Brute' observed with analytical coldness that the Burgomeister and the retainer had been struck by two different men. One was lefthanded, and the other righthanded which accounted for the blows to different sides of the head. The Burgomeister nodded that was right and volunteered the dead retainer's wife was in the reception room with his wife.

When they entered the room, they saw the old woman too was quite dead laying at the feet of the Burgomeister's wife who had a bloody and broken nose, and missing teeth behind swollen lips. It was the teeth being knocked out that partly was the cause of the mouth being cut so badly when she was punched in it. Both her eyes were blackened as well. It was plain the poor woman was in a state of shock. The bishop covered her trying to keep her warm.

The Burgomeister's wife said to the bishop through her torn and swollen lips, "All these years I treated her contemptuously and then she died trying to defend me and Brigitta."

"Brigitta! Where is she?" Gidon asked, fearing the spoiled girl might be lying in her own blood somewhere in the house.

But the Burgomeister's wife could only say, "They tore her nightgown open and now she is gone!"

What the woman meant by Brigitta being gone was still a question. Gidon noticed that the sharpness that once characterized the woman's features had been torn away only to be left by that look of vulnerability seen in so many victims down through the generations of men.

Brute' asked the Burgomeister, "What of your prisoner?"

The man shrugged and said, "They took the dungeon keys and one man went down to him, but I never saw the prisoner come up."

Gidon said, "I know the way so I will go down to check."

He found the prisoner laying, still attached by shackles to the wall, with his head smashed in. The man had been hit squarely in the top of his head as one might kill a steer. He correctly guessed the shackle key was not on the dungeon key ring. However Brute' later would tell him they never intended to set the man free because his face would now be known. The reward for failure has always been death among men such as these.

Brute' shook the Burgomeister and said, "Man, get your wits about you. You have not done too badly so far, but I can see you are wandering in your mind. How many men were there altogether?"

"Three, I think. It all happened so fast." The Burgomeister's mind needed to be stable. He not only had questions to answer but a wife and daughter who needed him to be clear minded.

Brute' said, "That was what I was thinking. But was there anyone here with a strange accent?"

The instability of the Burgomeister's mind showed through when he said, "Only you."

It was plain they would have to hurry before the man became completely useless.

Gidon asked the Burgomeister, "Do you know where Brigitta is?"

The man shook his head. "When they took her, they told me an enormous sum of ransom I would have to pay to get her back. It is far more than I really have. I could not even get that amount if I stole the village's funds. And the way they were touching and talking about her I wonder if I will even get her back whole?"

Gidon felt some disgust with the man. When he talked of not getting her back whole it seemed to him as if he was putting some value on her person above the love for a daughter and it rankled him. And that was partly because in the past he had done the same but in a different manner.

Gidon said to the bishop, "How did you know this had happened? You did, did you not?"

The bishop looked toward Heaven and said, "I only knew something bad had happened and I had to get back to Eastwatch."

Gidon considered. If he was told something had already happened before he returned to Eastwatch, that meant he had covered an impossible amount of terrain to get from the monastery back to the village. Once again, the bishop had made an incredible journey in a short space of time. It was a wonder.

Bishop Elisha walked to the door and opened it before the caller could knock. “It is good of you to come. We are going to be in much need of people who will help through tonight and the next few days.

Gidon is again in wonderment. *How did the bishop know they were there before they made their presence known?* In the years he had known this man, he was beginning to suspect he had not really known him at all!

It was then Gidon told Brute’ “I have to go and prepare to hunt these persons down.”

Brute’ said, “I make it out there are three men plus somewhere there is yet a Hashshashin to be accounted for. I also think the Hashshashin did not send these men. And if that is right there is no accounting for what might happen. A man like that could kill all three of them and the girl too.”

“Why do you think the Hashshashin did not send them?” Gidon was wondering about the conclusions he had come to.

Brute’ explained, “The Hashshashin could slip in and out undetected even by the householders. They are masters of concealment. He would not need the dungeon keys for he could open the locks with ease. I think he made the mistake of saying it needed to be done and they tried to impress or please him. And for that reason, what we have here is a botched operation that could cause them a lot of trouble.”

“What about Brigitta? Do you think there is no hope for her?” Gidon was surprised at his concern for the girl.

“Oh, there is hope, at least for a little while. The Hashshashin might consider her something to trade if he got cornered. But he would not have ordered her kidnapping for ransom. When he took the contract from whoever hired him that was all the wages he expected or wanted. With those people it is a matter of their perverted sense of honor.”

Brute’ continued, “We had better wait for morning when hopefully we will have clear skies for a little while.”

Gidon looked at him. “You are not at home with fighting with stealth in the forests are you?”

Brute' replied, "No, and after the Roman defeats by the tribes of Gomer in these forests I am leery of the forests. Many of my old brotherhood actually fear these woods. Fighting in these conditions is not what I am best at."

"Then sir, meaning you no offense, you are as likely to get me hurt as to help me." Gidon was rather matter-of-fact about this knowing straightforwardness was the best way to approach Brute'.

"Do you know someone you can take with you?" Brute' asked.

"My father would be the best one to take. But I am reluctant to take him away from Brunhild. I have not seen him so happy since mother died."

"You are talking about going up against four men and one of them a Hashshashin. That seems to me a good definition for foolishness." Brute' opined, "I think the three men might have some familiarity with the woods."

"Believe me sir I am not being foolhardy. I will try to not take them all at one time if I can help it. And when I attack it will be in an hour they think not if I can manage it. Beside the which, Snaggle Tooth is likely to meet up with me out there." Gidon had his plans, but he was aware things do not always work out as planned.

"Snaggle Tooth?" Brute' asked.

"Yes sir. That is my sabretooth friend."

Brute' laughed his weird laugh again. "So the Baron was not kidding. You really do have a sabretooth tiger."

"I have a friend who is a sabretooth tiger. I really do not think anyone ever has a cat, sabretooth or not." It was Gidon's opinion but he found Brute' in agreement.

"Do not get yourself killed. I am not sure the Baron would ever forgive me if I allowed you to do that."

At this time the Burgomeister walked up to Gidon. "Please save my daughter Gidon. You know Brigitta loves you, at least as much as she is capable of loving anyone more than herself."

Gidon thought it was the blow to his head that had so rattled him that he was capable of such honesty. But the Burgomeister's wife had overheard the conversation as well. "Yes, she loves you Gidon." Her mouth was so badly damaged she could say no more.

As they walked to the door Gidon asked Brute' to please tell Getrudis he had gone to rescue Brigitta and hoped to see her as soon as possible.

Brute' asks, "Is there a woman in all of Eastwatch who does not love you?"

Gidon replied, "Yes, most of them."

Brute' laughed and said, "I rather imagine an opinion poll would come up different, but it might make some fathers unhappy. They cannot all become your lady."

When Gidon got to the stable he discovered Begleiter was gone with the Baron. He knew he would be but he still missed him. So did the Baron's warhorse. He took a few minutes to pet and talk to the Baron's lonely steed.

Herman the Schmeid had not only come from his home with the things he requested but his father, Gid-visu had packed a complete hunting kit for him. He would not have to backtrack himself. From the amount of food packed in the food sack, it was plain that he thought someone, probably the Baron, was going with him. Gidon knew he never would have consented for Gidon to go on this mission alone.

When Gidon asked the Schmeid if he would oil his sword and take care of it while he was gone hunting, he could see the young blacksmith was absolutely thrilled to be trusted with it. He wished he had time to tell him of the plans for armor that involved him, but that would have to wait.

Once Gidon had changed into the forester's clothing and the other gear distributed on his body he set out back to the Burgomeister's house and then proceeded in the direction the pieces of information pointed to. He was surprised at the number of people who had seen something but said nothing.

The clues took him out of the village and into the forest where at one point he found a torn piece of nightgown to tell him he was on the right track. But the rain had washed away many clues quite thoroughly.

It was not until he was getting fairly deeply into the woods following his own instincts, he felt a head go under his hand and push it up till it was fully on Snaggle Tooth. The great tiger stood just above his elbow in height.

What a massive creature he is, Gidon thought.

The huge sabretooth looked at him as if he could read his mind. Proceeding on the way, rubbing that enormous head as they walked together, he said to the cat, "Things are going to be fine, if we are careful." Snaggle Tooth answered him with a deep growl as if saying, "I will do my part, I do not like whoever it is you are after already."

Chapter 7

The Hunt

Trying to get through the forests which were dimly lit on a clear day was often difficult. Nearly impossible was moving about on a dark night with rain now blowing and swaying the trees. It is always strange how things may appear in heavily wooded areas when light was badly diminished. Gidon did not wonder that so often stories of all sorts of mystical happenings were invented by people uncomfortable with the deep woods.

Tales of the walking trees were often thought to be invented by people who had lost their way. They would look behind them and it would appear the trees had moved because the way back looked differently than it had going through them. Gidon thought that was possible but probably not the case. No doubt woodsmen would observe that in an area where they had cut down a tree, coming back in a few years to the spot, they would see a tree similar to the one cut down growing just a little distance away from the first. They knew these trees came up from the roots of old trees capable of reproducing themselves in that way. But when they tried to explain it to people, unfamiliar with the different characteristics of trees, what actually occurred would be misunderstood. And sometimes woodsmen delighted in adding to the mystery of the forest.

It was kind of like the situation in the fall when bare limbs looked like evil grasping fingers in the moonlight. Scary to an overactive imagination, but completely harmless, that is unless a limb that had died happened to fall. But now the sap was up and limbs that had survived the winter were already displaying much green finery with the spring. And the forests would keep getting denser until the process reversed once again in the Autumn.

He reflected on the very old belief that ancient gods met under a giant Ash tree which had three roots. Below one of the roots resided the goddess Hei. Under another root lived the frost giants. But under the third resided humanity. Sometimes the gods and goddesses, along with the frost giants, would seek to invade the root of men. From these periodic invasions came the seasons. And it was because everything lived under the root of the giant tree, all trees showed the coming of the seasons as a sign. Gidon was very glad his tutor had delivered him from such ignorant ideas. But there were many who did still cling to them.

Gidon traveled at least two miles into the wood mainly guided by the instincts of Snaggle Tooth, who seemed to understand where Gidon was headed. At least he hoped the great cat was not just going for a walk in the rain with him. His feet could feel the heavy layer of humus under him built up by years of falling leaves. In spite of wide areas where no ground vegetation grew because of the thick canopy overhead, he realized he was on a trail but not such as animals might make. It was a little too wide and a little too straight to be a line made by the activity of forest creatures. It was a human trail, one that had not been worn bare by long usage. His confidence in Snaggle Tooth grew.

As he sensed the morning was about to come, he found himself in a spot where the wind was not blowing through the area because its direction was contrary to the little passage between two slopes of the wood. He began to think he could not be much farther from the camp of the men he sought. If so, the chances of an unwelcome encounter increased the longer he stayed on their path. It was time to start thinking smartly.

Moving up the side to his right because it had the longest slope, he walked into a bush that had found a place to grow in a depression barely twenty feet away from the path. Working as best he could in near dark, for some rays of the morning sun was just beginning to penetrate his little spot, he fashioned a shelter in the midst of the bush using the oiled cloth he carried for a little tent. His father had thoughtfully packed a gill net which he put over the tarp and platted pieces of the bush into it so the construction was camouflaged toward the trail. He did this in a manner where observation was directed toward the trail, but he and Snaggle Tooth could enter from the uphill side. All in all, Gidon thought it was not too bad a job. He hoped it would hide him from the trail while allowing the taking of one of the varlets if opportunity presented.

Gidon had considered the possibility of making a snare or trap to try and take out at least one of the men, but the problem was he needed to take them one at a time because he was seriously outnumbered. A man caught in a trap or snare that did not kill him outright would holler for help. It was too unlikely several could be caught at one time. Such a plan was obviously a bad plan. He had discounted the idea of a trap, at least to begin with. It seemed as though the best chance was relying on his skill as a bowman and taking advantage of opportunity that came along.

Gidon was content for the present to watch the trail out of the worst of the wet. He opened the container he had put his bow and arrows into to keep them dry then proceeded to wipe the bow, bowstring, and three deer hunting arrows with an absorbent cloth he kept for such occasion. Now Gidon exhibited the same patience as though he was hunting a deer.

He did doze a bit knowing he could rely on the keen senses of Snaggle Tooth who seemed very content quietly cleaning himself beside Gidon. But as he sat quietly, every once in a while, all sort of dire thoughts of Brigitta possibly injured or abased interjected themselves. In some way he felt responsible. But he knew the Burgomeister should never have built a dungeon into his home. His home certainly did not qualify as a Hold, which offered the lowest level of security for imprisoning dangerous men.

Later, as the day wore slowly on, Gidon divided some of his food with the sabretooth. He showed a positive appreciation for the roasted calf. He whispered, “You like that better than raw meat?” to which the cat responded with a purr. Gidon rubbed behind his ears and jaws. The cat appeared sleepy but Gidon hoped his senses were still working.

Again, his mind wandered to Brigitta. He still had his fears for her, but his mind went to the bishop being told about her gown being torn open. He had never seen her breasts, but in his youthful daydreams had imagined them before. Now his imagination had a specific event to focus and daydream on. He snapped his mind back to watching the trail. *Daydreaming can get you killed*, he thought.

It was not till the middle of the afternoon that Snaggle Tooth raised his head alerting Gidon to the fact something was moving down the trail. His senses strained to pick up specific noises that would tell him whether what was coming was animal or human. To be on the safe side he placed an arrow on the bow ready to pull back the string if needed. When the man came into sight, the sword at his side told him the man was the most dangerous of his quarry, the Hashshashin assassin.

Gidon was waiting till the man was directly below him to fire his first arrow. He wanted to make sure the man was alone. But when he got to the place where Gidon wanted to fire he stopped walking and turned looking up the hill directly at Gidon. Gidon felt the momentary hesitancy many hunters experience with their first deer that stops and looks at them. Gidon had never killed a man from ambush with a bow or anything else before. But the hesitancy was only just a second or two. When he loosed his arrow at the assassin, he was already running up the hill toward Gidon. He had not expected that.

He never saw a man move so fast as when the assassin brushed away the arrow with his sword and kept on coming. His father's training had taken over and he had replaced the first arrow with a second and fired it almost without thinking. The second shot went out when he was almost on top of Gidon and took the man completely by surprise and squarely in the chest just to the right of his heart. He went over backwards sliding down the slope breaking the portion of the arrow sticking out of his back.

Surprisingly the man was not dead. He turned himself in spite of what should have been excruciating pain and crawled toward the protection of a tree. Gidon's third arrow was fired at his legs but the man had moved out of sight so fast he did not know if he had gotten his target or not. Gidon readied a fourth arrow from his quiver.

For some minutes he could hear the man he had just put at least one arrow into breathing heavily behind a tree. Then the sound ceased. Gidon had been told such men are not easily killed normally and now he believed it. *Could he have found the strength to be hunting him now?*

Gidon considered how vulnerable he might be if the man was able to now sneak up on him. He remembered how a couple of years earlier, a bear shot by a huntsman had then come around to spring upon the man. He had actually gotten on top of the man, who had been able to get out his hunting knife and stab the bear repeatedly in the abdomen. The bear had died on all fours perched over the poor fellow. It was with great difficulty that he was able to worm his way out from under him. The huntsman would later say if the bear's legs had not locked above him, and instead fell down upon him, he would either have smothered to death or been trapped only to bleed to death.

The bear had been able to claw the man's face open, destroying one eye, and bitten him in the shoulder, taking away much of its movement forever after. It had taken the huntsman several days to get himself in a condition where he thought he could try to make it home. He was met by a search party of neighbors that came looking for him because he was long overdue. Gidon knew that if this assassin managed to turn the tables on him he would not have to hope for a search party to meet him. It simply would not matter.

By late evening, with nothing yet happening with his assassin, Gidon decided he should go out and see if he was still alive or waiting to kill him. But when he moved, Snaggle Tooth took the initiative. He went to where the assassin hid himself and pulled him out by one leg. He was quite dead. Gidon was pleased to see he had not only gotten the assassin in the chest with the second arrow but the third had done its job penetrating through the large muscle in the back of the upper leg. The man had died chewing on some substance.

Gidon supposed it was the pain killer the Hashshashin had gotten their name from.

The fact none of the men in the assassin's employ came down the trail meant he had either left the three watching Brigitta somewhere up the trail, or that he had killed them and moved on. Since he would probably have needed to recruit replacements had he killed them, Gidon opted to believe he still had a hope of rescuing the Burgomeister's daughter.

But his first order of business was to see if he could gain some information about who had hired him. He took the man's cloak. It was of a design not worn in these areas in the way it went around the head. With some difficulty he removed it from the assassin's body. He observed the dead weight of people was seemingly even harder to handle than the weight killed animals. The cloak had within it a recess to hold things but nothing was in it. So he laid it open on the ground to put the man's possessions in.

Gidon saw the man had six knives at an angle across his chest. They were completely flat. He assumed these were made for throwing and probably coated with poison. He took them and the straps that went over the shoulder and tied back to the belt and laid them on the cloak along with his Yataghan and a knife that was not unlike his own. All the weaponry went into the cloak. Then Gidon searched his pouches. One consisted of various forms of money. The other had two compartments. One compartment held the substance the man had been chewing when he died. He would have to share that with the apothecary. The other had some papers but they were not in a tongue or tongues he could read. Perhaps the bishop could decipher them. All was packed into the cloak and thoroughly tied up.

Snaggle Tooth looked at Gidon as if he had a question. Gidon nodded and said, "Go ahead." So he dragged the body off and hid it. Gidon hid the loot from the body in the bush they had used for a hunting blind, making sure he could find his way back to it. As soon as Snaggle Tooth returned they headed up the path the assassin had come down. Gidon's hopes he would yet be able to save Brigitta increased. When the thought, *Would the village think the less of me if*

I fail? came to mind, he felt ashamed. Her rescue was not about him, or what others thought.

It was fully dark by the time they smelled the wood smoke of the would-be assassins' camp. They had tried to make a shield to keep light from the fire from shining beyond the camp, but the men had made a poor choice in woody materials to burn. Gidon could see he had come up behind where they had tied poor Brigitta to a tree with her hands secured just far enough over her head that she could rest them on it. But how long she had been in that position he did not know, but it was plainly causing her some distress. He thought to slip up behind her and let her know he was there but he had no confidence she would not give them away.

Gidon began to work his way around to the far side of the camp to gain a perspective of the layout from there. It would not do if someone allied with these men should come up the path behind him. Snaggle Tooth was right with him, moving as he might when stalking a prey. Gidon got the impression he was enjoying himself, getting to do these catlike things with Gidon.

It was when they got to the far side of the clearing the layout of things became clearer. To his left they had taken an oiled cloth of some size to make a tent for the men. Across the clearing sat Brigitta looking the most abandoned, sad, and miserable person in the world. In her lap was a cloak they had probably used to cover her during the rain but these cads had pulled it down since the rain had ceased exposing her breasts for their lecherous pleasure.

Gidon was expecting three men but he saw only two. One was cooking something in a pot over the fire, and the other was walking about complaining. He would soon learn the cause was Brigitta herself.

He listened closely and was soon making out the man's words. "I do not care the Persian said not to touch her. They will pay ransom no matter what condition we return her in."

The man at the fire said, "The Persian did not want her taken at all. It would have been better had we left them all dead. Now he is concerned that the villagers will come out and search for her."

"You know yourself," the pacer retorted, "everyone in the village hates the Burgomeister and his whole family, and especially that spoiled little wench over there."

Gidon grimaced. Brigitta would truly hate being called a wench normally, but now she set listening dumbly, looking down at her lap. She faced the reality that people really did not like her or her family for the first time.

"Look at those tits," the pacer commanded. "They will soon flop down to her navel because she has never done any work in her life. We should get some pleasure out of her before that happens. He walked over to Brigitta and grabbed a nipple, tweaking it harshly. The muscle in it hardened and twisted, while Brigitta actually tried to remain stoic in spite of her tears. "See. She likes a little rough treatment."

Gidon whispered under his breath about the man, "For that alone I will kill you. God give me strength and your death will come slowly." He felt the heat of righteous anger rising in him. Snaggle Tooth looked at Gidon and positioned his body to attack. Gidon thought, *I have to be careful or we will be in the fight before I am ready.* He looked at the cat and thought, *Can you read my mind?* The cat looked back at him knowingly.

The third man appeared at the opening of the tent. Gidon now knew where the third man was. "Untie that woman's hands from over her head and let her cover herself with the cloak. Cannot you feel a cold breeze coming down from the mountains since the rain has stopped? She has no stamina for such treatment. I do not wonder no woman wants the likes of you."

The man from the tent walked into the wood on Gidon's side, and the sounds of his reason for leaving the camp were soon heard. Meanwhile the pacer did as he was directed, still taking opportunity as he undid the knot holding her hands to rub the front of his body against her. It was just another way he could abuse her.

The man who had gone to the woods came back just as the man at the campfire pronounced the food ready to eat. Each man filled a bowl from the pot but none was offered to Brigitta. While the men ate, the pacer said to the man who had been resting in the tent, "I do not understand why the Persian left you in charge. Why should you be boss over us?"

The man, who had huge hands, made a fist and said, "He left me in charge because I can whip either one or both of you at the same time. Besides this, I may not be too smart but I am smarter than both of you put together."

The stewpot man said, "If you are so smart then tell me why, since everyone hates the Burgomeister's family, what makes the Persian think they would come after this shrew?"

"There is a man, the fellow who hired him considers dangerous. His name is Gid-visu. He and his son are master foresters and they seem to think the village is their responsibility. That is why he left. He wanted to kill Gid-visu before the weather cleared, and they came after us. Remember Gid-visu's son has killed a Hashshashin, but the Persian thinks that if he cuts off the snake's head the body will soon not be a danger."

Gidon realized that by killing the assassin this afternoon he might have saved his father's life. That took any sense of guilt for striking from ambush away. Killing such men, who killed from ambush themselves was not dishonorable, he reasoned. Men who kill from ambush should not be surprised to die in the same manner.

The stew pot man was told he had the first watch. The pacer said, "Come into the tent wench and pull off our boots. It will be the first work you have ever done in your life."

Brigitta stood up and started trying to put her torn nightgown over her breasts in some manner. The pacer said, "Do not cover that. Even if I may not have it I ought to be able to enjoy it, I may just take the whole gown away."

Some of the old Brigitta showed up and she said, "My Gidon will come for me and you will regret the day you ever abused me! He will make you sorry!"

The man replied, "Just for that, after you get our boots off you will lay yourself on the ground and be the cushion for our feet."

The prospect of their stinking feet resting on her body demolished all the strength she had just mustered. She went about the duty of removing their boots and obediently lay down at their feet. Gidon saw her breasts sway in the motion of straddling each leg and pulling off the boot but he had no pleasure in it. Her torment only made him angrier at the men. The pacer planted his feet into her back none too gently.

Gidon had felt a sense of pleasure when she had expressed such confidence in him. It grew harder and harder to be patient, in order to win the day, the more he saw her abused. He might not particularly like her, but he hated to see her so disrespected, even though in the past she had mistreated others.

The wait for some opportunity stretched out as the camp settled down with two men in the tent resting their feet upon Brigitta and the stewpot man keeping the fire and walking about the camp. He really was not much of a guard.

Gidon slowly worked his way around to where the men had dug a hole to take care of their physical needs. He thought this his best opportunity to take his first prey of the night. Just before it was time for stewpot man to be relieved of the watch, he came to the hole. Gidon was hiding under a bush, so just as he was about to drop his pants and turn to sit on a pole over the pit Gidon rose up behind him. Then putting his hand over the man's mouth, he first slit his throat then shoved his knife under the man's ribs. Then he dropped the man and began shaking his left hand. The fellow had bit his hand! How he would like to holler! He thought through his pain that he would have to learn how to do that the right way.

Then he and Snaggle Tooth worked their way back around to his first location. He was just in time to hear the boss man tell the pacer it was his turn to watch. He also spoke to Brigitta saying, "Go get your cloak girl and come back into the tent. You can wrap yourself and no one will bother you tonight. I mean you no harm for I have daughters of my own."

As Gidon set three arrows at the ready, he wondered how this man would have felt had someone messed with his daughters as they had with Brigitta? In Gidon's mind he was only slightly better than his fellows. It would not be enough to save him.

Gidon noticed the man he called the pacer was slow to come out of the tent. Brigitta had acted much quicker to retrieve the cloak and wrap it tightly around her. So, when the pacer came out of the tent, delaying so as not to miss a little opportunity to ogle her, she was watching him as he was shot squarely in the groin, with the arrow appearing to extend out his anus. Gidon had chosen a small game arrow for just that person. The pacer lay on the ground screaming in torment.

The man he called the boss emerged from the tent not really sure what had happened. He had a sword in his hand but when the deer arrow went through his heart he did not run as some deer have been known to do. He was dead before he hit the ground.

Brigitta was standing there in shock as if she did not know what had happened. But when Gidon stepped out of the forest, bow in hand followed by a sabretooth tiger she fainted dead away. Gidon knew from the way she felt this was not one of her female affectations. She was out cold!

He picked her up gently and took her into the tent. Then he splashed a bit of water in her face and when she responded he gave her a little to drink. He said, "You lie here. I must take care of a few things and then I will come back in to you."

By this time the pacer was no longer screaming but laying on his side whimpering. Gidon squatted beside him. "When I saw you abusing Brigitta I promised myself you would not die easily."

Unbelievably the man answered through his pain with a chorus of curses.

"You know, a man about to stand before God should be thinking about making peace with his Maker, not adding up more sin to pay for." Gidon thought for a brief minute that the man who had seemed the worst was actually being blessed with an opportunity the others did not have.

"I do not believe in your God." And again, as the pain reasserted itself, he launched into another tirade of curses.

"I think you will believe in my God in but a few minutes." Snaggle Tooth walked over, put his paw on the man's chest, and looked at Gidon.

Gidon spoke to him, "You are right my friend. If I delay this thing, I will just be playing with my prey." Whereupon he slipped his knife under the pacer's ribs and into his heart.

Gidon went over to his ambush position and picked up his bow and arrows. He stopped long enough to warm the stew a little and then took it into Brigitta. He lifted her up and brought his spoon out of its pouch. With her laying in the arm with the bitten hand, he used his spoon to get some food into her. When she had recovered a little, she said several times the thing that kept her hopeful was the knowledge he would come. In some ways she almost seemed as the little girl he had first known when they were children. There was one exception; the ordeal changed Brigitta. She was no longer snooty.

When Snaggle Tooth pushed his way into the tent she momentarily tensed but then remembered she had seen him with Gidon when he first appeared. Gidon told her, "This is Snaggle Tooth, my friend. Snaggle Tooth, this is Brigitta. She belongs to me." The sabretooth seemed to understand completely and momentarily lay his head upon her stomach. Gidon rubbed behind his ears and soon Brigitta did likewise. Then the old cat lay down on one side of the tent.

Gidon was fairly sure all the evil gang was taken care of. He said to Brigitta, "If you do not mind, I am very tired. I have killed four men today and my hand is wounded. I need to lie down and sleep beside my cat."

Brigitta said, "I too am very tired." She picked up his injured hand and held it to her lips. "Perhaps you will permit me to also sleep in the tent where I can feel safe?" So it was, with two men dead before the tent and another before the waste hole, they slept as the carrion bugs came out of the wet ground drawn by the blood that had soaked it.

At one point in the night, Gidon awoke to see Snaggle Tooth get up and walk over beside the girl. She had been moaning, no doubt from bad dreams about all that had occurred. He stretched out beside her and she wrapped her arms around him without ever waking up. Gidon thought to himself, *That Snaggle Tooth. He never ceases to amaze.*

The sabretooth was up before any of them when the sun arose. Gidon got up to be presented by the cat with two freshly caught rabbits. Thanking him, he stepped into the wood and down by the creek found some herbs to give them flavor. Then he rewarded Snaggle Tooth with the rest of the calf that had been packed into his things.

When Gidon returned and came into the tent to retrieve the stewpot and his spoon he saw Brigitta was still sleeping the sleep of one who has been through much. The disarray of the torn nightgown left her exposed in a pretty and provocative manner. He averted his gaze. Already it was bothering him that he had fantasized about her being exposed as he came to rescue her. But when he actually saw her, he was filled with rage at the men. Now he thought part of the emotions was because he was ashamed at having taken pleasure in the thought of her gown being torn open on her body. It was quite a different matter when he saw it for real. It left him filled with self-loathing for having such thoughts.

By the time she arose, he had rabbits stewing, and had also found clothing among the stewpot man's things that would fit her, but very loosely. She took them into the tent and tried to put them on but fell over. Gidon called out to her, "Are you okay?"

She said, "I am sorry but I need help."

When Gidon entered the tent, she had pulled a blanket over her to hide her nakedness.

"Gidon forgive me. I know you probably think I am playing a game but I am not. I seem to be too weak to keep my balance and get into these clothes."

Gidon knew her well enough to know this was not a game. She just did not have the strength to hold up under what she had been through. Her body had never been hardened by challenges made upon it. He helped her to dress very gently, respectfully averting his eyes as much as possible for he realized she had been severely traumatized as well as physically challenged by what she went through.

Gidon spent the balance of the day inspecting the men's belongings and tying up the things he thought worthy of keeping. Unfortunately, nothing of what he found gave him a clue to who was behind the assassins who had come to Eastwatch. So Snaggle Tooth obligingly took the bodies away when he was finished.

An inspection of Brigitta's feet revealed they had been pretty badly bruised and would need a couple of days to heal before they could head home. In the meantime, he would have to fashion her some footwear that fit and not make her feet raw as well as bruised.

Gidon tried to tease her about taking his cat. She tried to protest till she realized he was teasing. It was the first time Gidon had ever teased her and secretly she was pleased. However it did surprise her to learn the cat had come and stretched out beside her and she had cuddled it like some stuffed doll. She tried to tease back saying just maybe she would cuddle the cat up every night. Teasing in this way was a new experience for Brigitta.

Gidon opened up the fire pit so they would have more light from it. And that night they shared a meal of fish caught in the stream below. Fish was also a great favorite of Snaggle Tooth and Gidon found out he preferred his fish cooked as much as Gidon did. As they sat in front of the fire sharing a bit of wine that had been found among the men's possessions, Brigitta relaxed by the wine, grew more open about her fears of going home.

She said, "No one will believe these men ever took me captive and did not deflower me. I am going to be marked for life as a tainted woman."

Gidon reassured her that something would happen to allow him to keep her reputation intact. He spoke over-optimistically, "By the time the whole thing is through everyone will believe you are a heroine!"

Later when they had retired to the inside of the tent Brigitta said, "There is something else about my reputation I am concerned for." She told him what had been said just before Gidon had rescued her adding other things the men had said about her the night she was taken captive. "I do not want to go back to the reputation I had before."

Gidon told her the only one who could change her reputation was her. He was about to say more when she started talking about what they said about her body. "Is it true I am going to be sloppy and heavy when I am yet too young to be that way?"

Gidon said it was very likely to be that way. "Men and women are made to work, and work helps keep the body firmer longer. It is not too late for you to get busy and do more with yourself, but you will have to make the decision to change the way you live. I do think you will be happier if you try."

The next morning Brigitta got up, and even though her feet were very sore, she went around the areas close to the camp and gathered what she thought would serve as firewood.

Gidon accepted her attempt, thanking her. Then he began the business of making her some shoes that would be soft to her feet. As he took each foot in his hand and held a piece of leather to the bottom of the foot, he instructed her to push against the leather in his hand so the foot was spread just a little from the weight. Then he made an outline on the leather with a piece of charcoal pencil." He marveled at how small her feet were. Brigitta had some vanity about her feet and mourned, thinking what they had suffered would mar them forever. Gidon sought to reassure her when the bruises healed they would be just as beautiful as ever. Perhaps even more so because they would be stronger!

On the fifth day of her recovery Brigitta said she needed to wash the clothes Gidon had given her and bath herself as well. Gidon tensed up thinking here it was, the moment of temptation was coming. But instead she asked if she could take Snaggle Tooth down to the stream with her as her guard? Gidon felt like shouting. He did not understand all that had happened with her but there was no doubt the girl was changed. And she was a woman.

That night he told her they would start their journey back on the morrow and he would need her to help carry some of the things they would be returning with. He would stop as often as she needed so they could rest. Brigitta gave no complaint or excuse, saying she welcomed the opportunity to serve her lord. Gidon decided to let that part of the statement pass.

They did have to stop a few times because Brigitta was still building strength. As they approached the village Snaggle Tooth gave his half growl mew. Gidon knelt down before him and scratched his ears and under his chin, till the sabretooth laid his right paw once more on his shoulder. Only then did the great cat take his departure.

Herr Brute' came to them first followed by his father and then others of the village. "The bishop said you would be coming this evening so here we are."

By this time a number of people were gathered around.

"Herr Brute', would you please carry this damsel to her father and mother?"

Brute' picked her up in his arms. Brigitta tensed when she saw his face but then she relaxed into his arms giving him her trust.

"Tell them she fought for her virtue, thoroughly defeating four bad men till I was able to get to her. She is like one of our warrior queens of ancient times. She only has one problem…"

The crowd waited expectantly thinking something to damage her reputation might come.

Gidon said, "She likes to sleep guarded by a sabretooth tiger!"

Chapter 8

New Outlooks

When Brute' picked Brigitta up in his arms he could see the woman was exhausted. He knew she had traveled some miles through the forest with both her and Gidon laden with packs. How far they had come he was unsure. But since it was evening, he assumed they had traveled all the day. It had not surprised him the woman had tensed when she saw his disfigured face. What had been surprising was how quickly she had relaxed in his arms.

"You do not fear me little warrior queen?" said Brute', adapting Gidon's words to describe her resistance to her kidnappers.

"No sir," Brigitta said. "Allow me to express regret for the unkind way I first reacted. I know anyone Gidon would entrust my care to must be a great man, worthy of my respect."

Brute' marveled. This certainly was not the shrewish, self-centered, spoiled child he had been told about. If her detractors had been correct about her, something had happened to change her greatly. For one thing the kind of girl he had been told about would have never consented to be dressed as a man.

He looked at the newly made footwear she wore. They could scarcely be called either boots or shoes. It appeared their primary function was to cushion the girl's feet. He suspected that in all likelihood her feet had been badly bruised as she was carried away and Gidon had made something to soften each painful step and prevent further injury while they made their way back home. Brute' decided Gidon had done a good job given the conditions.

"You are like one of the Alemanni warrior queens of the past." Brute' opined with the strange voice that had been described as eerie.

"Oh no sir," Brigitta said, feeling a need to be honest with this man in spite of the fact she was once seldom honest with anyone. "I am no warrior queen nor could I be even a warrior princess. The truth is that if those wicked men had held me one more day they could have done as they would with no resistance from me. I have never been so shamed or abused in my life. Gidon spoke as he did so all standing about would know they had not broken my flower. I remain a virgin. My great desire is to become that virtuous woman the Bishop Elisha has often spoken of when preaching."

"Then you are a warrior queen in the best of ways. A man would be honored to carry your favor in battle." Brute' said, "Allow me to call you as Gidon has so named you. You are Brigitta, our little warrior queen."

Brigitta shifted her weight and wrapped her arms around his neck, placing her head against his chest. She liked the idea of being this huge scary man's little warrior queen. And she liked the challenge of trying to live up to his opinion of her.

*****

When Gid-visu met Gidon coming home and safe, he first felt a bit of anger that his son went on such a perilous adventure without him. But the sheer joy of not only seeing his son home safe but also apparently victorious rapidly overcame all other emotion. He picked up the packs Brigitta had left behind intending to help with the burden.

But Gidon said, "Father would you let someone else carry the packs and instead tell the bishop, if he is still in town, and the Apothecary I would like to meet with them at Fox Home. Then perhaps you and I could take a sauna together? There we could talk of things that occurred where we are alone."

Herman the Schmeid along with Herr Brauner came to meet them together, both out of breath. They must have been together when they heard he was coming and ran to meet him. Perhaps that means they are already working on Baron von Krieg's special armor. Together they volunteered to take not only Brigitta's but Gidon's packs to Fox Home. Gidon suspected their eagerness to serve in the matter was some hope of hearing of the things that took place.

Being relieved of the packs was also a little like being relieved of some responsibility for Gidon. He suddenly began to feel very tired. As they walked through the town toward Fox Home and a place to finally sit in a chair, the way began to seem longer and longer. For Gidon it was not the miles he and Brigitta had traveled, nor the weight of the burdens they returned with. It was the heavier weight of responsibility and burden of taking human life that made for his exhaustion.

*****

Brute' walked up the steps of the Burgomeister's house with Brigitta still firmly held in his arms. As they had come up the cobblestones of the last street, a number of its residents had left their homes to follow them. Perhaps some wanted some gossip, but just maybe there were among them those with the genuine concern of holy charity. Brigitta asked Brute' to turn around and face the throng. Her words spoken that day were described as fair and gracious:

"Please allow me to thank all of you for your prayers for the safe return of Squire Gidon and myself. I am humbled seeing you come out to greet me as Herr Brute' sees me safely inside my home. I can tell you I am anxious to see how fares my momma and poppa. I imagine each of you know far more about their condition than I do right now.

"Once I have recovered, it is my hope to have some small part in the work for the protection of Eastwatch that Gidon told me about. Of course, I have no skills with needle and thread and hope some of the women of our town will have pity on a lazy girl and teach her better. God bless you all!"

A few cheers went up and Brute' turned to pull the bell string on the door. Brigitta found herself more shocked at seeing Herman One Eye open the door than when she first beheld the scarred face of Brute' As they went through the door no one heard her say to Brute', "You will not leave me will you?"

Brute' looked at her as kindly as he could. Brigitta had won his heart in spite of it being as scarred as his face.

*****

When Gidon came to the door of Fox Home, he was complete with an entourage made up of not only Herr Brauner and the Schmeid but some hangers on, who had originally come out to meet them. They had followed out of simple curiosity to see what would happen next. Eastwatch was seldom as filled with events as it had been these last couple of weeks. No doubt the townspeople, whether those with simple souls or not, all believed the next exciting event would happen around Gid-visu and Gidon. Only the two carrying packs would gain access. But some would linger on outside just in case some news filtered out.

Gidon was glad to see Judah the Hammer was on duty at the front. He stood there with the bishop, and just behind them was the new Mistress of Fox Home. Judah recognized the transformation in Gidon that made him a man of war even as he; they exchanged the hug appropriate to godly men of war. Bishop Elisha was more reserved, and Gidon simply said, "I owe you more than ever I can repay. Brunhild would have none of it and gave him hugs and kisses, so that his mind went back to when he was a small boy with a dying mother needing desperately motherly affection.

Brunhild directed Herr Brauner and Herman the Schmeid to lay out the packs on the big table where guests usually ate. But Gidon warned that some items might be poisoned, so the bishop hurried to inspect the lot and, if necessary, neutralize poisons. It was just as these things were happening Gid-visu arrived with the Apothecary, bringing an ointment for Gidon's damaged hand. As they got together to go inspect the goods, Brunhild grabbed his arm and gave it a little squeeze saying, "I have sent for Getrudis." Gidon wondered how much she knew or surmised?

The young lad who they had used to make the sauna fire and warm water had now become a part of the household staff so he was not hard for Brunhild to find when Gid-visu told her that he and Gidon would have a steam bath this night.

*****

Brigitta, seeing her father's head, shorn of hair and swathed in bandages, felt her heart moved. He was complaining of terrible headaches so bad he sometimes could only just lay on his pillows and moan. Her mother on the other hand was an even more terrible sight. The bishop's healing priest, part of an order of Hospitallers, along with a krankenschwester, a woman who cared for the sick, had sewn up her lips torn in three places and set her broken nose. Her face was very swollen still, so that she could scarcely see through two blackened eyes, and all she could eat was cold broth. She broke into tears when she realized her daughter was not only alive but in the room. Brigitta was suddenly very glad, and not for her own sake, that Gidon had killed those awful men.

She had intended to tell her parents of her plans for service as soon as she got home and inform them of the change in her heart she had experienced. But now she saw this was not an appropriate time for that. At the moment her duty was to be something she had never been before. It was now time to be a dutiful daughter and take care of her parents.

What she took the most comfort in was Brute' would not leave her as long as she asked him to stay. And she had no doubt that Herman One Eye would perform exactly as he commanded. After a few minutes of being with her parents Brigitta knew there was nothing she could do at the moment. She took the hand of Brute' and went to a spot in the hall where there was a chair meant for several people to sit while waiting for the Burgomeister. She asked, "May I lean against you and rest for a moment?" He nodded and she slipped herself under his left arm which had the hand with the missing fingers and lay her head against his chest. Immediately she was asleep and would remain so several hours. All the time Brute' held her without moving. Yet he had a glare for anyone coming through or making the slightest noise. When she awoke there awaited a most unpleasant experience. Her feet had swollen so badly she could not stand at all. So Herr Brute' picked her up gently and took her to her bedroom, placing her feet elevated on pillows. The krankenschwester came in and ordered Brute' out while she stripped away her male clothing and put a clean nightgown upon her. Then because Brigitta insisted, Brute' was allowed to come back into the room usually forbidden to men.

*****

It was hard for the men gathered at Fox Home to decide what should be inspected first. So, it was decided on a division of labors that would allow the work to go on simultaneously. Bishop Elisha took the papers only to discover it appeared they were written in two separate languages. Though he suspected what two languages, he was unsure and preferred to know with certainty before he spoke. He would have to go back to the monastery Scriptorium to see if any of the documents stored and copied there might give not only the languages but also the meanings of their message.

The Apothecary announced he would need to get to his shop to do analysis on the material the assassin had been chewing when he bled to death. But he declared his opinion that eating enough of the stuff might cause hallucinations. In any case what little they had, if they could get no more, would prove of limited value as an ongoing pain killer.

Herman the Schmeid took all the tools and weapons that had belonged to the men Gidon had killed. He left only those which had belonged to the assassin. Herman said the quality of the other weapons was very poor, but they could be repurposed. He was learning from the monastery smith and growing in ability. The priest had discovered how Herman the Schmeid learned best and was making great progress with him.

Gid-visu announced the Hashshashin weapons might be poisoned and the poison would have to be rendered inactive. He rolled them back up in the assassin's cape as Gidon had first placed them and bound them tightly. They could wait for the morrow.

Herr Brauner was asked to sell the goods belonging to the three varlets and put what little came of it to his labor in making the armor Baron von Krieg designed. Gidon suggested the tent material might go to the new fighting priests for use when they traveled to the king's muster. It seemed each man had some things to take care of as a result of this last adventure.

Gid-visu had asserted the contents of each would-be assassins' geldbeutel should by rights belong to Gidon. The money from all the men's money bags were counted and after the tithe of the tenth was turned over to the bishop, Gidon found himself with a fairly sizable reward. The one responsibility not spoken was what Gidon must do next. He felt like the only one who had yet realized the grave predicament before them. That was not true, but he now did understand better and would have to make the decisions of a mature man.

When Getrudis arrived, she was escorted by Oma carrying a package. Getrudis looked as if she was experiencing a mixture of embarrassment and excitement. Yet when Gidon looked in Oma's face he knew she had not had all of her conversations with Fat Max about Getrudis go her way. He saw Oma was intent on getting him off to herself so he motioned her to the little room where, what seemed a year ago, they had another talk.

"Gidon, do you know what I have in this package?" Oma was being very direct.

"I imagine you are going to tell me." Gidon had decided to be just as direct.

"In that package is Getrudis' wash-dress, and another item of which it is hard to speak. It is a new sleeping gown. She paid one of our village sewing women to make it. She does not have the money for such things, so it was purchased with great sacrifice. It is made with embroidery and a special decoration over her left breast of a sabretooth tiger. Now what is that supposed to mean?"

"Getrudis said she belonged to me when she was here less than a fortnight ago. The night we celebrated Brunhild becoming Mistress of Fox Home. And you told me to take care of her," Gidon said knowing full well the thing he had been supposed to take care of was her fears. "It looks like she meant it!"

Oma stood there wordless. She had expected many excuses for what she imagined.

"You do not worry. I have not touched her flower. We have been one another's very close friend and yet more than friends. I care for her very much and we will make some decisions about the future this evening." Gidon feared the decision if it caused him to lose Getrudis.

Oma reached up and patted Gidon on the cheek. "You are my good boy. I do trust you and I believe you will follow the best of a man's ways with a maiden." With that she turned to the door and into the hallway where Getrudis had been left standing, even as once Brigitta had been left in the same place, but with different intent.

*****

Brute' was trying to sort his feelings. He had lost a family when overcome in battle as a member of the Italian Band. Was what he was feeling toward this helpless young woman the emotions of a father long stifled or was it some deeper emotion of a man for a maid? Yes, a maid alright, but one less than a third his age. Could it just be gratitude that she accepted his disfigurement? She certainly was not just sympathetic to damaged men. He sensed she was very uncomfortable to find Herman One Eye in her home. He could not fault that. After all, he had felt the urge to kill him several times when he made a nuisance of himself at the tavern.

Brigitta had drifted into sleep as the pressure eased in her feet. But it was not sleep undisturbed. She began to dream the men who had kidnapped her were torturing her, sticking needles into her feet. She moaned in her sleep and the sound of her own voice brought her awake. The nurse heard her moan and fearing the worse might be happening to her from the ugly man inside, rushed in. She found him standing over her and his weird voice was what she heard before she understood the words.

"Little warrior queen, I know exactly how your feet feel right now. Having once been a soldier who moved by foot, I saw many men with damaged and even bleeding feet. When I was a young soldier I too was once badly bruised in my feet. I can work the bones and joints in your feet so they will get well and you will not be crippled. With your permission I will do so. It will be a little painful at first but it will help you get better."

"Oh please sir. I will try to not make you ashamed of me. Until I was carried away my life knew little of pain, But I do trust you, and will endeavor to bear any pain your ministration causes." Brigitta was determined to be worthy of the title used by this surprisingly gentle but fearsome looking man and endure anything he chose to do to her.

The nurse started to speak but instead exited the door. Brute' assumed she had gone for the healing priest. Instead she was back in scant seconds with a jar of ointment and handed it to Brute'. "Sir, rub this in and it will help the muscles in her feet. It will also help with the pain as you work."

Brute' found himself surprised at the krankenschwester's behavior, expecting to be upbraided for daring to touch a woman's feet so familiarly. He gratefully accepted the unguent and opened the jar. The odor that came forth filled the room and opened up the sinuses. He thought that if the substance worked as well on her feet as it did on his breathing it would be a miracle potion indeed. He sat on the bed moving the pillows under her knees, while all the time the nurse looked on as if supervising. Not knowing the strength of the medicine, but if the smell was any sign, he felt the application should be made sparingly.

The bottoms of Brigitta's small feet were facing Brute'. He marveled at how square her feet were with the line where the toes met the feet almost straight. With his hands grasping the right foot first he placed his thumbs side by side on the pad behind her toes. He began to knead the joints away from each other. Once he had worked that portion, he put ointment on the top and bottom and then moved to the left and harder to reach foot where he repeated the process. In all of this Brigitta neither cried nor complained. Her one comment was the unguent was really warm. Brute' took his time giving the medicine an opportunity to soak in and diminish its heat, fearing massaging might cause the rub to become overly hot.

When Brute' looked at her face, she favored him with a sweet smile. But he did notice a single tear roll down her cheek.

*****

Gidon walked over to Getrudis in the hall. "We need to go somewhere we can talk."

She was overcome with a sense of shyness not knowing what he and Oma had said to one another, but well aware she had taken her package into their meeting. Knowing what was in it, she feared that Oma would tell Gidon to give her up. She had heard quite a lot from the old woman when she discovered the nightgown on her cot back at the tavern.

But before they could get away to be alone Gid-visu yelled down the hall it was time to go to the supper. Oma said she could not stay but must get back to help Fat Max, making the point for Getrudis benefit, they were short of help at the tavern. Brunhild placed Getrudis beside Gidon on a long side of the table that had recently been filled with the material Gidon had returned with. She placed herself on the other long side very near to Gid-visu where she could see all who sat at table. The bishop sitting at the far end opposite Gid-visu blessed the food, the gathering, and gave praise for the safe return of Gidon and Brigitta. It was a pleasant supper but through it all Brunhild and Getrudis secretly worried that the bishop would be invited to join in the sauna. Both women intended to go in with their menfolk and would not be dissuaded, bishop or no bishop. What Getrudis did not know was the ever-foresighted Brunhild had already planned for just such a possibility. However, after the meal, the bishop declared he must be going to call at the Burgomeister's house; then he would sleep in a priest's cell in the church.

Gid-visu and Gidon excused themselves leaving the ladies at the table. They went out in the back and stripped naked. Then they poured a bucket of cold waters over them and taking a towel off the line entered the sauna, spreading out the material to sit upon.

Gidon had just finished telling his father the assassin he killed was heading back into town to kill him when Gidon was able to make the ambush. He had also said his henchmen called that assassin the Persian. He also expressed the fear there was a traitor living in the area. He would have said more but just then their women entered the sauna. Gidon felt a bit of disappointment because they were wrapped in linen sheets with wraps also around their heads. When he had heard them coming, he had anticipated the pleasure of seeing Getrudis naked once again, even though he did not wish to share the experience with his father.

Both women went to the side of their man sitting opposite the other. Then they lay their sheets back on the bench so their loveliness was confined to the man in their life. Gid-visu fully appreciated the beauty of Brunhild sitting beside him even as he continued wanting particulars of the way Gidon had managed the feat of killing the men. Gidon was not happy to talk about blood and death in front of the women so he simply said, "If it were not for the lessons you taught me about fighting it is highly likely I would not be here. Let us talk again at a more suitable time."

*****

The bishop's arrival at the Burgomeister's home affected people in different ways. Herman One Eye was none too happy to see him because he was, as he had often said, "Not a religious man." But Bishop Elisha could see into the man's heart and knew there were different ways to reach men. He began by complimenting him. "You have been given a great honor being chosen to protect the Burgomeister's home in such a perilous time."

"Bah," said Herman One Eye. "The only reason Gid-visu gave me this job was because I was getting on Fat Max's nerves, and that gargoyle up in Brigitta's room wanted to kill me. You should have seen him glare at me in the hall today. He still wants to." He conveniently overlooked the fact Herr Brute' was concerned he not waken the sleeping Brigitta.

The bishop could see old Herman was well aware of what was going on around him. While he might not have social ability, it certainly was not because he was oblivious to those about him. He would have to employ different strategy.

"How many retainers does Gid-visu have?" Bishop Elisha would work on his outlook by using only those things obviously true and ignoring arguments against the truth he pointed out. "Consider, he could have sent any number of men but he chose to send you. He must see something in you worth giving you this responsibility."

Herman One Eye was thinking, but he found it difficult to give up on his usual negative nature. "He once found me so worthy of responsibility he knocked a dent in my head."

The bishop knew he had him now. "Now Herman, were you not drunk at the time? And when you are drunk no one can reason with you can they? That means in spite of that unfortunate incident and the fact you were so foolish to fight his son he still saw some good quality in you."

Herman One Eye tried to carry his negative attitude forward one more time. "Well, no one likes me or my family."

"Herman, Herman, Herman. That just is not so. As you know Baron von Krieg has left on some important mission. You may have not known that in spite of being so rushed with his duties he took time to take a package of food out to your wife. Listen to me. Prove yourself in this great responsibility and you will be trusted with greater things."

Herman One Eye found himself making a commitment to the Bishop to try and do his best. Then the Bishop went on to talk with others in the household.

*****

The women were first to flee the heat of the sauna. Gidon looked at his father seriously. "I am going to have to do something about Getrudis. It seems to me both Brunhild and her are in danger. I am either going to have to break with her or keep her here at Fox Home where she can have a bit of protection."

Gid-visu said, "She is a good girl and will be welcome here. I am thinking we need two more girls for the tavern. You decide what you want to do and I will support you."

"No. I am going to let Getrudis know the danger. Then I will let her decide." Gidon was now grimly ready to leave the sauna. He was glad his father had not mentioned his hope that his first experience of knowing a woman would be in the state of marriage.

After all, what if his father had arranged a marriage this year and the woman had not liked him? What would the experience of their union have been like then? He wondered how many people in a world of arranged marriages, where people were sometimes bought and sold in marriage covenants, had unions that went loveless? He had a love and feared he might have to give her up.

*****

Bishop Elisha went directly from Herman to Brigitta's room. The nurse, sitting in a chair in the hall, warned him that Herr Brute' was with her and she would have it no other way. As the Bishop announced himself and walked in Brute' had just finished massaging her feet and again applying the pungent unguent for the second time. With the power he had to read men's hearts he could see how this man who had seen so much and suffered great losses in life had become attached to this girl. He knew of his desire to take her feet in his hands and kiss each toe separately making it better. She truly was his warrior queen and he fully adored her.

When the bishop came in Herr Brute' begged to be excused and went out to take care of his person so he could set more easily waiting her call.

Brigitta was extremely joyful to see the old priest. Finally, she felt she had someone she could share her desire to learn the use of needles of the kind needed to make the armor Gidon had told her of. She told him how she regretted having been a careless and useless person in the past. Then she talked of her desire to be a person of worth and character such a person that a great man like Gidon or even Brute' might love. She said, "Herr Brute' calls me his warrior queen. He started that because Gidon said I had been like one of the warrior queens of old when a captive, but of course it was not true. I told him as much and yet he still calls me so." She realized she had been gushing on and on.

Bishop Elisha asked, "Will you keep your vision of being worthy of such a man? Days pass away and emotions are often fleeting."

Brigitta became very serious. "I have seen what I was and what I would have become had I stayed on that path. I am not sure I can ever be worthy of a man like Herr Brute' but I intend to try. It may sound strange. It has happened so quickly. But I have seen things in him that draw me to him. I simply adore him!"

The bishop promised to send one of the hearth women to instruct her in needlecraft as he left.

*****

Brunhild and Getrudis had changed into wash dresses and were waiting to douse their men with water and then towel them dry when they came out of the sauna. They had brought each man one of the short inner tunics men often wear for working without other clothing. Tucked up through their belts, when doing certain types of work, this spared more expensive garments from damage. Gidon had grown so much since his was made it barely went half way down his upper leg. He needed to replace that one with a garb that could be tucked.

Brunhild said Gid-visu was going to use the tub first. So Gidon responded that Baron von Krieg had taught him an exercise they could do while they were waiting. Gid-visu laughed and said "I think I know the exercise whereof you speak. I will have to teach it to Brunhild." This left Brunhild with a suspicious look on her face, especially when Getrudis seemed so merry about doing it with Gidon.

Gidon led Getrudis to his chambers, and the girl, eagerly expectant, announced she was going to sit on his shoulders without her gown. It was too much for Gidon. He grabbed her in his arms and wrapped them about her squeezing so tightly she was almost breathless. His lips found hers and they melted into a long embrace with lips and bodies pressed tightly to one another. Finally, Gidon said, "This will not do!"

He stepped away from her, leaving her not the first time naked before him. "Put on your wash dress. I cannot speak to you of this so overwhelmed I am by your beauty."

Getrudis' face got serious and of course she blamed herself for the situation as women are too often apt to do. "What have I done to offend my lord?"

"Do you remember the morning of the heavy rain when I sent you with Gwynedd back to the tavern?" She nodded, saying nothing.

"Do you remember I put my cloak on you because you had only come with a shawl?" Once more she nodded her head and bit her lower lip. She felt like crying and did not yet know why.

"There could have been an assassin lurking about out there in the rain and I did not have enough sense to realize the danger. I am so very sorry. I could have lost you. I could have gotten you killed and I did not even realize it at the time. I was only thinking about getting you in trouble with Oma and Fat Max."

Getrudis said with typical female logic, "There was no assassin out in the rain. Everything worked out fine."

"You don't understand. I killed a Hashshashin on the trail to rescue Brigitta. When I found the camp with the three varlets, I listened to their conversation while they were tormenting her. If that had been you, I would never have been able to restrain myself till I had an advantage. But the thing was I learned the man I had just killed had been on his way back to kill my father. If he had been successful, he might also have killed Brunhild as well. These are evil men."

Getrudis pertly answered. "Well I am glad you did not tell me you had fallen in love with Brigitta while you were rescuing her."

"Getrudis how can I make you understand? Ever since I have been filled with fear something might happen to you because of me! I either have to take you into my house or send you back to the tavern forever. I will not make this decision. It is your life. What will it be?"

Getrudis walked right up against Gidon. "I told you before, you are my lord. You are my master, even as Sarah told Abram he was her master. As long as I live, I am yours. As long as you want me, I am yours. So do you want me or not?"

It is difficult to say who initiated the next long embrace and kiss.

When Brunhild walked into the room, she found Getrudis naked sitting cross legged, buttocks spread out on Gidon's shoulders as he pushed them both away from the floor.

Brunhild crossed her arms over her gown and adapted a smile that was both sardonic and somewhat expectant at the same time. "So this is the exercise Gid-visu wants to teach me!"

Chapter 9

Return of the King's Rider

Twice Gidon woke thinking it was now time to be up and about. Each time Getrudis held him tight and said the hour had not yet come. He should go back to sleep. As his body tried to relax, the part of his brain over which he had no control would begin to work. He found no real joy in killing men no matter how wickedly they had been doing. But he did not mourn them either. His mind sought to reconcile the deeds he had performed with his belief life was sacred.

The third time he woke, he knew the waking hour was near. His injured hand throbbed. His mind dwelt on how sweetly Getrudis had applied the salve the Apothecary had brought. The hand bit by a man fighting for his life, even as Gidon killed him, had hurt for nearly a week. Its healing was slow. The sweet girl had tears as she looked at the ugly cuts and bruises, teeth marks made around the joint where thumb and hand meet. He remembered her sobbing as she treated the Baron's back in the sauna in what seemed a time so long ago. What a sensitive and sweet heart she had. But she also had a bit of impishness about her. When he lifted up the sheet last evening so she could come in, as he had done the first time they were bedfellows, he teased, "Shall I put a fur between us?" She had said, "If you do, I shall bite you!"

How his hand hurt! Gidon had his arm under the small of Getrudis' waist. Her waist was very tiny, but his arm was very thick thanks to exercises and hard work he had been put through since his father came home from the last war. He had his arms about her waist most of the night. He did remember how after one dream he had taken her buttocks in his hands and held them firmly pulling them toward his body. Getrudis had taken it for passion in his sleep and perhaps it was a little bit. But it was also a reassurance to him that something precious was in his life and he could cling to that. But the arm had to be extricated from beneath her now no matter all that happened in the night.

When Gidon removed his arm Getrudis rose and did her customary stretching of arms toward the ceiling. It mattered not to Gidon whether she was facing him or not, that stretch was a fascinating gesture. Quite aside from the beauty of her body was the tremendous grace with which the ritual was performed. Gidon decided he deeply enjoyed just watching her move at any time. He would not be satisfied till he carried out his plan to publicly bond her to him so it looked to the world as if a lesser transaction had occurred. But all the while he would accomplish a greater one clandestinely with the bishop's help. He would have to find a way to contact him. He hoped a subtle plan would cause any enemy to place less value on Getrudis' importance to him and not target her because of him. Yet he would keep her closer than ever before.

This morning he lay aside his woodland green clothing for that of a squire. In truth the forester's clothing was filthy from the long adventure that had just occurred. But he knew by evening two women would see that situation changed. No, today he would don his chainmail and even put on his sword. He had no illusion receiving instruction from his father with wooden swords and shields as he grew made him more than a novice with the sword at his side.

When finally he went to the breakfast table, Gidon saw Brunhild and Getrudis had jointly prepared the meal and were waiting for Gid-visu and Gidon to ask them to join them. This formality from old times was followed this day because the women expected very weighty matters to be discussed; matters the men might not wish to burden their loves with.

Gid-visu looked at Gidon and he made the decision to ask their loved ones to sit. Gid-visu already knew some things he had anticipated discussing would not occur as they ate. Gidon waited till the servants withdrew, not because they were not trusted, but because he wanted no word of the plan to slip out. It was then he laid out his plan to openly purchase Getrudis from the tavern, making her his personal servant. Then because a marriage would have to be at least as public as Brunhild's establishment as Gid-visu's mistress and Mistress of Fox Home, he would draw up privately the formal establishment of Getrudis as Gidon's mistress. Then when things improved, she would become his wife. It was not the way he would like to do things but he hoped this would give her a measure of safety. Neither Brunhild nor Getrudis was thrilled with the limited and misleading action but they understood Gidon's concern for safety when there might be unknown enemies lurking about. And as Getrudis said, "At least I will be legally all Gidon's when it is done."

*****

Brute' had been reluctant to leave Brigitta's side. But the unmarried men of war age were gathered outside the Burgomeister's house. Someone told them when they first assembled on the village square to come to the house instead. These were only men of the village that had been summoned to this training. First selected for the special force of Eastwatch were only to be unmarried men living in the village. Baron von Krieg had ordered if fifty men of the village who could meet Herr Brute's standard were not found, then only could they look farther.

Brigitta insisted Brute' leave her to do his duty. The last time he massaged her tiny feet they had little pain. They were back in as good condition as when she and Gidon had begun the journey home. After the last massage she had been able to spread her toes a little and Brute' gave in to temptation. Beginning first with each of the large toes, he began kissing them all singularly and in order. It had shocked the nurse terribly and sent a thrill of pleasure up Brigitta's feet and legs. She had never dreamed it was possible for a woman to experience such a feeling. And the nurse secretly wished she had a man like that in her life when she was young.

Brigitta told the nurse to bring her the ladies' chair when Brute' left. She was going to use it, then go and spend the day with her parents. The nurse insisted that she must return to her room and put her feet up for a time after each visit to a parent. She did not want a relapse in the condition of her patient's feet.

Brigitta's last words to Herr Brute' before he departed was, "My lord. When you finish your day of duty will you come back to me?" Brute' could not speak. He could only nod in assent.

Going out from Brigitta to the motley crew gathered outside was like leaving a clear spring for a pig's wallow. But he had not really expected anything else. You would not have known that to hear him. With all contempt one might expect from a centurion of the Italian Band he growled, "Herman One Eye, come out here!"

Herman came out at the trot. He recognized the tone of voice. It belonged to a soldier who orders men, even when it came through Herr Brute's damaged larynx. None had to tell him to stand at attention.

"How dare you, a pike man of King Gregor the Second, allow this bunch of human dung stand outside where I am quartered in such a manner?" Brute was enjoying being back in a command.

"No excuse sir." No one had told him he was supposed to take charge. Then, to his shock he saw Herr Brute' wink. He remembered well the games played in the military.

"Herman One Eye, you take this glob of human maggots and teach them how to stand in a formation, instead of looking like some confused birds waiting for someone to come along and kill them. Then you take their lazy young asses and teach them how to march as if they were real soldiers. You march them around the village until every one of them can do it right and in step. And then I will take them on a little hike." Brute' had to work to make his voice function, but it was worth it to see Herman's hidden grin while the others groaned.

Brute' stepped back into the house enjoying the sound of Herman barking out instruction and moving men into position.

One fellow thought he could protest Herman being in charge of the formation since he did not live in the village. Herman One Eye knocked him cold with a single blow from his huge right hand. That, as it has done for centuries, settled the question of who was in charge of the training going on.

Herr Brute' went to find Herman One Eye's youngest son of fighting age. "Bolt the back door and then go find the schmeid and tell him to come here. Then you will resume your post walking back and forth between entrances to the house," These were all the instructions he had for him. How he carried them out would tell Brute' the value of the boy.

By the time Herman the Schmeid arrived, Herman One Eye was beginning to move the group of young villagers in unison from one end of the street to the other while its residents called out encouragement. The schmeid was not sure he wanted to talk to Herr Brute' at all, wondering what he had in store for him. He was actually relieved when he was instructed to get a large pony cart and have it ready for this afternoon. Then Brute' went to inform Herman One Eye's son who he learned was called Ohtrad, meaning fearsome, that it would be his duty to drive the pony cart behind and just out of sight of the men Brute' would take on the hike.

Brute' was having fun and knew he would be out late. He would go and see his warrior queen which sometimes he thought of now as his virgin queen and tell her what he had to do.

*****

Gid-visu and Gidon went together to inform a very unhappy Fat Max that Gidon was buying the indenture of Getrudis. Oma was pleased even though she was not told any other event was in the offing. One thing about Oma was she loved to talk too much to be trusted with the secret of Gidon's other plans. That is, if she saw the importance of a matter you could not have torn a secret out of her even with torture. But without a threat to visualize, Gidon would not take a chance with Oma keeping this secret.

Fat Max was grumbling about having to find and train a new girl. In reality he was very affectionately attached to Getrudis and fearful of losing his daughter-in-law Gwynedd to the Baron as well. He wanted his daughters in law happily wed, not just turned into mistresses, even mistresses with legal standing. No not even to such fine men as Gid-visu and the Baron. And Gidon did not even offer any part of his plan to Fat Max. His opinions Fat Max would grudgingly keep to himself. He had been a tavern keeper a long time.

It was then the young boy, who had recently become a part of Fox Home staff, came into the tavern with the announcement Baron von Krieg was back and had stopped first at Gid-visu's house. He announced the Baron had five horses with him and a boy who did not seem interested in talking with anyone. He said the Baron ordered him that he should, after finding Gid-visu and Gidon, tell the Schmeid to come for the horses.

Fat Max and Gidon agreed on the purchase of the indenture and planned to meet at Fox Home to conclude the transaction after the tavern closed. On this day of the week that was normally about two hours before midnight. Max grumbled that with the Baron back he would have little help waiting tables since Gwynedd will be in a hurry to get away as well.

The men hurried home glad to have part of their business done. But when they arrived in Fox Home, they discovered things were not quite as they hoped. The two women were sitting with the strange boy who was still wrapped in a large cape and seeking to hide his face.

When Herman the Schmeid arrived, two particular horses less heavily built than war steeds were described to him, The Baron's orders were that those should not be fed. Instead take them to the outskirts of the western side of the village and turn them loose at an hour when all were asleep. The Baron was very specific. He wanted no one to see him take them there and turn them loose. One could tell from the look on Herman the Schmeid's face he had never before heard an order like that. The remaining three horses, which included Begleiter, were to be taken care of, for they were the Baron's.

The boy who had notified Gid-visu and Gidon was sent to get the Apothecary with instruction he should bring healing ointment for damaged skin. And he was told that on his way back he should again go by the tavern and tell Oma to come as soon as possible.

Baron von Krieg turned to Brunhild and asked, "Can we make do without the household staff for the rest of the evening or need we wait till they have prepared meals?"

The Baron then turned to Getrudis and said, "I am glad to see you. I will need my little wash girl this evening."

Getrudis said, "I may not m'lord, unless my lord says I should." She gave the Baron one of her smiles that were both sweet and full of mischief.

"Have things changed so much in Eastwatch since I have been gone that I must find a new wash girl? Who is this new master that would deprive me of my wash girl?" The Baron growled, but only with pretended anger.

Gidon spoke up. "That would be your squire and much as I hate to disappoint you, Getrudis now washes only me!" Both Brunhild and Getrudis broke into laughter.

The Baron said, "I know there must have been some major changes since I have been gone. On our way into town I saw a remarkable sight. I saw Herman One Eye teaching men to march. And who is responsible for that?"

Gid-visu said, "I sent Herman One Eye to guard the Burgomeister's home after it was attacked, the household harmed, and the man you had taken prisoner killed. This attack happened even as you were leaving. What has happened since I do not know, except for the fact Herr Brute' has quartered in the Burgomeister house since Gidon put Brigitta into his arms after rescuing her from abductors. You see, Brigitta had been carried away as well."

"It sounds like there is quite a story you have to tell. I want to hear all of it." If there was anything that could be said for Baron von Krieg; He was a stickler for detail. So Gid-visu told the story as far as he knew it while Gidon kept mum. There were some things about the adventure he did not want to share before women and other things he did not care to share at all.

When Gid-visu finished the recounting, the Baron asked Gidon, "Did your hand get injured fighting the varlets or did Brigitta bite it?" Everybody laughed together. That is, all except the boy who sat quietly keeping himself tightly covered.

Then the Baron was asked about his adventures? He said that he would tell them when they were all together this evening for the story affects his companion and some need to hear her part in particular. No one missed the fact he referred to the boy as her.

When all the staff had retired to their quarters, the household was relatively quiet except for the group gathered at table. Only the fighting priests were on the main floor, ever faithful to their duties. They knew the priest who arrived at the entrance well. He said the bishop had sent him with the formal document making Getrudis to become Gidon's mistress. The bishop had not come in order to avoid witnesses he said. Once again Bishop Elisha had acted without anyone yet giving him the plan behind the actions. Truly it had to be said the source of his knowledge was the Invisible God Himself, who is present at every conversation of men.

Once the papers were signed, Gidon thought wryly, *The woman has become my mistress before she has become my servant.* The idea events had been so ordered pleased him strangely.

With the priest's departure there came the Apothecary's arrival. The Baron told him that if he breathed one word of what he saw and heard at Fox Home this night he would be dead as quickly as lightning flashed from East to West. The Apothecary appeared wounded. "Surely dear Baron you know that keeping confidence is part of my stock and trade. Not to mention I would not speak of anything you said to keep secret, not even to my wife." That was an important reassurance because it was well known his wife was a notorious busybody.

The Baron shifted his weight in the chair and an involuntary groan escaped his lips. "I am afraid I have been wounded. But I have not been able to see to it till my responsibilities were completed." Brunhild took charge, immediately removing his tunic and mail, with the woolen garment it rested on. The Baron was sitting before the whole group clad only in his under breeches. There was revealed a deep gash along the ribs on his left side. "Even the most incompetent spearman can get lucky once in a while," he said.

The Apothecary said, "My friend the potion you asked for was not made for wounds such as this. But fortunately I do have some things with me in my case…"

The Baron interrupted, "What I asked you to bring was not for this wound. You will see what I asked that unguent for soon enough. But in truth I admit that I did not know this wound was as bad as it is."

It took over an hour for the wound to be cleaned, stitched, and bound. Just before the work was completed Oma and Gwynedd arrived. They announced Fat Max would be along shortly. Aside from the young men of the village being out training to be soldiers and giving the tavern no business this night, the only people frequenting the place was a few village elders who were eagerly waiting to hear from Baron von Krieg. Oma said Max had told them to bar the door after he left and when they were finished slip out through the kitchen. He was on his way.

Gwynedd had stared at the place where the Baron was wounded ever since she arrived. Plainly she was upset to see him hurt. Oma said to her, "Do not worry. Haki will be just fine. He was tough even as a little boy."

The normally jovial Fat Max was a bit taciturn when he arrived. For a man who normally enjoyed good conversation this was highly unusual. However, the transaction of ownership of Getrudis indenture was accomplished with Gidon insisting on paying the full amount instead of a reduced amount on the basis of the time she had served the tavern. Gidon said that she was too precious for him to pay less and this pleased both Getrudis and Oma. He told neither Fat Max nor Oma that she was already legally his mistress.

When all the formalities were done everyone began to look to the Baron, wanting to hear of his most recent adventure and what the girl disguised as a boy had to do with it. He began the story with some facts known to just a few of the group:

"You know Gid-visu, that our friend Herr Tweitman raises horses mostly for the king's use. He also keeps carrier pigeons for communication between him and the king's castle. We needed more steeds to replace the one Herr Brute' lost and also to replace Begleiter, the horse my squire won the loyalty of." Just to make sure Gidon knew he was speaking with humor, he looked at Gidon and smiled.

"It was the cause of reporting to the king and receiving instruction that was the reason of my urgency to make the trip. Begleiter carried me on a normally three-day trip in just over two days. The king needed to know we believed Goraleck to be behind the attempt on your life last fall and the events this spring. I personally think there is a traitor living in or around Eastwatch. You might be interested to know Gid-visu, you are not the only key person in the kingdom who has had someone seek to take his life. Others have not fared so well.

"It had been my idea that Gid-visu would become the Baron of Eastwatch and have the Keep we are preparing to build to defend against eastern invasion. That construction had been the king's order so I had just assumed it would go to Gid-visu, but I was mistaken. He intended it would go to me. And by the way, the king has approved my marriage to Gwynedd. That is if she will have me." The noise that came out of Gwynedd obviously meant there was no question about that. And Fat Max began to show a better disposition. Gwynedd would be a Lady.

Gidon advised they make a secret document making her his mistress until the unknown traitor could be found and then they could have the public wedding with all the pomp and ritual required by von Krieg's position in life.

The Baron picked up the narration. "When the problem I am about to tell you of, that caused me to hunt down three varlets occurred, I had already made the deal with Herr Tweitman for two horses and was waiting to see if the king would send further instruction. The two new horses now in the Eastwatch stables were outside at Herr Tweitman's, kept in a small fenced in area when they were stolen. I told Herr Tweitman they were already bought and thus my property to be recovered and not his loss. Then I set out on Begleiter to get my horses back. And I had to make sure these people did not ever steal another horse from Herr Tweitman's Hold.

"I had followed them for a day when I came upon the dead body of a young man who had not been very cleanly killed. I could see from the material left behind they had enriched themselves by two horses and one young damsel. That is the young woman sitting here in Fox Home as your guest. I will let her tell you some of her story now."

The women displayed their compassion for the young woman who had suffered at the hands of ruffians. Oma spoke to her in her grandmotherly way. "Come my dear, you do not have to be ashamed to be dressed in man's garb after going through such an experience. Why our Burgomeister's daughter was carried off by terrible men and when Gidon rescued her she was wearing some awful men's clothing."

Gidon did nothing to correct this idea since it was better than the fact he had to provide her clothing from the dead men, because Brigitta had been carried away in her nightgown. The idea she was rescued in a torn gown and having trouble keeping her breasts covered was one that did not need to be emphasized.

"You do not understand," the girl said. "I was not wearing men's clothing because they were given me by my captors. I was wearing them because after Baron von Krieg rescued me it suited my purposes no one should recognize me and tell my stepfather I still lived. The man whose body Baron von Krieg discovered was not just my bodyguard but in a sense my guard. My stepfather is very jealous of me and very strict about any action he considers a transgression of his rules. I do not always know what those rules are until I break them. So I did not want to return to what was no longer my home and perhaps even be punished by him for being captured."

The Baron said, "This young lady hopes you will allow her to work at the tavern and try to start a new life. She has a fine education for a woman, and can be helpful in many ways. And we hope no one traveling through will recognize her, because this would appear a movement down in her station in life. After all, she would be working in a tavern at least four or more days from home in a village that gets very few visitors."

Oma was dominating the women's side of the conversation. "What is your name child? And, how old are you?"

"I choose to call myself Durchgefüweg, and I am seventeen years old. I do not care to mention my real name, for the family name is too well known. Thus, I have taken a new name."

Fat Max opined, "Carried Away is a good name for a woman who has been carried away from her home. But taking her in could pose a risk. It is apparent the Baron thinks this a good thing to do. We respect his opinion. But why should we take the chance?"

The Baron spoke to Durchgefüweg in that voice that would not be denied. "Turn your back to us and take off your clothes."

Durchgefüweg hesitated but a little before she quietly complied. She dropped her head in shame as the people in the room saw her damaged flesh. From the top of her shoulder down the legs to just above the knees it was quite obvious she had been recently brutally whipped. Oma said, "Oh poppa, look beneath her skin. This is not the first time she has had such a beating."

Getrudis, of the gentle heart, cried. She and Brunhild walked up and hugged her. Brunhild said to her, "You do not have to be ashamed that we see you naked. We are people interested in your welfare. These men are honorable men like the Baron. Our men would do you no harm or wish any thoughts unbecoming. As we trust them with our entire being, so can you."

The Apothecary walked up behind her and began cleaning the wounds. "Do any of you ladies happen to have a clean gown you are not afraid to have ruined by drainage from her injuries? After this solution is applied you must lay down on your stomach to sleep. I will leave the remaining unguent with Brunhild and she can take care of you."

The Apothecary then said to the Baron, "You can depend on my discretion. But this is one of those times I wish I could be a man capable of violence like Gidon or yourself. The man who did this deserves to die." He meant no insult to either Gidon or the Baron. How he said things simply reflected the thinking of the small village.

Oma sought to make the matter plain. She had come around in front of Durchgefüweg, "Child you say that your stepfather did this?" The girl could not find voice but could only nod. "Why in the world would he do such a thing?"

Durchgefüweg said, "I love to ride. This last beating was because he said I talked too long to the stable boy. We were only talking about my horse."

Oma said, "What happened to the stable boy?"

Durchgefüweg began sobbing so hard her breasts shook. "Nobody knows. No one has seen him since, but I overheard one of the farm hands say his things were still in the cubicle where he slept in the stable."

Gwynedd brought out her clean wash dress and put it over Durchgefüweg's body. Up until she acted, she had only sat at the Baron's feet holding to his leg as she cried. How she loved this hard man who would put things aside to take care of a hurt girl!

Oma asked for more information. "Has he always beaten you?"

"Yes, he started right after he married momma. But as momma sickened, he beat me more frequently, and then after she died it became unbearable. He got harder and more frequent in what he called my training. This last time, after he reduced me to just trying to endure and live, he touched my flower. Had not some friends of his came unexpectedly, I fear what he might have done to me."

Oma looked past her to the Baron, "Haki, what are you going to do about this?"

The Baron looked at her seriously. "Her stepfather does have a Hold granted by the king. I cannot just go administer justice. I would have to cut down at least thirty men with my sword before I got to him. I will speak to the king soon when we are face to face. I am sure her stepfather's days are numbered.

"As far as her person is concerned, I think I have a plan. As her rescuer and dispenser of king's justice I have the right to claim any unmarried girl I have freed from a captivity. I will do this and after she is healed sell her into indenture to the tavern. If any question arises you can truthfully say you bought her from me. Truth will protect both you and Max."

Brunhild wrapped up the man's clothes saying she would personally burn them tomorrow. "We will work out a way to make you appear differently Durchgefüweg. Though you may not feel so lovely right now, the truth is you are quite stunning. If we try to hide that fact it would make you all the more obvious to others a great beauty. So, we will emphasize your beauty by altering the appearance of it."

Gid-visu changed the subject slightly. "From the time you found Durchgefüweg's dead guard how long did it take you to catch up with the horse thieves?"

"I rode all the remainder of the day and seeing they were following a path I continued after them when night fell. "I stayed on their track through the early night. When I caught up with them, I rushed upon them suddenly. I had removed two of their heads when the third hit me with a spear. That was when I was wounded. Then I turned Begleiter and removed his head. I left their heads on spikes I made and drove in the ground so people finding them would know this was the king's justice. The young lady stripped off her torn dress, putting it in the fire and dressing in men's clothing, intending to run from her stepfather. This was when I saw her wounded back and asked what happened to her? I am frankly impressed by her fortitude."

Gidon said "There is not a big market for so expensive animals as war horses. Where did they plan to sell them?"

Durchgefüweg then spoke up. "The thieves were headed west toward Goraleck's territory. I think they were willingly running the danger of him simply taking the horses and killing them. But they did have a plan for me as well and that was selling me to the Norsemen. I do not think they were very smart. Vikings and their lot prefer to simply take what they want unless those who trade with them do so from a position of strength."

*****

Herman One Eye had nearly run the men into the ground marching them up and down streets and round about the town. But their day was not over when they were formed back up in front of the Burgomeister's home. Herr Brute' then gave a course of instruction on how to do a marching shuffle to cover a great deal of land quickly with a minimal effort. Roman legions were known to cover thirty-five miles each day in the manner he taught and get to their destination in good enough condition to fight.

Leading the men by example, Brute' started out moving with the shuffle that is faster than a walk and less tasking than a run. He had planned a circuit of roughly ten miles but some began to fall out before they had made even five. They would be picked up by the cart of Ohtrad. To the credit of some they would rest and then rejoin the march. Some were made of less sterner stuff and content to quit for the night. By the time Brute' got back to the front of the house where waited his warrior queen, it was late but he was happy. Once a soldier, nothing else makes you quite so happy in the same way.

But in Brigitta, there was something he had never known…

When he got to her room, he found a girl who also had a successful day. She patted the bed and said "Please come here." He positioned himself as before at her feet "No, please come up here beside me."

As he moved up to lean against the pillow beside her, the scandalized nurse could take no more, not even for the sake of being a good chaperone. She left the room. As he sat beside Brigitta she took his arm and wrapped it around her leaning into his chest as they did in the hall just the day before.

Brigitta said, "I have a problem I am helpless to do anything about. It is about my poppa. He complains about terrible headaches and the priest says it is because he will not stay on the pillows so swelling in his head can go down. He keeps getting off the pillows and if he keeps doing it he will die. I have tried to talk to him about it but he just will not stay on the pillows."

Brute' said, "I can fix that. Let me go talk to your poppa. I will be right back." He got up and walked down to the father's room. He found the man was laid out more or less flat on the bed. Brute' grabbed the front of the Burgomeister's nightgown and unceremoniously set him on his pillow. The fat old man opened his eyes to see Brute's scarred face just far enough away so he could get the whole of it.

Brute' spoke to him in his best evil sounding voice. "They say you are going to die just because you will not stay on the pillows. That is good. You just keep doing what you are doing. I am going to get your house. I am going to put your wife out on the street. I am going to take your daughter. And there is nothing you can do about it because you are choosing to die. So go ahead and do it!" With that he walked out of the room and back to Brigitta.

She motioned for Brute' to come back and sit beside her as he was doing before. "What did you do?"

"I just had a talk with your father. I think he will stay on the pillows now."

"How did you do that?"

"I think I just scared him into living," Brute' said. And it even came out funny through his broken voice.

"What did you say?" She inquired.

"I told him if he died I was going to take his daughter."

"Why Brute', does that mean you will not take me if he lives?" She made a cute expression of shock.

"He does not have to know everything!"

Chapter 10

Durchgefüweg and the Bishop

Durchgefüweg had found Gwynedd's wash dress difficult to adjust to. A wash dress was made to fit tightly on the wash girl so it did not get into the water when the girl is working. Durchgefüweg was taller and more strongly built than Gwynedd, with the exception of the hips which were narrower with more muscled buttocks from much riding. It had been difficult getting the dress over her and pulling it down without hurting the skin that had been so badly abused. The ladies had worked carefully under Oma's supervision, but it was a slow process. Yet when it was in place it was like a tight bandage against the body. But there was still a problem because it held her ample breasts too tightly and parts of them wanted to squeeze out the sides of the sleeveless garment. Gwynedd completely loosed the laces of the bodice but that only helped a little. To anoint the wounds and change the garments daily, another wash dress would have to be found. The one she was now in would have to be modified a little when it was washed.

The dress, because of its extreme tightness, did nothing to hide her womanly attributes, and neither she nor the other women wanted to summarily bundle her off to bed. As badly she needed rest, after days of riding, she needed the warmth and acceptance of good people who meant her well. And too, she should not be excluded from any conversation which might also affect her. For the sake of her modesty, they got one of the clean sheets sometimes used in the sauna and wrapped her in it.

Gid-visu said, "Now that we have Durchgefüweg here it is more critical we find any traitor that might be in the village right away. If such a person got even a whiff of her situation there is no telling how he might use it to cause a problem. Quite frankly the girl has been through enough."

Baron von Krieg asked, "Does anyone have any idea who might be a traitor yet? Failing that, does anyone have any idea how we might catch a person like that?"

Fat Max had never been part of the inner counsels related to assassins before. He found the idea someone, probably someone he had known a long time, might betray both village and king profoundly disturbing. He liked to think well of everyone. He did have one question. "Is it more likely such a person might be among the village elders or would it likely to be one of the less notable citizens?"

Gidon said, "I think that is part of the quandary; we really do not know." He looked to the Baron, "What do you think the more likely?"

Baron von Krieg always tried to analyze problems. "I would think the higher up a person is the easier it is to gain information and to influence decisions."

Brunhild asked, "Could it be a woman instead of a man?"

Durchgefüweg was amazed. It was the first time in her life she had ever seen women take part in such a council or be treated as if their opinion mattered.

Gid-visu stood up and bowed to his new mistress. "Then we should consider women who dominate their husbands. A man in the right position could be used to gain information while his wife influenced his opinions and colluded with our enemies." He began to pace as he thought. Then he stopped and reached into the closet where the cape with the Persian's weapons had been placed. "Gidon, I forgot to tell you I tested the Yataghan when we were waiting for our meeting today. This one has no poison on it. It is safe to put with your other one."

Durchgefüweg gasped and stood up. Everyone looked at her waiting her words, but she was unsure she had permission to speak. Oma said, "What is the matter child?"

She asked Gid-visu, "May I ask sir, where you got that blade?"

Gid-visu said, "My son Gidon took it from an assassin he killed. Actually, he has two such blades from killing two assassins. Now what is it to you girl?"

Durchgefüweg said, "A man came to our Hold maybe two or three months ago. He wore such a weapon. It could even be the same one. I saw he had a knife with a matching handle and other flat knives across his chest. He had come on some secret mission to meet with my stepfather before going on to meet another person of importance."

"Do you remember the name of the person he was going to meet?" Gidon asked.

"Alas I do not right now. I believe it may have started with a J or a G. I was very upset because he saw me and asked if he might buy me for a harem when he came back through? My stepfather apologized, saying he could not sell me because I brought him power. I do not know what he meant by that but I never heard his voice sound so sinister. He told the man that by the time he was finished with me I would be all used up. I think my mother died because he used her up, perhaps by beating her too."

"Do you know any more about this?" the Baron asked.

"Only that my stepfather seemed to know the person he was going to meet with. And this man had five very evil men with him who seemed as intimidated of him as I was scared. He made them stay in a storage hovel near the stable and they were not allowed to talk to anyone. Not that anyone would want to talk to such vile men. That is all I know."

The telling of these things seemed to completely exhaust the poor girl. So Brunhild gave her a glass of warm wine and honey to help her sleep. She led her to the Baron's room and made her comfortable face down on his bed. The Baron had already announced he would be sleeping on Gidon's floor again.

Fat Max and Oma said they must be going. They were very unsettled about what they had heard. But it probably was necessary they should be aware in case their help was needed in any plan that should be devised. One thing was sure. Oma was sufficiently alarmed to be sure she would keep Durchgefüweg's secret.

When the Baron entered the outer room of Gidon's chamber with Gwynedd, they could see through the arch Gidon was doing his exercises again. By now the hand was not as sore as before. As Getrudis was elevated on the side of Gidon's cot opposite the arch she said, "You two should not be peaking in here!"

Gwynedd said, "We are not peaking, but my master cannot exercise tonight for the stress would pull his wound open." She had quickly opened the pallet on the floor and Haki lay down on his uninjured side facing the fire. Gwynedd said, "I have lost my wash dress and have no gown with me to wear to bed. I was not expecting things to go as they have. Let me lay behind you and I will press my breasts against your back."

Haki, for a little bit was more the mischievous boy than man. "I have a better idea. Why do you not rest facing me and put your breasts against my chest?"

Gwynedd spoke teasingly, "I know you are a man of iron will. But I am but a woman who has wanted you from the first day I saw you. Should I lay before you I fear I will consummate our union before the time."

Haki laughed. "Tonight, if you should lay before me, what would happen would be my fault alone."

Gwynedd took her place at his back. With teasing words they sealed their bond to mutual respect and restraint.

From the room where Gidon and Getrudis lay came a little voice. It was not a squeal but more a sound of discovery and anticipation. All was quiet for several minutes. Then came a low sound from Getrudis that was close to a moan and a prayer of gratitude in one sound. Only two words were heard in that sound. "Oh, Gidon!" Then all was quiet if not still.

When Gidon awoke it was to watch Getrudis make her usual morning stretch to the ceiling. Beautiful as always, it was different somehow. Some might say it had more of the grace of the woman and less of the girl. Gidon started to get up only to discover he was sliding through blood. "Getrudis are you all right? I am afraid I have hurt you!"

"No, I am fine. I have had the best night's rest in my life. You have not hurt me."

"But there is blood in the bed and it is not mine. I fear you are hurt."

"It is my blood, you bad boy. You have broken something. You have broken my flower!"

*****

During the hours when at Fox Home weighty matters were being discussed and a union consummated, a pious priest was in fasting and prayer in the monastery chapel. No longer was this man the respected Bishop but a humble servant of the Invisible God who he was calling on by his Name, Yahweh-Jireh, which means in the common tongue The Lord Provides.

The provision he was looking for was the answer to a great unease that had been haunting him. The worried man had again and again been driven to his knees seeking an answer. What was it he needed to know that this great burden had been laid on his heart so finally he had forsaken food and at the last not even thought to drink water?

His body was near exhaustion and had become totally divorced from the considerations of human need when the vision took place. The floor opened up before him and he peered into a basement that had been turned into a dungeon. Tied to a rack that was a horizontal bar bolted to a short cross was the body of a young man more dead than alive. His clothing appeared that of a person who worked about stables. It hung from him in shreds. He had been brutally whipped just short of death repeatedly. It would be impossible to describe the agony the lad had suffered.

The occult symbols in the dungeon the praying priest recognized as common to the occultists of Lower Lotharingia that had once been connected, but rebelled against the Frankish Druids to focus on dark works against the True God. They had in their secret language a connection with a tongue once spoken in Persia where the god of death was brazenly adored.

The vision ended after the priest of Lucifer cut off the young man's manhood, thus extinguishing his life as the last of his blood spilled on the floor. He then began the Ritual of Summoning, incantations to bring fallen angels known as daimōn to the Greeks. The opening into the vision closed, leaving the servant of God bathed in sweat and only a little closer to the answer for his concern.

As a young supplicant he had come across some of this evil wizard's kind and had to learn of them in order to recognize them. He had to learn how to fight them in unseen worlds, a calling that required he be utterly committed to the True God and Lord of Creation known in the Ebiru tongue as Elohim. It was this Name for the True God that was most important because in their satanic delusion they worshipped a goddess of rebirth instead of the God of Creation. The initiate to the vile order was placed in complete darkness, with utter isolation and sensory deprivation many days until the succubus goddess came to him and ate him. From there he was supposed to enter her belly and finally be reborn with creative genius for whatever evil goals he desired. No person who had surrendered himself to this satanic delusion ever seemed to recognize the discharge of the man through the goddess bowels symbolically said he was human offal. As his lord Lucifer does, the wizards often present themselves after rebirth as a light bringer and doer of good. But always his benevolent actions came at a terrible price to men.

The priest lay on the floor sick to his stomach. He knew not how long he had lain in this position when he became aware of two men dressed in shining garments in the room. Only one of the men spoke yet it was as many voices were speaking: "Hail Elisha, much beloved of the Lord. We have traveled and fought many days to come to you."

The light that emanated from these men was almost blinding. Even the mail that covered their bodies was like molten silver so that when he looked at it his own face shined back. "Take this scroll and swallow it. It shall be bitterness in thy mouth, yet in thy belly it shall renew thy strength." Elisha took the scroll and it was terribly bitter in his mouth but when he swallowed it he was renewed not even needing water to drink.

"When we say we have fought many days to come to you fear not. For in this world it has been but a watch in the night. But our God is the El-Olam, the Everlasting, who exists outside of time and commands time. So that what has been weeks to us at this time has been but hours to you. Even now the Fallen Ones have arisen and been bid to go out searching for a young woman he has been persuaded brings him greater power in her pain. We shall go forth to meet them and overcome them. Tarry here till the vision returns and you will see what happens when we are victorious." And with that the two men disappeared.

Elisha lay on his face stretched out before the Lord in abject supplication for success in the battle. He knew this was the way in which mortal man entered into the battle between demons and angels. And then the vision in the floor opened again as the wizard was thrown across the room of his dungeon. Those he had summoned now attacked him. They spoke to him in voices that sounded akin to the growls of beasts of prey.

"Stupid human you did not say a true servant of El Shaddai stood in the gap between us and the prey you seek!" The most grotesque of the demons picked him up and again threw him across the room. One of his legs striking a torture hook tearing the muscle.

The wizard held up a hand as if to hold away another blow. "Forgive me, I did not know!"

One of the beings batted away his hand and backhanded him. "You fool! We do not deal in forgiveness. Still our Infernal Master has ordered we shall not kill you because he has further use for you. Thus we will torment you and leave our marks upon you before we go."

The vision closed and Bishop Elisha rose and prepared himself. It would soon be time for morning worship.

After worship and breakfast with his priests he took the pony cart and accompanied by the two newly consecrated fighting priests, who had now chosen names which in the common tongue meant stability and strength, headed out for Eastwatch by the Rising of the

Little Dan. The warfare against unseen forces had just begun. The evil people who served the darkness nearby must also be defeated.

The trip to the village proved uneventful, but then that was what he expected. The spiritual attack would come in another manner, from imbedded enemies or he missed his guess.

For reasons he did not understand he was headed first to Fox Home even though he knew the men would be out at work this time of day.

*****

Durchgefüweg's sleep, even aided by honeyed wine, was not completely peaceful. She was plagued by evil dreams including one where her wicked stepfather tried to simultaneously grab her breasts and her female part often referred to among the Aleman as a flower.

After the morning meal Gwynedd had come to the girl's room with a full heart. The endearing things Baron von Krieg, who she now thought of as Haki her beloved, had said to her as he rested filled her soul. She brought with her fresh bread covered with butter and honey as well as milk that had chilled in the always cool below ground storage. When she walked in she saw the young woman was still asleep. But the bread would nourish the body and the honey encourage it to heal. She sat the food on the table and tried to shake her without hurting her damaged flesh.

When Durchgefüweg turned over Gwynedd saw the twin mounds of Durchgefüweg's breasts had managed to work their way between the two sides of her bodice so they were captured and held closely together by the fabric. The girl in great embarrassment tried to quickly bring them back into captivity within the garment.

Gwynedd said to her: "Do not be embarrassed. All women have breasts. I long for the day when mine might be held captive by my Baron's hands."

Durchgefüweg said, "I have no such longings. In my dreams the person who wants to grab my breasts is my stepfather." She gave a little shudder.

"Do not worry," Gwynedd replied. "Such ungodly pain will pass with time and safety. One day a man will love you and say 'Thy two breasts are like young roes that are twins' and find his delight and peace among them."

"That sounds poetic and is a beautiful thought, but I will never have peace as long as I know he is out there and may again get his hands on me." Durchgefüweg looked very sad.

"You do not worry while you are at Fox Home, for in the house there are no less than seven great warriors. There are four fighting priests, Baron von Krieg, the master of the house Gid-visu, and his son Gidon who at sixteen has already killed many evil men. You could hardly be any safer than in this place."

The sound of the door clapper was amplified through the hall and sounded very loud in the room. "You rest a little longer and then we will take Brunhild's wash gown and modify it to fit. When your back ceases draining, we will make you a brand new one to fit your body."

By the time Gwynedd met Brunhild at the front door the bishop was already inside. The two new fighting priests had seen Herman One Eye marching his trainees, at least the ones able to walk after the previous days training, and asked to join them. After they had done the legionnaires' shuffle Brute' was heard to say that what he needed was a group of fifty fighting priests.

The bishop asked Brunhild if any of the menfolk were about the house, and he learned that for the moment, as he expected, none were present. The Baron had gone to see how Brute' was progressing with the training of what he hoped would be fifty fighting men from the village. Gid-visu had learned the scabbards holding the throwing knives of the Hashshashin were filled with poison so each time one of the knives came out it was freshly laced with destruction even through the slightest scratch. And Gidon was off to encourage the workmen to go ahead and plant since the thinking was that no further really heavy rains would come. Then he had to go to the stables to inspect the horses and finally make sure all was well at the tavern before he could get back to Getrudis.

The bishop said, "I need to speak with the men on a matter most urgent. In the meantime I shall talk to my priests who are here.

Please wake those who are sleeping for me." We will meet by the front door so the house is not completely unguarded."

When the men were assembled, he warned them of the need to be on guard against demonic forces as well the normal problems of evil people. Without telling the particulars he said the battle had already been joined. It was Judah the Hammer who told the bishop of the young woman dressed as a boy who had been brought to the house by Baron von Krieg yesterday. He told him someone had beaten her in a way he considered tortuous. Other than those facts, he confessed he knew no more of the matter. But he thought it took someone allied with the forces of darkness to treat an innocent woman in so cruel manner. The bishop sent the men back to their duties.

It was then Bishop Elisha asked Brunhild about the young woman and learned she was beaten very badly by her own stepfather. Brunhild said she thought he should talk of the whole matter with her master, Gid-visu, and the Baron. He noticed she did not include Gidon in her suggestion. He wondered her motive? Perhaps she thought he was too young and should be spared. Or perhaps she thought it might be a dark cloud that would overcast the next few days between Getrudis and Gidon? Whatever her motive he would consider her words but his thinking was that Gidon should know.

Brunhild, Gwynedd, and Getrudis were all addressed by the bishop before he departed. He said he would come back to meet Durchgefüweg in the evening. He cautioned the ladies there was some evil afoot which he might not speak of at this time. But they should know that they should be in continual prayer until these things be reconciled.

Taking his leave, the bishop then walked to the tavern and on an impulse entered through the kitchen. He met Oma there and found her highly distressed. Oma took him to an out of the way place and shared with him her concern for Durchgefüweg, telling him the decision had been made to say little of her story for the sake of protecting her. The bishop said he considered that a wise decision. But Oma told him there was more. The bishop knew, with the loss of help, they needed to find girls that would not be a drawback to the reputation of the tavern. Max, before those other things were known, had the town crier announce he was looking for new serving girls.

Today Oma had entered the tavern to see about customers' needs only to see there was a comely girl whispering in the ear of Fat Max. He seemed to be getting very agitated. When Oma came in relief showed clearly on his face. Oma in a voice that lacked none of its usual pleasantness said, "What is going on here?"

Max looked at her with a sigh of relief and said, "My dear, this woman has offered to service me if I would give her a job in the tavern."

"DID SHE NOW!" Oma reached for a fire poker used to warm mead, now cold behind the counter. When she came up with it there was no girl in sight.

Fat Max loved his wife dearly. For many years they had been inseparable. "Thank you dear. I did not know what to do. She just kept talking and talking. Why some of those things she said she would do I did not know were even possible. I feel like I need to take a bath."

She confessed to the bishop she had been remiss in her duties as a wife but would correct the matter this night beginning with Max's bath. The bishop commended her for being a good wife saying that always taking care of one another builds a hedge against the wiles of the devil.

She then asked him for a personal favor. Would he disguise himself so that each time a girl comes in looking for a place she could count on his counsel? She did not want the women who came seeking work knowing who he is, for obvious reasons. He promised that as much as possible he would do this thing. After all, the women who should not be hired are unlikely to come to the church and thus know who he is anyway. For the moment he set in the dark corner favored by the King's Rider and had a bit of whipped goat's milk, waiting in the off chance one of the men he hoped to see would come.

Just as he was finishing his milk a little girl came running out of the back and through the front door of the tavern followed by an angry Oma who moved surprising fast, beating the girl with a broom. Fat Max said loudly "Momma what is going on?"

Oma had stopped moving at the front door where she stood for a moment with her whole body shaking with the effort she had put forth. Then she said, "That slut came in back looking for a job. She is small and claimed to be but twelve, however she has lines around her eyes and mouth that would not belong to a young woman, the little liar. And the worst of it was she said she was a virgin and her whole body smelled of men."

The bishop went to get himself a disguise. But he thought as he went, *Oma does not really need any counsel when it comes to picking out the bad girls.* Within the hour he was back as a doddering old man, dressed very poorly and leaning on a staff to keep him upright.

There would be one more woman to come in. As she entered and walked through the tavern to the kitchen, she paused but a moment to look back at the bishop disguised as an old man. There was a leering look on her face that was quite unsettling. The bishop waited a moment and then followed her into the kitchen where she was already trying to ensnare Oma. As he came in behind her she stiffened, then, turned toward him saying, "I know you, the holy man of God." The bishop said, "I adjure you by the power of the Son of God that you reveal who you are serving in this village."

The visage of the woman grew even more sinister and a look of cunning was apparent. "I am in service to one Wilhelmina."

The bishop said, "I perceive thou art a lying spirit. Would you be cast into hell before the time?"

"Very well the name is Jacklyn." the demon spirit said.

"Is that a spirit name because she is a supplanter?" the bishop asked.

"That, I cannot say. I only know that name. Now let me go."

"By the power of Yahweh-Tsidkenu in whom dwells all righteousness I command you in his Name not to go back to the one who sent you; neither shall you communicate to any other whether man or demon, and that your lying mouth be closed till the Judgment. Now go."

The bishop said to Oma, "I do not think any more of this sort will come in here today. But to be safe, tell Max that if any women come in today, he should say they must come back tomorrow. I need you to come with me to Fox Home now."

The bishop and Oma arrived at Fox Home to discover Durchgefüweg had gotten out of her bed. The women were making final adjustments on her replacement wash gown before again treating her back and putting the clean fabric on her. When the visitors were announced she drew the sheet around her in modesty.

Without wasting time Bishop Elisha said, "Durchgefüweg, your stepfather is an evil wizard of the Druids. Last night he sent two demons to find you."

The girl nearly fell over in shock at his words. Brunhild came beside her chair and held her against her side so she would not fall completely out of it. "I should have known," she said.

The bishop gave her a little time to collect herself. "He failed in his attempt and the demons returned to him, hurting him severely. Now I want to ask you a serious question. Are you a true follower of the Invisible God?"

She said, "Yes, before my father died our family worshipped the Invisible God. We even have a chapel in our Hold where a priest came at least once a month. Then we and our father's retainers went to worship right there at the Hold. When my father died and Bruno seduced my mother, he expelled the priest and closed the chapel except..." The girl paused.

The bishop spoke gently, "Except for what my dear?"

"Except sometimes he was seen slipping into the chapel near the witching hour."

The bishop had not missed that the girl had given away the personal name of her stepfather but made no mention of it even though he recognized it as common among Druids.

The bishop continued, "Now I must ask you some delicate questions and you must answer me truthfully. To your knowledge did he ever carve any of the vile symbols of Satan into your body, particularly buttocks or breasts? Had he ever tattooed you or made piercing in your body, especially the lips of your womanhood?"

Durchgefüweg had not thought with all that had happened she could any longer blush but under the questioning of the priest she found her whole body had gotten hot and turned red with embarrassment. "No sir. He once took out a thin sharp knife after beating me and I thought he would cut me then, but something happened and he did not."

Then the bishop spoke to the ladies. "Dear women of faith. I must call on you to do things most delicate for this young woman has been most sorely mistreated. I cannot go into her private chamber to aid in this for she is most attractive and I learned as a young supplicant even the consideration of temptation can separate a man from his holy calling. And that not easily to be regained. For her sake you must inspect her body and look for the things I have named lest evil was done to her when she was in a stupor. Look even to the soles of her feet and hidden in her hair to see if there are any tattoos. Oma will know what is best to look for about her female mystery. She must make sure there are no piercings on her there and that her maidenhead is intact."

Durchgefüweg was almost in a panic at the thought of further humiliation after all she had been through yet she knew these people were acting for her benefit and not for evil. It further comforted her that this holy man did not want to be present at the inspection of her person. Still she could not help sobbing over the matter.

The women went with her into the bedchamber. When the ladies returned, they reported that nothing was found of the things he had mentioned. The priest gave a visible sigh of relief. They did not know why these things were of so serious a nature but saw that Bishop Elisha did and he was more at ease that nothing he was concerned for was discovered.

He spoke again to Durchgefüweg, saying, "Dear child, though you do not understand the reasons for all of this, let me assure you that you have indeed been protected from above. Had you not gotten free, worse things than what you have already endured were coming. Because none of those things I have mentioned are upon you, no evil force may lay claim upon you, however false. Finally, I do not think you will ever see your stepfather again. But if you do, you will find he walks with a limp because as a result of his evil the muscle in one of his legs is torn. Justice is coming for him. That is just a foretaste of what awaits him because he chose to follow the Evil One.

The ladies finished the adjustment to the wash dress and took Durchgefüweg away to privacy. This was in order to clean and reapply the ointment and get the dress upon her. When she returned again, once more covered with a sheet, her composure was also with her.

Bishop Elisha blessed the women and then he spoke a special prayer for Durchgefüweg, calling on the Invisible God by His Name, Yahweh Rapha, the Lord who heals. By the following day her back would be close to completely healed.

Brunhild made the decision to ask the washerwoman to scrub the soiled wash dress and hang it on the line overnight. Try as she might, it was obvious the stains of the unguent and the bloody drainage could never be completely removed.

Oma told the women of the events of the day at the tavern with the evil women who had come in. Some of it, like Oma chasing the woman who falsely claimed to be a twelve-year-old virgin, brought peals of laughter from them. Oma cautioned the women they should never neglect their husbands and leave them vulnerable to temptation. And the bishop chimed in saying that men should never neglect their women for the Old Serpent loves to target women.

The difference between the return of Gidon and Gid-visu were scant seconds. Like all young lovers every minute they had been separated from their true loves had been an eternity and they were eager to get home.

The Baron came more slowly. When he had given his body some rest, the wound had intensified its discomfort making him very sore. But when his eyes fell on Gwynedd it was obvious that his heart was full of love for her. During his business about the village, he had even stopped to buy her a gift of fine linen and lace. These were items of finer value than any she had owned in her life. All the women professed those things were wonderful.

Durchgefüweg thought in her heart that these women, including Oma, must be some of the most blessed women in the world because of the devoted men who inhabited their lives. She began to long for a man who would love her and cherish her.

Chapter 11

Many Adventures Begin

Bishop Elisha took the men aside, first to explain the events of the previous night more fully than he cared to share with the women. In his opinion they had been subjected to far more than he wished. And the men must be impressed with the seriousness of the spiritual challenge. Men are sometimes more ready to face physical challenges than things in the area of spiritual warfare. And he wanted to stress to them the necessity of guarding their women because the Evil One has often targeted women ever since the Garden.

Then he spoke about the events of the day that happened in the Eastwatch tavern. Of course, two of the women were nothing more than people who followed the course of destruction set by the Prince of the Power of the Air. However, the third was a woman under demonic possession. He confided he had not expected so open a movement to destroy the tavern and the elders who made it their center for meetings. He considered the attacks that had happened previously to have been for the ultimate purpose of harming the kingdom through attack on two key men, Gid-visu and Baron von Krieg.

He did tell the men he got the name of the person controlling the local insurrection from the demon inside the last woman. The name was Jacklyn. And he told them he did not know if this was a spiritual name for it meant supplanter, or whether it was an actual name.

Baron von Krieg volunteered that when he had found the murdered guard, he had thought he was on Hold land a man named Bruno was in charge of. He knew Bruno had not won or been awarded the right to the Hold, but had it because it had been given to the man whose widow he married. He also shared at the time the rightful master of the Hold had died, his death had been questioned. He had been a hale and hearty man in the prime of life. But so many pressing things kept the matter from being investigated as it should. He said, "I now can see that King's Riders should have united to look into the matter. King Gregor has a man who can look into a body and tell exactly how he died. He is as adept as King Arthur's Merlin, I am told."

After the men's conference they invited the women to join them including Durchgefüweg. The meal of the evening began to be served. Gidon declared he wanted to clean up later, beginning with the sauna. His father said he and Brunhild would join them. Gid-visu started to ask the bishop if he would join them, but he beat them to it saying he needed to confer with the wounded Baron, who, for reason of the wound, could not enter the sauna. The young lad whose duty was now to tend the fires was called for and sent out to start warming things up.

But things were also rather warm at the supper table. It seemed no one except the bishop was truly willing to wait till the meal was finished to talk about local situations. Baron von Krieg told the Bishop of his visit to Herr Brute'. He had sent a request to the bishop. That is, thanks to the training Stability and Strength had received from the older fighting priests, he wants to borrow them at least for a few days to teach the basics of fighting with the one hand double edged sword. "Brute' said, and I quote, Herman One Eye is an excellent pike man, but he is a lousy swordsman." That was good for a laugh with the group.

The first six wooden training swords had been delivered. Herr Brute' wanted to waste not a minute in training men with an aptitude. He was in a rush to make up fifty elite guardsmen for the day Eastwatch Keep would need to be manned. And he wanted to cull out those who should go to the king's castle for general training. To this need the bishop willingly assented.

Then the Baron gave a different type of report that soon had all the people at the table laughing. He recounted how he had stopped in to visit Brigitta, mainly wishing to see the change of heart he had been told of, for himself. He found her resting with her feet up at the krankenschwester's demand. He said when she began talking to him, she became effusive praising Brute'. She praised the Baron for bringing such a wonderful man to Eastwatch, and she had nothing but kind words to say of Gidon for delivering her to him. She said that was one of the most wonderful days of her life. She told the Baron, Brute' had saved her father's life. The Baron asked her how he had done this? Brigitta replied he had told her father that if he died, he was going to take her. Then she had leaned forward and told the Baron with a confidential air, "He is going to take me anyway!" Once again, the scandalized nurse had found it necessary to leave the room and when the Baron told that, they laughed a bit more.

Then the Baron recounted how he had left Brigitta and visited the Burgomeister in his room to find him sitting up on his pillows with all appearance of good health except for the bandages around his head and blackened eyes. His opinion of Herr Brute', the Baron said, was quite different from his daughter's. He told the Baron that Brute' had told him to die because he was going to take his house, his wife, and his daughter! He begged the Baron to protect him from this evil fiend. But the Baron had one game to play on the Burgomeister himself:

"My dear Burgomeister, If you have him wed Brigitta you must realize he would be honor bound to protect his father and mother-in-law?"

The Burgomeister said, "Yes! Yes! I had not thought of that. I must get to work on that as soon as they allow me to get about again!"

Baron von Krieg said, "This day my friends I have performed a miracle. I changed a fiend into a suitable son-in-law."

Everyone laughed at it all except for Durchgefüweg. She was trying to imagine a man so fearsome looking that he could fill a Burgomeister with fear while at the same time filling his daughter, who they all said was beautiful, with ever growing love.

Gid-visu opened up the subject of the current threat stating that this Jacklyn, the bishop had learned of, was probably the sole traitor in Eastwatch. But the Baron thought this person more likely headed a conspiracy. There had to be co-conspirators. And he reminded the group attempts had been made on the lives of important persons in other places in the kingdom. He said, "The more a person wants to do right, it seems the more springs up to oppose him. And we have a very good king."

Brunhild, who always seemed to have ideas worth considering, said "If this name was a spiritual name and not its actual name, could it be the person was a man who had a name like Jacoba, which is a male version of the name Jacklyn and meaning the same thing?"

The room went very quiet. Durchgefüweg thought Brunhild might really be in trouble for speaking this time and felt uneasy. She did not yet realize how much respect these women had from their men. The truth was they were all thinking of one village elder, Jacoba, who bought the rough, locally woven goods, many of which were made in the winter, and sold the villagers fine goods such as the local folk were not capable of producing. It seemed a fine business.

The thing about Jacoba was he was slightly built like a woman but with no female form. But he had long fine fingers like many women; was never seen when he was not clean shaven, and he also was not married. Perhaps his name rose too early in the conversation. But after that no one could think of another possible candidate.

Baron von Krieg addressed the bishop. "King Gregor has approved my marriage to Gwynedd. For the sake of her safety till the crisis has passed I want to take her for my mistress privately. But I want it written into the contract that she will be the Lady of Eastwatch Keep when I have completed it."

Gwynedd was a widow and should have behaved as a completely mature woman about these things. But she had discovered a new youthfulness in the love of this older man. We can forgive a little squeal as loving arms went around the Baron's neck. Indeed, he received hugs from the women and congratulations from the men as he formalized what he had previously announced.

Oma said, "I have to go. I have promised Max a bath tonight," She gave a little wink to her girls and Durchgefüweg. It was to be an interesting night in many places and Durchgefüweg longed more and more for a day when such joy might include her as well.

As the room emptied out with each person going to their respective plans for the evening, the bishop reached into his case and pulled out parchment, quill, and ink. His skill would make the document not only a thing of law but a thing of beauty. Long hours in the Scriptorium had honed his skills. He still took great pleasure illuminating books and especially the Holy Scripture. Tonight, he would produce a holy document that was also a thing of art.

*****

Gid-visu and Gidon entered the sauna clad only in the towels they would sit on. The ladies were coming from the washroom clad in the sheets. This gave the two of them a little time to talk. Gidon asked his opinion of the bishop's warning?

Gid-visu said, "Just over three hundred years ago I was warned that I should pray. My failure to heed that warning cost me the joy of the woman I loved and the pleasure of seeing six children grown and well situated. I shall never make such an error again."

There was quiet for a little space and again Gidon asked a question. "I had promised to go back to Herman One Eye's hovel. I said I would inspect his sons' work getting a crop planted. What would you think of me taking a little food for his wife and some extra in case I meet Snaggle Tooth along the way?"

"That would be fine," Gid-visu said. "But you have something else on your mind as well."

"Yes, I thought I would take Getrudis. I believe Begleiter could carry the two of us easily. Do you think the Baron would mind?"

"You did not pay good attention my son. The Baron said he was replacing Begleiter because you had stolen his affection. The horse is yours. All that remains is to thank him for this fine present to his squire." Gid-visu did not see how that fact could escape his attention. But then his mind had been in softer places at the time.

The women entered the sauna and slid behind their men before removing their sheets. As one they began to wash the men's backs, missing no opportunity to tantalize them with little touches that had nothing to do with getting clean. Getrudis was learning from Brunhild, who did have womanly experience from her previous marriage. One day she planned to ask her how it was she could give herself first to one man and then to another even after being widowed so long? She could not imagine giving herself to another man should she lose Gidon.

Gidon turned around so that he faced Getrudis standing behind him. He had quite forgotten Brunhild was also behind the bench tending Gid-visu. "How would you like going with me on an adventure tomorrow?"

Getrudis could barely reach around his neck from this position while Brunhild slipped around the bench to get beside Gid-visu. "Oh yes, I would love it."

"Very well, we will be up and at the stables before the sun, so none of the townspeople will know we have gone."

Getrudis wrinkled her nose, "Then I had better get you to bed so we can be well rested."

Neither Brunhild nor Gid-visu could keep from laughing at that.

When Gidon and Getrudis entered their chamber, Baron von Krieg was already in the pallet before the fire. He said, "Can you two not be quieter? You woke me up."

A little voice came out of the covers in front of his body. "He's lying!" she said. Her head was just under his chin and it was plain their cuddling had been intensely pleasurable to both. The love long denied expression in the flesh was infinitely more pleasurable for the wait.

*****

Gidon and Getrudis thought they were first to rise. In quiet and darkness, they dressed with the help of a single candle. They did not wish to waken the couple sleeping in the next room still locked in love's embrace. Gidon hated donning the chainmail because it still felt cold even with the inner garment, and it was a barrier of separation between him and Getrudis. But Getrudis had to rely on her woman's cloak for warmth in the early morning air since too heavy a dress would make riding behind Gidon the more difficult. She was excited both by the prospect of being close to him for a day as well as the thought of the new experience of being on the back of a horse.

When they got down to the kitchen, they found the ever busy Brunhild had already packed them fresh food, plus a small wineskin for the noon meal. Gid-visu was there with her but he was impatient to finish seeing the couple off and get back to bed for a couple of additional hours of closeness before they must be about the day.

Gidon and Getrudis now equipped with the needs for the day hurried to the stable, intending to saddle Begleiter and be clear of the town before the sun's rays began to waken the village. They were mistaken in thinking they could do that quietly. The horse seeing Gidon and sensing a new adventure about to begin noisily spoke his welcome. It frightened Getrudis who had no experience of horses and it took a little coaxing to encourage her to come up next to the animal and make friends. But once she saw Begleiter respond to her, she became thrilled with the horse and he sensed it in her.

Herman the Schmeid slept in the stable boy cubicle. It was also convenient to the smithy. He could keep some watch over both businesses fairly continually. All the activity roused him and he was put to work setting things in order. It was the first time he had seen Getrudis for a few days. He used to prolong visits to the tavern just in the hopes of seeing her. He had never thought of any romantic possibilities, but she was a pretty girl and he a lonely man with little talent and fewer prospects. He was glad to see her with Gidon whom he considered his friend.

As he helped them get ready to depart, he confided to Gidon the monastery smith was going to begin teaching him how to mend chainmail and he was looking forward to repairing the suit of the King's Rider. He also told Gidon that he hoped he would not need his mail repaired from damage in battle. This idea caused a little worry line to appear on Getrudis brow. Much as she adored seeing

Gidon looking so bold and brave in his chainmail and tunic, the idea he might be seriously hurt or even maimed was not something she liked to contemplate. It had devastated her when the man Gidon had fought with bit his hand. But since he had not treated it as a serious matter, she had not been overwhelmed by it. Gidon, seeing the little worry line appear, made a mental note to later warn the schmeid not to frighten his lady with talk of injuries.

Little things like getting the two of them positioned on board the horse with weapons appropriately in place proved a bit challenging but they were well on the way to their first stop at the monastery by the time the sun spread its light and warmth about.

Gidon spotted Snaggle Tooth working along the tree line and pointed him out to Getrudis. It was the first time she had seen the sabretooth and when Gidon promised to introduce them later she was not sure that was something to look forward to. But she did ask what the cat was doing? She had the idea he was stalking them. But Gidon said he was watching out for them. He was being protective. The idea of a sabretooth tiger being protective of a human was a new one to her. So, for part of their ride he was explaining not all sabretooth tigers were the same even as the bishop had once done with him.

As Gidon was coming to the spot where the attacker had shot Baron von Krieg's horse, she wanted to know every little detail of what happened. She asked, "Were you not afraid as you attacked the assassin?"

Gidon said, "I did not have time to be afraid because Begleiter turned and went after him so quickly."

"You mean he knew what you wanted to do just like that?" Getrudis asked.

Gidon decided it would be too hard to explain Begleiter knew what he wanted to do, not what Gidon wanted. After all, it is fun to be a hero in the eyes of your love.

As they approached the monastery, they could hear the priests singing hymns of praise as they came out of the Chapel. Gidon told Getrudis that when he was a boy going to school at the monastery, he used to enjoy the singing very much. She said it was her opinion that they should let boys and women sing also. She said, "They have good bass and tenor singers but could surely use some altos and sopranos as well!"

The priests invited the two to join them along with their families, hearth women, and children for a fellowship breakfast consisting mostly of Landesbrot, butter, and some fruit preserves. The children got the eggs that were available because, as it was explained, the monastery chickens were not laying well. Many hens were past their prime and new hens were not yet producing much. As one said, "We will soon be having more chicken broth in our meals in a few days."

The leave taking was pleasant indeed. New connections had been forged as people worked together with various projects such as armor for the fifty who would defend the area. Many of the older men had known Gidon since he was a boy. And they knew Getrudis to be Gidon's lady, else she would not have been with him without chaperone. Getrudis was more quickly comfortable with the motion of the horse on this next part of the journey. With her arms wrapped around Gidon she was very happy. Even Begleiter seemed into the spirit of the day.

Finally they got to the place Herman One Eye called home. Gidon circled around the hovel area so he might inspect the place where the people lived and the outbuildings as well from a direction they might not expect people to come. He was surprised by what he saw. While he had seen fields tilled and planted as he made his circle the real surprise was at the hovel itself. He saw two of Herman's sons working on the thatch on the roof while two others were constructing an addition to the house. It no longer looked as if the animals had better accommodation than the people. It was plain the son, too young to go to war, had taken charge of his older brothers when they were sent back to finish the spring planting. He was keeping an eye on them as they worked. But one son of Herman seemed to be missing.

Gidon began riding down toward the hovel looking forward, he hoped, to learning what had happened. The young lad saw Gidon and raised a hand in welcome. He called to the house and his mother appeared. She actually looked better than when last he saw her. He held Getrudis as she slipped off behind him and then he took the long descent from horseback to ground. Begleiter was ready for a cool drink and stretched his head toward the water trough. Gidon inspected it suspiciously but was pleasantly surprised to find all in good shape without any scum in the water or on the wood. This place had really changed.

The wife of Herman One Eye approached the two of them actually trying to curtsy to Getrudis. "Squire Gidon, our home is honored by the presence of you and your lady." She tried to be polite according to custom but had never had the opportunity to learn.

Gidon said, "The improvements you have made are worthy of praise madam. I perceived some of the improvement as I rode down with Getrudis. No doubt it is due to the son I did not get to meet on my last visit. I also see one of your sons is missing. Is all well?"

The youngest son said, "He is here m'lord but I am afraid he is in no condition to come out to greet you right now."

"What is the cause of that?" Gidon asked.

The lad replied quite calmly; "We had some dispute about whether he would work or not. So, I did to him with my staff what you once threatened to do to my father."

"How were you able to best him? He is a pretty big fellow." This was adding up to a pretty interesting story, Gidon thought.

"You see sir, this woman is my mother and not the mother of the other boys of Herman One Eye. Her father was well known for his skill with the fighting staff and his daughter watched him train from the time she was a little girl till her father's last day. The death of her father was the sad cause of her marrying Herman. She taught me how to fight with the staff and none of my brothers knew how to use it. No one had taught them."

Gidon laughed, "And where is your brother now?"

"He doth lay in the goat hovel. I give him a piece of bread each day and all the goat milk he can catch. And sir, the goats do not like him and his head hurts too badly to move fast! I told him if he wants to eat more then he must work. He was too fat and lazy. I might not cure him of being lazy but I will certainly cure him of being fat!"

Getrudis spoke to the woman, "I perceive you have a good son who will do well in the future. We ask if you will favor us by accepting some provision we have brought?"

The woman began to tear up. "Though we are much improved in our circumstance, partly because Herman has found some employment from which he sends us a bit, we are yet limited in our daily bread and we are most grateful. Will you join us in having a meal Lady Getrudis?"

Gidon did not correct her error in Getrudis status. For to him she was his lady forever. Gidon spoke, "My lady and I have an appointment with my sabretooth for lunch. They have not yet been formally introduced and she is anticipating meeting him. So we cannot linger."

To Herman One Eye's youngest son Gidon said, "I perceive you are a fellow of possibilities who is likely to do well in life. May I ask your name?"

"If it pleases you, I am called Wolfgang as was the name of my mother's father."

"So you are a lone wolf who sets the path. It seems you are already living up to your name with your brothers. Fare thee well Wolfgang till we meet again." And with that Gidon mounted Begleiter and pulling Getrudis up to him they rode out of the camp of admirers as he had done once before, when there was animosity to turn his back on.

When the two, in their journey back to Eastwatch, reached the point where Gidon had once put the fear of his sabretooth into Herman One Eye and his sons, the sun was still high in the sky. Movement along the way was much faster when not slowed by a goat cart. Gidon looked expectantly up the hillside. He was rewarded with seeing the tawny coat of Snaggle Tooth as he came running with the fluid motion of a great cat. Gidon wondered why he was not already in his spot? But when Snaggle Tooth reached the very spot he had been at when last he met Gidon here, he sat down as if to say, "Well you are finally here, so what!"

Gidon thought, *Only a cat can do that!* But then he amended his thought to add, *Or a woman!* He slid down from Begleiter in a complex motion that moved Getrudis into the saddle at the same time. This marked the first time in her young life she had ever been on horseback alone. But Begleiter was on his best behavior. He, like many male horses, had a fondness for human women and small children.

Gidon and Snaggle Tooth went through their familiar routine together where he scratched those areas behind jaws and ears cats can never seem to get enough of, till finally the large cat put a paw on his shoulder and reaffirmed their bond.

Getrudis in the meantime slipped from the horse to the ground and began to approach a scene between man and beast seldom seen since The Flood. Snaggle Tooth was watching the approaching woman intently. Gidon looked over his shoulder at her and said, "Come here my love and kneel beside me and scratch behind his ears."

She did so a little squeamishly at first but as the tiger responded to her caress, she became more enthusiastic. Gidon addressed the cat, "Snaggle Tooth, this is Getrudis. She belongs to me."

There are times when great cats seem to show expression on their faces. This was the first of two times Snaggle Tooth seemed to look surprised this afternoon. When he said 'she belongs to me' the old cat looked genuinely confused as if to say, "Are you starting your own pride?" He had said exactly the same thing when he had introduced Brigitta to him. The tiger began to smell the girl all over but when he thrust his nose into her crotch, he stopped for he recognized Gidon's mark upon her. To say the least, both Gidon and Getrudis had been surprised by that last move.

Gidon, Getrudis, Snaggle Tooth, and a reluctant Begleiter walked over the crest of the hill to see an indent that looked as if some giant foot had once stepped there. Getrudis laid out their cloaks on the ground at the heel side of the impression. There two people and a sabretooth shared a meal while the horse grazed the opposite side of the depression, all hidden away from the road. Perhaps it was the wine, but warmed by the sun, Getrudis removed her outer dress and kicked off her shoes to stretch and reach upwards clad only in a shift that went down to just below the knees.

Gidon remembered she had been raised on a farm and this was probably the first time she had been free of the village since her indenture. As she set by Gidon, Snaggle Tooth reached out and licked the sole of a bare foot. The rough tongue tickled her so she giggled. Then on impulse she stood up and danced, with Snaggle Tooth bounding around her. He liked this girl!

Gidon looked on with amusement. He was learning things about both the cat and the woman such as he had never imagined. Getrudis saw Gidon watching and decided she would stalk him like a tigress. She pulled up her shift so it would not catch on her knees as she got down on all fours and slinked toward him like a cat stalking her prey. He marveled at the roll of her hips that was both seductive and did indeed mimic a cat. This was the second time Snaggle Tooth could have been said to have expression. He looked very sad and walked up to the crest of the hill sitting where he could look over a wide range of territory. Who knows what is in a sabretooth's mind? But his breed mated once, for the life of the mates. Perhaps at that point he mourned for his mate, lost so long ago.

The group lingered in their hideaway long into the evening. The plan was to return to Eastwatch after darkness set in. They would enter from the opposite side of town in order to draw less attention. While their time together had been so pleasant, increasingly they felt the sadness of its ending. Who knew if or when there would be such an opportunity again?

As they entered the village from the eastern side Gidon pointed out a little rock house with thatched roof. He told Getrudis his father said it had been his home over three hundred years before. Today he once again owned it but it was used by his tenants. By the time they got to Fox Home it was fully dark. Gidon was tempted to just turn Begleiter loose to go to the stables on his own but he decided against it because he knew the horse deserved better. But still he had to take a moment just inside the front door. He wanted to take his sweet tigress in his arms and thank her for being the beautiful woman she was both inside and out. Then he went to Begleiter and they walked together to the stables.

When they came to the entrance to the stable Begleiter paused and stood, ears pointed forward, listening intently for sound coming from the stable but no greetings sounded. Why were the horses standing so quietly? Gidon, knowing it was not necessary, still told the horse, "Easy boy."

He left the animal standing with his reins tied over his neck. Quietly circling the building, he came to where a ladder was built into the side of the wall. Up he went, this time trying not to make a creaking sound on a rung or worse. He looked into the darkened loft and tried to make out any movement. Not seeing anything he slowly eased himself in through the barn loft door. At the moment he was grateful for having stopped to leave Getrudis at Fox Home.

At this time of the year the loft was nearly empty of hay and some boards had even been moved off the floor joists to allow for better circulation of air to keep hay from getting moldy. He could see down into the stable area from a variety of positions.

In the pen that held Schlachtross, the Baron's war steed, a body was on the floor. He supposed it to be Herman the Schmeid. But if the intruders were expecting the war steed to stomp whoever was there, they did not understand these horses. And if it was the schmeid you could be sure Schlachtross was not about to step on the man who fed and curried him, not to mention daily caring for his wound.

Gidon positioned himself above the man he presumed was the farthest back in the stable. He and the one other he could see both had crossbows, preferable for a job such as this where there was little maneuver room. It was as much circumstance as choice that put Gidon where he was. The second man was positioned across from Schlachtross' pen. And he suspected, there was a third located close to the stable doors.

The action started when the man immediately below Gidon was hit by a piece of falling straw and looked up swinging the crossbow upwards at the same time. As soon as he started to move Gidon dropped through between the joists, sword almost magically leaping into his hand, going up and coming down in a motion that cleaved him from shoulder to breast bone. His crossbow shaft cut Gidon's cheek and hung inside the hood of his protective chainmail.

Even as Gidon fell from the loft, Schlachtross kicked with his powerful rear hooves sending the gate on his pen across the stable knocking the second man off his feet. The other two horses began to neigh buck and kick adding to the confusion.

There was a third attacker located near the entrance to the stable revealed as he loosed his bolt at Gidon, just before Begleiter came through the entrance and ran over him. Then turning to stomp him once more, he demonstrated his displeasure to the man with powerful hooves. Gidon felt the sting of the front attacker's shaft as it barely split the mail to wound his skin. He would have a scar but no serious damage from it.

The Baron's war steed, after kicking out the gate, spun to attack the middle man. Schlachtross had been just slow enough to have been spared the front bowman's shaft and just fast enough so the assassin he knocked down with the gate would never get up.

Gidon spoke his praise telling all the horses how wonderful they were as he worked his way past them to the schmeid. Schlachtross had to examine Gidon's wounds while at the same time pushing him toward the schmeid. The horse did not realize that at this point he was doing more hindering than helping.

Gidon could never explain what happened next. When he discovered that Herman the Schmeid was not dead he somehow swung himself up on the back of the Schlachtross taking Herman with him. He could not have done that under normal circumstances. That big horse galloped out of the stable followed by Begleiter as Gidon rode bareback and reinless to the Burgomeister's house, where he knew he could get medical attention.

Herman One Eye heard Gidon yelling even before he got to the front door and came out to take the now moaning schmeid in his arms and into the house. Gidon swung down and felt a momentary bit of weakness. But Herr Brute' caught him as he stumbled. He and Schlachtross were both covered in blood and when Gidon looked at the horse he finally realized much of it was his own. The horse's wound had not been reopened. It was only later he learned, though bloody, none of his wounds were truly life threatening.

Brute' spoke to Brigitta who had come out in her nightgown, "Get back inside my warrior queen. I cannot act if I am afraid for your safety. Beside this, you will be needed inside." As she turned, he was caught by the movement of her backside through the nightgown. Before he caught himself, he gave it a friendly swat. She looked back and made a little 'o' with her lips, then grinned and bounced back inside, not realizing the deed had been recorded on her nightgown by the blood on Brute's hand.

Brute' handed Gidon to Ohtrad to keep him from falling. Gidon said, "Where is my sword?" And then he became even more wobbly on his feet. It was then Brute' flung himself upon Begleiter, and with the Baron's warhorse deciding on his own to go along, he rode to Fox Home to get the Baron and Gid-visu.

It would be quite an endeavor to keep Getrudis from rushing right over that night. Her fear of one day losing Gidon in war seemed more real than ever.

CHAPTER 12

NEW ADVENTURES CONTINUE

The bishop's plan went into motion about the same time Gidon and Getrudis had made their way to the stable to get Begleiter. It was full daylight and they would hear the singing from the monastery before a blind beggar, guided only by a staff to feel his way about, made his way down the street where Jacoba had his business.

He was a pitiable creature with a long unkempt white beard. A single strand of material covered his eyes so all could tell he was blind. Only a blind beggar would have chosen the wrong side of the road upon which to sit. For most of the side he chose was wall, the back side of residences. And who would cross the street to put something in the bowl of a blind beggar?

When the man had sat down and leaned his staff against the wall where he could readily find it, he had pulled his garment about him and seemed to fall instantly asleep. Who would care a thing about a sleeping blind beggar? From the looks of his garment he probably smelled awful. It certainly did not look as if he could expect a profitable day, so he surely would not return for a second day of begging. And who would want to encourage him to?

It had taken some hours and not a little expertise to get the blind beggar disguise exactly right. The skill had been learned from a summer spent with a group of Romano wandering about the country some years earlier. Bishop Elisha had learned many things from the Romano. Among the things he learned was they were extremely hard to convert into followers of the Invisible God. They had already been committed to their form of religion for millennia before he had the opportunity to try.

The street on which Jacoba had chosen to place his business was most interesting. As a place for the purchase of rough fabric it was probably fine, but it did not seem the best location for the selling of fine items in return. The bishop did learn something about the trade in products made by local serfs and farmers over the winter months when opportunity for them was limited. The winter product was still coming in at this point because people were driven by the priorities of their primary concerns, such as preparing the ground for planting. He also saw how much of a vicious circle it was for those locals doing trade with Jacoba. For instance, people producing feather mattresses often traded much of their gain getting the fabric that would be stuffed with material for the next round of mattress making. He saw people making feather mattresses who could never afford one for themselves. They slept on hay or rope beds if they had beds at all. The bishop had a rope bed in his cell which was covered with a woven hay mattress. He felt very thankful for it knowing many he served had far less.

To the blind beggar's left, as he watched Jacoba's shop, was a little business built up by three floors, as high as anything stood in the village with the exception of the Church. The first floor was a place where people could stop and have the simplest of fare to eat as they went about their business. The second floor was simple sleeping accommodation such as might be used by people who took the products from Jacoba to other places for trade. But not all who stayed there were cart drivers or petty merchants. The blind beggar saw three men emerge just before the fifth hour after noon who were all dressed in the exact same simple but new garb, carrying packages all wrapped in the same way. He thought this strange. After all, few men tried to hide what they carried for there was normally no accountability for such things in Eastwatch, where no taxes were collected.

Further left was a house where women sold themselves to whoever wanted the use of them. One of the people Bishop Elisha saw that day was a woman who looked like a scraggly young girl. He was sure this was the same woman Oma had chased through the tavern.

On the immediate right side of Jacoba's business was a storage facility, and from the traffic it was discernible to see was part of Jacoba's business activity. As the day wore on Bishop Elisha became increasingly certain everything on the street, including the whores, were part of his business empire. No wonder the Deacon had reported to the bishop he never saw Jacoba in Church! Jacoba was a purveyor of human flesh, a Zuhälter. It would be enlightening to know to what depths his catering in human chattel went, considering there seemed to be a link between someone in Eastwatch and the Druid Bruno.

It was about the fifth hour after noon when Jacoba emerged from his business, neatly dressed as always, headed in the direction of Fat Max's tavern. He obviously preferred better food than what was to be had at his own business beside his shop. The bishop decided to go to the tavern as well. And somewhere along the way he was transformed into a wandering minstrel.

*****

The two newly consecrated fighting priests Stability and Strength were completely thrilled to have the opportunity of working under the command of Herr Brute' to build up a defensive force for Eastwatch. Even though their time was limited because they soon would depart for the king's muster, they knew that when men thought they had peace it would not be long before trouble again reared its evil head.

It was not easy putting together a unit trained and dedicated to Eastwatch. Many forced to train simply did not wish to. Others lacked in physical ability. And there were some who were not opposed to the defensive force as long as it was others doing the defending. For these priests it was about defending people of faith in the Invisible

God from those who were not only against accepting the faith but were against those who did.

Like the men gathered for the training they knew nothing about conspiracies and intrigue. Things were more straightforward to them and therefore easier to deal with emotionally. They had to teach the rudiments of onehanded double-edged swordplay to a group of men whose number had already been cut by ten for reasons of physical stamina. They would, without doubt, build stamina on the long march less than a week away.

Since the singlehanded sword would be the main single combat weapon for these recruits, those who failed to have an aptitude for it would also be cut and go forth in the general muster. For some of the recruits it had not yet occurred to them that doing their best was the better way to avoid a month of intensive training after a week or more of travel to get to the king's castle.

What the priests would gain from their role in the training at Eastwatch would be a honing of skills through working with the novices as well as a promise made by Herr Brute' to teach them the rudiments of fighting with sword and knife in combination. Judah the Hammer had been particularly encouraging to these younger priests saying "Anytime you have a chance to learn from a member of the Long Knives you should do so."

This would be the first day Herr Brute' would wear armor other than Haubergeon chainmail since coming to Eastwatch. One reason for change was that even though it bore no insignia, it still was of Roman design. And Romans, which locals often called children of wolves, were not well liked among the Alemanni. His preference was for light armorment, to which he only added chainmail extending mid-thigh when battle was sure. Plate armor and the like too badly restricted movement in his opinion. He noticed the fighting priests preferred the Hauberk style, which was a longer shirt of chainmail without a chainmail hood. The Celts, it was said, originally invented chainmail primarily as a protection for the throat. Brute' was not sure of that, but it was certain many different styles now existed including the new one Baron von Krieg had devised.

The main reason for Brute' putting on his armor had been Brigitta. She considered him quite dashing in his armor and not only that, she had stated emphatically, "I do not want a sweet hair on your head hurt, not even by accident!" Brute' did have one other reason for donning his armor. The helm design signified authority. He had heard of the murmuring of a few villagers against him being in charge of training. He decided that since he could not avoid the criticism, he might as well face it head on.

*****

It was hard to say whether the Baron was acting in his capacity as a King's Rider or as the Baron, soon to be Baron of Eastwatch Keep. As he began his workday all he could focus on was how soon he could be through and get back to Gwynedd. But he also knew the women had planned a busy day of their own.

He had previously chosen what he considered the best site for the Eastwatch Keep even when he thought he would build it for Gid-visu to be lord over. A water-witcher had been used to douse and make the decision on the optimal position within the proposed site to get the best flow for a well. And this day would begin the process of proving whether they would have the well they needed or not.

It had been the Baron's decision to hire and not conscript serfs for the digging of the well. They had been told the best workers would be staying on to work when the master masons came to build the Keep itself. It would be a long-lasting job, building the whole of the Keep. It would last several years. This income would be a boon to villagers and nearby farmers alike. Some men would send their sons to earn income for the family with the hope they would gain skills as well. He hoped to build a more resilient and loyal community, like the one about King Gregor's castle, over time. Thus, people were paid for work.

With the successful establishment of the well he would have the first step toward the making of a defensible Keep. After all, if you cannot provide the basics, you cannot defend your Keep any more than without assault resistant design you do not have a fortification you can hold.

A great deal of thought went into the production of the Keep. He tried to learn the hard lessons from past designs that ultimately failed. Even the loyalty of surrounding populace was a key component to having a defensible keep. That was another reason people would be paid and given opportunities for advancement. Even the force that manned the walls would be better if local people were the ones trained to do it. They would also be defending their home.

Baron von Krieg knew without a doubt that the plans against the kingdom had to fail in Eastwatch for the sake of the village as well as the kingdom.

*****

Durchgefüweg was the target of Brunhild and Gwynedd for the day of new adventures. This was the day she had been promised when her back was healed enough. Today they would do what women have loved to do since right after The Fall and that is change their appearance with dress and beauty applications.

Bishop Elisha had prayed a prayer for healing for Durchgefüweg and subsequently all saw a remarkable overnight recovery from damage the terrible beating produced. Now he was asked if it was acceptable for women to employ makeup and ornately plait their hair? He thought about it for a moment and said, "If that is all there is to a woman and her motives are wrong then it is wrong. But if her motives are pure, such as to please her husband, then there is no sin." But the Bishop did not end his statement there. "I have considered the warrior women among the Britons. I think they paint their bodies blue in order to frighten enemies. I am not sure that is bad. But I also think they believe that painting their bodies blue makes them more attractive, even distracting to their enemies. Would you think that was good or bad?" He always loved to leave people something to think about.

One of the first changes was the way her abusive stepfather made her wear her hair. He made her wear it combed out and straight. The ladies chose a five braided style with a crown braid favored by many

Viking ladies. This made her look more like she came from a more northern part of the world. They had discussed cutting away her beautiful hair but the effect would have made her look more like she had once been a beautiful slave. And they did not want to do anything to make someone suppose her modesty had ever once been compromised.

The ladies solved problems like hair and makeup carefully, changing Durchgefüweg into a new appearance that was both modest and appealing. Then they set about preparing appropriate clothing. The ladies produced a wash girl garment that was both tight enough to keep from getting into the baths and modest enough so she would not show too much of her femininity. Of course, she would have to be trained in how to properly and somewhat modestly perform the duty of the job. The first had to precede the latter, and they began by practicing on a young lad a wealthy father had sent to Fox Home for training named Manfred.

The second dress item was an appropriate dress for a tavern serving girl. Oma had provided the material, but the shape of her body, with the bosom exceeding in balance the hips, was a bit difficult. But the ladies produced a fine garment that was almost too good to adorn a simple tavern wench. All in all, it turned out they had put forth a fine day of work. Tonight, Durchgefüweg would have to sleep in the shift undergarment of the dress. They would worry about a good nightgown on the morrow.

*****

Bishop Elisha was pleased his minstrel disguise fooled even Fat Max, but he was not so sure about Oma who several times gave him sidelong glances. She wisely said nothing. Fat Max asked the fake minstrel if he planned to sing and play this night for his supper? The bishop said, “Alas I may not for I am stricken with a malady.” The bishop did not explain that of all the priests at the monastery his malady was he probably had the poorest singing voice of them all.

The minstrel/priest found himself a spot near enough the table of elders where he might hear what was going on. And it was very enlightening.

When Jacoba had entered the building the sole person at the table of elders was Heller von Swabia, a man who made his living through investments. Heller had imbibed a number of beers even before Jacoba arrived. When Jacoba set down, he lost no time working on the man getting him upset over the fact Herr Brute', a foreigner, and Herman One Eye, a low-class man, were the people appointed by the King's Rider to train the good young lads of Eastwatch.

Jacoba was definitely influencing Heller von Swabia to make it an issue before the other elders whenever they arrived. It was highly unlikely anything he would say should bear fruit this night but ideas repeated enough develop a life of their own. Who knows what might happen since people from Roma were not well liked anyway?

Heller von Swabia, tugged at the garment of Jacoba. It was plain Jacoba did not like being touched. "Do you know what I saw just today? I saw Herr Brute' wearing the uniform of a legionnaire!"

Jacoba said, "Perhaps you should tell everyone about that." Bishop Elisha saw he was very careful how he phrased his words. If someone brought it up, he could truthfully say that he never told anyone to tell everybody Herr Brute' dressed in the uniform of a legionnaire. The bishop recognized that whether Jacoba was a man or a woman he was cunning.

Bishop Elisha would need to speak to the Baron and Gid-visu right away, but he would not hurry lest by rushing he be spotted by Jacoba. And his bowl did contain a very good meal.

So it was that as he arrived at Fox Home, he was just in time to see Herr Brute' appear riding Begleiter and followed by Schlachtross.

*****

Herr Brute' said, "Get your swords. Gidon has been wounded!"

"How badly? Will he live?" shouted Gid-visu.

"Hard to tell, but he took two bolts up close. I think maybe not badly." Brute' had added the last part for Getrudis sake because the poor girl was beginning to shake and cry. He could not tell his condition in the short moments he had seen him. And he was not going to mention all the blood in her hearing.

At the sound of alarm all four priests manned the posts without discussion. Those resting were nearly as quick as those already at their posts in the response.

Brunhild, Gwynedd, and Durchgefüweg surrounded Getrudis who was now crying "I must go to him!" The sisterhood was established among these four women in that instant. It was a bond that declared whoever Durchgefüweg should ever find to love, he must be a man that could be part of the brotherhood of the men they loved.

Gid-visu was handed his sword with belt by one of the staff, and he leapt upon the back of Begleiter behind Brute' with the equipment still in his hand. The Baron had already grabbed his sword when he first heard the alarm. Schlachtross placed himself beside the Baron who swung up on his back as if the height of the great horse was nothing.

Someone watching the scene might have said the horses had hardly arrived and the alarm "to arms" called out than three men were galloping away, the Baron holding on with his legs trusting the war steed to know the way to go. The horses' iron shoes rung on the cobbles bringing heads leaning out of windows as the curious wondered what was going on? Brute', who had just recently lost a horse because of a misstep, hoped none would occur this night.

The horses safely delivered their three riders to the Burgomeister's house where Brute' saw Herman One Eye standing at the top of the outside steps. The other two men rushed inside and past what they thought was the scullery maid cleaning up blood in the hall while still in her nightgown. Brute' however lingered asking Herman One Eye, "Why are you standing outside exposing yourself to possible arrow shot?"

Herman said, "It is not my fault. The little mistress would not let me look out through the guard window in the hall."

"And why not?" Brute' asked.

"She said I could not stay at my position and watch her backside."

"And were you?" Brute' looked at him so sternly Herman dropped his head.

"Yes." Herman was looking down but Brute' thought he saw a hint of an unrepentant grin.

Brute' stomped past him but became quieter as he entered the hall. Even without the bloody handprintz he would have recognized the buttocks beneath that nightgown. For a minute he was transfixed watching its movement as the girl scrubbed the floor.

"Herman One Eye, I told you not to be gazing at my backside!" Then she twisted to look and saw Brute'. Brigitta then turned, rose to her feet, and came into his embrace in one fluid motion.

Brute' said, "Warrior queen are you trying to get your guard all flustered?"

She knew Brute' was teasing and said, "Nay my lord, but that view is only for your eyes."

"And what were you doing down on your knees scrubbing up the blood? Do we not have enough help to get that done?" He said, looking down at her with his broken smile.

"The scullery maid said that scrubbing floors was very good for firm breasts." Brigitta said with a smile that said she was doing it all for him. "And the scullery maid appears to have firm breasts, have you not noticed?"

Brute' was not going to fall into that trap so he changed the subject.

"Where are our wounded?"

"The doctor is attending them in the guest bedroom." Since Brigitta would not allow Brute' far away at night, beginning in the first days after her trauma, he had never used it. He had first slept in a chair and then on the floor where she could see him and feel secure. She was still haunted by memories and dreams of when she was a captive. It was a comment by one of the varlets about her breasts sagging because she was lazy that had really caused her to be scrubbing the floor. That and the need to release nervous energy caused by her fears pushed her to do something.

When Brute' arrived at the bedroom Herman the Schmeid was conscious but could not remember anything that happened. Gidon told him Schlachtross had probably saved his life. The Schmeid tried to nod his head but it hurt too badly. He simply said, "He is always a good fellow."

Seeing Gidon sitting up with his left cheek sewn together, Brute' said, "Are you trying to get as pretty as me?"

The men began to question Gidon about the details of what had happened. He did a fairly good job of recounting events but admitted things began to happen very fast. Brute' said, "Ohtrad and I will go and clean the mess up at the stables and see if we can find your sword."

It was then the bishop stepped into the room and said, "Ohtrad will have to go it alone. We have more pressing matters!"

*****

It took only a few minutes for the bishop to tell the men what he had observed and been able to surmise from the events of the day as well as including what happened at Fat Max's tavern. It did not answer all their questions but certainly gave them cause to investigate to see if Jacoba might truly be the Jacklyn the demonic spirit confessed to be helping.

"We will go past the stable on the way to the tavern and Ohtrad can make sure the bodies are not moved until we have opportunity to inspect them," the bishop said.

Gidon started to get up, "When we get there, I will take a quick look for my sword."

"You are in no shape to be getting up and moving about, my son. You have done your part this night." Gid-visu had not seen the wound to his side, but did not want it pulled loose.

The Hospitaller said, "It is unlikely he shall do too much damage to the wounded side as long as he does not get into a pitched battle. It might keep him from getting stiff if he moved about a bit." So it was the matter was settled by the doctor.

When the men started out the door Brigitta met Brute' with his helm. "Come back to me my love." If anyone saw she was still in her nightgown or that it had a bloody handprint on her right buttock they did not say. But the krankenschwester pointed it out as soon as all the men but Herman the Schmeid left the room. He was feigning sleep and within seconds it caught him for real.

The Hospitaller said, "The best thing this man can do is sleep. Perhaps with rest memory will return." He went on to advise the nurse on the differences between a head wound that requires rest and the ones that require the injured be kept awake. He said to her, "We do not know all there is to know about head wounds but perhaps one day we will. For now, we try to keep as many alive as possible."

The trip to the stable took more time than planned. Schlachtross and Begleiter walked into their shared pen as if nothing had happened. To them it was of no concern whether it had a gate or not. The gate was still on top of the fallen assassin who Schlachtross had kicked to death. The two horses that had not gotten out were happy to see men they knew. They responded to them before concerning themselves with the returning horses. They nickered back and forth the remainder of the night.

Gid-visu picked up the first crossbow he came to. After looking at it and the others he knew he recognized the handiwork of its maker. All made in the same place.

The Baron spotted Gidon's sword lodged halfway down the breastbone of the man he had killed. When it stuck, it was plain to see he just left it and went to aid Herman the Schmeid. The Baron told Gidon, "You should not make a habit of losing your sword. You might not get it back next time." But secretly he was pleased.

Herr Brute' remarked to the Baron, "I think you made a good choice in taking this boy to train as your squire. He does run off on his own a bit, but still I think he is a good choice."

The Baron said, "I think you have made a good choice in Ohtrad. He has possibilities."

Brute' was about to say he had not yet chosen Ohtrad when the bishop said, "We are wasting too much time here. We must get on to the tavern."

Now with his sword firmly sheathed by his side, Gidon was ready to get on with it. The men left Ohtrad to take care of business in the stable and walked in silence to the tavern. It was useless to make plans. Each man would play out his role when he came to it.

As the men quietly slipped through the door Heller von Swabia had grown committed in his opposition to Herr Brute'. And like some men who are prone to talk too much about what they know little of, he had put himself in a position where he could not see who was coming in to listen. As they had heard part of his oration on the outside, Brute' had taken the lead to enter the room first.

The elders could see the group entering the room and became transfixed. It was something Heller completely misinterpreted as he said, "We should go to them as a delegation and say we will not have it!"

Brute' as quiet as death itself was now directly behind Heller. "What will you not have, Heller?"

The man nearly fainted and his water ran down a leg to puddle in the floor. He turned to face the scarred face of Herr Brute'. "I uh; I mean we uh…" And he lapsed into silence.

The bishop struck a sharp blow to the face of Jacoba with his staff, knocking whatever the person was to the floor. "You move one more finger witch or murmur one more syllable under your breath and it will be your last."

Gidon pulled his sword and stood there, still with blood all over his tunic and chainmail, the tip pointing down at Jacoba's heart. Gid-visu stood to one side with a crossbow in one hand and a sword in the other. Jacoba stared at the crossbow and it was plain to the friends he or she knew whence the weapon had come.

Baron von Krieg said, "I am the King's Rider. What are men who are supposed to be elders of Eastwatch doing listening to this drunk? The King's Rider appoints whom he will to what he will in the name of the king. Do you men question the king?"

It was the elder who dealt in jewels and was mainly dependent on Gid-visu's merchandise who answered. "You know we are honor bound to listen to all men of the village whether we consider their voices nonsensical or not."

"And what do you consider this voice?" the Baron asked.

"Plainly nonsense!"

Then there was a surprise for them all. The Burgomeister entered the room, dressed in formal garb with the chain of his office about his neck. Though he was still swathed in bandages and had lost considerable weight, he had just made the longest walk in many years. "Who is this that speaks ill of Herr Brute'?" No one answered. "That is good, for to speak ill of him is to speak ill of my future son-in-law!"

Fat Max yelled out loud, "Oma, bring Herr Burgomeister a mead." She immediately came through the door from the kitchen area with the drink and a hot poker. Plainly the woman had anticipated her husband's command. A couple men laughed and the Burgomeister took a table beyond the place of the elders looking like a man holding court. In all of this Gidon's sword had not waivered.

Herr Brute' was motioned over by the Burgomeister. He had intended to say something nice to the man but Brute' spoke ahead of him. "You have announced Brigitta's betrothal to me this night. But what if she will not have me?"

The Burgomeister looked at him and smiled. "My boy, she will have you alright. Do you think I am as big a fool as some take me for?" Brute' tried to smile back but the Burgomeister had not yet come to recognize it for that, so he drank a bit of mead.

Heller von Swabia addressed the Burgomeister. "Please do not exile me from Eastwatch. I have lived here these past twenty years without being anything worse than an occasional drunk. On this day, years ago, I was exiled from my home in Swabia because I listened to my wife and spoke out of turn. It took me all these years to recover and build a new life here while my old wife has dined sumptuously and lived richly on my lost fortune. This night I have again played the fool. If you decide to exile me, please kill me instead. To go through that twice in a lifetime is more than I can bear."

The Burgomeister looked at Baron von Krieg who nodded at him. It was his judgment to make. "I am inclined toward leniency on the happy night I announce my daughter's betrothal. But we will not have insurrection happening in Eastwatch. We will put you on probation for let's say six months in which time you will do many acts of charity reporting weekly to Bishop Elisha. Then we will consider your case once more."

The bishop said, "There is another matter we must settle tonight." He looked at the merchant laying on the floor. "I think thou art an Hexe. Art thou male or female, Jacoba or Jacklyn?"

Gid-visu said, "Stand up witch. Whip it out and we will see whether you can piss in the fireplace." The accused did not move.

The bishop ordered men to take off its clothes in front of all. "We will know whether you are male or female." The men pulled away the garments while all the time she protested. She had pancake breasts with large nipples for she was woman. Her body, though skinny, was female. But the betrayal of her true self lay in the occult tattoos on parts of the body, even soles of the feet that would be hidden were tattooed. Clearly this was a Druid servant of Lucifer.

The subject of what to do with her was then the question. But it was answered by the accused herself. From some unknown place she brought forward a small vial whereupon almost immediately she began to foam at the mouth and within minutes was dead. The shamed elders volunteered to take the body to the garbage pit called Feuer der Hölle or Fires of Hell and burn it that very night accompanied by Bishop Elisha.

*****

Brute' with his future father-in-law on his arm walked home together. Brigitta, who had been waiting anxiously, was amazed at the sight. But she gave a squeal of delight when she learned he had announced her betrothal in so unorthodox a matter. Brute' was looking forward to going upstairs with his warrior queen when he suddenly remembered and gave out a groan.

"What is the matter" my love," Brigitta said.

"I forgot Ohtrad. He should have things a bit straighter by now and needs to return here."

"Then," Brigitta said, "You and I shall go and relieve him and we shall take care of the stable the rest of the night. Just let me change into an appropriate dress."

As she walked away Brute' thought how much he admired the way the fabric of a nightgown moved against her hips, with or without his handprint.

When Gidon walked into Fox Home accompanied by his father and the Baron, the minds of their women were greatly set at ease. Having no idea at all about what had transpired they were simply glad that this time all had returned.

Getrudis wanted to hug and kiss Gidon. She was not hindered by all the blood on him or the fact his face would now have a scar. She could not tell exactly where he was injured and feared she might hurt him further. She did not know it all looked much more serious than it was. She took him to the unheated sauna room where there were the long seats one could stretch out on and there with the help of Durchgefüweg they carefully removed his clothes down to his short under breeches.

At this point Durchgefüweg excused herself and left the couple together. Getrudis cleaned his body while tears began to flow.

Gidon asked her what troubled her? She replied that she hated to see him injured at all and she feared the day his calling to be a soldier might cost his life.

Gidon spoke carefully. "I did not choose to be a soldier. I am content even now to be a forester. But this life seems to have chosen me, and for what purpose I cannot tell. But all things have risks. A forester might even be attacked by a wild stag he only wounded. Even a soldier might die of good old age. I believe the Invisible God has a plan for us all, and if we do not follow His plan, we cannot be happy. I am content with the day, for we have no guarantee of tomorrow." The two lay happily together on the bench, thankful for the time they had.

Chapter 13

The Next Step

Bishop Elisha called Stability and Strength to aid him in what had to be done before much time had passed. The property of the now deceased Druid priestess Jacklyn had to be secured. He was convinced they had done nothing more than cut off the head of the serpent. In a few hours this belief would be confirmed by reports several well-known people disappeared during the time between the witch's death and the first morning light. The following night a few others would also be gone. It was fortunate none of these sat among the elders. If any traitors remained in Eastwatch they considered themselves well hidden. And they undoubtedly were.

It was the third level of the building, beside the false Jacoba's shop, that yielded the first information on the activities of the evil Jacklyn. It was dedicated to the study of astrology and divination by that means. A perusal of how its tools of augury were set revealed the two stars known as Sirius was the center of the astrological investigations. They appear as one in the night sky. No doubt the woman Hexe thought, like many of her occult sect, this was a goddess who caused men to weaken and women to become aroused. Jacklyn would have sought the goddess' help in accomplishing her designs through these means.

Since no building was higher than three levels in Eastwatch, there had been no building tall enough for people to be able to see into what happened in the open area of the third floor used for astrology.

Otherwise many would have been outraged. The Church building was the only exception to the height of buildings in Eastwatch. But the tower was not yet completed and in use. Bishop Elisha thought the destruction of this conspiracy would likely mean the setbacks and slowdowns in the construction of the Church tower would now cease.

The most disturbing thing about the third-floor astrological design was equipment apparently used for sacrifice. It was easy to tell these were not confined to just small animals. Druids have a long history of human sacrifice. Since Jacklyn as Jacoba also had the house of ill repute at hand this probably was one of the sources of victims. And as observed in many places and times; who notices or cares at the disappearance of an occasional whore now and then? The bishop sorrowed such evil could have been taking place under his very nose.

When the astrological observatory was first found, Bishop Elisha considered bringing Gidon to see it as a means of encouraging him to continue his studies. He had often thought Gidon showed some promise as a scholar. But the darker the scene became, the more he realized that this would be a bad idea. He well remembered how painful his own first looks into the forces he would spend his life fighting had been. The Baron would need to know, however. as the future Baron of Eastwatch Keep. He would have to keep guard against those forces that were part of the Mystery of Iniquity that renewed itself in every generation.

As morning came the two priests Stability and Strength became hungry and visited the first floor of the building where many of the folk making their living had a bowl to start their workday. The report they brought to the bishop was disgusting. He immediately shut it down and decided the food area should be completely cleaned out. It is entirely one thing to eat weevils and maggots in food, but the roach and rat droppings could bring plague into the village. That just would not do. Perhaps Fat Max would want to take over the establishment to meet the need for simple fare among the poorest people who lived and worked in that portion of town?

*****

Gidon and Getrudis found it necessary to flee the sauna and head for the warmth of his cot and furs in the early hours. The boy, who now had regular duties regarding baths, had set a fire the earlier evening. When he found it was only to be used to clean the blood from Gidon's body, using the hard, flat benches, he ceased his labors and sought his own cot. Thus the fire declined, and the morning chill crept in. He never expected Gidon and Getrudis would linger in love's embrace on the hardwood boards.

Even in the softness of the furs and linens it was impossible for Gidon to lie on the left side. Both side and face did not appreciate having pressure upon their wounds. The two found themselves positioned differently than was their custom and it took a little adjusting. Once in the cot Getrudis lay with her back to Gidon and positioned his hands so her breasts comforted the hands that had been so violent earlier. He would never speak of the emotional wounding violence does whether forced or not. But her instinct to meet her man in the area of his need seemed always to guide her. And in this case, he also brought comfort to her as well. Had it not been for her warmth those hands would have been struggling with the pain of violence in what remained of the night. Getrudis was comforted with the knowledge the man those hands belonged to had again survived and reached out for her alone.

With the morning Gidon would first go by the stable and then on to check on Herman the Schmeid before joining the men the fighting priests were training for combat with the single hand double edged sword such as he possessed. Though he had now swung his blade twice in a fight and won, he did not consider himself at all skilled. He knew if he was to go in harms' way and return to his beloved he must train. Natural ability must be developed or death comes from the man without natural ability but with hours spent honing the skill.

Getrudis dressed to go out with him since it was likely, if the threat had not been eliminated the night before, it had been greatly diminished. They were very surprised to find Brigitta and Brute' in the hay loft above the horses. It was not surprising to find Brute' there but it was the last place she would have thought to find Brigitta. She really had changed since being humiliated by kidnappers.

Brigitta reached out to Getrudis as if they were old friends. "I just could not leave him to spend the night alone," she said by way of explaining her presence. "Especially after poppa announced our betrothal at the tavern." This was the first time Getrudis had heard that part of the events of the night before. She wondered how everyone could have omitted to tell of so wonderful and important a declaration?

While the men went to care for animals and look about the stable for more evidence from the fight, Getrudis turned to Brigitta and asked, "Does it not frighten you when your man goes into danger so boldly?"

Brigitta answered, "My yes! It seems like there is something every day. But what is a woman to do? I think his boldness is part of what keeps him alive in the midst of danger. And he calls me his warrior queen. How could I be what he expects of me if I allowed myself to be seen by him consumed with fear?"

Getrudis would ponder that in her heart. The girl she once considered flighty in her mind now seemed to have begun to become a woman of great understanding.

When Gidon and Brute' came back to the ladies, the animals had been given their morning ration of grain and seemed none the worse for all the excitement the day before. It might have been true they were already anticipating new adventure. The smithy from the monastery was there and he proposed to work, even with Herman the Schmeid not being present. He said there was too much to do and could not afford waiting for him to heal.

The four decided that since the tavern was as close as the Burgomeister's house they would go to the tavern and find out the news. It would mean retracing steps later but it could be worthwhile to find out what was being said about town.

Gidon would decide he wished they had not made the trip to the tavern. One of the first things they heard upon entering was someone saying Gidon had stripped the clothes off the witch and stabbed her in the heart. Gidon had to hurriedly tell Getrudis all he had done was hold a sword to her heart to keep her from making enchantments. Others had torn her clothes off to find out if she was man or woman, and also look for signs of witchcraft on the body.

One fellow started to say something about what Herr Brute' did to Heller von Swabia. He did not start off as if he was going to tell what actually had happened and a look from Brute' stopped him in midsentence. Gidon told Getrudis he had not seen either of those men at the tavern last night, so they had only gossip to tell.

An entertaining story told and retold was the witch had burned with a blue flame. And another said they had heard when she was set on fire she stood up and ran around the garbage pit shrieking terrible screams as if being chased by demons. At last he had enough, Brute' spoke up and loudly announced none of them knew what they were talking about. This did not sit well with the people who were really enjoying their rumors and gossip. And it did not stop them from continuing when he had left.

Brigitta and Getrudis would have been happy to leave without eating, but their men stubbornly declared they were going to have full breakfasts. Fat Max finally announced everyone should thank Gidon and Brute' for saving the village from such an evil person. Then he said "If anyone wants to know what really happened, ask me later." He winked at Brute', and the man knew Fat Max was going to have his little joke on them.

*****

Neither Brute' nor Gidon were happy to learn from Fat Max that Bishop Elisha had called Stability and Strength to him in the night. Both had goals that would be delayed because of it. And this just had to happen when the woodcarver had turned out more training swords as well. Brute' had long believed in an unwritten rule; in a soldier's life it never fails that just when you begin to make progress in one area, you lose ground in another. Gidon was beginning to get a lesson in that frustrating reality as well.

But, Brute' was a man of action. He was determined he would show some progress in his assigned responsibility. He turned to

Gidon and asked him to teach his village conscripts the proper use of the long bow. Meanwhile he would ask Gid-visu if the captured crossbows might be turned over to him for training purposes as soon as he finished looking them over.

The timing of his decision to act was perfect. For no sooner had Brute' decided to ask Gid-visu about the crossbows than he walked into the tavern with Brunhild by his side. So Gidon was transformed from a man looking to get training into being a trainer. And Brute' would not only receive three practically new crossbows but enough shafts to train a home guard destined for Eastwatch Keep in their use.

Fat Max volunteered the information that Heller von Swabia had once served as a crossbowman in a war, or so he said. Brute' borrowed a boy from his kitchen to go and summon the man telling him to say Brute' needed his help, and emphasize it was a request. The messenger arrived at the home of Heller just as he was securing a rope to a beam in the one room in the house high enough for him to hang himself. It was the wording of the message, "Herr Brute' needs your help," that kept him from immediately completing his shame by suicide. Perhaps there was reason for hope yet.

Gid-visu had not only arrived with Mistress Brunhild but an entourage of his own. Behind them followed Gwynedd and Durchgefüweg. It seemed these ladies were on a mission of their own to introduce Durchgefüweg to the tavern and take the first steps toward getting her situated in her new position. Oma was thrilled to see them. She declared the place was just falling apart without her girls. She bustled about apparently hoping the impossible, that Durchgefüweg would learn it all in one tour of the place.

It was a little tense when Getrudis got up and tried to involve Brigitta in the group. Outside of Durchgefüweg who had no experience of Brigitta, the other women were more used to her looking down on their work. It took a while for them to get comfortable with her. As Brigitta was watching a kitchen wench stirring a savory stew in a black pot for the lunch, an innocent question broke the ice. "I imagine all that stirring must be good for firming the breasts. Will you not let me take a turn?" The women broke into laughter. Brigitta happily got her turn.

Baron von Krieg arrived and immediately asked if Gwynedd was there. Her safety was ever on his mind. He was told she was with the other women in the back when their joint laughter was heard. He could pick out the sound of her laugh from all the other women and it was the sweetest sound in the world to him. His mind was at ease.

The men joined together in the dark corner to speak of weighty matters secure in the thought their women were both safe and happy together. Gidon did not sit because the only position left to him would have placed his back to the entrance. Instead, he stood where he could both see and hear, acting as the security for the three others.

Brute' acquainted the Baron with the situation concerning training and proposed that Herman One Eye be given a cart and provision to take the twenty villagers already eliminated from the selection of fifty on to the king's castle. The cart would be for the supplies and not the men since it was expected the march would harden them. Gid-visu suggested Herman be allowed to use his two-pony cart and carry enough provision for a hundred and so send up some of the young men in the region who had not before been to war. In that way they could get additional training as well. The Baron approved the plan after Herr Brute' assured him Herman One Eye was much more dependable than he had once been. The trip would be a test to see if the man could be trusted with even greater duties in the time to come.

The group considered whether to move two of Herman One Eye's sons up to guard duty at the Burgomeister's house since the threat had been diminished and his son Ohtrad was doing well. Instead the decision was made to alternate four of the young men of the village who were doing well in their training to become part of the fifty. That way it could be a test to see if any of them could be considered for advancement later and Ohtrad would not have to contend with the problems that come when you must give orders to relatives.

Heller von Swabia arrived. When he saw the four men he had been in trouble with the night before his limbs visibly shook. He wondered if the summons was a cruel joke. Brute' tried to give him a smile but that only increased his fear. "Max says he heard you were once a crossbowman. Is that true?"

The question took him by surprise. He recalled only mentioning that fact once in the tavern. It had been several years ago when he was trying to impress some of the elders. Today he did not want to make too much of it lest he be embarrassed. "My lord, it was more than twenty years ago when I was a crossbowman on the wall of the king of Swabia's castle. I have not shot my crossbow since."

"Do you mean you still have it?" Gid-visu asked.

Heller von Swabia nodded, already sorry he had not taken it out and practiced from time to time. He was not sure why he was sorry. It was just that these men had that sort of impact on a fellow like himself.

"Do you remember what you were taught? Do you remember how to do it?" Herr Brute' wanted to get something going right away.

"Maybe with a few extra bolts and a day or two of practice I might be able to do it. It has been a long time."

Gid-visu said, "I can give you twenty new bolts."

Herr Brute' said, "I will order the making of three straw-men. They will be set up in a spot where no one can watch. You will practice two days and on the third you will instruct others in the crossbow. Any questions?"

Heller looked at the man. "What if I fail?"

"Don't!" Brute' growled out a curse word and said, "I need a couple of messenger boys. Anybody know of two lads I can have available day and night who knows the area well?"

Heller was glad to have something clearly positive to contribute. "I can provide two orphan boys of about twelve years. They are the twin sons of a whore who died when they were about five. I have had them ever since."

"Waste no time, man. Get them to me."

*****

Bishop Elisha walked into the tavern. He had been up all night and now he was hungry. Even though regular fasting was part of his spiritual life, he recognized the necessity of food particularly after spiritual battle. And what he had observed this night, beginning with the confrontation with the false man and continuing on to the lair of the witch made for types of spiritual battles. Now he must eat and allow his mind to rest.

He saw when he entered the tavern that though he would get food, rest for body and mind would yet be delayed. Here was his opportunity to inform Baron von Krieg and get that over with. Then he recalled he needed to talk to Fat Max and Gid-visu about providing a place to eat for working people across town. He had to get food and rest. He was rapidly running out of energy.

Baron von Krieg called the old priest to come and sit with them in the chair Gidon would not use. He at first turned them down saying he must eat. But the Baron called for stew and bread along with a tankard of beer for the Bishop, so he had no choice but to comply. Oma and Brigitta brought the food quickly. To see Brigitta willingly serving others might have at one time brought comment. But today it was the admiring look for Brigitta on the face of Brute' that made for nudges between Gid-visu and the Baron. Gidon watched the interplay remembering when he had attention from Getrudis as he sat at the very same table.

The first sip of stew made a warm flow through the bishop's being. So as soon as the women departed the bishop spoke to the Baron of the things he had already found. He warned him it is not the way of these servants of Satan to give up territory once claimed. It would be the Baron's particular duty to guard Eastwatch against the workers of evil who might come just as it was his duty as the Baron of Eastwatch Keep to guard the kingdom against foreign invasion from the East.

Gid-visu, who had his own adventure with an occult enemy that ended with his return to Eastwatch, began the conversation concerning how one might keep guard against such an enemy. But when they turned again to the bishop with a question, they discovered he had fallen into a deep sleep. Baron von Krieg and Gidon picked him up and carried him to the nearest bed, leaving the bowl of stew half eaten and the beer untouched. Gidon was surprised at how light his body was. He set a chair at the door of the room and began his watch over the bishop.

The Baron reentered the tavern room to see two children standing at the door. If these were the twelve-year old boys promised by Heller von Swabia something was very wrong. They looked closer to nine than even ten. They were down to skin and bones so that even the shape of their skulls was obvious.

Herr Brute' spoke to them, suspecting who they were. "Who are you boys?"

The result of his voice and his scarred features sent the boys cowering into a corner, clinging to one another. They did not speak.

For once Fat Max did not yell for Oma. He instead walked through the arch into the kitchen areas looking for her. And when he returned all the women came with her. Oma took one look at the boys and said, "We will try to feed them some of the broth of the stew we made today. It may be their little stomachs cannot bear even that."

As Oma walked toward the boys, they cowered even closer together. Apparently they did not view women as the warm refuge common to most children's ideas. She told Brunhild to order water heated for a bath, and said to Durchgefüweg "Put on your wash dress. After we get a little into their stomachs, you are going to have your second experience of giving a wash. These boys may look nearly dead but they smell like they already are." The women fairly herded the two little boys out of the room.

Fat Max told the Baron it was his opinion that Heller von Swabia would do just as well without his head since he obviously did not use it. But the Baron said he had need of Heller, at least for now. He said, "Justice comes in its season."

Brute' looked sad, except on his scarred face it only made him look meaner. He said, "How often in Roma I saw children in as bad or worse condition, and I passed them by without a thought. Now I am thinking of the children I lost. They will be long grown now, if they have lived." He took the bishop's untouched beer and drank it straight down.

Baron von Krieg laid his hand on Brute's shoulder. "I am sorry my friend, but if I had not carried you off the battlefield you would have died. That would have done them no good either."

Brute' replied, "There have been times I have wished you left me as I lay, after you struck me down. It is the times when I am alone usually. But Brigitta has filled much of the loneliness. She is a delight. Right now, it is memory of the pride I once held in who and what I was that haunts me. Such pride did not care for the hurting of this world. J was probably a terrible husband and father because of that pride as well."

Brute' called out to Fat Max, "Another beer."

The forward momentum Brute' had tried to achieve had been stalled for a moment. But it was just becoming time for the midday meal and some began to trickle into the tavern. It would not be fair to Max to use any of his people to carry messages this time of day. So he and his two companions did what good soldiers do when given opportunity. They ate and drank, enjoying one another's company.

Only once was the companionship disturbed. Brigitta came in to ask, "Do those boys belong to us?"

Brute' reached over and putting his hand on her hip pulled her to him without ever getting up. He looked up at her and asked, "Does my warrior queen mind if we keep them?"

"That will be wonderful. But we have a problem. I have never seen so many fleas and lice on two people in my life. They will need treatment after we get them another bath. We used the first bath to kill the bugs. When we poured it out in the backyard the chickens went crazy eating them. I do not think those boys had ever been clean in all their lives. And we are going to have to make them some clothes. The rags they were wearing had to be burned."

Brute' then stood up towering over her. "I must go out. I will send the Apothecary and a seamstress to help you while I take care of other matters. You take charge and tell them we will pay all in coppers."

Brigitta said, "You need not worry about a seamstress. Oma has already sent for the fastest worker in town."

Brute' had just thanked the Baron for the gift of his horse and was about to walk out the door when Herr Burgomeister, with a staff in one hand and Ohtrad holding his other arm, walked in the door. Brute' barely nodded at his soon to be father-in-law but focused on

Ohtrad. "Go down to the stable and saddle my horse. Take it and ride to the thatcher and order he build straw men for targets. I want the first one ready by morning. Tell him to take it directly to Heller von Swabia. Then go to the Apothecary. Tell him to come with ointment for flea and lice bites."

The Burgomeister sat down heavily. Since he had started walking, he was gaining in strength and shedding pounds. But he was not yet nearly where he should be.

Brigitta said, "Oh poppa, is it not wonderful? Brute' and I have two sons!"

The old man nearly had a heart attack right then. Brute' started to correct what he meant by keeping the boys, but when he saw her happiness and the Burgomeister's stricken condition he decided that it was too enjoyable to say she had misunderstood his words.

Ohtrad finally caught Herr Brute's attention. "I am sorry my lord but I have never ridden a horse."

Brute' looked at him sternly, "By the time you have finished doing as I command you will have.' And that was how Ohtrad broke his arm. But even with a broken arm he still completed all Herr Brute' commanded.

*****

Bishop Elisha had been down a scant four hours when he came out of the bed and headed back into the tavern area followed by Gidon. The noon business had ended and the lull between it and the evening business had begun. It was the perfect time to get Max and Oma aside with Gid-visu to offer the proposition they take over the druid's building and provide a good eatery and inn in the poor section where Jacoba once had his businesses and schemes. He wanted the poor to have healthy food they could afford.

As the men continued to discuss the proposition Oma got up to leave. Fat Max said, "Where are you going momma? I forbid you to go into that filth! We can hire people to clean."

Oma said, "Since you men have already decided what you are going to do, someone has to set things in motion. I know a woman who has three of the biggest, meanest, and ugliest cats around. I think we should begin by getting rid of the rat problem."

Fat Max looked at the men and grinned. Leave it to Oma.

It was true the seamstress who came worked fast. And she also worked efficiently. The two boys had a second round of broth and a bath that was thorough. This time Durchgefüweg caused a few squeals as she turned skin pink from a thorough scrub. The women took the boy's squeals as a good sign, compared to what little noise they made before. Earlier sounds only seemed to be attached to fear. The boys were showing the resilience of youth.

Getrudis teased Durchgefüweg, "You do not scrub those places on grown men you know. That is unless the grown man happens to be yours." There was a round of tittering about that. Then Brigitta added, "I can see I have so much to look forward to." This prompted another round of laughter.

The Apothecary arrived and covered virtually all of their bodies with ointment, prescribing they sit naked until dry. That would take quite a while since the medicine was a bit oily. He said he would check them in a couple of days and left.

When the boys were thoroughly dry, the last requiring patting the skin, it was not very long till they were dressed in nice new nightshirts. The seamstress promised they would have a complete set of clothes to wear by the morning. Brigitta gave the seamstress four coppers for the material and work on the nightshirts, and a bronze coin for material for the rest of the garments before she left. The women all said she was paying too much.

Brigitta said, "I cannot spend too much for Brute's sons."

Oma said, "I do not think Brute' got those boys for sons."

"Oh, I know," Brigitta said happily. "But my mother once told me that one of the things a woman does to make a man happy is to get her man what he does not know he wants and then convince him it is what he always wanted!"

The men enjoyed hearing the women laughing together in another room. They never would have guessed the last laugh was about them. Durchgefüweg felt really happy to have these women for friends. She was determined not to fail Oma in the least matter.

People were just beginning to come into the tavern for their evening pleasure. Two men were sitting at the Tracht table, which had the board pattern inscribed and painted into it. For each draught, as well as the game, money would change hands when they gambled. Usually they did not gamble on a night when work had to be done the next day since sometimes that action would last into the wee hours. But Fat Max liked the game because it drew onlookers, and onlookers and players alike would enjoy a few beers.

Herr Burgomeister had seated himself at the elders' table, surprising them by buying all the elders a beer. If anyone noticed they cared not, he did not order the more expensive mead. It was enough the well-known spendthrift would actually buy at all. The four men who watched but did not participate sat in their dark corner. They nursed one mead each, waiting for their ladies to tell them it was time to go home.

Then one of the workmen came in from the site that would be the new Keep with the news they had struck water. It was not just water seeping into the well either, but water running through the well. They had hit an underground cavern with water running through it, and all the workmen were pleased even though a death had occurred as the bottom fell into the underground river. Baron von Krieg purchased a small cask of beer for the workmen to share with their fellows. Tomorrow, he said, they would start to widen the well shaft and install shoring in the hole. It looked as though the Keep was going to have plenty of water.

Ohtrad came in. His broken left arm had been set and splinted by the Hospitaller. It was plain that pain was getting fairly intense, but he was committed to being tough about it.

Herr Brute' said, "When you are going to fall from a horse you should always pick someplace soft."

"Thanks," replied Ohtrad with a crooked grin, "I shall try to remember that."

"You still have your right arm, so stand beside my chair as Gidon does for the Baron. You might as well start training in your other duties." In this offhand way Herr Brute informed him he was going to make him his squire.

Durchgefüweg came in, now changed back into her dress. She was serving tables, holding three tankards in each hand as if she had been serving all her life. She asked Ohtrad, "Does your arm hurt much?"

He replied, "Only when I smile. And seeing you makes me smile a lot!"

Durchgefüweg blushed, but she did not miss the opportunity to be the coquette. "Well then I must depart. I would not be the cause of your pain."

Ohtrad lost his words and only could watch in silence as she walked away. Had he lost or won the first round of wooing with the fair maid? Only time would tell he supposed, but with the news he would one day become a squire, he felt his prospects improving.

*****

The bishop returned to the businesses of the wizard. He brought food and drink for the fighting priests. They had been hungry and thirsty all day and it was greatly appreciated. What they had seen thus far had been a spiritual challenge. Lacking food and particularly water had weakened them in a time they needed to be strong. It was a challenge in this place to live up to the new names that completed their vigil, Stability and Strength.

The noise coming from the brothel was the only sound on the street until the snarling and growling of rats and cats commenced. Bishop Elisha told the priests to bunk down in the warehouse. He was quite sure no one would invade these buildings seeing it sounded like the demons of hell were fighting in there. The battle of cats and rats would last, it seemed nonstop, for three days.

Chapter 14

Brute' and Brigitta

Herr Brute' picked Brigitta up and put her over his shoulder like a bag of horse feed. She said to him, "If you think I am going to yell and kick you are wrong. You can just keep your hand on my fanny all night. I like it!"

He sighed and put her back on her feet. "Listen my warrior queen, your father has had plenty to say about us being out all last night. We have to go home this night."

"But the boys! We cannot just go and abandon them!"

Brute' thought, *She surely has her motherly instincts going.* He said, "For the last time, sweet woman, they will not be alone. Oma and Durchgefüweg will be right there with them. They have had more attention and better food and treatment today, than they have had in their whole lives."

"Did you know when we asked their names, they answered Eins and Zwei?

"My beloved woman, I did not know that till you told me ten times ago!" Brute' sighed.

Brigitta sounded her disgust, "What kind of person gives little boys numbers for names?"

Brute' thought about saying, *Someone who could not tell the twins apart.* No, levity would not go over well. Then he thought about saying, *Someone who believes the old wives' tale that twins are bad luck.* He decided neither response would help the situation so he said nothing.

Brigitta leaned into him and looked sweetly up into his scarred face. "Are we having our first lover's quarrel?"

Brute' looked down at her. He could command men to charge into the face of death but he was helpless with her. My, he loved this woman!

"My beloved, of course we are going home. Anything you say," said Brigitta.

They spent the night in a room in Fat Max' inn area of the tavern.

Stripped to undershirt, which came midway down his thighs, and under-breeches, which went below the knee. Brute' was scandalously clad in the presence of his virgin queen. She no less so, for she was in the linen garment worn beneath the dress. But they were in their favorite position. He was propped against a pillow, and she under his left arm with her head against his chest.

"Brute'," Brigitta asked sweetly, "why do you love me?" She never asked him if he loved her. That was too plain to be questioned. She saw her imperfections and wondered at his love.

Brute' looked down at her. She was so different from the wife he had known in Rome. The Roman woman had been dark of hair with very classical features. And she was shapely with every portion of her body in proportion with all others. Her feet had been long and angular, in proportion to her height like the dancer figures often painted onto jars and murals. She had been well educated and was therefore quick to be critical of many ideas. And she could handle discussions and debates on many subjects. She was also a senator's daughter, so she could help his career as long as things went well.

His Roman woman's main flaw was she did not come to his bed a virgin or as a woman who placed her husband at her head. In Roma sexual promiscuity going back to the days of pagan worship in the temples was taken for granted. She thought it perfectly fine to play her own societal games without concern for his opinion. Things Brigitta would never do.

Brigitta had an oval face, fair complexion, and long blond hair. She had her own gracefulness that complimented her short stature. She was named for the great warrior queen of old, and lived up to that in more meaningful ways than the veil of illusion cast by the Roman elite. Lips, breasts, and hips were full and rounded in proportion to her small size. It communicated strength and beauty on the outside that was a testimony to genuine inner strength and beauty only recently revealed. Her beauty was not a sham or delusion.

Here was a woman woken by ordeal, not diminished by it. She might not ever discuss great literature or philosophical ideas of the Greeks. But behind cute remarks there lurked a woman's perception that can be of great value to her man. In the transition from spoiled child to woman she had discovered a new world whose center was a man who called her his warrior queen. Her modesty, self-interest, and even chastity is his to command as he will. And as a man of character he respected what she was.

Brute' answered her question about why he loved her, not by extolling her beauty or any other singular virtue. He simply said, "I love you because you are you, and it would be impossible to do otherwise."

The problem with lovers resting in one another's arms, smelling their scent, feeling their warmth, and when stirred, listening even to their breathing is that morning must always come. And when it comes, the duties of the day come as well.

*****

Ohtrad had not found it easy to separate himself from the Burgomeister. He had been extremely unhappy with that duty. The man simply did not know how to use his guard. Since told of his promotion, the primary job was to stay with Herr Brute', and he and Brigitta were staying in the inn portion of the tavern. The Burgomeister wanted the whole family to go home together. Not doing so would pose a conflict of responsibility for Ohtrad because he also had a duty to guard the Burgomeister and his family. Finally, the Burgomeister decided to take a room as well, rather than to be seen going home alone. He did not recognize this eased the conflict Ohtrad had in his duties. It was not the Burgomeister was intentionally inconsiderate. That attitude had changed with his own part of the recent ordeal. It was just simply in his life of ease these things had never before had a place. It was outside his area of customary thinking.

Like Brute', the Burgomeister well knew the two boys had plenty of supervision and he was scandalized his daughter would be alone with her betrothed another night. How villagers loved rumors and taverns were the hotbeds of all gossip. But no arguing with Brute' was possible to be sure. And his daughter would agree with her poppa and then do what she wanted. That is, unless Brute' got stern with her. So, he slept in his room beside theirs and could hear everything said or done through the thin walls.

Ohtrad dutifully took his position in the hall in front of Brute's door. Durchgefüweg, passing down the hall, saw his discomfort as he tried to lie on his back and prop the broken arm upright against the wall. She made up two pillows and brought them back to him so he could lay on his right side with both arm and head elevated. Ohtrad thanked her but she treated the matter as if it was a thing that did not matter. It kept him puzzled about whether she cared for him more than other persons or not. But when she walked away from him down the hall it did seem as though her form had a bit more swish with each step. He would be awake first because the throbbing arm just never allowed him any deep sleep.

Ohtrad had been hazily aware when Durchgefüweg had walked down the hall from the rooms previously shared by Brunhild, Gwynedd, and Getrudis in the early morn. Their absence left a significant gap in the efficiency of the tavern. Durchgefüweg was determined to try and learn all she could about the various duties they had performed so the burden would not be so heavy on other staff. Worthy girls, women with the mindset that would complement Fat Max and Oma's vision for their tavern and inn, were not that easily found. Until that happened there would be less rest than one might hope for, and less time to spend with her new friends.

The preparation of the tavern for the day began with the fire boy stirring up the embers in the kitchen, then a little kindling to burn hot and quickly build up coals made by hardwood burning just right. As the fires developed, he would stack sufficient wood for the day where it could be readily used. Step by step the kitchen would come to life with the preparations for breakfast meals to be readied. By the time these things were moving in earnest, Oma would be there supervising all. Most tavern staff had been happily employed for years, so the functioning of the kitchen moved like a choreographed dance, where people did their jobs without getting in one another's way. It would be Durchgefüweg's responsibility to learn the dance and her part in it. How quickly she adapted to her part would impress all.

By the morning Brigitta had made some decisions regarding the names of the boys. She decided the boy named Eins would be called Wolfdregel, which in the common tongue meant Wolf-Runner and the boy named Zwei should be called Vulfolaic, which meant Wolf-Dancer. This should be their names she told Brute' because they came to him to be messengers and his symbol should be the dire wolf. She whispered in his ear, "You are the great big wolf of great power all men must respect." To that Brute' made a flirting reply.

Brute' had agreed to the new names, noticing by her explanation for her choice in boys' names she revealed that she had known all along the real reason for their coming to him. *She is as cunning as a she wolf,* he thought. What he did say was, "These names are of great warriors from the past, it will give them something to live up to." Then he said, "I guess it is appropriate their mother should be my warrior queen." Brigitta gave him her sweetest smile.

The boys woke ravenously hungry. Hunger had been part of their everyday existence in the past, but they had quickly adapted to their new circumstances. Brigitta was glad she had not yet changed them from their nightshirts to their new clothes when she fed them. She would have to teach them not to eat like wolves.

The value of these boys would be proven their very first day in the Burgomeister's house. His wife, embarrassed by her scarred face, had been increasingly withdrawn. When shown two boys who Brigitta claimed to be hers and Brute's she found herself in a quandary of mind in which she was unsure even how much time had passed. In deference to her mental state, she readily accepted these children were her own grandchildren. The boys Wolfdregel and

Vulfolaic, though initially frightened by her damaged features, soon responded to her unrestrained love and were wrapped up in her arms like two puppies against their mother.

Brute', seeing these things take place, marveled at the understanding Brigitta had shown about how to bring healing into the house. Whether called womanly wisdom or intuition, her impulse to adopt the boys had worked miracles. In spite of the boys' lack of social understanding they had brought happiness into a house that became more of a home because of them, and were themselves blessed with a joy they had not known before. They had something they had never known. Love!

*****

Brute' wasted no time giving Herman One Eye marching orders for the trip to the king's castle. He told him to take the culled-out village boys and add to their number eighty of his choosing from surrounding farms for the first conscripts to the king's muster. Surprisingly two of those he chose were his own sons including the one who was the laziest. When questioned Herman told Brute' he hoped the trainers would soon knock some sense into his head. Brute' laughed at the simple solution for laziness.

Gidon, accompanied by Getrudis, was at the formation when it gathered in front of the Burgomeister's house. He had but five bows to use for training. After asking whether any of the young men had any experience shooting a longbow, he proceeded with demonstrating the simple procedure of stringing the bow in preparation to use it. Each man had to string and unstring the bow placing one end in front of the right ankle and using the back of the left leg as the block around which the top end was pulled. They quickly found that doing this repeatedly made for sore places where so much pressure had been applied. This encouraged them to work the more to get the thing right so the bow could be passed on.

Getrudis laughed watching the men's struggles. Gidon asked her, "Do you think you could do better?"

"Of course, it does not seem that hard." She said this with such certainty he decided to play a trick on her. He handed her his bow. To her credit she placed the bow in the proper position the first time. All the men training stopped to watch her. She grabbed the bow high with her left hand, holding the string in her right. But when she leaned forward to bend the bow and put the bowstring on the end, she found it would not move.

The men laughed and this made Getrudis red of face so she tried harder. But try as she might, she just could not move the bow far enough to seat the string. A few men made comments about how weak she was.

Gidon said to them. "You should not be laughing. My bow has more than twice the pull of any of yours. I daresay some of you could not bend the bow as much as she did, and if you managed to string it you could not shoot it with accuracy because the pull is too great." He then explained the different amount of pull between bows. The more strength it takes to bend the bow the farther the arrow will fly. But accuracy demands the bowman must be able to pull the bow comfortably. The more you practice the greater the bow you can use.

Getrudis spoke to Gidon where the men could not hear. "You tricked me. You knew I could not bend that bow. But then you took up for me. Sometimes you are hard to figure out!"

Not caring who was looking, Gidon put his arms around her and pulled her close to him. He looked down into her face and strong emotion flowed through him. "Yes, I tricked you because I wanted you to appreciate shooting a bow is not as easy as it seems. But more importantly I wanted to teach something to the men. You see they watched you closely because of your beauty and the good humor made it easier for them to hear me. They learned because of you. You were of great help, you see."

Getrudis wrinkled her nose, "I just think you liked tricking me."

What more could he say? She was right!

After teaching the group about the different kinds of arrows Gidon selected five to be receiving the first training in using the long-bow. He took them away to a place where they could continue training in privacy and safety.

Herr Brute' came out of the house and selected four men to act as guards for the Burgomeister's home, turning them over to Ohtrad for their instruction. The remainder he drilled on the wooden swords until they thought their arms would fall off. When they became so tired they were beginning to make increasing errors, Brute' was concerned someone might get hurt. Only then he dismissed them for the day. In this way he also avoided having them learn bad habits as well.

In the evening Herr Tweitman arrived at Fox Home carrying messages to Baron von Krieg and Gid-visu. These contained orders that included a commission for Brute'. A messenger was sent to Herr Brute' and he came straightaway.

One of the things Herr Tweitman arrived with were a pair of new ponies trained to cart and plow. Gid-visu had sent him a messenger saying he anticipated the need for more of these little horses in the months to come. He had been wise in anticipating the need, even ordering a new two pony cart from the local cart maker. He thought they would be needed in the building of Eastwatch Keep if nothing else.

Supper that night was full of merriment as Herr Tweitman was visiting Eastwatch for the first time in several years. They even had a local minstrel in to play for the group. The supper table was full. Gid-visu had Brunhild by his side. Baron von Krieg had Gwynedd by his. Gidon and Getrudis sat together, and Herr Brute' with Brigitta were pleased for this was their first formal function together. Herr Tweitman was in position of honor at the far end of the table. Even the Fox Home staff was excited by the occasion, though it did make for more work.

When the meal was ended and the table cleared the women rose up to leave the talking to the men but Herr Tweitman said, "With Gid-visu's permission I would like to ask the women to stay. What we have to discuss will impact their lives as much as ours."

Gid-visu nodded approval, for messages from the king always had weighty importance.

"I think you had better read this first message Baron, since from the content I think this is based on your recommendation to King Gregor." Herr Tweitman had a little smile on his face. He handed the message to the Baron. Each message was on very thin paper of about two inches height wrapped tightly so it could fit in a capsule attached to a pigeon's leg.

The Baron looked at it intently. "Brute' you are commissioned the King's Master at Arms for Eastwatch Keep. This makes it an anointed position that comes with a king's allowance. The King says you are now to be known as Brute' von Aleman, which means you will wear the King's crest and your own as I do. It says that you have served our country well so you are from the whole according to the pleasure of King Gregor II, a citizen of Aleman. You are further ordered to send your banner to hang with the King's men in the great hall of Almanya as soon as possible."

Brigitta clapped her hands delightedly. "I have already designed it," she said.

Herr Tweitman then said, "This next message involves both you Baron, and Herr Brute'." He handed it to Gid-visu so he might read it. "Baron von Krieg and Lady Gwynedd as well as Lord Brute' and Lady Brigitta are ordered to marry within the fortnight. Said marriages to be consummated before Gid-visu and his son depart from Eastwatch for the muster. The King regrets he will not be able to attend because of matters of State. This means both you women are officially ladies of the realm. We must speedily contact the bishop."

It seemed there was nothing but good news but yet a third message remained. Herr Tweitman decided to read this message himself. "It is to Gid-visu." He paused and everybody was filled with anticipation. "Through Gid-visu, Master of Fox Home: The Mistress of Fox Home, Brunhild, is ordered by her King to establish dovecotes, in the absence of Gid-visu, for the raising of carrier pigeons for fast communication between the king's castle and Eastwatch. Mistress Getrudis should assist her in this. I think the king is thinking that since Mistress Getrudis was raised on a farm, she should know the way this is done. Twelve carrier pigeons that home to the castle will be brought by Herr Tweitman." Brunhild looked at Getrudis. King Gregor's order was not to be ignored.

Gid-visu excused himself from the group for a few minutes and when he returned presented to both Gwynedd and Brigitta matching necklaces. "These are from Brunhild and me to commemorate the day of your wedding." They were awesome necklaces, each with a highly polished diamond as the central piece. There were two strands of necklace strung with fresh water pearls of great luster, plainly selected for their matching quality. Many were the admiring comments made by the women. What they did not know, and Brunhild did not tell, was that Gid-visu had previously given her a similar necklace with three strands against the day of their own marriage. Brunhild wore her precious necklace, with the red stone that held a star in it, daily.

*****

The morning came and there began a flurry of activity in the household of the Burgomeister. The command of King Gregor concerning the wedding had pleased him well. He was not the only one to wonder at the basis of the king's knowledge concerning the relationship between Brute' and Brigitta. After all, Baron von Krieg had departed to get horses from Herr Tweitman and to send pigeons to the king's castle before the intrusion into their home had even been noised about. He tried to discuss it with his wife, but she only said, "He is the King," as if he had some source of special knowledge and that settled the question.

Brigitta sent for the Hearth Woman, who was key to helping her learn fine stitchery. She needed her help in producing the banner of Brute'. She had already designed his insignia as the head of a blue grey dire wolf on a red background. Brute' said it perhaps should have three heads like Cerberus but she would not have it. She said he was not a dog to be kicked, but a wolf to be feared. Brute' conceded to her wishes.

Below the wolf head were two long knives pointing in opposite directions, as if on guard against danger however it came. Since it would hang in the castle of King Gregor only the finest yet durable material was used in it. She did run into one snag in her plans. Brute' insisted his motto was duty and honor, and that was that. He was very adamant on that one point.

Brigitta had two tunics made for Brute'. One was of fine fabric and embroidery. King Gregor's ensign was above the heart and Brute's on his right side. He would wear it at the wedding. The second tunic was made tough enough to be worn daily. But she was not yet through with her tunic making. A tunic bearing Brute's ensign was made for Ohtrad and for the two boys Wolfdregel, or Wolf-Runner and Vulfolaic, meaning Wolf-Dancer. The boys were proud of their new names and their new tunics. Though they were not able to explain it, the names gave them personhood and the tunics belonging.

*****

The Hospitaller stopped at the small table in the kitchen often used by staff to eat. It had become a favorite place for Brute' and Brigitta to meet and just hold hands and look into each other's eyes. Brute' was alone as his warrior queen waged her special war against time doing all the things that must be done for her marriage.

The priest said, "The time when I am needed here grows short. But I thought there might be something I can do for you. May I look at the wounds on your neck?"

Brute' allowed him to do so, opening and closing his mouth on command as well as forcing air out to make sound.

The priest asked. "Do you often choke on your food?"

Brute' shook his head.

"Does your throat often feel sore?"

Brute' nodded his head to that question.

The Hospitaller said, "I have read material by a great Greek named Galen who studied the area where you are damaged. I think you do not have one injury there but two. That is what makes your voice sound strange. I believe that with the help of the Great Physician I can make it much better."

"Who is this Great Physician and where does he live?" Brute' asked.

The priest answered carefully. "The Great Physician is the Son of the Invisible God. He is always present when people like me try to help our brothers. The problem is we do not always listen to Him as we should."

"What will happen if you fail to fix me?" Brute' wondered out loud.

"As far as your voice is concerned, you might not be able to talk at all. The worse thing would be if I hit the wrong place, you might actually be suffocated by food or water." The priest spoke frankly because this sort of man appreciated frankness. "Your condition left alone could get worse as you get older."

"What would you do?" Brute' was curious because the prospect of his problem getting worse was something he often thought was happening.

"I would make a little hole in your throat where you could breathe, and another hole above it where I could try to fix your problem. After I finished you would not be able to talk for a week or have anything other than cool water. And, it will hurt while I am doing it, and for a few days after. Before I could do it I would have to make some special tools so I could not do it immediately. What do you think?"

"I think this should be discussed with Brigitta." Brute' was not afraid of the pain but what happened would affect her greatly.

"It would have to be some weeks after the wedding because of all I must do."

The priest nodded then said, "By the way, there will be no kissing while the throat heals. You might tell her that as well."

*****

Gwynedd and Brigitta entered into a conspiracy. They would not let their future husbands see the wedding dresses till the wedding. Brigitta got the woman who had made the boys clothes in on the secret that both dresses were to look exactly the same. Though neither woman was very tall, Gwynedd was a bit taller. Yet they thought it would be great fun if someone, anyone, got confused about who was marrying who. It could be possible seeing their faces would be covered with veils. When the two women confided to the cobbler their desire to play a joke, he obliged by making the soles of Brigitta's slippers with more leather so the women appeared to be of the same height.

Then the two went together to Jacoba's old shop to get enough matching material for two dresses. They were also committed the material would match the necklaces given them by Gid-visu and Brunhild. The priest told them they were just in time. Because of the cats having done their jobs, the priests would soon set loose noxious fumes to kill the roaches and such. And who could know where those fumes might appear?

He told the women the strange story of three cats Oma had described as "three of the biggest, meanest, and ugliest cats around." It seemed even these cats responded well to praise. They could not eat all of the rats they killed and after the first incident where one brought a dead rat outside to be rewarded with the bishop's praise they took to coming out with every kill and putting it at his feet waiting to be praised again.

Some of the rats they were killing were almost as big as the cats. They got to know the bishop's hand was not going to strike them but put ointment on places where they had been bit or scratched. The cats finally got to the point over three days where they looked for the bishop to scratch behind what remained of ears and so forth. The one thing they had difficulty understanding was why the bishop kept putting the dead rats in a barrel instead of eating them.

Bishop Elisha told stories about the mighty rat killers in such a funny way the women found themselves laughing several times. They were good stories and what happened later when the priests started fumigating the place made for better stories still.

The bishop would not allow the women to pay for the material they chose. He said the Druid had made much wealth by taking advantage of the poor of the region. He said that he knew they were going to make the world better for Eastwatch and its environs so they should have the material for free as an investment in the village future.

*****

During all the activity around pulling two weddings together training still had to go on. Heller von Swabia had arrived and done his part, though he did come close to getting a drubbing over the condition the two children had been in. Brute' had learned the fake Jacoba had told the impressionable Heller he might need them back very quickly at some time. To his mind it made the investment in them of even the simplest things not very worthwhile. They had begun their new life after their mother's death mainly depending for their sustenance on a bitch dog which had lost her litter.

Herman One Eye, with a cart loaded with his large frame and provisions for the journey, had departed with one hundred young men who would be taught the skills of fighters afoot. Though he had never shown much interest in the wellbeing of his wife before, he made a detour past his hovel and stopped to see her. When he saw what the youngest son had done with the place in short time and the improvement of his wife's appearance he actually cried. Perhaps he had been inspired by the sweet romance between Brute' and Brigitta. Or perhaps it had been the loving relationship between Gidon and Getrudis. Maybe it was a combination of many things. Who knows? But he pulled a somewhat reluctant woman into his arms and apologized for not doing better. He held her and cried. Then she was holding him and crying. It was a very tender moment between the two. Perhaps the most tender in all their married lives. The two parted actually hoping to see one another again.

*****

The day of the wedding, the priestly choir overlooking the spot where the ceremony would take place began to sing. Herr Burgomeister escorted his veiled wife down the center aisle and seated her along with the two boys on the left side. Fat Max led Oma down the aisle and seated her with Durchgefüweg by her side on the right. Behind them sat Gid-visu, Brunhild, and Getrudis. The village elders and their wives took position on the Burgomeister's side, with other village people filling in the cathedral according to status. It was quite a dignified affair and everyone was dressed in their finest attire.

While Max and the Burgomeister were seating their wives, Gwynedd and Brigitta switched positions, a thing not easily done with their full dresses. The trick worked and both men tried to take the arm of the wrong women. The laughter at the front of the Church made many in the pews wonder what was happening?

Both the Baron attended by Gidon, and Brute' attended by Ohtrad, took their places in front of the priest dressed in tunic and cloaks with their insignia. A short space of time was given the men to engage in knightly prayer for blessings upon their unions. When they again stood as one Fat Max and the Burgomeister began escorting the veiled brides to the altar. It was all quite beautiful and dignified.

Once Max and the Burgomeister had delivered the women to their intended husbands they again sat down by their wives. The ritual of ages progressed smoothly, that is until it came time to lift the veils and kiss the brides. When the veils were lifted the Baron and Brute' saw the lips of their loves painted and moist above breasts uplifted and adorned with the diamond and pearl necklaces. Their breasts in the revealing confines of their dresses looked as if they were straining to break free the imprisonment of fabric into the embrace of their lovers. Both men were awestruck even as the women had intended.

One of the priests in the choir would later remark, after having two tankards of beer, that those twin visions of loveliness came closest to making him want to break his vow of chastity, more than anything since he became a supplicant. He would later become one of the married priests.

Though Herr Burgomeister could see nothing, he was so moved by the emotion flowing down from the two couples. He lifted the veil his wife wore to hide her scarred lips and damaged face placing a great kiss upon her, whereupon she collapsed into his arms.

Fat Max, ever ready to embrace a good idea, pulled Oma to him and gave her a great kiss, followed by Gid-visu and Brunhild.

The elders, perhaps carried away by the emotion or thinking a new twist had been added to a ceremony so seldom seen in Eastwatch, embraced their wives and renewed their commitments to one another. After this it can be truthfully said that not a couple in the Church failed to kiss and renew their commitment as well.

When Gidon later told Getrudis what he had observed from his position by the Baron she only laughed. She said, “I am not at all surprised, those two mischief makers would do something to make the day different.”

But for many years after, whenever a couple married in Eastwatch by the Rising of Little Dan, all gathered would kiss their wives and renew the commitment they had one to another.

Chapter 15

Gidon, Fair Lady, and Leviathan

After the wedding, the celebration moved to the village green where a steer had been slaughtered and cooking began. Village lads slowly turned the animal over the fire. The Burgomeister had provided quantities of beer and wine, while villagers brought breads and pies to the occasion. Spring had hardly begun, and there had already been a number of occasions for celebration. Men were going off to train for a month, but not to war this time. That alone was a cause for rejoicing, for the terrible cost of wars had been paid by the village many times. The building of Eastwatch Keep had already helped the local economy as well, with the promise of future benefits. This year held out the hope of being a very good year.

But there was one person who did not seem at all happy. He did not participate in the hammer or pole throws. He did not wrestle or do any of the things he normally would have liked to participate in. He only took part in the archery competition, and that because his father had made sure his bow and arrows had been brought. He tied his father for the longest shot to hit the bulls' eye, but he lost to him when it came to being closest to the center of the eye when it came to a common shot. A few other archers had competed but Gid-visu was still the best archer in Eastwatch.

Gidon only demonstrated the throwing knives because his father had brought them. One of the villagers said they should have some of those made so a target could be set up in the tavern to compete all the time. The truth was Gidon was getting glummer and glummer as the evening wore on. Getrudis watched him with a little frown on her pretty face. It was plain he was not himself. After what he considered an appropriate time, Gidon walked over to the Baron and whispered something to him. The Baron gave a nod. He then went to Herr Brute' and shook his hand, stopping to hug the new brides where they were seated on small elevated thrones. Then he turned to walk toward Fox Home. Getrudis followed him, now sad because he had not asked her to come. She was following only as a dutiful mistress of her lord.

When he got to Fox Home, Gidon went out to the sauna and set it up. With the fire he had going it was plain it would not take long till the room was very warm. Still without speaking he stripped his clothes hanging them on the line then walked into the building. Getrudis did as he, without even bothering to wrap herself in a sheet.

As Getrudis entered she saw he was sitting on the very bottom bench. It was several minutes before Gidon spoke, "Come here my love and sit on my legs."

Getrudis looked and saw his request was not motivated by physical passion. She stepped up on the bench and in a move that was a combination of awkwardness and flexibility set on his legs wrapping her own limbs around him and crossing her ankles. Then she slipped her arms under his and tried to get them around his chest. She pulled herself into him in as tight an embrace as possible. There they stayed until the rising heat caused perspiration to slip between their bodies and she was beginning to have trouble holding on to him.

Gidon then put his hands under her buttocks and she moved her arms up around his neck. Once she had him firmly gripped around the neck he stood up. Her legs slipped from their grip around his waist and he stood her on her feet. The two of them were still facing. He kissed her firmly and meaningfully.

The two dumped buckets of water over their heads and fled back into the house as the fighting priest on guard dutifully averted his eyes.

They toweled each other dry and went to their chamber. They knew they would not be disturbed because Haki and Gwynedd would be again going to the guest bedroom to consummate their wedding night.

They lay together in the familiar cot and Gidon began to speak. "I am very upset King Gregor did not order our marriage. I had said we would marry once the danger was past. Yet I fear this is about as good as we can hope for in this world."

"You should not worry about that," Getrudis responded. "I am quite content being your mistress as a matter of law. Our children will not be bastards. I am very happy, having for my own the love of the most wonderful man in the world."

"There is something else. The king said he was giving you the job of helping Brunhild with the pigeons because you were a farm girl. It felt like a slight to me." Gidon was not ashamed she was a farm girl. In the sense that they planted crops now, he was a farmer.

Getrudis said, "You know very well that Gwynedd was a farm girl before she wed Fat Max's son. I do not think he meant a slight. A pigeon message is not much space on which to write so he had to choose his words carefully."

Gidon looked her in the eyes and said, "You are a better woman than me."

That got him a pert retort, "I hope so. I am thinking a man lies in my bed!"

They cuddled and teased for a good while before Gidon said, "I asked the Baron if I might go fishing with you for two or three days before I have to leave."

She reached for a special place and said, "What will we be fishing for?

They fell asleep wrapped in love's warm embrace.

*****

When morning came for Gidon and Getrudis, Brute' and Brigitta on the far side of the village were still discovering the mysteries of where perfect love and perfect desire meet. Gidon, dressed in his favorite garb as a forester, took down from the wall the bow he had used as a lad along with a quiver full of target arrows. His one exception to customary dress was his sword, already attached to his weapon belt. Getrudis dressed for the forest excursion and they made their way to the stable where a mountain pony was laden with their camping equipment.

Begleiter noised his objection to not being included in the adventure, but beyond that the stable stayed quiet. Herman the Schmeid had returned to his pallet and was enjoying this holiday from all but essential work within the village.

The couple made their way toward the construction site for the future Keep. Gidon intended to pass north of the Rising of the Little Dan and then cut back on the far side of the river. They stopped for only minutes to watch as the first stirrings of life in the camp of construction workers began. So far, the work had been only minimally costly in terms of human life. The Baron was more thoughtful of workmen's lives than many.

The first life had been lost when the workmen reached the bottom of the well shaft and broke through to the chamber where the water rushed through. During the dig the ground had proven sufficiently firm there had been little fear of cave in, so minimal shoring had been required. It had been the lowermost workman who had cried out and disappeared. Most thought him swept away by the current of underground water, but he never popped up in the river.

The second loss occurred when a man working on the walls at the twenty-foot level from the underground supply cried out. The rope that had held the seat from which he worked looked as though it had been cut. But nothing was found along the walls sharp enough to do the deed. Then it was presumed not enough care in keeping serviceable ropes in use was the cause. The Baron berated the foreman till he promised to daily check ropes personally.

A third man died, and it was at the twenty-foot level as well. A number of workmen were involved making a flat floor circling that level, intending the well hole was wider up to the top. The idea was to make two caves in opposite directions to be used in case the Keep was ever overwhelmed. Soldiers could pass down to the floor around the hole and hide in the manmade caves. Then when the enemy was at rest they could come back up and take them unaware.

It was assumed the third man had been lost by slipping and falling down the well shaft to be swept away. But one of his fellow workmen said he had seen a great beast, a Leviathan, rise up the well to grab the lost man. His report was put down to the delusion of working in a place of shadows. Many reasoned his mind was just trying to explain the sudden loss of his friend. There had not been any report of Leviathan or Behemoth in this part of Alemanni for many years.

Gidon felt disappointment he would not get to watch the construction of the Keep. But the Baron would also miss some of the work since he had to go with Gidon to stand before King Gregor II. It was likely he would be home to Gwynedd before Gidon got home to the darling Getrudis now sitting by his side. Gidon skirted the construction camp so he would not have to talk to other people, or see them fearful of Snaggle Tooth, who almost magically appeared by the cart to the dismay of the mountain pony.

As they circled the camp Snaggle Tooth kept looking toward the construction site and growling. Something about it was unsettling to him, and he would not be comforted, no matter how much Getrudis stroked him and spoke sweetly to him. Gidon started to think the sabretooth had showed up when he did simply to protect them, but from what he knew not.

It was with some relief that he finally got to the place on the far side of the Little Dan to follow his old trail going up toward the mountains. Gidon had a special spot he had often retreated to as a boy. He thought of it as an almost idyllic spot. The couple arrived there before midday. It was a pleasure making their camp in the warmth of the spring sun before the coolness of evening reasserted itself.

Gidon stripped down to his inner breeches for the work of setting up the old camp site and getting things situated. Getrudis, following his lead, wore only an inner shift she had intentionally chosen because it barely covered her hips and was tight to the outline of her breasts. She wanted to distract Gidon from the sorrowful mood that kept haunting him. In truth he felt like, having just discovered the true joy of his life, that joy was about to be stolen away.

In the evening, Gidon caught fish in the mountain stream below the camp and the three of them feasted on fish cooked over an open fire. The mountain pony, having been allowed to graze in a clearing frequented by deer, was staked inside the campsite for the night. He still did not like the presence of the great cat. But with the stoicism of the breed accepted he had not yet been attacked. So, he would grumble but not panic because of Snaggle Tooth.

After sitting by the fire for a little while the two spoke of hopes and dreams of the future when they spoke at all. Snaggle Tooth lay first by one and then by the other listening as if he understood every word. They talked and cuddled as the night deepened, then moving under the tent shelter the three bundled together shielded from the morning dew to come. Getrudis was protected on one side by a great cat and on the other by a man, barely more than a youth. But she knew many already thought of him as a great warrior. She saw him as her hero and love.

*****

When the morning of the first day of their freedom from obligation came, Snaggle Tooth rose first and departed to find some nice rabbits for breakfast. Getrudis went to the fire pit. There was something special about using for their fire the same area that Gidon had built when he was but a lad. In her mind's eye she could imagine the young Gidon gathering and carefully selecting the stones that were still in position today.

But there was an ulterior motive in her plans for getting the morning fire stirred up today. She positioned herself intentionally so her back was turned to where he lay under the tent shelter as if completely oblivious to him. Then after she stirred the embers up and added kindling, she stood and leaned over carefully placing each stick of wood and shifting her weight so the visual impact displayed the strength of her upper legs where they met the roundness of her hips. After some time of fiddling with the fire she heard a deep voice behind her say, "Come here girl."

She twisted her body and looked back at Gidon with the twin mounds of her hips still exposed and said teasingly, "Are you talking to me?"

They tumbled and played under the tent until Snaggle Tooth returned with three rabbits for breakfast. The fire needed stoking back up.

*****

The rabbits went for good purpose. The three of them enjoyed the rabbit breakfast and the skins Gidon pulled from their bodies was made into a target that would be used for Getrudis to practice on.

Gidon was a stickler for practice with basic moves even before ever a shaft was loosed. Getrudis had to make sure she always pulled and seated the bowstring beside her face at the same place each time. The left wrist had to be bent just right so the string would not burn her arm. And very importantly she had to learn the secret to siting the arrow so she could hit what she shot at.

Getrudis had to practice and repeat the operations so much she became a bit frustrated. But Gidon said, "This is the way I learned on the very same bow, and I am the greatest huntsman in the world!"

Getrudis snorted. Yes, she actually snorted, and they laughed. But when Gidon allowed her to release the first shaft at the rabbit skin target, she hit it in the center. Whereupon Gidon exclaimed, "My fairy huntress!"

"What!" Getrudis exclaimed. "I thought I was a woods nymph huntress!"

Laughingly Gidon said, "In that dress you are the rare creature hunters dream of and spin stories about to children in their beds."

Getrudis made a number of poses with her bow, imitating the idea of a fairy or wood nymph huntress. The last pose was after she had untied the strap to her left breast and tucking the loose material inside her shift pretended to be a fairy huntress once more.

Gidon kissed the freed breast and said, "I always wondered why so many fairy huntresses appeared that way!"

Getrudis promptly said, "So how many fairy huntresses do you know?"

Gidon again took her in his arms and said "Only you my dear, only you."

Getrudis bent her knees a little and looked around Gidon on every side. She spoke in a very low voice, "Do you suppose they are listening to us now?" Later they talked of what might be said around the fairy fires concerning the two humans in their wood. It was great fun.

*****

The morning of their second day, Gidon and Getrudis rose together. They were feeling a bit somber knowing this would be their last day. All the time in the wood they had not made love. They had been as children, excited with just being in love with one another. The day proved exceptionally warm for this time of year so they shed all their clothing and walked together in the wood like a new Adam and Eve in the Garden. They both wondered if they should ever have such a wonderful time again? It was quite a picture. A man and woman as they might have appeared in the Garden with a great sabretooth tiger walking beside them. It was a magical time marred only by the knowledge this was the last day.

They had not made a breakfast fire and after a while hunger intruded. Down at the creek they harvested mussels intending to make a stew. There was a spot where the creek had a large pool made by water cascading down a long sloping drop. On one side was a large rock that rose up beside the pool about eight feet. Snaggle Tooth lay on the rock looking into the depths of the pool below.

Suddenly Snaggle Tooth launched himself so his forward momentum stopped just as he was directly over the pool. He landed in the water with a tremendous splash sending drops even down to where Gidon and Getrudis were. The couple waited expectantly for the sabretooth to emerge. He was under water so long they began to become worried and walked toward the pool. Then the great cat emerged, walking out of the water toward them. In his mouth was a fish, if it might be called a fish, bigger than anything they expected to see in the creek. And it was fiercer looking than anything they expected to see as well. It was actually a little scary to see, and imagine they might have swam in water where it lay hidden.

Gidon said, "I had thought we might swim in that pool this evening even though the water is cold. Now I am glad we will not. I have seen such a fish once before in the river. I never expected to see it here."

The fish had a long narrow snout with a mouth filled with several rows of razor-sharp teeth. His hide was not scaled for the most part but was covered with a tough skin. He looked every bit a predator.

Getrudis gasped, "Why he might have bitten something off!"

"They have been known to bite people and inflict horrible scars. But the good news is Snaggle Tooth has made a great contribution to our stew pot. He will go well with the mussels and wild onions." Gidon went on to tell her he had seen one much bigger than this one. He now noticed they change a little in appearance as they grow. Since they were not fish but reptiles, he wondered how big they might become?

Getrudis said, "Do you suppose they might grow to be some kind of Leviathan?"

Gidon replied, "It could be possible, I suppose, if they could live long enough."

That night after supper, Gidon announced he had been neglecting his pushups. So Getrudis dutifully positioned herself on his back while Snaggle Tooth went back to lick the stewpot. Upon completing ten pushups he dumped her over onto some furs announcing he was going to do a different push up now. He had Getrudis come and sit in his hands with his fingers cradling her buttocks, his strong thumbs inside her thighs. It was not the most comfortable grip he might have made on her but she cooperated without complaint. He lifted her straight up ten times without waiver or wobble. When he brought Getrudis down the tenth time he kissed her which caused her to fall over giggling. They made love that night, sweetly and gently knowing one another.

*****

It was very hard to get up with the morning light. Their time of freedom was coming to an end. They must return home. Both dressed in their outer clothing after finishing the bread and butter they had brought along. Snaggle Tooth enjoyed getting his portion, then finishing the butter that remained.

The mountain pony had enjoyed his days of grazing and was unwilling to be on his way again. But mountain ponies think they need to start their work being disagreeable so they can get praise for the improvement in their behavior later. Getrudis could always sweet talk the pony into good behavior just when Gidon was ready to give him a good slap. But finally, they got the now lighter load adjusted properly.

On the way down Gidon was very quiet till they came to a little patch of spring flowers growing together to form a bouquet. Getrudis said, "Mountain fairies!" They both laughed but secretly wondered at the strange occurrence.

*****

It was noon by the time they came to the Eastwatch Keep construction site. New workers had arrived with wagons and families. Experienced in making new working communities, they established their campsites outside the construction area and closer to the river. Both the future Baron of Eastwatch Keep and Master at Arms, Lord Brute' were present with their Ladies. Master of Fox Home, Gidvisu, was also present with Mistress Brunhild. At first glance it had already occurred to Gidon they should not all be here. Not with their departure for the king's castle imminent.

Instead of heading for the wood as usual, Snaggle Tooth had ignored all the humans hollering and calling one another's attention to the sabretooth tiger. He had stayed right at Getrudis side. He was however making a low growl from which the girl could not distract him.

Gidon walked over to his father and asked, "Why is everyone out here?"

Gid-visu said, "Early this morning another worker went down the well and did not return. Two men who were with him are claiming they saw a monster. Perhaps some kind of dragon is down there."

"Do you believe their account?" Gidon asked his father.

"This world is full of strange things. That I know. But I also know that if we do not solve this problem in a way that satisfies the workmen this project could be stopped for a long time."

Gidon walked over to where the Baron was sitting on Schlachtross. The war steed was chomping at the bit and pawing the ground nervously. "What do you propose we should do?"

"Well, if there are any dragons here, as the King's Rider I am expected to kill them. But I have not figured out how I am supposed to do it. I have been trying to think of all the stories about dragon slaying I have ever heard, but nothing seems to fit. Many who have slain dragons end up dying in the process. Somehow getting my name sung by bards and minstrels does not seem a thing worth dying for. I need a good idea."

The women had congregated to Brunhild, who was their natural leader. That is all except Getrudis who neither wanted to leave Snaggle Tooth or create confusion by walking around with him. The women were ready to solve the dilemma by walking to her when it happened. The Leviathan emerged from the well.

He had a face that was somewhat like a horse and a little like the fish Snaggle Tooth had caught the day before. Tentacles like a moustache hung down from either side of his head just in front of the nostrils. At the front of his body below an area that appeared to be the neck he had two arms that were not as long as his legs. Both arms had hands with three clawed fingers that could grasp or tear. There were four small wings of webbed construction, two on each side that appeared to be somehow jointed together. Obviously, they were useless for flying, so they must somehow be an aid to swimming. There were spiny finlike ridges that ran from behind the neck to the tail nearly forty feet in all. All this Gidon observed in mere seconds.

The creature was heading straight toward Getrudis!

As the Leviathan neared her, Snaggle Tooth hit the monster with all his great strength. The blow was so powerful, with his mouth biting into the neck region, his teeth literally imbedded into the beast so he could not pull loose to bite again. He had knocked the animal to one side and that was enough to convince him to turn back toward the well, dragging the tiger who had been ripped open by one of the great claws.

Gidon acted instinctively. The thought this thing would hurt his love made him see red. When he saw him hurt Snaggle Tooth he was utterly mad with rage. All his inhibition and caution departed. His sword had leapt into his right hand and a knife into the left. Moving with incredible speed he had caught up to the tail as the front of the beast headed down the hole. With a great leap he landed on the animal's back driving his knife into the beast up to the hilt. The tail raised him up in the air and Gidon slashed down with his sword with such force the entire end of his tail was severed from the body, dropping him onto the ground beside the still writhing tail.

"Now that was smart!" He said in disgust when he stopped rolling. Not waiting to retrieve his knife, he pulled the spare blade from the sheath behind his back. And then he jumped into the well to rescue his cat.

Getrudis was overcome with fear for her beloved as seconds that seemed like hours passed with no sound coming from the hole. The women, having reached her, clung to one another. All feared the worst.

The Baron and Brute' drew near the well with swords drawn. Gid-visu with his long knife drawn pulled his son's blade from the still moving end of the tail cut off Leviathan. It was he that had to be restrained from going down the well immediately.

The tension mounted among all who had watched what had already happened. Then there came from the well some of the most awful sounds ever heard in the realms of men. These continued for the space of about a minute, though they seemed interminable. Then all was quiet once more till the sound of a lop, lop came up the hole.

Gidon's voice sounded strange as he yelled, "Hey, someone send a rope down for my cat."

One of the workmen said, "We are afraid of that sabretooth." To which Herr Brute' responded, "What are you more afraid of? The cat down there, or me up here?"

A rope was let down in remarkable time. When the cat emerged, he still had part of the dragon in his mouth. Gidon had lopped the neck in two on either side of the cat's face. Gid-visu cleared the piece of dragon locked in his jaws while Getrudis breathed into his nostrils. Brigitta shocked everyone as she compressed his chest trying to make him breath. They had quite forgotten the story of Brigitta sleeping with a sabretooth guarding her.

The Hospitaller arrived saying he had wondered why the bishop had told him to be here this day, but now he knew. As the cat sucked in great breaths of air the priest inspected his side to see if anything inside needed to be sutured. Satisfied at last, he pulled the hide back together coating it liberally with a thick greasy substance. People looked and wondered what it was? The priest said, "One taste of that and he will not lick the wound."

From below Gidon commanded men come down and haul up all the pieces of Leviathan so the well would not be contaminated. Then he finally emerged, covered one more time with blood. Brute' took one look at his face and said, "Now I am sure you are trying to get as pretty as me!"

Gidon had a deep cut on his cheek that was about half as long as the one on the same side of Herr Brute's face. "I think I did that when I jumped on his tail."

The Hospitaller said, "You will have to get it cleaned out." He smiled, "It is going to hurt. But you will have to wait till I finish with our friend Snaggle Tooth. His wounds are more interesting than yours." All that heard him laughed and some of the tension eased.

Some of the masons that had come to Eastwatch on the King's command said they had never heard of people having sabretooth tigers for pets. One of the local wags said, "Oh yes, many of our children grow up having them for pets because many of our women are secretly tigresses." There was quite a bit of snickering before they caught on; they were being teased.

It was about then the shirt of Gidon's foresters dress split on the same side where his face was cut. The spines had cut Gidon's clothing all the way down to the undershirt. The spikes of the Leviathan had gone through the undershirt to make a series of holes in his flesh from chest to abdomen. They had bled into the nightshirt but not so much as to soak it.

Some men rigged a litter for Snaggle Tooth and lifted it onto a cart so the big cat would not have to move much right away. Getrudis declared he was going home with her till he was well. But then she remembered she was a guest in the house of Gid-visu and Brunhild.

They made it plain the arrangement was fine with them. After all, once before he had acted to protect Gidon, and now he had protected Getrudis.

The Hospitaller stripped Gidon all the way down to his under breeches seeking to make sure he had found all the wounds. The Baron said, "See, if you had been wearing your chainmail you would not have been embarrassed. But maybe you are not embarrassed. I see you have a suntan." He glanced meaningfully at Getrudis who blushed. Once again everybody laughed.

Already people were getting ready to celebrate the death of the Leviathan. There would be a party at Eastwatch Keep tonight but two people would not be there, nor would Snaggle Tooth. He was transported to Fox Home where he was placed in Gidon's cot. As soon as he caught the smells of Gidon and Getrudis he was quite content to rest in the human cave and recover.

Brigitta came over to Fox Home and petted Snaggle Tooth till he fell asleep, while Getrudis took Gidon to the washroom once again to cleanse his body. Once she had hot water in the tub, she dismissed the fire boy. When she washed her beloved, she knew he liked it best if she did not wear a wash dress. He would always find some way in which to have an excuse to touch her as if to prove she was no dream.

Brute' brought the boys, Wolf-Runner and Wolf-Dancer over to meet Snaggle Tooth. He thought they would be afraid of the great cat since they were afraid of nearly everything. But they responded quite differently. As for the cat, he liked children.

Getrudis asked Gidon, "Why did you attack the dragon like that?"

Gidon thought about it for a minute. "When I saw he was coming after you it drove all reason from my mind. I really did not think about it."

"And after Snaggle Tooth had turned him, why did you continue to attack?" She asked.

"That is more complicated. Snaggle Tooth and I have made a bond with each other. He has kept his part of that bond so I could do no less for him."

It was then Gid-visu and Brunhild could be heard in the hall speaking with Brute' and Brigitta. The two got up from the bath and hurriedly dressed. Gidon had no choice but to don a nightshirt. His forester's clothing had been destroyed and he had none of his clothing as squire in the washroom. The state of dress put an air of informality upon the three couples meeting in the dining room.

Brute' had a suggestion for Gidon. Plainly he was going to need a new suit of forester's clothing. He suggested it might prove worthwhile to have some good chainmail sewed into it since it seemed he never knew when danger would threaten.

Gid-visu said he thought this was a fine idea but it would have to be carefully designed. He thought he might look into getting such a suit for himself as well.

Brigitta said to Getrudis that she ought to change Gidon's insignia from that of a sabretooth cat to a sabretooth with a dragon in its mouth.

While they did laugh about it, Getrudis began to think about the idea in earnest. She then had an idea, but it was one full of mischief and for Gidon's eyes only. It would have to wait till later.

Herr Brute' asked when he thought the Baron, Gid-visu, and Gidon would leave for the king's castle? Gid-visu said they had been supposed to go in two days but he thought they might have to delay a little to let Gidon's inner bruises heal. He had suffered many a pulled muscle in the fight with Leviathan.

They promised to meet at the tavern around noon on the morrow to coordinate getting ready for the journey. A thing overlooked at the start could become a big problem before they arrived in Almanya.

Back in their chambers Snaggle Tooth kept calling Gidon and Getrudis to come and be with him. But Getrudis was not yet ready to cooperate. She said, "Gidon you know Brigitta's idea about changing your ensign is a pretty good one. What do you think about it?"

He said, "If it pleases my little huntress, it pleases me."

His words surprised Getrudis, for this was the first time since the day in the woods he had referred to her again as his huntress. She would have to figure how to live up to that even as Brigitta was trying to be Brute's warrior queen.

"Wait a minute," she said as she disappeared into the adjoining room. In a few minutes she came back wearing her nice nightgown with the sabretooth tiger over the left breast. It looked different somehow but the room was dimly lit. He looked closer and saw what was peeking out the mouth of the tiger.

Gidon said, "You realize this will be the first time I ever kissed a tigress!"

Chapter 16

Virtuous Women

Gwynedd, Lady of the Eastwatch Keep, which did not yet exist, was worried. The reason she was worried was precisely related to the fact Eastwatch Keep did not yet exist. Her new husband, Baron von Krieg, the Baron of Eastwatch Keep, was going away. And, when a King's Rider went away, who knew how long before he would return? Here she was a girl who began life as a farmer's daughter; became the wife and then widow of a tavern keeper's son; suddenly elevated into the position of being the lady of one of the greatest heroes in the land. With his departure eminent she now found herself overwhelmed with concern she might fail him while he was away.

She had thought of communicating her concerns to her husband. But she knew that to burden him with her fears would only put an additional burden on shoulders ladened with responsibilities. Life was more than the joy of being in love and loved. It was also duty to the one loved, whether they be absent or present. She wondered if her man had any doubts about her? Did he just assume she would do her devoir and so mount his horse and ride off with no more thought on the matter? Though she doubted he had any misgiving about her ability, she did. He was so self-assured. Did he ever wonder if he would be able to accomplish the challenges set before him? She certainly doubted herself.

She was glad that during the winter after her first husband died, the bishop sent a teaching priest to stay at the tavern to help her and

Brunhild with their sorrow. He had not only imparted wisdom from the Holy texts, but he had also taught her and Brunhild to read and do numbers. In the days when they were snowed in there were few patrons at the tavern. They often spent the bulk of the days reading. She could now read fairly well in the common tongue, but the knowledge of working with numbers beyond simple addition and subtraction eluded her. It was certainly not what was required to build a Keep. She was sorry the priest had not stayed longer. He had left earlier than planned because he feared widows were too much temptation for him to be able to deal with. It had to have been temptation in the mind because she and Brunhild, in their loss, were not open to succumbing to the lusts of the flesh. Consolation yes; seduction no.

Without the ability to talk the matter over with her beloved Haki, she turned to the woman who had been like her sister since they first married the brothers, sons of Fat Max. Brunhild was not much older than her, but she always seemed a woman of foresight and keen understanding. But this was a conversation she hardly knew how to begin. Not only must the questions be right but the three men presently living in Fox Home could not know of her secret fears. Exposure, she felt, would at the very least embarrass her lord Haki.

She waited for the opportunity to question Brunhild. She did not bring the subject up till just after the men had left to go about organizing the events to come. Then she did not delay. Even though they would not return for some hours, she wanted time to talk. They must not be embarrassed by interruption. Getrudis had gone back to the chambers she and Gidon shared to care for Snaggle Tooth. It was in the private chambers of Brunhild and Gid-visu they met. There they could hope for minimal interruption by staff.

Brunhild even had reason to be in the private chambers at this time. She had clothing to make for Gid-visu's trip to Almanya so he could stand before the king well attired. She did not know her husband had stood before both King Gregor I and II with torn and bloody clothing in time past. But clothing is a lot like horses. When the need is great, the desire is for that which endures. But when peace and ease arrive people seek out that which looks good. Some hold the same standard in choosing women. Gid-visu and the Baron both believed the women they had chosen were not only what looked good but also would endure.

Gwynedd tried to open the conversation by asking, "Do you think our men ever doubt they might be able to do what they set out to accomplish?"

Brunhild stopped and thought a minute. Then she said, "I think men have more doubts and fears than we poor women do. But they are somehow more stubborn than we, or perhaps I should say, stubborn in a different way."

Gwynedd looked puzzled. She knew from the terrible scars on her beloved he had been terribly treated when someone once held him prisoner. She also understood it took real stubbornness and dedication to survive through such an ordeal. Was that what Brunhild meant?

Brunhild continued. "Women see the problems and dangers on every hand, and it makes us afraid. Men will focus on an objective, and will not see the danger to their self. They will see the danger they pose to anyone who has gotten in their way."

Gwynedd said, "I fear failing Haki. Do you think he ever fears failing me?"

"Ah yes," Brunhild smiled. "Men fear failing their women more than anything else in the world. They fear that even more than they fear the king. How they see themselves is dependent on how you and I communicate to them how we see them." Brunhild had made it personal.

"I am afraid of failing my lord as his Lady. All that must be done to build on the Keep while he is away just seems beyond my ability." Gwynedd had finally confessed.

"Yes, I fear failing Gid-visu." Brunhild replied.

"But you always seem to have everything together", Gwynedd said.

"People need to see you as their lady. Be calm outwardly, never panicking. Appear in control. It does not matter how you feel on the inside. It is how you behave on the outside. This is how you communicate you are the Lady of Eastwatch Keep. Remember you have help in meeting your husband's goals. While you should never trust people completely, like the foreman of the construction project. You must listen to his counsel and then if you feel it is needed remind him he will one day account to the Baron of Eastwatch Keep who is a King's Rider." Brunhild stopped talking and waited.

Gwynedd rose up and hugged her. "You are my greatest counselor. I have learned a lot today. Now I must go and prepare things for Haki. He must not see me idle."

Brunhild only smiled.

*****

The women were congregated together at one end of the dining table. Only Gid-visu had sent a message to say they were not coming to eat the noon meal. Gwynedd took this as more proof of men focusing on an objective to the exclusion of all else.

Brigitta had joined the group escorted by one of the young men who had been given the special duty of guarding the home of the Burgomeister. It was plain he was very much smitten with Brigitta, a fact she was not unaware of. She dismissed him to the guard's room, and then confided, "We are going to have to find him a girlfriend!"

The women laughed at the foolishness of such young men. Many a young fellow had competed to wear the favor of a married woman. The code was he should always admire from afar but entertain no hope of ever winning her. If she was a true woman of virtue, he could not. This was part of the role playing in chivalry. The woman was outwardly treated as the young man's ideal of womanhood. And sometimes it was actually true. But to take it seriously was folly.

Brigitta had come bearing news that Bishop Elisha had finally let loose the fumigation smoke in the basement of the building located beside the false Jacoba's shop. It seemed the dangerous combination of noxious odors had driven more than just roaches from the area. The buildings on that short street were discovered to be interconnected in a myriad of ways.

Some things the smoke revealed the bishop sadly needed to keep to himself. Those unpleasant things, constructed into the very buildings, allowed great evil to occur. Were it to have become known would have caused the whole village to feel shamed.

It was what had been disclosed and was now being noised about town Brigitta had to talk about. It seemed all the buildings on that side of the street had a multitude of secret passageways, including the house of whores. People could come in and leave through underground passageways. The smoke, with its noxious chemicals, had penetrated upwards and outwards emptying the house of ill repute even as it killed roaches. Some of those who fled the building were men of standing in the village and would have much to explain when they got home. Many were even missing garments and could not reenter the building because of the deadly gas.

The women laughed at the account, visualizing potbellied old men walking home naked. Getrudis said, "It serves them right for being unfaithful to their women."

Brunhild, always more thoughtful, said, "Sometimes a man seeks another woman because he is not getting something he needs from the woman he has."

Gwynedd said, "You mean things like respect?"

"Yes," Brunhild replied, "it is more important than sex. But men will sometimes substitute sex with another woman when they cannot get respect from their wives."

Brigitta winked and said, "With a man like Brute' it is not hard to give plenty of both!"

The women all laughed together before they settled down to discussing all they must do in the days to come and how they would work together after their men had gone to see King Gregor.

The subject finally came to their new friend Durchgefüweg. Gwynedd said, "I had thought she might like Ohtrad. But I have not been entirely satisfied with that."

It is your woman's intuition," Brigitta volunteered. "He is always making passes at my scullery maid."

"You mean the one with the firm breasts?" Getrudis asked meaningfully." The scullery maid had talked Brigitta into scrubbing her own floors as a way of firming her own full breasts.

Brigitta did not pause a second. “Yes, and I am still scrubbing the floor in our bedchamber. Brute’ seems to like me taking care of that floor personally.”

“You mean while he is there watching.” Brunhild said that with such a straight face all the women laughed and laughed.

“Herman the Schmeid is watching the scullery maid too. I am glad he is going back to his stable today.” Brigitta was afraid there might be some conflict between him and Ohtrad. While the schmeid was far stronger, thanks to Brute’s training, Ohtrad was now more dangerous.

Brunhild said, “Men often are more violent than they need be when it comes to settling conflicts with those over whom they have authority. Brigitta, we will save your husband much trouble when we make peace wherever we may while the other men are gone.”

*****

A message arrived, brought by one of the trainees going to Almanya. Gidon had him bring the women word their menfolk desired their presence for the supper hour. Getrudis said she had to finish something that was a surprise for Gidon. She took her project and worked on it outdoors, letting Snaggle Tooth lie in the evening sun in the backyard where the walls would protect him from the eyes of the curious.

Brunhild instructed the messenger he should wait with the guards of Fox Home till it was time to escort the women to the tavern.

Brigitta called for the young guard who had accompanied her to Fox Home. She said, “You…uh…What is your name again?”

He replied, “Herman, my lady, son of Herman the Barrel Maker.”

Brigitta looked at him seriously. All the women knew she had mischief on her mind. “Does Squire Gidon know what your name is?”

The young man was quite serious. “I do not know my lady. We have not spoken before today, not since we were children.”

Brigitta said, "When we get to the tavern this evening, do not volunteer your name is Herman to Squire Gidon."

The young man looked perplexed. And the women could scarce hide their grins. They all knew Gidon's distaste for the name. But Brigitta had made it sound as if being named Herman might even be dangerous when it came to Squire Gidon. And everyone knew he had stabbed Herman One Eye in the leg even if they knew not why.

After Brigitta sent the young man back to the guardroom, Brunhild and Gwynedd felt free to laugh. The offer was made by Brigitta to help the two of them finish their work before it was time to go forth and meet their men. Brigitta did not have so much to do before the men departed since Brute' would not be making the journey. She was using the wealth her father always said he did not have to pay people to work on her projects as well.

*****

When it came time for the women to get together for the walk to the tavern, Getrudis appeared again. All the women were well dressed. But Getrudis was dressed differently. She had constructed an outfit entirely from woodland green material and she was carrying the bow and arrows Gidon had given her.

The top portion of her garb had a bodice with string lacing, common to a working dress. But the whole looked a cross between forester's garb and that womanly apparel commonly worn by workwomen. She had a sabretooth cat with a dragon in its mouth embroidered over her left breast as a man might wear the ensign of his lord. This was certainly not something ordinarily worn by a woman. But it was a communication saying Gidon was her lord. Her back was laced holding the common girdle that fit below the breasts and goes to the hips showing the figure to advantage. But the lacing was covered by a short cape that went over her left shoulder and under the right arm. It seemed something a male child might wear. It also made it possible to have a cape without interfering with the use of the bow and arrow.

The dress was not one but two. The long dress stopped scandalously above the ankles so it revealed hosen breeches that went all the way to slippers made for walking quietly in the wood. The shorter dress which lay over the long one stopped at the knees. The effect was quite stunning. It was all topped off with a hat that had a peak in the center and a short brim all around. A feather stuck out of a band which circled the hat. The women were speechless. What she was wearing was very modest but at the same time a scandalous departure from normal dress.

"What do you think Gidon will say when he sees that?" Gwynedd asked.

"If he has any sense he will love it." Brunhild answered.

"I wonder what the bishop might say?" Brigitta asked. "But I am sorry I did not think of it," she went on to say.

It is fair to state that when their two young escorts entered the room, they could not take their eyes off Getrudis. And the next month several young ladies of Eastwatch appeared wearing their own versions of Getrudis' dress, but they bowed to convention so their dresses barely cleared the floor. After all, the dresses they made would never go to the wood.

The entry into the tavern was no less attention getting than the one Getrudis made in Fox Home. One of the elders said, "She is wearing man's clothing."

Brunhild looked him dead in the eye and said, "We would have to do something about any man who would appear in that dress." Gid-visu supported his wife's words saying simply, "I like it." That was the end of the criticism. It is always interesting to observe who has influence.

Gidon stood up. You could tell he was about to say something quite serious from his expression. Getrudis looked at him and gave a little tremble. Was he pleased or would she be sent home in disgrace? Finally he spoke. "You men of Eastwatch; and especially you elders gathered this night. I marvel that men so respected for their wisdom could be so appallingly ignorant. Surely you have not lived this long and cannot recognize a fairy huntress when you see one!" Gidon never allowed his expression to give away the fact he was being humorous.

After that many came round to kiss Getrudis hand and say they wished their women had the ability to dress so delightfully. Gidon told them all Getrudis would be wearing this dress to the forests with him when next he came home.

*****

Supper turned into a business meeting. The tavern's seldom used special room was opened for that purpose. At times the elders of Eastwatch would be invited to join the group. To make things simpler they joined the meal and the business concerning the entire village was handled first. As usual the Burgomeister was late. But he came wearing his chain of office because it was an official function. All were pleased to see his wife on his arm though she still wore a veil at all times. She was very self-conscious about her recent scarring.

The ceremonial anointing of Brute' in the name of King Gregor II by Baron von Krieg would have to occur on the morrow along with a simultaneous consecration of Ohtrad as Brute's squire by Bishop Elisha. The elders expressed regret that due to time constraints delay was impossible. It would be a significant event in the history of Eastwatch by the Rising of the Little Dan. But the remaining men of the area that were part of the muster must get to Almanya, the home of the king and center of the national function.

Communication had been made with the bishop and it was agreed it would take place at Eastwatch Cathedral, even though it was not completed. The Bishop Elisha pointed out it would probably prove better if the ceremonies happened there because it would be good if as many as possible could then witness the occasion. Opposition to Herr Brute' because of his origin had greatly diminished, but not altogether. It was important the people see his commitment to them manifested.

One of the elders remarked how times were changing and wondered if some of the local young men might stay in the capitol city lured by its charms? The Burgomeister said it was likely more of them would return with city women than the other way around. A lot of the people living in the places about the castle would be likely to consider the young men of Eastwatch country bumpkins, with the result they should not like to linger among them. Another elder said he thought they would be so busy with military training that they would have no time to socialize. When free they would want rest. To this, one of the older elders pointed out, young men and women tend to find one another no matter what.

The town crier was ordered to call out the news of the anointing through the first hours of the night watch along with the departure of the men for the king's muster on the day following. The Baron was not happy with noising about the day of their departure. He was ever the military man and did not want a potential enemy to know their plans. However, when so many of the local families were involved, there was little doubt the date of departure was well known. Already young men from outlying areas were encamped upon the village green. It was hoped the trip would begin without a problem. But those who knew the way of things understood, no matter how thorough the preparation, the unexpected always appears.

The next order of business was the properties that once belonged to the woman who had called herself Jacoba, who had been in reality the Druid witch Jacklyn. It was agreed that the whole should become the property of the Church under the supervision of its bishop. This had the result of putting the bishop officially in charge of a house of fornication and adulteries. It was a most uncomfortable position for them to be in. However, the Bishop did have some ideas on that, and he was developing more to be announced later.

One of the plans he had already set in motion insured poorer workmen in that area could get a bit to eat as an extension of the tavern of Fat Max and Oma. All that portion to be overseen by Lady Gwynedd and Lady Brigitta, with the help of Mistresses Brunhild and Getrudis.

It was then, for the first time since their home was attacked, the Burgomeister's wife spoke in public. "I rode down the street with our two grandsons earlier out of curiosity. When my boys came to Jacoba's three-story building they went into a complete panic, crying about their momma. They had seen something awful at the age of five and were still horrified by the memory seven years later. Perhaps there are other children who have bad memories of the place as well."

She offered a solution to the problem of bad memories in Eastwatch. "It would be good to do alterations on the facade of the building and perhaps the whole street, then it would not be recognizable as a place of horrors for our villages' children. I would like to oversee a remodeling, first that building, and ultimately the whole street. Would not such a change benefit the whole village?"

This signaled a change in her as a woman. Once she thought of doing things to make the Burgomeister and herself look good. Now she saw the pain of bad memories in another and wanted to make things better for the benefit of all. The elders agreed alterations should be made under her supervision in coordination with the village wives. And, almost miraculously they decided the burden of these changes should be borne by the village.

Fat Max and Gid-visu proposed the acquisition of the house adjacent to their tavern. The elderly wife of the city elder who lived there had recently died. Having no children, he made an agreement that in exchange for the services of the tavern he would keep only several rooms to live in. In return for the property, he would receive the benefits of the tavern without charge. He wanted to be free of responsibilities for the time he had left.

Max wanted to put in a narrow area for the throwing of knives like Gidon had. Several had made that suggestion since the joint marriage celebration. Having a target in the tavern for regular use would be most fitting, they thought. Max planned to use a type of wood for the targets that would heal perforations by being soaked in water. The demonstration of the balanced throwing knives had been a big hit. Max thought this would make a great game for the tavern as long as nobody got hit by a knife. He knew it would draw people to the tavern as well. He never expected that over the next twenty years the game would spread all over Aleman.

Additional sleeping areas were also going to be in increased demand because of the increasing movement of people through the village as Eastwatch Keep was built and the village grew. Max anticipated the space would be needed at least for a decade. If demand eventually declined, they could put in other amenities to keep the tavern profitable. The elders heartily approved the tavern expansion.

The elders departed the conference and returned to their familiar table in the tavern proper, very pleased with the decisions they had made.

*****

The Burgomeister and his wife left the tavern anxious to check on the boys. The old familiar krankenschwester had stayed on, after much deliberation, to act as a nanny to the twin boys Brigitta had adopted. They had made space for the old nurse so she was never far from them even at night. Because of her and the Burgomeister's wife, the boys were much improved in overall health of mind and body. They were now showing signs of growth as well.

The four couples remaining discussed at length the challenges to come at Eastwatch and how much benefit Herr Brute' could be to the several women. Gwynedd was much pleased to learn about the sort of education he had acquired during the years he was a member of the Italian Band. She had not known that wherever they went they adopted and adapted to their store of knowledge the skills of many peoples. That part which Herr Brute' knew of would contribute to success for Eastwatch.

It was fairly late by the time they had finished talking. Fat Max and Oma had talked about the future of the little business across town. They had even discussed the project of building the dovecotes. After taking leave of their friends, three couples made their way to Fox Home. It seemed as if each step brought the closeness of the hour each pair of lovers would be separated from one another nearer, and the unhappy event began to weigh heavier.

*****

Later in the night Gwynedd told her beloved Haki that after tomorrow's ceremony of knighting Brute' they must hurry home. He smiled with anticipation and said, "Why is that my love?"

“I need to get you in the sauna to soften and clean the scars on your back so I can rub them with the ointment treatment before you leave,” she said.

“Is that all you had in mind?” he inquired.

“Well…I am sure other things will come up.” She started to say more but her mouth was smothered with his kisses.

*****

Upon entering their chambers, Getrudis hung up her bow and arrows before preparing to change into her nightgown.

Snaggle Tooth had obligingly gone into the adjacent room and laid down on a pad before the fireplace, even though no fire had been made. He seemed to understand they wanted to be alone.

As Getrudis very slowly began removing her huntress dress, she asked Gidon to help with the lacing of the girdle where it joined at the back, as if she could not manage it alone. She asked, “Do you really like my outfit?”

“Of course; It looks so appropriate on you. I think you may become the leader in women’s garment choices for Eastwatch. However, you need to know right now that when we go to the forest after I return, you will not be needing the long skirt!”

Getrudis laughed. She planned to tease him with the hosen that embraced her legs when they made that trip.

After a few seconds Gidon said, “There was a minute there back at the tavern when I first saw you and realized you were wearing my insignia, that you had me worried.”

“What made you worried?”

“I was concerned about what might be peeking out of the tiger’s mouth beside a dragon.”

They laughed together and her nightgown never made its way over her head.

*****

Gid-visu and Brunhild were quite passionate in their love for each other. But it was more reserved for much was kept between the two of them. When they finally got to their chambers, he took pleasure in watching her undress for bed. He was so busy watching he forgot, and not for the first time, to remove his own clothes. He felt a little ill at ease when he undressed because he saw her body as being so perfect and knew his own to have many scars from wars and hardships.

She did not mind that he had not undressed because it gave her pleasure to undress him even as it pleased her to wash his body and be close to it in the sauna together. She preferred for them to be in the sauna alone and enjoyed him washing her as well. A trip to the sauna for just the two of them was a rare event. And it made it hard for her to maintain a semblance of modesty when others were around, let alone freely give pleasure to each other.

Gid-visu started out complimenting her. He said it always pleased him when she so quickly responded when he called her to him. He said he thought it set a good example for other women when she honored him in such a way.

Brunhild smiled and said half teasingly, "I am pleased to serve my lord. One day bards will write of such dedication, and minstrels will sing, extolling my virtues of constancy." She did actually think it important for others to know she reverenced him and considered his presence a blessing.

It was unexpected when he reached out and cupped her breast. She knew he liked to see them move as she did things like remove her clothing or help him out of his. He said, "Do my eyes deceive me or are your breasts growing?"

"You know my breasts swell every month as part of my body's cycle. It was on the night we first knew one another my breasts were going through that cycle." Brunhild paused and gave a little frown. "Gid-visu the finish of my cycle did not come."

"Is that bad? What does it mean? Do we need to see the Hospitaller?"

"No, it may mean nothing more than I am with child." The importance of what she said had just settled in her mind even as

Gid-visu was wrapping his mind around it. "Oh my dear man, you probably made me that way the very first time you lay with me!"

It was an enormous idea that God who opens and closes the womb had kept it closed in her first marriage but immediately opened it when they were joined.

*****

It was nearly midnight before Max and Oma had managed to close the tavern and take their selves to bed. Their passion was usually consumed in exhaustion and age at this time in their lives but the sweet spirit of dedication and commitment to one another remained.

Though the lives they had made together had held sorrows like the deaths of their two sons in the king's wars, they had also shared many pleasures and accomplishments. Both considered the joining of the widows of their sons to good men as accomplishments to be enjoyed together. The three women—Brunhild, Gwynedd, and Getrudis—had begun as servants in the tavern. All three had become treated as daughters-in-law, even though Getrudis was not in fact, and now they were truly as daughters in their relationship with Fat Max and Oma.

For Max and Oma, the intimacy of being together physically had become pushed to the background of their daily lives. And it might have remained dormant and unattended, like a neglected flower bed growing weeds choking out the beautiful plants, had it not been for a woman acting seductively toward Max and making him confused. It had made Oma aware of her need to put a hedge of protection around him with her love. She had expressed this as a promise to wash Max's back. Her showing him that he was still desirable to her meant he had nothing to prove to feel as if he was still a man and therefore able to ignore vain flirtations and worse.

Even for two people as portly as they, and in spite of the difficulties of obesity, a new dimension was added in their relationship by working at the physical as well as the spiritual side of intimacy. Max had once said the relations between men and women were wasted on the young because they tried to make it into a physical contest.

Since the night Oma said she had to wash Max's back, the truth of his words had been reality in their lives. Thus, the impromptu wedding kiss had been an expression of that new dimension.

Now very tired from an extra-long day, they lay in the bed looking at one another waiting for sleep to creep up. Oma said, "Max, how old are you?"

He had to think about it for a minute. "I think I am almost sixty. If I am right that would make you about fifty."

"Max, you know my time as a woman seems to have passed. I have not bled, for as near as I can figure, for the space of almost two years."

"Okay. What does that mean?"

"Max it should not be but I think I am with child!"

Max was instantly wide awake.

Chapter 17

Ceremonies and Farewells

The morning brought the heavy fog of spring, depressing many spirits. For the next couple of weeks, the people knew they would have this annual phenomenon to begin their day. Some still influenced by the old religions believed this was the time when demon gods who rode in clouds came down to the earth and went about seeking to seduce people into sin. The glum among the people saw the fog as being like a funerary pall, stretched over a dead body. In actuality as soon the sun rose but a little, the droplets of the water in the mist diffused its light, so the mist was much lighter than so dark a cloth.

Farmers and travelers were most bothered. In the worst of the fog, great difficulty finding their way presented itself. For the farmer just moving between structures holding various animals could be a problem. The ever-necessary morning feeding had to be done. After feeding the animals, fog would allow an excuse for a few extra minutes at their own breakfasts. Until the mists lifted, even very familiar fields could be hard to locate or work. In the same manner many an early traveler would take a wrong fork in a forest road and wind up traveling many miles before discovering he had gone the wrong way.

In the Burgomeister's house the fog could not enter but its heaviness could be felt. His wife rolled off her bed to pull the chamber pot out from under it. She was suspended over it held by her husband's hands as the poor woman began her morning sickness. For the first time in a long time the Burgomeister had lain with his wife. The first time they had coupled was after, overcome by love and desire flowing down from those being joined in marriage, he had lifted her veil and kissed her, so she genuinely swooned in his arms. The second time was the previous night. The Burgomeister had seen something of the girl he once wed. Her selfless act of wanting to cover the shame of the street on which the Druid Witch had hid, for the sake of their adopted grandsons and the other children of the village had moved him.

When they got home from the tavern the night before, he had taken her in his arms and bussed her properly. Right in the hall! In front of their guards! She had leaned into his body and said in a voice that sounded as she did at eighteen, "If I had known you were so attracted to scarred women, I would have gotten myself beat up long before." They laughed and proceeded together up the stairs. When they came to her bedchamber, he found the strength to sweep her off her feet and twisting sideways carried her through the door, even though the effort made his damaged skull ache. It was then Brute' and Brigitta discovered how thin the wall was between their bed chamber and her mother's. She covered her mouth so not to laugh in joy.

Brigitta whispered in Brute's ear, "Do you suppose they heard us on our wedding night?"

Brute' replied, "I hope so. Maybe it gave them some ideas." But no more was said because Brute' had an idea of his own that made morning come all too soon.

When Brute' appeared on the porch the fog was still too heavy to see the back rank of his men assembled. He could barely see the tips of all seventy of the wooden spears standing upright. He said, "You men are the ones who have done well in your training. This morning fifty of you will be chosen as the first guard of Eastwatch Keep. In a few minutes Baron von Krieg and Lady Gwynedd shall arrive to call out your selection and award you the first armor of your station. And then, from this point, your training will grow more intense. Leaders of ten shall ultimately be picked from the fifty after you are divided into each of your groups.

"Those of you who are not selected to be part of the fifty will join the men going to the king's castle on the morrow. You should not consider this a failure but an opportunity. In recognition of your achievement you will march as a special squad and be given the honor of protecting the rear and flanks of the troop of your friends and neighbors as they make the journey. This is a most responsible position and I know you will not let me down."

Herr Brauner arrived with fifty pieces of armor of the Baron's unique design. And Herman the Schmeid, along with the monastery smithy, appeared with fifty swords and twenty iron tipped short pikes of about ten feet. Three chairs were set out at the top of the front door steps. From this vantage the Lady Gwynedd was expected to sit in the center, flanked by the Lady of the Master at Arms on her right hand, and the wife of the Burgomeister on her left. This seating arrangement had been thoroughly discussed the night before. It was decided upon to reflect the dual mission of the fifty both to the village of Eastwatch and the Keep.

Baron von Krieg and his Lady Gwynedd, arrived almost simultaneously with the bishop even though they came from different directions. Behind the Baron and his Lady followed Gid-visu with Mistress Brunhild and Gidon with Mistress Getrudis. As Lady Gwynedd mounted the steps to take her seat, the Lady Brigitta and her mother came out of the house on cue to sit beside her. The two boys Brigitta had adopted stood by their grandmother's chair. Gid-visu led his entourage to where they stood opposite the side of the stairs where the weapons were placed. Quite a few of the village was standing on either side, especially the parents of the men soon to be given their assignments.

All five men, the Baron with Gidon; Herr Brute' with Ohtrad; and Gid-visu were resplendent in their best tunics and chainmail. The air of solemnity had steadily increased from the beginning of the assembly till now. The fog had now cleared till all the rows of new soldiers were visible.

Bishop Elisha stepped up on the second step leading to the porch. He looked over the group, many of whom he had known from birth. They had little thought of what might really come into their lives should things not go well. He raised his right hand, making the ancient priestly sign of blessing, and said, "Let us pray."

Seventy men went down on their right knee as one. The five standing before them drew their swords and, holding them before as crosses, also took their knee. Village men removed their caps and women bowed their heads. All waited expectantly. Bishop Elisha prayed:

> "Our God who created the heavens and the earth,
> Setting all things in motions by the might of thy power,
> Who suffered all things for our Redemption,
> Attend our prayer we plead.
> We pray Oh God, even as thy mighty angels wage war against evil in the heavenlies,
> These men might learn war on earth in the power of thy Holy Names.
> We pray, Oh God, even as thy Son is the Captain of the Lord's Holy hosts in Heaven,
> So might He be the true captain of our guard on earth.
> We pray, Oh God, that thou wilt lead and guide the men thou hast raised up on earth to be the visible leaders of our troop,
> May you ever guide and protect them for thy purposes, even those objectives unknown to men.
> We pray, Oh God, thy blessing upon these before me, who follow your anointed leaders, who bear the sword not in vain.
> May they ever be faithful and true, keeping holy purpose before them.
> And may the land of the Alemanni ever be thine.
> Amen.

And, all the new soldiers and the people said amen. Though it must be said many questioned, "What was the meaning of the bishop's words?"

Baron von Krieg moved to stand before the men. "My lady will now read the names of the twenty men who will receive metal tipped pikes today and the first mission. You will be protecting your brethren going to the king's castle, but she is also entrusting you with the protection of her lord, my person. And since Mistress Brunhild is entrusting you with the protection of her lord, Gid-visu, she has prepared for you a special surprise. Each of you will also receive from her a golden yellow cloak as a symbol of the trust you have earned."

As each man's name was read, he stepped out of formation and went forward to receive his pike and golden cloak. The Burgomeister had given himself the job of shaking each man's hand before they received either pike or cloak. He made sure to congratulate each. After receiving their equipment, they went to form a new formation separate from the first.

Then Herr Brute' stood before the fifty remaining. "You all know that you are going to be part of the first guard of Eastwatch Keep. But Lady Gwynedd will read your names so all gathered will know them. Now you will be that guard under my command. We will serve according to the good pleasure of King Gregor II and Baron von Krieg. You will notice the armor you are being given has little to protect your backs. We are the men of the Keep. We do not run. We stand our ground before any enemy we may face." A great cheer went up.

Herr Brute' raised his right hand. "My Lady Brigitta has also prepared a special surprise for you. She has prepared for you fifty red cloaks. On the back of each you will find the symbol of the Keep and the Eastwatch village set side by side. From this day forth we are committed and willing to give our lives in defense of both."

Lady Gwynedd read the names and as they stepped forward each man received, after the Burgomeister's handshake, his cloak and breastplate with weapons girdle and sword. They found trying to put on the new equipment difficult, especially in the confined area of the formation. It was solved by learning to cooperate in getting the whole accomplished. It was an achievement that pleased both the Baron and Brute'. Lessons of working together and cooperation are some of the most important lessons men at arms might learn. As soon as all were dressed, they returned to positions of attention with their wooden spears pointed straight up.

Then the four young men who had been separated out to be guards over the Burgomeister's home were called forth and given blue cloaks which had the symbol of the city on the back. They were pleased not to be forgotten in this ceremony.

Herr Brute' announced, "Tonight there will be an anointing service. Then Ohtrad and I will stand vigil and pray. I expect you all will be present for the anointing service, but I want you to know any who would like to stay at the back of the Cathedral will be most welcome to fast and pray during the time of the vigil." All the guard would be present to fast and pray through that night. But the time of that vigil was yet hours away.

The new guardsmen had been dismissed into the loving and admiring arms of their families. Twenty of the men still had the duty of preparing a kit for the trip to Almanya. But most of those had already expected they would not be among the ones chosen to stay, so they had set some things in readiness. There were those who felt keen disappointment, but being reminded the difference between being chosen and passed over had been small was some consolation.

Each one of the women wanted to be alone with their man for the short hours remaining but Gidon had the duty of accompanying the Baron to inspect the men on the village green. There were always some last minute items to be attended to among so many conscripts for training. Though a number might not be happy with the circumstance, most were now caught up in the excitement of events. A number of them had been present to see the ceremony that took place before the Burgomeister's home. And the ambitious could hope for future advancement.

Herr Brute together with Ohtrad had followed the bishop to the Church where they discussed the ceremony and vigil which would come in the evening. Though he never said a word, it appeared Ohtrad had been disappointed neither his brother Wolfgang or his stepmother had come for the events of the day. He did not yet know they would be in the congregation at the Church that evening. Travel by goat cart was slow business and Wolfgang could not be away from the farm over long. In fact, because of the demands of the farm they would make their trip home in the dark of night.

Gid-visu made the final checks and loading of three two-pony carts. The first contained the bows and arrows he had been working on the past three years. In addition, it also contained the banner of Brute' von Alemanni and many other things of precious consideration. The cart was more carefully covered and sealed than the others. The second cart contained victuals for man and horse alike. It was the heaviest of the carts starting out for there was a large number to feed. And it was the only cart that did not have water and beer casks mounted on its sides. The third cart rode at the rear of the troops. It was almost as heavy as the food cart because it held tenting and tools. The least expendable part of its load was the tools.

Each man was expected to carry his own weapons, blankets, and water for the day upon his person. The water skin he carried alone would weigh about eight pounds, and any man who carried less than enough would soon have cause for regret, for the plan was to travel more than twenty-five miles a day. That meant a body used a lot of water. Unless the individual carried some food, meals were eaten morning and evening. Only the ponies got a measure of grain at the noon halt. Game could never be depended upon to be adequate to the need of the company but it was hoped some deer would augment the food carried on the way. They would not be allowed to stop at taverns as they traveled to the king's castle.

Once the Baron had finished his work, he dismissed Gidon. The Baron suggested they might meet at the tavern with their women for a supper before the anointing ceremonies.

Gidon lost no time getting to Getrudis. They walked together through the town rather aimlessly. It was enough to be in each other's presence. He held her arm on his like the great lady he considered her to be. It was interesting to observe that all who greeted Gidon also greeted her as they passed. She had been well respected in the village of Eastwatch as a working woman of high morals before meeting

Gidon. Their union had only served to elevate her the more in the eyes of the people.

The couple did stop to watch some boys at play. They might have been working at various occupations since they appeared nearly ten years of age. But today was a festive day when only the essentials were seen to. So, the boys with homemade swords played at being soldiers of Eastwatch. Gidon thought to himself they had no idea what war was all about. But then he realized, neither did he. He had never been in a pitched battle or even seen one. If this muster proved to be a training exercise, this summer would end with him still never having seen a battle. But he had seen enough that now he was grateful that experience had not yet come his way.

Finally the young lovers did wind up in front of the tavern, and went in to discover Brunhild and Gid-visu had already arrived. Gid-visu explained they had come straight to the tavern from inspecting the carts. The schmeid had promised to harness the animals and have them ready to go in the morning. Gidon said, "Herman is doing us a better and better job. We need to think about building him a house attached to the stables and smithy when we get back. And then we must find him a good wife to make it a home."

Gid-visu said, "I did not think you liked Herman at all."

Gidon simply said, "He has changed a lot during this spring. Or perhaps it is the case that this spring has given him the opportunity to show what he is capable of."

Gid-visu laughed.

Brunhild told Gidon how Brigitta had toyed with Herman, the Barrel Maker's son. Everybody laughed about it. Gidon said, "I remember him from when we were children. But in truth I had not recognized him. We will still never name one of our children Herman, but I know just because a man is named Herman it does not mean he is a lesser person. I guess what I am saying is I have learned we must judge every man on his own merits."

Getrudis frowned, "I know the village boys are attracted to Brigitta for she is a comely woman. But I do not think Brute' will suffer their attentions to her gladly."

Gidon said, "I will not suffer any of their attentions to you gladly. But we know men are attracted to beautiful women, and it is lonely when you are full of passions and no one is there to be the object of those passions."

Getrudis had not missed the fact he called her beautiful and she lowered her head in a manner that only heightened her attraction to him.

"Brigitta will handle any situation, I am sure of that." Brunhild offered.

Oma came to the table with four glasses of wine. "This will put some of the color back in your cheeks Brunhild."

"Thank you dear Oma. When we got to the tavern, I was feeling a bit tired, and so early in the day." This was a very unusual thing for this woman who was constantly busy.

"It is not uncommon when you are with child," Oma said. She then said, "I will tell you a secret. I am with child as well, and at my age!" Both women reached out to her. Then she said with a smile, "I guess I still have to be careful how I wash Max's back!"

The remainder of the morning passed pleasantly. A number of customers moved through the tavern, each only pausing for refreshment. It seemed everyone's activity was either centered around the anointing at the Church this night or the departure of the men on the morrow.

Oma said she thought Eastwatch village would have a great baby boom about nine months from this week. "The whole place has been breaking out in romance since the Baron wed Gwynedd and Brute' married Brigitta."

Getrudis said, "But I am not with child."

Gidon gave her a meaningful look and said only one word, "Yet!"

The afternoon passed quite happily among friends. Many had stopped by the table wishing Gid-visu and Gidon good fortune in the days ahead. Even the construction workers the king had sent to help build the Keep seemed to catch the spirit of the events. The foreman came through dressed in the best he had and asked whether he and his chief men might find a seat in the Cathedral? The much hoped for involvement of the people was definitely coming to fruition.

The Baron and Gwynedd did not appear for the supper meal as planned before the ceremony. As time grew short, Gidon reluctantly said he had to go and find the Baron so he could be prepared to do his part. The four of them decided to walk together to the Cathedral. It seemed better to go now. Arriving early meant Brunhild might rest a few minutes before the ceremonies began.

The Hospitaller came into the Cathedral and approached Brunhild. He gave her a small chilled pot, made of baked clay, filled with a yellowish substance. With a small silver spoon, he dipped an exact measure out of the pot and gave it to her to eat. He said, 'Take this spoon and dip out the same measure each morning. Keep the jar in your cool storage between uses, and when this runs out, I will bring you more. Take this till you deliver your baby, and then for three more months."

Brunhild smiled and said, "Thank you sir." She had scarce eaten it when she began to feel better and then stronger. "May I ask, what is this miracle concoction?"

"It is called Royal Jelly. You must treasure it because much effort is expended to get only a little amount. But it will keep you well and help make any worthy baby greater and wiser in its days. Bishop Elisha saw your condition and knew you should have it. It is worth more to the health of a woman than its weight in gold."

When Brunhild returned to Fox Home that night she put the clay pot in a strongbox, along with the silver spoon, before having it deposited in the cool cellar. Thereafter she wore the key around her neck below the beautiful red stone Gid-visu had given her. It was her dearest hope that she would give her beloved a strong and healthy child to comfort his old age.

When all the notables were assembled and the troop of fifty were gathered round about the sides of the Cathedral, the time had come to begin. Baron von Krieg, with his squire Gidon proceeded down the aisle between the pews toward the altar. This investiture of Herr Brute' along with the anointing of Ohtrad as his squire was going to be carried out with all pomp and ceremony. Gidon carried the Baron's Battle Sword on his shoulder in the appropriate position of attention, his own sword sheathed at his side.

As soon as they reached the steps leading up to the altar the two men turned. They were resplendent in their best dress. The bishop stood at the top of the steps dressed all in white trimmed with gold. He literally shone in the lights of lanterns and candles. Had not every port been opened to the outside air, the heat and smoke from so many lights would have been stifling.

Herr Brute and Ohtrad appeared between the great wooden and bronze doors at the front of the Church. They too were resplendent in their finest garb. The dire wolf insignia of Herr Brute' was quickly noticed by all. Children were raised on the stories of dire wolves and their importance to the tribes of Gomer including the Alemanni. Perhaps this was an omen. Many present considered the possibility. A warrior wolf had come to them from the wolf men of Italia.

When Brute' came within two paces before the steps to the altar he knelt down on his right knee placing both his sword and his long knife before him. Ohtrad knelt as well following the example of Herr Brute'.

The Baron was first to speak. "In accordance with the command of his Majesty King Gregor II, I dub thee knight of the order of King's Riders, Brute' von Alemanni, and invest thee with the position Master at Arms of Eastwatch Keep." The Baron took his sword from Gidon and touched both shoulders and finally the head of Brute'. When the sword was raised again in the first element of the salute position it was handed back to Gidon.

Bishop Elisha took a step forward holding a shepherd's staff in his right hand. His words were few but full of import. "In the Name of God, the All Seeing, I anoint you lord Brute' von Alemanni and Ohtrad, son of Herman One Eye to the service of God, by serving the King and the people. May you always use your holy anointing as the means of living with honor, ever diligent to perform your duty."

A priest poured the anointing oil over the heads of both men and another held a small basin below their heads. When they stood a cheer went up from the troop of fifty. This alerted the twenty standing guard on the outside and they too lifted up their voices. The sound carried throughout the village.

The recession left Brute' and Ohtrad before the altar on their knees. The vigil had begun. The bishop came down, and the Baron with Gidon took their position behind him, followed by the anointing priests and then choirboys. As they walked out of the Cathedral prominent citizens took their places according to rank or position led by the Burgomeister and his wife. Once the church was cleared of all witnesses, pews were moved up to make an area for the fifty to kneel, pray, and ultimately sleep on the Church floor.

Outside the Church, on the steps ascending to the doors, two of the group who would begin their march to Almanya took the first watch. They had divided the watch into ten, so that two were on guard always as the others tried to sleep on the steps. They would not leave this post till the dawning and the vigil ended. It would make tomorrow a hard day but it was something they wished to do as a group, to honor their Master at Arms and their village.

Throughout history, when the armies are composed of men with loved ones and families, the times before a deployment are particularly hard. Some use the last minutes to go over the preparations they have made for departure. Some choose to use the time in making love to the woman they must leave. Others will play with children or pets, savoring the essence of home life around them. Not a few gather and lift tankards of ale and beer among friends and relations. What is the best way depends on the character and values of the individual. But people do not change much through millennia and neither do soldiers.

For the three couples who now resided at Fox Home, the most natural stop enroute was the tavern. For all, Fat Max and Oma were an integral part of their lives. The men knew Oma in particular would have been terribly disappointed had they not stopped by after the most consequential ceremony to take place in Eastwatch for many years. The men could not miss Oma's hugs and tears. She considered them as her boys and must be given their farewell before they could leave in the morning.

There were people stopping by, glad to be given a minute of time with these most notable people. Many would point to conversations that occurred this night as evidence of some personal relationship with these heroes, when gossiping with others in the future. It is an amazing thing to watch people do this. A sense of frivolity and merriment descends over people gathered to celebrate what is no cause for celebration at all. The movement toward war!

When the three couples finally made it to Fox Home, each spent the evening in exactly the same way, that is, after Gwynedd had cleaned and treated the scars on Haki's back and Brunhild had put away her jar of Royal Jelly. They lay naked in one another's arms. There was no sexual play, only the closeness of desperation knowing they would be separated from the one person dearest in all the world.

Snaggle Tooth stretched out on the rug beside the cot of Gidon and Getrudis. The big cat sensed something was happening he was going to be left out of. And that did not meet with his approval. He was healing nicely from his wound inflicted by Leviathan. He already had the scars of a long life. Though his human friend Gidon was just starting out in life, the scars on both sides of his face already had begun to make him look fearsome. They were quite a pair together, though soon to be separated for a time.

But scars did not deter the strong attraction Getrudis had to her sweet love. They were first the reminder of the dangerous role life had chosen for him. And the second more terrible scar, just beginning to heal, reminded her of the rage that overcame him when what he loved was placed in danger. She would watch him sleep in her arms till it was time to wake and go to the stables for the men's horses.

Breakfast was a solemn affair. Brunhild, who was usually mindful of everything, had to be reminded to take her Royal Jelly as the Hospitaller had directed. So Gid-visu said to Getrudis, "I am counting on you to look out for her while I am gone."

Getrudis only glumly nodded. Like them all her mind and heart were full.

The cook who often had little to do other than assist Brunhild, packed a lunch for the men to have on the road. She tucked her hands into her apron and looked crestfallen.

Brute' upon leaving the Cathedral had sent Ohtrad to check the guards at the Burgomeister's, while he proceeded to the stables. He would sit his steed in review as the men passed out of the village. It was not his legionnaire background alone that prompted him to do this. He wished to show respect to the men going to the king's muster, particularly the twenty gold cloaks who had stood watch outside the Cathedral during the night.

He found Herman the Schmeid had already saddled Schlachtross and Begleiter, as well as loaded the Baron's new pack horse. The schmeid was most apologetic, saying he had not known Herr Brute' would require his horse this day. Brute' said he really needed to spend more time with the animal anyway.

It was then the Baron appeared with Gidon by his side. They set their weapons in place on their horses as Gid-visu made last minute checks on both carts and animals. He planned to drive the lead cart containing his prize bows and arrows himself. The leading of the troop would ultimately be the responsibility of the Baron, with Gidon often conveying the orders down the line. When the carts were taken out and lined up on the road to Almanya, men had to be directed to their position in the formation. They were told sternly to remember their place because this was where they were expected to form up throughout the trip. It was not easy to get everything together in the heavy morning fog.

As Gidon rode up and down the line checking things for the Baron he noted the twenty iron tipped pikes standing straight up in the back of the formation. He knew that beneath them stood twenty young men in their golden yellow cloaks. He was sure that because of Herr Brute's tutelage they would stand fast against any problem that came their way. He did not really expect a problem. Surely bandits and the like would not dare take on their great company, but in this world something unpleasant was always possible.

When the order to march finally came, the formation of men started off like an accordion. It seemed the fog might be dampening the sound of the command or it may have been some were inattentive. The Baron was not at all pleased. He did what was for him a very unusual thing. He swore. "If I have to start and stop this formation all day, every one of you mother's sons will step off at the same time. We will not look like a bunch of country yokels going down the road." But in truth that was what many of them were.

Many villagers had come to line the side of the roadway. Not a few brought early spring flowers to throw before the men as they passed, men they could scarcely see for the thickness of the fog. It was a cheering thing but it did not help the company keep step within the formation.

Finally the Baron sent Gidon halfway down the line with instruction. He yelled to them that when they heard him yell the command, "Company," they should be ready to step out and when he said, "March," the first foot should come out. He then yelled out the cadence their steps should fall in. So when the Baron yelled "Company!" Gidon repeated him. And he did the same when he called out "March!" Gidon did likewise. They were not perfect but the accordion effect was not so pronounced. The Baron swore they would be marching like the king's regulars before they got to Almanya.

As things settled down and the group was fairly underway, Gidon found he enjoyed riding along upon Begleiter beside the Baron. He also enjoyed the occasional trip up and down the formation speaking to various men. Some he had known as men when he was but a boy, and others whom he had grown up with, all made occasion for words of encouragement and camaraderie.

And now they were off on what was to him a great adventure. In spite of the perils he had faced in the last few weeks this was all a big exciting experience. That is the beauty of youth. It can put a gloss on very serious matters.

He hoped that during the trip the Baron might tell how he came to be so scarred on his back. And perhaps his father might fill in some of the gaps related to his claim to be over three hundred years old.

The farther he got from Eastwatch, the more deeply he missed Getrudis. It was now a matter that each time he was separated from her he was consumed with fear for her safety.

This soldier's life may have chosen him but it certainly was not the life he would choose for himself. He would like to be home wearing woodland green and playing with Getrudis and Snaggle Tooth in the wood. Such joy seemed very far away now.

Reality would set back in when they finished the first day of travel. The decision was made to stop early so the men would have plenty of time to sort out the experience of pitching tents and making their evening meals. It turned out this took even longer than what they had planned for. But by the time they reached their destination they would be seasoned pros at making camp and breaking encampments.

CHAPTER 18

MASSACRE AT HEIM

The first twenty or so miles on the road to Almanya could only be described as hard slogging. There was not enough traffic on that portion of roadway from and to Eastwatch to keep grass from growing on the trail. The early spring growth wrapped into the spokes of the cart wheels and hid ruts, holes, and rocks. When it was possible to move more quickly because of low grass, the carts still could not roll faster for fear of damaging or breaking wheels. If Eastwatch was to prosper commercially this section of roadway would have to be improved.

While the excuse of an early stoppage on the first day's journey was to allow the men time to learn to set up tents and make meals in bright daylight, the true cause was more complex. Both animals and men had worked harder to make headway than they would after they reached the first fork where the main road heading south turned back southeasterly. Their way lay north. The road was so seldom traveled the company just camped in the middle for this night. At least where they had stopped a clear spot would be left in the road when they moved on.

The hard part of the first encampment was breaking it up in the persistent morning fog. In spite of their leader's insistence on returning tools to the carts when not in use, some items were lost the very first morning. It went hard with the few who could be identified as the careless culprits of those losses, but most equipment had simply been lost with no one knowing who was to blame. Strangely enough, former conscripts of past years were seen to be no more careful than those young men who were called to serve for the first time.

The second day they found the fork in the road and continued northwards. The going was easier and the spirits of the men increased. Until the noon day break. Then a man stepped out of the wood on the western side of the road. He held his hands high. Four men surrounded him as another ten of the cloaked guard with pikes turned toward the direction from which he came. Gidon rode Begleiter toward the wood but could not enter in because the brush was too thick for a man on horseback. He sat his mount peering into the massive undergrowth for movement.

The Baron brought some of the older men to back Gidon up. He also set men to watch in the opposite direction should it be a ruse to misdirect their attention. It would be a great way to have a successful ambush, getting people looking in one direction and hitting them from the other.

The man continued to hold his hands up with palms outward. He shouted, "I am unarmed. I mean you no harm."

With four men of the company guarding him on every side he was brought to Gid-visu at the lead wagon. The Baron, once reasonably sure the area was secure, joined them there.

"Who are you, and why do you approach us?" Gid-visu asked.

"If it please you sir, my name is Jotham. I come from a hamlet located maybe two miles west of here."

"What is the name of your hamlet? Do I know it?" asked the Baron. As a King's Rider he knew more of the land than most people. He knew even hidden places where people of every sort and intent made their home or resting place.

"Sirs, I perceive thou art king's men from your tunics. I ask you to help my people and deliver king's justice to men who now hold all those who yet remain captive," Jotham replied.

"You are getting ahead of yourself man. The Baron asked you a question. What is the name of your hamlet?" Gid-visu returned.

"We call it simply Heim, which in the old tongue means hamlet. We set up our homes on good ground away from others. We only sought for a peaceable life. Thus far we have not been able to decide on a better name. Now we have been taken over by evil men. Most of my neighbors are dead already." Jotham said.

"How is it that you were not taken?" Baron von Krieg asked suspiciously.

"When they came in the night, my father told me to hide myself, and I obeyed. I was close enough to hear the question they asked. When our people would not answer they struck the first down; then hung the second. Finally they resorted to torture. My father was among those tortured but none would speak and tell them what they wanted to know, even to save wives and children." Jotham looked entirely defeated by all he had seen and heard.

"What is it exactly they wanted to know?"

"The varlets had become lost in the woods and fog. They thought it might be they passed the road they sought in the mists. They are planning to join with another group to kill all at the monastery near Eastwatch by the Rising of the Little Dan. They still do not know they are within two miles of the road they seek. They seem to have grown more interested in shaming the women they have not killed already." Jotham said, "We have done our best to save the servants of the Invisible God. They particularly want a man named Bishop Elisha."

"How did it happen you came to the road now?" Gid-visu asked.

"I had thought to get to the monastery to warn them. It was God's good fortune I found you here." Jotham answered.

The Baron called Gidon to him while Gid-visu broke out their woodland green clothing from the wagon. He told Gidon very quickly what the man had claimed and said, before they acted presumptuously, they must check to see if it were true. If it were, they would need a plan before committing themselves to action.

Gidon went to the wagon and began to change his dress. Jotham was still standing there with guards by his side. He asked the man, "Do you know who these men were sent by?"

Jotham answered, "They are the same sort of men we fled from in the kingdom of Goraleck. One man I had seen wearing Goraleck's ensign and working for the tax collector when I lived in his kingdom. That is all I know."

Gid-visu and Gidon dressed in the woodland green and armed with bows and knives back-tracked the path Jotham had taken. It was easy for these two, so familiar with reading sign in the forests, but they doubted that anyone less skilled could have backtracked Jotham's route from the hamlet to the king's road. The undergrowth was heavy much of the way and Jotham had claimed they had been unaware of his presence before he made his escape.

When they came to the hamlet called Heim, it was soon plain these varlets were so self-assured in the remoteness of their location they were not even posting lookouts. Those who were not actively mistreating the captives were amusing themselves watching them be debauched. After making sure they were thoroughly familiar with the terrain and the shape of the hamlet, the two men stealthily withdrew and brought back their report to the King's Rider.

The decision was made to make up a company of men under the command of Baron von Krieg. Some of those chosen had woods experience. And the twenty, who now were nicknamed gold cloaks, would go because the Baron thought it good to broaden their experience. It was thought their dress would intimidate the intruders when the confrontation came. They were repeatedly warned of the necessity to be quiet as they approached the hamlet. They would prepare to retake the village in the clear night and launch the attack at first light using the morning fog to their advantage. They were counting on the eerie impact of the fog to make the situation more confusing for people just waking up with hangovers and tired bodies from forcing fornication on the hamlet's women.

Gid-visu and Gidon moved in close. They could listen in on conversations of the hamlet's captors. They had decided since no menfolk were left, and what remained were women and some girls to sell them as slaves. The invaders decided four men would seek to retrace their steps with the captives they had taken. One laughed to think not only had they enjoyed the women, but now they might be sold in Goraleck's kingdom. King Gregor did not allow unwilling slavery in his kingdom.

It was during this night of stealthy listening Gid-visu discovered all the women who appeared to be with child had already been put to the sword as had most of the older women. This was strange in a way. Women who were pregnant often received a greater price at the slave market. But these men were fearful of being slowed in their retreat. With so many dead and apparently no man left alive in the hamlet of Heim, there was no immediate concern. They had time to plan but knew it would not last. Yet, the place had been turned into such a carnage house Gid-visu and Gidon felt sick just having to spy it out. How could these evil men stand it?

The information would be relayed to the Baron after they completed their own grizzly work. As men fell into stupors caused by drink and debauchery, Gid-visu and Gidon would come upon such and end their lives with a quick slice of the blade. So effective were they in the night's work, a dozen of the evil men would not stir with the morning. And eight women had followed them quietly as they worked their way out of the camp. Some could not, for they were chained to pillars and they could not be released for the noise it would make. But each was quietly told to be of good cheer for their salvation was near.

Gid-visu returned to their encampment to take charge there. It must not fall into disorder while the retaking of Heim was being completed. Most of the men at the camp had not been able to sleep fearing what might happen if Gid-visu or Gidon was discovered, or should the rescue of Heim prove unsuccessful. With the return of Gid-visu, with eight women already freed, the men felt more at ease.

Gidon, who was now very familiar with the way, returned to their camp to slip into his chainmail and tunic in preparation for the morning. He then returned to the attack force. He felt sick at heart for all he had learned about what had happened in this place. Inside welled up a great anger at these invaders. He could not comprehend the minds of those who would slaughter so wantonly as these men.

As the sun rose the first of the invader's dead was found. There arose a general sense of panic among the evildoers as others were also found. It seemed to them, in the wicked agitation of their minds, more of their number were dead than actually were.

There were quite a few eyes looking outwardly now, then as the mists receded the tops of the pikes became visible. It seemed to the fevered imaginations of the evil doers as if they were completely surrounded on all sides. A voice rang out over the hamlet stern and unyielding, "Lay down your weapons!" It was the Baron.

The sound of weapons clattering to the ground was the response to his command. For the present no one could truly see the other. Only the sounds of weapons being dropped and the tops of the pikes were evidence of what was going on. Gidon had found himself an elevated spot looking down into the encampment. Any sign he saw at all to indicate someone was beginning to recover a more-sound state of mind caused him to launch an arrow in that direction. From the sounds that came back he was being effective. Four men would later be found to have been fatally touched by his shafts.

The Baron once more commanded, "Do not move!" He never promised that by complying they would be allowed to live. One noise was unmistakable; someone had fallen on his sword.

As the fog abated a little more, the experienced men among the company moved into the village binding prisoners and directing all toward its center area. This included the surviving women. The gold cloaks tightened their ring around the hamlet, inspecting each hut to see if there was anyone hiding in them. Any who showed reluctance to move received strong encouragement from them. They had no mercy for this enemy after the discoveries they had made checking the area.

Gidon came down and put his bow in a safe place. He thought he would have no more call for it as they dealt with these men. He went with the Baron to look at the man who had fallen on his sword. The Baron remarked coldly that he was probably the leader of this band of killers. Then he said something that struck Gidon as odd. He said, "He was always a bastard butcher." *The Baron had known this man!*

Gidon asked, "Do you think he fell on his sword because he recognized your voice."

"Doubtful. When last he heard my voice, I was screaming and crying," he answered.

Gidon could not ever imagine the Baron screaming and crying…Unless it had something to do with the scars on his back. But he was not going to pursue the subject further with so much to be attentive to.

As the fog cleared away, some older men were working without need of being commanded. They began setting things up for a trial. They brought a goodly chair found in the central lodge hovel. That was the place where the town would often gather. A cart was provided for the chair to set in. The Baron went to mount the cart and sit on the seat when it momentarily became imbalanced. A few of the men and former captives of the invaders laughed, but none of those who had been taken prisoner did. They did not want to further antagonize this man who wore the insignia of King Gregor over his heart. The tongue of the cart was hurriedly weighted down so there would be no further mishaps. It was plain these men were going to be tried before given the King's justice.

One of the fighting priests came forward with table, parchment and ink to record the proceedings. It would go to the king. The other priest set up a separate table where the survivors of the town massacre could record their name, condition in life, and the former occupations of murdered husbands and fathers. There would be two copies of the survivors' names made.

The Baron planned to ask four questions of each prisoner.

1. What is your name?
2. Where are you from?
3. Who is your master?
4. Of what deeds are you guilty of in this place?

Baron von Krieg would then call for all who would give testimony against the man. It would be a long day, but the survivors of Heim would be able to say justice was served to the full.

When the first man was brought forward, he refused to answer any of the questions. But a woman stepped forward. She wore a rag that barely covered her nakedness. Her clothing had been ripped away. She may have been a little over twenty but in the stresses of the past events she looked older and tired. "I would accuse this man m'lord."

"Of what do you accuse him, dear woman?" The Baron spoke to her gently.

"This is the man who entered into our hovel in the middle of the night, killing my husband. He grabbed my crying baby from my arms and smashed its head against the center support. My husband and child are in there still. He came back later and tore my garment off even as I mourned my dead. He then had his way with me." She was embarrassed even to mention what he had done.

"By the raising of your hands did any others see this man do evil?" the Baron asked.

Four women raised their hands. The Baron motioned one of his older men to come to him and whispered in his ear. He nodded and got a small piece of unsplit firewood and set it up below a tree limb, tossing a rope over it.

The Baron said, "Inasmuch as you inflicted pain on many over a short period and refused to cooperate with this hearing, I sentence you No Name to die by slow strangulation. Whereupon your head shall be severed from your body and put on a stake."

Though the man tried to struggle, the rope was tied to the strap that held his hands behind his back. He was pulled up to where he stood flat footed upon the upright tree log. Then the rope was put in a single loop around his neck tightly shutting off some of his wind. As long as he could keep his arms pushed upwards, he could breathe. But if he dropped his arms or lost his balance he would strangle himself. He took a long miserable time to die.

The Baron was about to call for the next prisoner when one hidden behind others worked free of his bonds. He reached down and grabbed one of the spears that had been dropped to the ground hurling it at the Baron in an act of defiance. Gidon reacted almost instinctively. His sword came out of its sheath and brushed aside the spear. He swung his sword in a wide arc cutting down two as he moved toward the attacker. He was about to come down and split the man in twain when he heard the Baron call, "Gidon!"

The man who had hurled the spear was on his knees with one hand held up. He was eager to kill but not eager to be killed.

"Gidon, your swordsmanship is improving remarkably. But let us give this man justice." The Baron spoke very coldly. He had the man brought forward and asked the usual questions. Then after taking the testimony of the survivors he passed sentence. "Because you like the spear so much I sentence you to be thrust through with spears. Then your head will be removed and placed on a pole while your body is burned."

It was plain the ministration of justice would take all the day. At the noon hour the Baron called Gidon to him. "You must ride with all haste and return to Eastwatch. Carry the warning so the monastery is defended. I believe the number they will have to face will be about fifty if there is but one other group. I do not think Goraleck would send three. Also tell them to prepare to receive these who survived this atrocity. Let them have some idea of the number involved." Then he winked. "Tell the Lady Gwynedd I send my love and say hello to Mistress Getrudis for me."

One of the men brought them some drink. They had removed and left their supplies to move speedily to Heim and had been without fluid for several hours.

"When all is secured, catch up to us Gidon. Do not wear your horse out to do so. We have much to do before we resume our march even if we work late into the night. I want to know all is well to our rear when you return." The Baron was worried for Gwynedd. It was a new emotion to him. The concern for his men was far different than concern for his love.

Retrieving his bow Gidon hurried back to their encampment and saddled Begleiter. Gid-visu cautioned him to be careful, reminding him that if he lost Begleiter he would not be able to fulfill his mission. On the way back he spotted the bones of Herr Brute's horse that was lost as he first traveled to Eastwatch. They had probably passed it unnoticed in the fog when first they came by. It served him as a reminder the road was treacherous because of obstacles unseen.

It was quite late in the evening by the time he stopped in front of the Burgomeister's house and informed him of the threat. The

Burgomeister asked, “Do you have any knowledge of a threat to Eastwatch?”

“When I left Heim, we had not yet heard anything mentioned about attacking Eastwatch, but I would do what I could to see to the security of the women.” Gidon replied.

Brute’ sent one of the household guards to rouse the red cloaks. The other three he assigned to take the Burgomeister and the women to Fox Home which was more defensible.

“Gidon, how is Begleiter holding up from your journey?”

“Once he gets a little water, he will be ready to go. I can tell he senses the adventure is not yet over this night and he is up for it.”

“You need to ride to the monastery and warn the priests.” Brute’ said.

“That was also part of the Baron’s orders,” Gidon replied.

“I am sorry you cannot go to Getrudis right now. I know you want to. I cannot travel with Brigitta across the village to Fox Home either. I must check with Fat Max to see if there have been any strangers in town today before I see my men. We will position ourselves to attack the enemy from the rear when they attack the monastery. Be sure the bishop knows that.”

Gidon imagined an enemy behind every bush on the way to the monastery, but the ride was uneventful. Begleiter was showing a little lather and would need to be walked and cooled before put to rest. But the monastery was still at peace. He hailed, and the drawbridge was lowered to him. Bishop Elisha was standing at the portal.

Gidon hurriedly told the bishop of the enemy’s plan. He told Gidon that since they expected to find the defenses down, they should make it appear that way. When a priest took Begleiter and promised to see to his care, the drawbridge stayed down. It was as if the people had not a care in the world. Priests hid along the parapets with crossbows waiting. The two oldest of the fighting priests, Judah the Hammer and Jonathan the Sword, having been released from duties at Fox Home, joined Gidon. So it was that two swords and a hammer would block the way into the monastery, while bolts rained down on those seeking to cross the drawbridge.

Judah told Gidon, "If the attack comes tonight, I suspect it will come before we normally get up for sunrise prayer. You have been going for many hours now. You will be of more use if you rest a little bit. We will put hay just inside the gate and you can spread your cloak upon it. Rested, you will do better when the battle comes."

Gidon quickly agreed. It seemed like he was falling asleep on his feet. But as soon his body got relaxed his mind flooded with the number of men who had died under his hand in the past two days. And now he was waiting to kill some more. It did no good to tell himself these men needed to die for their evil. The fact to him was he had taken that which he could not replace, and when he struck down the last two, he hardly saw them for the rage he felt.

Just before the fourth hour they came. So stealthily they crept forward, the first group was halfway across the drawbridge before even Judah and Jonathan knew they were there. Gidon woke to the clang and thud as the first two men stepped off the drawbridge and through the portal to die by the hands of the fighting priests.

An alert priest began to ring the bell that would let Brute' and his red cloaks know the attack had commenced. It was a miracle how a sudden wind swept the fog away from the bridge and those with crossbows on the parapet covered every square foot on the drawbridge with a prearranged bolt. Not a living soul remained on the drawbridge and the response made the rest hesitate to charge into what looked like certain death. But crossbows take a little bit of time to reload.

As one man, Judah, Gidon, and Jonathan charged out on the drawbridge their blood now singing with the energy of battle. The two swords side by side seemed to give Judah no chance at hitting an enemy, for the swords' wide arcs passed over the whole of the drawbridge width. But the thuds behind them meant some had slipped past the swords. Perhaps when some clangs sounded of metal on metal, the men had blocked blows and twisted by in the darkness. When they had fought to the very end of the bridge, with crossbow bolts flying overhead, they retreated again to the portal. But a roar of fifty throats sounding as one meant the enemy had been caught unawares from the rear.

When the battle was done the red cloaks had lost eight men killed and ten wounded. The monastery had lost none. Brute' thought this an acceptable number considering men who had never been in battle had just utterly destroyed an armed group twice its size. The Baron had been wrong in his estimate of enemy strength. It mattered not to Brute' fully half or more enemy had fallen to crossbow bolts shot from the parapets. The men of the red cloak, who lived to fight another day, would be even more formidable the next time they met an enemy in battle.

The commander of the enemy force survived. However, he had a bolt in one shoulder, where it lodged. He was a hard fellow who plainly had seen many battles. His one comment was that he should have waited for the rest of his force, but it looked like an easy victory. Gidon could not resist saying to him, "If you had waited for the rest of your force you would have had to wait into eternity, for that is where they are."

When the enemy commander was told of the conduct of his men at Heim, he was genuinely apologetic. He said that he had not chosen the man who led that band. The man was thrust upon him because he had favor in higher places. He considered him no more than a man whose mind reveled in causing others pain. Knowledge that he fell on his sword rather than go down fighting, and risk capture, surprised him not at all.

The commander would answer no questions, but the bishop took his papers saying they would no doubt give some clues. But Gidon knew the one behind the whole attack had been Goraleck because of what had been said without trying to give out secrets.

The enemy commander had but two requests. He asked leniency for his men who survived and begged for himself an honorable death. Brute' personally thrust him through, allowing him to keep his head. A cairn of huge stone was later built for him on the side of the road between the monastery and Eastwatch.

The ride back to Eastwatch went slowly. Gidon was thoroughly tired. Before he had left the monastery, he asked Judah the Hammer if he also felt weakened after the battle. He said, "Yes, both I and my brother do. There is always a kind of exhausted let down after a fight, whether the battle was quick or prolonged. But I and my brother have a source of strength from the Invisible God you do not yet know of. It will come."

He rode into the stable and saw Herman the Schmeid. "Take care of Begleiter for me, please. Give him our very best for he has well-earned it these past few days."

"You can depend on me," said the schmeid.

"I know I can my friend."

The schmeid was speechless. Gidon had just called him his friend for the first time.

"Oh, and by the way Herman. There is a woman coming here from a place called Heim. They should be here tomorrow or the next day. There are many women coming, but this one is the newly made widow of a blacksmith. She is a comely woman with a good head on her shoulders. She has been through a lot but would make some man a fine and dependable wife after her time of mourning is over. When they get here, you might want to seek her out." Gidon had surprised himself telling this, but it seemed the right thing to do.

Herman was amazed that Gidon had been looking around for him a suitable wife even as he was making war and getting himself covered with blood again. Herman thought, *What a friend I have in Gidon!*

When Gidon got to the door of Fox Home he was met by one of the Burgomeister's guardsmen. But inside the door he was overwhelmed by the sweet embrace of Getrudis. She was not one bit discouraged by the bloody clothes he wore, only asking, "Have you any hurt, my love?"

As soon the noise of Gidon's return had rung through the house the boy who tends the fires had begun heating the sauna and wash water. Soon Gidon would be cleansed. The fire boy sneakily hoped to catch a glimpse of Getrudis' body. The little scoundrel!

Gidon, holding Getrudis in his arms, said to Brunhild and Gwynedd, "Your men sent their greetings and affections."

Brigitta said, "How is my darling Brute'?"

"He is without harm, my lady. He has eight dead and ten wounded that must be attended, before he can march his men home. But as far as I could see, he was without injury."

The house staff took Gidon's tunic and chainmail into another room to be cleaned. Blood had soaked through the chainmail even into the woolen undergarment. It too was carefully pulled over his head. The scar he had gotten from Leviathan had opened up a little sometime in the fight. He was left in his under breeches with his bare chest disclosed. Someone thoughtfully brought him a sheet to wrap himself in. He did feel a bit of a chill.

Gidon told the women about the survivors of the massacre at Heim. He relayed how the men had died rather than reveal how close this enemy was to the road to Eastwatch. All of the men had died and not a few women and children, except for one man. Gidon said he expected the man would be taken with them to stand before King Gregor who would want to know more. He did not elaborate on how the women had been shamefully treated. He did not enjoy the thought of any woman being treated badly and supposed it likely the women would know even more about it than he did in the days to come.

Snaggle Tooth quietly sat on his haunches, straining his neck forward to lay his great head in his lap. Gidon found petting the sabretooth strangely soothing. He told Getrudis the whole village knows she has the tiger. He did not want her going out without him for the next few days.

Brunhild had the staff bring Gidon boiled eggs, cheese, and bread. With a few drams of goatmilk, it was a truly refreshing meal. Everyone wanted to know what had happened at the monastery so he told about the priests with their crossbows and Judah the Hammer with Jonathan the Sword at the portal. Someone said, "Where were you during all this Gidon?"

"Me? Oh, I was asleep on a pile of hay!"

A silence filled the room. If he was asleep how did he know all that had happened? If he was asleep how did he get so covered with blood? After the long silence it got through to all he was not going to talk about what he had done, and that was that.

Shortly thereafter Getrudis and Gidon, wrapped in the same sheet, walked together as they made their way to the sauna. Both had towels about their waists to sit on, but they enjoyed the closeness of sharing the sheet as they entered into the building. Only the fire boy was disappointed.

The sauna brought much relief to the stresses his activities had put upon his body. But the loving ministrations of Getrudis left him thoroughly relaxed through and through. He thrilled to her touch and to touching her. He wondered if she was as moved as he was until a little sound escaped her lips and he knew her body was responding deeply to his caresses. It could have continued forever had they not gotten too heated in there. They doused their bodies with water and rushed out toward the washroom giving the fire boy more to see and dream about than he had ever hoped for.

The wash proved more a cause for cuddles than for washing. Getrudis did get Gidon's hair cleaned of other men's blood. She rejoiced that except for some new bruises, which were ugly enough, he had no new cuts. Snaggle Tooth had wandered into the room and seemed to be thoroughly enjoying himself by just being with them.

To make accommodation for new sleeping arrangements for the night, Gwynedd and Brunhild became bedfellows, leaving the Burgomeister and his wife the room normally set aside for the Baron. Brigitta moved to the room where the fireplace was in Gidon's chambers, leaving the guards instruction where to send Brute' whenever he came in.

Gidon and Getrudis were back in the cot that was beginning to smell a lot like a sabretooth tiger. Gidon said to Getrudis, "I have not done my pushups lately."

Getrudis laughed and said, "Are you planning to do the one where you lay on your back again?"

They never got around to doing his workout that night. There was too much joy in simply looking into one another's eyes and feeling their bodies touching.

Fox Home's fire boy thought he had finished his day of work. He found out differently when Brute' came. Brute' began snatching off his tunic and chainmail when he was scarcely through the door, giving orders the fire boy should be roused and set to work. Brigitta rose up and smothered him with kisses. She said, "I shall have to inspect you thoroughly to make sure you are unharmed!"

It was past noonday on the second day after the Battle of the Monastery before the survivors of the Heim massacre appeared. Lady Gwynedd and Brigitta had blue cloaked messengers running every which way all morning to try and find ways to honor them for their sacrifice and provide for their immediate need. It was a big undertaking that proved beneficial to many.

Chapter 19

Heim Grows Eastwatch

The staff of Fox Home had been well chosen by Brunhild. They had every bit of Gidon's clothes and chainmail cleaned and pressed by morning. Getrudis rose before Gidon. He always waited so he could enjoy watching her stretch. She put on her huntress garb to please him, and they walked together with Snaggle Tooth. Not as many dared to come up to them when they were with the great cat, even though the village knew he bore mankind no ill will. They did make for quite a picture though. The gallant squire in chainmail, tunic, and cloak; His lady dressed in woodland green, holding his arm; and, a sabretooth tiger by her side.

They walked down to the stables where Gidon asked Snaggle Tooth to wait outside. He wanted no animal hysterics this morning and the stable now held several ponies which had never seen the sabretooth. Begleiter bugled a welcome as soon as he heard Gidon's voice, stamping his feet as if to say, *I am ready to go, if you are.* But when the couple walked over to his pen he held his head out to Getrudis.

Gidon asked, "How is it all my animals like you better than me?"

"Are they all not males?" She pertly replied. "You like me better too!"

Herman was standing by waiting to hear Gidon's inspection of his work.

"Herman, you like me better than Gidon too, do you not?" Getrudis was teasing him, but his face turned all red and he could not speak coherently. He wanted to run.

"Dear heart, do not tease Herman so. He is all alone with no woman of his own. Such a question can be unsettling to a man." Gidon said. "Besides that, look at all the hard work he has put in getting my equipment clean and Begleiter checked over. I imagine he has been up most the night so his guard is down."

Getrudis walked over to Herman the Schmeid, touched his arm, and gave a little curtsy, "I am sorry sir if I have caused you disquiet. Gidon and I consider you among the very best of our friends, and a trusted enabler of our work."

There is no doubt Herman would never forget this morning, and he would hold a secret love for Getrudis to his dying day.

After Getrudis' words to Herman, Gidon could do no less than shake his hand as he praised his good work, before they departed for the tavern.

The sabretooth could cause some discomfort in the confined space of a tavern so they entered through the kitchen. This caused the immediate exit of a little pet goat that had taken to wandering in and out of the area looking for a treat.

Oma, after giving them both a hug, went into the main room to announce Squire Gidon and Mistress Getrudis were about to enter with their pet tiger. In this way no one was taken by surprise. Gidon told Oma he wished to speak to her and Fat Max when they had time.

Gidon, as a matter of course, now took the seat in the corner leaning his sword and staff against the walls on either side. If Max thought anything at all about this change in behavior from the days before the King's Rider came, he did not show it.

Oma brought the couple Gidon's favorite morning meal, called a farmer's breakfast, with a special plate for Snaggle Tooth that she sat before him on the floor. He ate very delicately. He even got a bowl of goat's milk as a special treat, which he lapped without getting up, holding the bowl between his great paws. People in the tavern became fascinated with watching him. One jokester was heard to say Snaggle Tooth had better manners when he ate than some of the people who came in the tavern.

The people lingered longer than usual, but finally most of the morning crowd had departed. Max and Oma came over and joined the couple. Gidon filled them in on the invasion of Heim and the pitiful condition the survivors had been left in. He told them it was likely they would arrive today, and if not that, sometime tomorrow. He pointed out the refugees would be composed of young widows, maids, and girls. All had suffered great indignities, as had Durchgefüweg before she came to them. He said these people had shown themselves people of character since they had not told their captors how to get to Eastwatch. He was sure the tavern could find good and reliable helpers amongst these people. Max and Oma were hopeful.

Gidon and Getrudis talked during the morning with some more of the villagers about the folks who were coming from Heim. Many of the unattached men hoped that in time they might find suitable wives among those who were coming. It was not known to very many the depths of mistreatment these people had suffered. When Durchgefüweg came to the table she was told a little more than others. She would not only be more sympathetic because of her own ordeals, but she would also keep confidence.

Brute' and Brigitta came in for the noon meal. It was then Gidon learned the commander of the attacking force had asked for those men who had survived clemency. They were now in the Burgomeister's dungeon guarded by Squire Ohtrad, and some red cloaks, while the blue cloaks guarded the home. The young squire had been hurt in the fighting, though not badly. He had kept it secret until it became a problem. It showed up as they brought the captives back to the dungeon. It was commendable, that upon discovering how much greater the force than estimated, Ohtrad had called on inner resources of his young manhood to try and see the job completed.

Herr Brute' asked Gidon what he thought they should do with them? Gidon appreciated the honor of being asked. He replied, "If the local people learned all that the other force had done at Heim their lives would be worthless. But if we could have their pledges of good conduct, we might put them to work outside the village. If they could be guarded with a minimal number of men, they could serve useful purpose in building the road out of Eastwatch toward Almanya. Perhaps we would not ever again lose a good horse to that difficult stretch."

Brute' said, "I do not think any will be interested in soon returning to Goraleck. He does not reward failure. It might work. We would only have to feed them and provide tools."

"And they would be out of the village," Brigitta added.

"Brute', the wolf men are known as road builders. We are talking about around twenty miles of road. How long would such a project last?" Gidon asked.

"It depends on just how good a road you want." Brute' replied. "But I am sure we can find more for them to do after that little job is finished. We could get carried away with the project and build a solid road all the way to Almanya."

They all laughed, but in the conversation an idea was born.

It was not long after news of people coming from Heim was noised about Eastwatch a group was seen arriving. It was being escorted by those seasoned veterans of the village the Baron had decided could be most spared from the king's muster. Their families would rejoice circumstance had brought them home early.

Some of the first to hear the news came out and lined the roadway. Notables like the Burgomeister and his wife waited on the village green. Lady Gwynedd and Mistress Brunhild were also there with them, flanked by the village elders.

Master at Arms Brute' found he did not have to call out his red cloaks. Neither did he have to call for his war steed. Herman brought his horse, saddled and ready, while thirty men fell into formation behind him. Of the eight dead and ten wounded, plus two on guard at the dungeon it was evident not one man of those available for duty was absent. Brute' was proud of them.

Lady Brigitta stayed with Gidon and Getrudis, a woman on either side of the tiger, watching the events unfold.

To Gidon it seemed the women and girls of Heim were only slightly better dressed than they had been when first rescued. Many could not endure reentering their hovels. Not for the sake of getting some clothing and meager possessions in any case. It was too painful to witness the awful condition a loved one's body was in. Most dead lay where they had been murdered. And when a few of the clothes brought out were discovered to have pieces of dead fathers, husbands, mothers, or children in them they could not bring themselves to wash and put them on. Anyone with no idea of what had happened would consider them a sorry lot to look upon. Gidon saw a certain nobility in these survivors of atrocity. He knew what they had been through and for what cause many had sacrificed their lives.

As the women and girls were escorted into the village it seemed they were first caught up with the enormity of it all. More than one pointed out the sabretooth cat standing between the two women; one dressed in woodland green like a huntswoman, the other in finer garb than they had ever known.

A woman pointed Gidon out, "That is the man who came in my hovel at night and slit the throat of the invader who had been hurting me."

One woman was heard to say to her fellows walking beside her. "He is a wild man. Did you see the way he cut those men down to get the spearman?"

Another woman asked, "Are they his women?" This earned Gidon a glare from Herr Brute' who had heard that remark too.

"He looks so young to be so scarred. He is as frightening as the knight on the horse. Yet, I am glad he came to rescue us."

Things were going fairly smoothly but as the red cloaks began to try to help in guiding the women toward the green, the women and girls began to feel as if they were being herded. This brought up the memories of what they had just been through. Beginning with the youngest more and more were sobbing and crying.

The people of Eastwatch began to go among the women embracing them and trying to reassure all was well. It was in the midst of this Bishop Elisha appeared. He said, "I know many of you women and especially you girls are very footsore and exhausted. But if you will follow me to the Cathedral, and not the green, you will have places to sit. We will bring you water and food and then see to other needs. If any must lie down, you may do so on the pews. None will think the worse of you for taking rest in God's house."

His demeanor brought great comfort to the women. Could this be none other but the Bishop Elisha their captives had wanted to kill? He seemed so kindly and good compared to those who had wished him ill. Why would anyone want to harm so godly a man?

The men who escorted the survivors tried to give a list of the people they brought; first to Herr Brute' and then to the Burgomeister. The Burgomeister, pleased to get rid of some of the responsibility for the people, directed them to give it to the bishop. Some of the escort, seeing they were more familiar to the women, offered to stay close at hand to help them feel more secure. Most of these men had wives, and those who lived inside the village soon joined by them. Each effort helped the people who had suffered so much get back to a semblance of normalcy.

Gidon came into the Cathedral with Getrudis. Snaggle Tooth waited patiently on the steps with Brigitta. Some of the people Gidon had rescued came up to thank him, meet his lady, and inquire how he came to have a sabretooth tiger?

Brigitta walked in beside Snaggle Tooth. "I could not stop him. He just decided to come in." The women of Heim began retreating away from the great cat.

The bishop called out, "No need to fear Snaggle Tooth. He is one of God's special creatures. I suspect he is interested in the children. He had a great time awhile back playing with the children at the monastery. He would never intentionally hurt a child."

Snaggle Tooth walked over to Gidon and Getrudis. Gidon got down on his knees and scratched under his jaw while Getrudis scratched behind an ear. He put his right paw on Gidon's shoulder as he often did, but this time Gidon was a little off balance and nearly fell over. A titter came out of the lips of the children as they watched this strange sight. Brigitta scratched him between his shoulder blades and the purr that sounded from inside him was heard throughout the sanctuary.

Bishop Elisha told the children, "I would not advise you to do that with every great cat. Most are very dangerous. Snaggle Tooth is only dangerous to someone who he thinks threatens those he considers his."

One little girl came forward, "Can I touch him?"

Getrudis said, "You can stroke him as one might a house cat."

The little girl stroked the big cat and she began crying. Brigitta was on the same side she was standing. She put her arms around her and said, "Why are you crying sweetie?"

"The bad men came and they beat my kitty to death. He was the same color as this kitty, only he was little. But he was sweet too like this kitty." The tears did not diminish, but grew harder. Snaggle Tooth responded to her tears trying to rub against her.

"Maybe your mommy can get you a new kitten soon." Brigitta was trying to comfort the girl but now the tears really flowed.

"They killed mommy and daddy too!"

The Burgomeister brought his wife into the sanctuary in time to hear the little girl's words and see Brigitta clutching her tightly. Brigitta's mother moved forward to kneel beside her daughter and also wrap an arm around the little girl. "My husband, we have another grandchild." That night a little girl named Geliebter would sleep in the softest bed she had ever known in her life. And in keeping with her name, she would soon become the beloved of the Burgomeister's house.

Bishop Elisha, however, had a problem. It was true the Cathedral's building offered the largest shelter in Eastwatch. What was lacking was any kind of privacy or convenience. Narrow pews made poor beds for the very reason they were hard and narrow, not designed to give comfort to the body. It was the best to be had at the moment, and the situation was pressing. These people had seen much misery.

Some of the problems with providing for people would sort itself out with the offer of employment from such people as Fat Max and Oma. Max was not able to come to meet the women right away, so Oma came bringing Durchgefüweg. She had proven herself an industrious and hardworking young woman. They wanted to get a look at the women straight away. This way they had a greater selection of people to choose from and offer work.

Oma went to the bishop, who had the list of women and their backgrounds. He could not offer any direct suggestions about who among the refugees to talk to. Heim had been so poor a hamlet there was no tavern, nor even a place where one might buy food. In fact, there had been no gold or silver in the place. They had not even the basest coin that might be directly exchanged for goods and services. All things were bartered or traded, goods for goods, as it had always been over most of the world. No one had any experience of working in a tavern or inn. Most had an idea they were all alike; the most disreputable places they had ever heard of.

Finally, the bishop stood at the top of the steps to the altar where he could be readily seen. He spoke directly. "Women of Heim, we have Oma, the wife of the proprietor of our local tavern. She is here with Durchgefüweg, who works at the tavern. Our tavern is a reputable place to work. It is expanding and they have recently acquired another place on the far side of the village. They need help from honest hardworking women like yourselves. They are not offering you charity but an honest place to work. Many who are part of the tavern staff have been there many years. If you are interested in such work you may speak to them tonight."

About twenty women and a few girls lined up to talk to Oma and Durchgefüweg. All were thrilled with the idea of getting clothing of their own, along with food and a place to rest. They would even be cared for while learning their jobs. Oma kept emphasizing that all employees must always keep clean. They had to take complete baths at least once a week. Most considered themselves fortunate to have gotten a complete bath once a year in the past. Four women and two girls went home with Oma and Durchgefüweg that night.

Herman the Schmeid came into the sanctuary and approached the bishop. He had of course removed his cap as he entered the sanctuary but instead of folding it and putting it away, he kept nervously fidgeting with it. The bishop looked upon Herman with some amusement. "What is it that you are wanting, Herman?"

Herman could not keep from stammering in his shyness. Finally, he managed to blurt out, "A wife!"

"Now what would you do with a wife?" The bishop asked.

"Love her! That is, Gidon told me a woman was coming who might suit me for a wife. It would be good to have someone to talk to and be with." Herman was all red and deep down he was questioning what would a woman want with him?

"Where would you put a woman Herman? Do you expect she would live in the little space you have at the stables?" The bishop went on to say he would need to build a home.

"Sir, the Mistress of Fox Home and Mistress Getrudis have made certain promises about that. But you are probably right. It was folly for me to think about a wife and I should leave." Herman stared at his feet miserably. His hat was beginning to come loose at the seam.

"Wait a minute Herman. I did not mean you should forget it. I just want to make sure you know how serious is the thing you are talking about. If you have some plan to provide for a wife that is another matter." The bishop saw the abused women of Heim were not the only fragile creatures in the sanctuary.

Once again Bishop Elisha stood up and spoke in a loud voice. "Who is it here that was related to the schmeid of Heim? Herman, the schmeid of Eastwatch, would like to meet you." Not one but three females came forward. One was a woman of about thirty years; the next was a woman of probably fifteen years; the third was a girl of about nine years. The older woman stood nearly as tall as Herman and looked to be very strong. The second was a head shorter but also appeared to be familiar with work. The little girl was just beginning to show the evidences of her femininity.

The bishop crossed his arms. He had not expected this. After all, he had not had much time to study the list of persons his priests had recorded at Heim.

Herman had set down on a bench in his discouragement. Now with three females before him, he hastily regained his feet. But he stood there mutely not knowing what to say.

The older woman said, "He is tall enough and strong enough to make a good blacksmith I would think. The question is if he is smart enough?"

Herman had thought he was going to interview a prospective wife. Now he felt himself under inspection. He simply said, "There are a lot of things I do not know, but the smith at the monastery is teaching me. I am under indenture to Gid-visu of Fox Home. It is his son who is over there with the sabretooth."

The woman said, "I met Master Gid-visu at Heim. It was he who rescued us in the night. He killed two men to set us free."

The younger woman said, "Momma, he is not bad looking. Do you think he will be gentle with us? I could not bear to have a man who is mean or violent." All this time the young girl was shyly looking on, standing with her toes pointed in so her legs were tightly together where they met.

Herman said to the younger woman, "I am very lonely. I do not have much and probably never will. But I have never been mean to people...Well I did hit a bully once, but only once. If you want to consider me, I can only say I will work hard so you never regret it."

The older woman said, "Do you know what has been done to us?"

"I know it was something awful. That is all I know." Herman said.

"Neither of my daughters still have their flowers unbroken. But it was not of their will. Can you accept that and never find cause to hate them for it?" The older woman was quite serious with him.

"How could I blame someone for something that was not of their making?" Herman replied equally seriously. The girl slipped her little hand into his huge, hard right hand.

The older woman looked at the bishop and said, "Okay, we will take him."

When Herman left the Cathedral with three women following him, he was not quite sure which woman he had become engaged to marry. But he was sure it would work itself out. For tonight the women would have to content themselves sleeping on the straw in the stables. Tomorrow they would begin making a place to live.

Getrudis had spotted a young woman who appeared about fifteen sitting apart from the rest. She was footsore from the trudge from Heim to Eastwatch. All she owned had been carried on her back. In a strange way she reminded her of Brigitta after Gidon had rescued her from the kidnappers. In spite of her small size and youth, she brought more than most of the refugees. She had even tied a cooking pot and a wooden ladle to the bundle whose rope straps had worn her shoulders sore.

For some reason the other women seemed to ignore or avoid this particular girl. There really did not seem to be anything to distinguish her above the rest. Perhaps she might be considered prettier than some, but that would hardly be cause for segregating her from her fellows. Getrudis' curiosity was aroused. She went to her and brushed her blond hair from her face. The girl looked up and Getrudis looked into the prettiest blue eyes she had ever seen.

"If you sit apart from the others you might not get help for your feet when the Hospitaller comes." Getrudis said.

"The other women do not want me to sit with them." She answered very definitely.

"Why is that poor girl? You smell no worse than the rest." Getrudis said.

In spite of herself the girl snickered. But then she said, "The women never want me around because I am not like them. Even before the bad men came, they would often drive me away."

Getrudis patiently sought to get to the heart of the matter, sensing the girl had an interesting story. "Why did they drive you away?"

"My momma was violated by Norsemen who came up the river on which our old home was located. It was their raids and the cruelty of the servants of Goraleck that caused us to migrate to Heim. Momma bore me when the time became full after her misfortune. She was always weak after I was born and died not long after I was weaned. Her father, my grandfather, blamed me for momma's death because I look a little different from the other girls in our hamlet. He said there was no possibility his son had been my father. He named me Freyja, to shame me I suppose. He meant to imply I would sleep with dwarfs or turn those who loved me into boars. It was as if he was wanting to put a curse on me. He did tolerate me most of the time because I kept home for him. But he let everyone know that I was not the child of momma's husband but of some Norseman. They shunned me because they hate the Norse. Then I began to dream dreams that came true. They started whispering maybe I was the seed of some kind of witch-man, and I was a vala. I learned to keep my dreams to myself. But when I dreamed Goraleck's men were coming to invade Heim, I thought that too important not to tell. I might have been burned for a vala, had not the dream proved true the night after I told it. They all think it was my fault." The girl looked down as she was doing when Getrudis approached. She expected that by being honest she would be rejected again.

"Tell me," said Getrudis, "who is your god?"

"I worship the one True God, the Invisible God and His Son." My mother taught me from my birth to do so. She believed the reason the Norsemen had their way with her was because the Evil One had put it in the Norsemen's hearts to abuse her. She said the Norsemen worshipped the Evil One through their false gods."

Getrudis made a decision. "I do not think you are a vala nor any other kind of hexen. Would you like to come with me and be my handmaid? I am a common girl, like yourself, who is the mistress of Squire Gidon. If you wish to come with me, the one thing I can promise is that no one would dare to mistreat you while my lord and master lives."

The girl looked up and smiled through her tears, "Yes, thank you. I am a violated woman by Goraleck's men, but I am honest and true. I pledge you will find me so."

Getrudis called Gidon to her side. "My darling, this is Freyja. She needs people who care about her. I have asked her if she would like to be my handmaid and she said yes. May I keep her? She will be the first member of our house separate from your father's."

Freyja looked at Getrudis and Gidon. "I will begin a new life with you. Perhaps it would be alright for me to have a new name as well?"

"Do you have a name you would like to take as your own?" Gidon asked.

"No m'lord, but the one I have was given to shame me." Freyja felt afraid. She was putting her future name and its power into this man's hands.

"Then I suggest you be no more called Freyja, but Frauke, for you appear to me a little lady indeed." Gidon said.

Getrudis spoke out, "I think that is wonderful! What do you think Freyja, shall you be Frauke for ever more?"

Frauke was amazed that she had been asked her opinion. But she knew also, after the custom of the people, if he exercised lordship over her by giving her a new name, she was bound to him and his authority always. The girl got on her knees before Gidon and Getrudis and kissed their hands. She said, "I am Frauke, and I am yours now and forever."

Gidon had not realized what he was doing until it was done. He looked at Getrudis and she smiled up at him with that wonderful smile that always melted his heart.

Snaggle Tooth was trying to figure out what was going on, so he smelled the girl and looked up inquiringly first to Gidon and then to Getrudis. It was Getrudis, not Gidon, who spoke to the great cat. "It is alright Snaggle Tooth. She belongs to Gidon too."

You could almost see the tigers mind trying to process it all. *What kind of pride was his human building?*

Bishop Elisha came over and said, "From what I was seeing from the other side of the sanctuary, I think you have something to tell me."

So Gidon explained the name change that would have to be recorded as well as the commitment that was made.

The bishop asked, "Do you intend to take her?"

Gidon had not thought of that part of her agreeing to be under his authority. "No, she will be Getrudis handmaid. Anything I do will be for Frauke's good, not my pleasure. I never knew a man could be so happy as I am with Getrudis."

A little sound escaped from Getrudis' lips. Frauke thought to herself that she had never known two people could love one another as did her new master and mistress. Dare she hope one day someone might love her like that in spite of all that had happened to her?

Gidon apologized to Frauke that she would have to walk again on hurting feet. But the distance to Fox Home was not far. He shouldered her pack and promised to treat her feet when they got there. So, the three of them, with Snaggle Tooth leading the way, walked through the village.

It was a good thing the Burgomeister and his people had left Fox Home, Gidon thought. The place was getting a little crowded. Frauke would make her pallet in the front room with the fireplace, in Gidon's chambers. Gidon was trying to avoid the reality that tomorrow he would have to mount Begleiter and once again head north.

Gidon and Getrudis had left too early to know Getrudis had started a fashion trend. Several of the younger women from Heim found employment as handmaids to some of the elder's wives. By the time all that could be done the first day was accomplished, less than ten women were still uncertain about their immediate futures. The bishop was pleased.

*****

Of all the women abused by the invaders of Heim, only one resulted in the conceiving a child. It was as the bishop expected. Traumatic assault upon a woman rarely does end in pregnancy. But there was still to be a baby boom in Eastwatch. It could be dated back to the night of the double wedding. Romance broke out among the villagers at that time, and then again around the first and second anniversaries of Heim coming to Eastwatch. With time wounds even of the heart heal, and love is the reward of patience.

*****

Fox Home stayed up late with the arrival of Frauke. Getrudis spoke in front of Frauke saying Gidon should do what he had done for Brigitta when she was carried off to get her feet better. Gidon responded that he did not think making her a pair of fur lined shoes would help in Frauke's case.

Getrudis said a little teasingly, “You did rub Brigitta’s feet, did you not?”

Gidon grinned at her and said, “It was Brute’ who massaged her feet and rubbed ointment into them.”

Getrudis was not through teasing. “Well maybe we should send for Brute’.”

Gidon came right back and said, “I would not advise that if you want to keep Brigitta as a friend. From what I have heard she believes all his foot rubbing belongs to her.”

They both laughed. Frauke was amazed at how they acted with one another. She had never in her young life seen a man and a woman behave this way.

The fire boy was disappointed that after he had water heating for the tub he was sent to the Apothecary for ointment. He was very curious about the pretty woman Gidon and Getrudis brought home. Unfortunately for him, Getrudis knew it.

*****

The next day was a busy one for almost all residents of Eastwatch. And it was a sad one for Gidon and Getrudis. Most people were stirred into action because of the sizable increase in population survivors of Heim made in the village. The bishop was out early making his rounds to the homes where the women of Heim had found a place. He was distributing fabric from the former business of the Druid Jacklyn for the making of garments. He often found people were already getting busy making clothing when he arrived.

At the tavern Oma had told him the four women and two girls she had hired were up and wanting to work before the sun. They had been amazed to discover that Oma was very serious about the fact they needed appropriate clothing as well as recovery time before they could serve the tavern. This was as important as the training she would give them.

Getrudis had taken her time dressing Gidon for the journey while the kitchen prepared him food to eat till he caught up with the company led by the Baron and his father. They walked slowly to the stable where they met an almost deliriously happy schmeid. Herman told Gidon he had woken to discover the mother he had brought home had made him breakfast, and the daughter served it to him before he left his pallet. They had industriously fed animals, which even the little girl took part in. And the little girl followed him everywhere. Much to her delight he had given her a ride on his broad shoulders.

Begleiter was ready to go, so it was only a matter of positioning his weapons and loading the other things he had brought with him. He could hardly drag himself away from Getrudis but he knew he had to go. He was not going straight up the road to Almanya, but by way of Herman One Eye's hovel, now being farmed by Wolfgang the youngest son. He wanted him to know of the women who had not yet found homes. He and his mother might like to meet them to see if suitable wives might be found for him and his brothers.

Gidon sighed, It was going to be a long day, and who knew what might happen other than the Invisible God? His arm encircled Getrudis little waist and he pulled her to him. He saw her wince and knew he had held her too tight. But she had not complained. He kissed her long and deeply wishing the moment would not end. But the lonely road ahead would not be denied.

Chapter 20

Company for the Journey

Riding away from Getrudis this time was even harder than leaving her had ever been before. It had only been a combination of tragedies that had returned him home before the training waiting at Almanya had been accomplished. Through those tragedies Gidon came to see how each person who was made a victim at Heim, was not only victimized in multiple ways, but their rescuers truly became a kind of victim as well. He had taken human life at Heim and later in defense of the monastery. His ledger of killing had reached the point where he was no longer sure how many had died because of him. But each death coalesced into a burden that had not gotten any lighter. He began to understand more and more how men without some softening influence would outwardly appear so hard.

At least the first few hours of Gidon's journey had some immediate purpose. He had thought to bring beer in a pottery bottle so he and Wolfgang might share a drink while he told the news. He needed to know there were women needing homes and husbands. Gidon considered Wolfgang the best of Herman One Eye's children, with Ohtrad running a far distant second. He knew that at least Wolfgang might benefit from a good woman. The other brothers had too much of their father in them. It was likely they were not ready for the responsibility of a woman. It would really take some special kind of women to turn them into better men. Just any woman would not benefit any of them, was his opinion, and they would only cause the wrong women pain.

When Gidon got to the hovel, he could not bring himself to ride straight into the household area. As he looked about for a possible threat, he could not help being impressed how Wolfgang and his mother were rapidly turning their former hut into a cottage. There was no longer any question about who was better sheltered, animals or people. Yet the animals were faring better as well. It made Gidon feel better about sharing the news of the women from Heim. Possibly a wounded spirit might find a new start in life with Wolfgang.

Wolfgang was not in the household area but out with the goats when Gidon rode into the farmyard. His mother sounded the hunter's horn. It was made from a cow horn of about two spans length, and its tone not unpleasant. No doubt its sound would soon reach wherever he was on their small bit of land.

Gidon rested by the well with Begleiter taking a sip from the trough every now and then. The warm sun made him feel like dozing, but even though he did not consider this family a threat any longer, it seemed napping was a luxury he could not afford. Diligence was not only a matter of survival but also a matter of establishing how others saw you. He was beginning to appreciate the importance of people's perceptions.

"Good day, Squire Gidon. I thought you now well on your way to Almanya. Are you bringing me word of my father or my brothers?" Wolfgang was speaking even as he came into the area. From his belt hung a brace of rabbits that had no doubt run afoul of his traps.

"Greetings, Wolfgang. The only news I have of your brothers was that Ohtrad was wounded defending the monastery from a band who appeared to be sent by the false king Goraleck. He was not badly hurt but I do not doubt he is using it to get attention from some of the girls of the village." Gidon responded.

Wolfgang laughed. "I think he has a lecherous eye. If any woman takes him as husband, she will have to be willing to do something to keep him in line. I hope Herr Brute' rides him hard." There was no doubt Wolfgang understood his brother.

Wolfgang's mother spoke. "We have had no visitors or passersby since we returned from Ohtrad's anointing as squire to Herr Brute'. We did not even know there had been a battle at the monastery. We hope Bishop Elisha and the rest of the people there are well?"

"All at the monastery are well but we did lose some men of the guard in the fighting." After answering some questions, Gidon went on to say, "But there was another conflict at a place called Heim. A group of the people sent to attack the monastery had taken that hamlet and behaved shamefully. The company led by Baron von Krieg and my father took it back and freed the survivors, most of whom were women and older girls. They left Heim escorted by a group of our veteran fighters and came to live in Eastwatch. There were about ten women, still housed in the Cathedral when I left. I thought maybe Wolfgang might find a wife, or even wives for some of his brothers among these women."

Wolfgang grinned and said humorously, "And I bet you had no part in the deliverance of these women."

"Well, the Baron and my father did have me do a few things not worthy of mention,' Gidon spoke modestly.

Wolfgang's mother spoke. "I think I might be a better judge of the women, and see if I can find some who might make Wolfgang and his brothers' wives.

"Wolfgang, hitch the goat cart and I will travel to Eastwatch to see about this".

To Gidon she said, "My son does not have time to leave the farm right now."

Gidon thought she might be right at least where Wolfgang's brothers were concerned. He gave her two coins, one to present to Herman the Schmeid to care for her goats. The other coin would buy her lodging and food at the tavern. Otherwise she might be in a situation where she had to go hungry and without shelter.

Gidon handed them the pot of beer saying, "I must go. I have many miles to travel before next I rest." He was not going to stop and share a drink after all. He had already stopped longer than he intended.

It was good to depart with people waving in a friendly manner behind him.

*****

The journey down the road, farther and farther away from Getrudis was not pleasant to his heart. He had traveled for no more than an hour since leaving Wolfgang before the aching loneliness and yearning for her reasserted itself. All other thoughts were expelled from his mind when her face and grace pushed itself back in. Gidon knew he was going to have to pay more attention to his surroundings if he wanted to arrive in one piece at Almanya. Riding a fine horse and wearing goodly garments, as well as traveling alone, were a signal to any band of cutthroats and thieves this was likely an easy target with a fat purse. There was a lot of wisdom in the King's Riders, who often traveled alone wearing simple garb. They might be taken for that of a poor penniless mercenary seeking employment. That is until one was ready to reveal himself.

Gidon tried to play the game of bushes where he looked sideways for any that moved wrong and so forth. But the forest was heavy on either side along this way. Any ambushes would come from the forest and hardly anywhere along this stretch of forest. It was just very heavy growth. He remembered it was such where the road from Eastwatch joined the road from the left going on to Almanya. At the very least that junction was still four hours away even moving at a good pace, as he was.

It happened so suddenly it took him totally by surprise. Begleiter came to a complete stop, his ears pointing forward. Something up ahead was not to the great horse's liking. Gidon said to Begleiter, "It is a good thing one of us has their head in the right place. What is it you see?" The horse snorted with anger.

Gidon thought about bringing out his longbow. But a longbow is difficult to manage from horseback. And if he stepped down to the ground, he surrendered some of his rapidity of movement. A wild boar, bear, or wolf pack would be best managed from horseback. It is not sport when the wild game hunts you. And if it were thieves and robbers, he was more concerned for Begleiter than his self, for the horse had no armor. He thought out loud, "At least I have chain-mail." The practicality was the loss of the horse would hinder him accomplishing his mission. But the reality was he just plain loved the horse and did not want anything bad to happen to it.

He and Begleiter sat perfectly still in the middle of the road as if he had all the time in the world. He watched the great horse's ears. Whatever the threat was, it was on both sides of the road. Man, or beast, there were more than one of the critters.

Begleiter snorted in a way he had never heard him snort because of an animal, not even Snaggle Tooth. Gidon made the decision it had to be men he was keying on. He called out loud and clear, "I see you. Step out in the open and make yourselves known."

Four men came out of the forest, two on each side. From Begleiter's action he knew this was not all. "I did not mean some of you come out. I meant all of you come out."

Two more men emerged. One of these was as big as Herman One Eye. He was definitely the boss, but leader by brawn, not intelligence. Gidon thought he had some advantage. He gave them commands and they obeyed. He looked at the man in charge of these scoundrels and said, "I just fought a man your size the other day."

The fellow's curiosity got the better of him, "What happened?"

He looked at the man and said, "If you happen to see a big one-eyed man come down the road driving a pony cart you might ask him."

Gidon felt he had not lied. If they chose to believe he had knocked out an eye it was not his fault.

"Did he give you those scars?" one of the others asked.

"Oh no! The one on my left cheek was from a bowman who was not as fast as my sword. The one on the right cheek was from a dragon that I slew."

One of the others said, "I think he is lying."

Gidon said, "If I was lying, I could have turned my horse around and fled. But I have not killed anyone today and I wish to not lose my touch. So, I thought I might give you bunch of knaves a chance before I killed you and cut off your heads to plant along the road on poles."

The big man was again curious, “Why would the likes of you want to take our heads?”

“I suppose you are blind as well as dumb. Do you not see my tunic?” Gidon wanted him to think the way he directed his thoughts. “What insignia is above my heart?”

“I think it be King Gregor’s.” Said the man who had accused him of lying.

One man had not said anything and that worried Gidon, so he pointed him out directly. “Do you know whose insignia is upon my right breast? Can you make it out?”

“I know not m’lord.” Gidon felt he was making some headway now even with this man because clearly using that address had been involuntary.

“That is the insignia of Baron von Krieg, who is one of the King’s Riders and Chief of the Long Knives. I am his squire. Do you know what a Long Knife teaches his squire to do best?”

The men stood there dumbfounded. They knew very well this young man with the scars was claiming to be a master killer, and his boldness made them suspect it was true.

“What is the insignia on your cloak?” The man who had at first said nothing asked.

Gidon was afraid he might be piling it on too deep but if he had read these men right, they were a superstitious lot. “One of my women made the insignia for me. I can become a sabretooth tiger at will. She likes me that way because she can become a stalking tigress as well.” He remembered Getrudis playing at stalking him and reminded himself he needed to keep his mind focused.

One of the men had become suspicious again. “Let us see you turn into a sabretooth.”

“When I get ready to kill you I will. I think I want to taste your blood.” Gidon licked his lips in imitation of Snaggle Tooth and imitated his growl like he was about to change.

The leader cried out, “Mercy, do not kill us. What do we need to do to be right with you?”

“Lay down your weapons now. That includes any hidden weapons you might have.” Gidon commanded.

The thoughtful one started to attack instead but while they were talking Gidon had closed the distance. Out came one of the throwing knives and he threw it, hitting the man in the eye. The thin blade passed through and hit the brain. He did not die immediately but lay on the ground writhing in pain. Gidon breathed a sigh of relief. Actually, Gidon had been trying to hit him in the chest.

"Now, shall we play or will you lay down your weapons?" Gidon's heart was racing but they did not know it. "Do you have any hostages for ransom?" Gidon asked on a hunch.

"We have two that are probably not worth your concern m'lord," the boss of the crew answered.

"There is none in all the land of the Allemande not worth my concern, for I am a servant of King Gregor. You also are my concern. Bring me the captives and their mounts. You will go to Almanya to answer the king's muster and I will be waiting for you there. If you do not come, I will come after you, and I know your scent." He made like an animal smelling the air.

They brought out from the forest two maidens and their steeds. He now had company for the road and for the moment was glad.

Gidon waved the women to the right so they would start out ahead of him. He wanted to get away from the gang of cutthroats, but he could not appear to them in a great hurry without giving away the game he had been playing. Thus far he had pulled off his deception only having to kill one person. He did not want to have to kill any more or risk being killed or injured in the process. He now also had a responsibility to the women he had freed.

He gauged the women's horses as they turned north and away from him. They were excellent horseflesh that had been hard used. He would have to exercise some restraint to allow these animals to return to their full vigor. More and more Gidon wished he had brought a pack animal so he could have extra grain. But he had planned on rapidly catching up with the Baron. Another lesson on how important it is to make allowances for the unexpected.

It took over five hours to reach the junction with the road from Eastwatch. Gidon toyed with the idea of taking them there and starting back out again. It would give him a chance to see his beloved

Getrudis once more. But these were foreign women who talked together in a language he did not know. His guess was they were heading to Almanya when set upon. He had a number of questions to ask after they made camp for the night. He did turn down the road to Eastwatch in order to be passed by, should anyone be following him on his journey to Almanya. He grinned at thinking it would really be something if the men he had bested this day really showed up for the king's muster. They could just be that dumb.

Gidon had thought about making a cold camp but decided the women needed the warmth of the fire since all he had to offer this night was some meager fare. The two ladies seemed to be pretty close to exhaustion. Considering their fatigue and the condition of the horses he concluded they had probably not begun their ordeal in the last day or two.

He began the conversation. "Ladies, I am Gidon von Eastwatch, son of Gid-visu. I am squire to Baron von Krieg of the King's Riders, lately appointed Baron of Eastwatch Keep. I know not your speech, or accent when you speak the common tongue. Would you tell me who you are and how you come to need rescue?"

The older woman spoke. "I am the Lady Dolores. I am chaperone to the Princess Loretta, daughter of the King of Andorra. We departed our home with a great escort to see King Gregor II in the hope of an alliance through marriage…"

At this point the princess interjected, "Oh, just call her Lady Lolita as I do, for she is more my pet than my chaperone."

Lady Dolores sighed and said, "What she is saying may be true Squire Gidon, for being chaperone to her is an impossible task. Though my princess may be pure as her name implies, it sometimes bedevils me how she can remain so with all the mischief she gets into."

The princess stuck out her tongue and said, "I do not understand why they would send only one mere squire to rescue me. Where are my knights in shining armor come to rescue the damsel in distress?"

"I am afraid you believe too much the tales about the rescuing of fair damsels told by minstrels and bards. I think about as many of them get rescued as dragons get killed these days. I have seen only one dragon in my life and I am the one who killed it. As for rescuing maidens, the only maidens I have known needing rescuing was one Burgomeister's daughter. I rescued her and there was one poor victim of a wizard my master rescued. Then that one preferred to stay lost." He had given them a riddle to ponder at the end of his speech, for how could a rescued maiden remain lost?

The lady Dolores began once more. "We left Andorra at an inappropriate season so our ships were buffeted in the winter storms. Some of the horses died in the rough weather at sea. Then we were attacked by pirates who appeared to come from the land across the narrow sea. We fought them off but lost a number of our bowmen in the fight. Arrows were constantly flying between ships for what seemed hours. We escaped finally in a fog bank."

"Then they were not Norsemen?" Gidon asked.

"No Squire, for the Captain of our ship identified them. We finally came to harbor at Stadtgemeinde Bremen on the Weser River. We found that pirates also made harbor there. One of the pirates, who had become a robber baron, looked with favor upon our Loretta and would have taken her had it not been the city has its own army to back up our escort. However, we lost several knights and other men in that dispute.

Lady Dolores continued the story, "Then King Goraleck heard of our dove and wanted her in spite of the fact he already has wife and mistresses. Since the city is independent of his kingdom, as you no doubt know, the soldiers of the city withstood him as long as we were there. But we had to make our way to King Gregor on our own. We could not even hire mercenaries that could be trusted. It came about that for safety we left the city by night. However, there must have been many spies about. We were repeatedly attacked as we traveled through Goraleck's kingdom, losing many soldiers as well as the princess' possessions and jewelry."

Princess Loretta picked up the story. "By the time we were beset by this last group of brigands we had only five knights left. They fought bravely to the last. These highwaymen were so depleted by the time you encountered them, you had only six to contend with and you left all but one alive." She said the last accusingly.

Gidon stood up and bowed saying, “My but you are a blood thirsty wench.” The Princess turned deep red at being called a wench and started to speak. Even in Andorra they knew a wench was no princess. But Gidon did not allow her opportunity to get started. “But you are right,” he continued, “I should have taken all six captive and roasted them over a slow fire cutting out their livers while they still lived, and then placed their heads on poles by the side of the road. That would have taught them!”

The princes sputtered, “You mock me sir!”

“Well at least you caught on to that!” Gidon retorted.

Lady Dolores smiled. Her princess had found someone who was not awed by her beauty or overwhelmed by her tongue.

“In my homeland the Andosins are a brave and stalwart people.” Princess Loretta boasted. “It was in our valley the Carthaginians were withstood when they sought to cross the Pyrenees. Even the name of our people, Andosini, means big or giant! We may be a small people but we are giants in bravery!”

“Well judging by their princess, they may well also be giants in boasting.” Gidon retorted. The princess who had made many men speechless now set in a huff speechless herself.

Gidon gave the two women his blanket to wrap themselves in. Then with his cloak around him he lay at Begleiter’s feet confident that if trouble came, he would not be taken unawares.

When morning dawned Gidon watched Lady Dolores stir up Princess Loretta so they could slip just inside the woods to take care of their needs of the morning. He was surprised they did not go in more deeply than they did. When they came out, he gave them just a sip of the water explaining the horses needed the rest. He had also given his little bit of grain to the horses the night before. But he was not without a plan. He planned to get the horses watered and waterskin filled at Heim. He hoped there might be some grain to be found, left by the refugees. Getting the women and horses hidden from the road while he went to check out the remains of the village was a thing that worried him.

It was a pleasant surprise to discover, when they came to where the Baron’s former encampment had been made, a path had been cut through the wood to Heim. Gidon determined he would use it as far as practical, though it meant the ladies would have to walk to avoid overhanging limbs. The trail had been cleared by footmen. The ladies' footwear was not designed for the woods. It was better suited to a courtyard than to the uneven path of the forest. They stumbled often.

He had noticed, when he started the women on the path, they seemed very ill at ease, though their steeds would willingly go wherever Begleiter went without fear. Gidon had looped the reins over his neck so he could pick his own trail. These two women plainly did not care for the woods itself. He wondered why? And the answer was soon forthcoming.

Princess Loretta spoke with some humility for the first time, "Please sir, do not get so far ahead of us. We fear being lost in this wood."

The path might not be the best in the world seeing it was made for a temporary use. But it was clear enough no one could easily lose it. Gidon said, "Why are you so afraid?"

Lady Dolores explained, "We do not have such woods in our homeland though great forests are on every side of the kingdom. In fact, our homeland is sometimes disparagingly called scrubland. We have little land, and many years ago some thought it wise to cut timber and use all for farmland. We did not know what devastation cutting all the wood would cause."

"Lolita does not tell you that everyone fears the evil creatures that lurk in the forests." The princess went on, "It is not just the wolves, bears, and boar; we really fear the gnomes and elves and all manner of other wicked beings that lie in wait to do harm."

Gidon replied, "I do not think you have such creatures to concern yourself with here. We may have some fairies. My woman and I thought we were left a live bouquet of flowers growing on our path when we took a small rest time in our forest."

"You have a woman?" Dolores said. "We thought you very young in spite of your scars."

Gidon did not think reassuring about his youth would enhance their willingness to trust him flawlessly and without question.

"Yes, I have a woman and her handmaid is also mine by choice. We have no slaves in Alleman." Gidon did not know why he had boasted about women. He was not at all sure it really had anything to do with his influence over these two. Maybe he wanted them to think him more experienced in the ways of women.

They were now within a hundred yards or so of the hamlet when he heard a loud voice coming from it. He handed the reins for Begleiter to Dolores. Taking his bow and arrows he instructed the women to stay in this spot and make no noise till he returned.

Slowly he slipped toward the hamlet being careful not to make any sound that might give him away. He thought it not likely they would hear because those in the camp were making enough noise to hide his own sounds. Then he came in sight of the sources of the noise. It was the robbers he had rescued the princess and her chaperone from the day before. His first impulse was to withdraw and go, but then he saw several women from the hamlet who had apparently chosen not to leave. He also saw two men tied hand and foot. He could not leave these people to their fate.

He set five arrows for bigger game straight up in the dirt beside him. The remainder he kept attached to his person in their quiver. Making sure he had his targets firmly secured in his mind he fired five arrows in quick succession, each one at a different man. Then he moved quickly to a new location he had already picked out. From the new position he looked to see what was happening.

It was the first time he had tried five shots at men like that. The laughing and singing had been replaced with another sound. This time he heard men moaning and groaning and rolling about on the ground. He located all five before he made his next move. He made the growling sound he had once heard coming from Snaggle Tooth. He thought it a fairly good imitation. The camp became still except for women rearranging their clothes and untying men.

From behind him he heard a voice. "You still did not kill them."

Without thinking he turned around and grabbed the disobedient princes most unceremoniously. He pulled up the four slips under her skirt to expose a bare bottom which he proceeded to thoroughly spank.

Another voice said, "Not so my lord!" Gidon looked at Dolores who had also come up with the horses.

"What! Do I now have to spank you?" Gidon growled menacingly.

Dolores fell on her hands and knees before him. "I will be your Lolita, your pet whom you may kick, spank, or whip as you please. You may spank me for her if it please you. But not so my princess! Please my lord, I beg you, mercy!"

Gidon turned and walked toward the men he just shot. Over his shoulder he said, "There may be two women who will not be able to sit before we get to Almanya if they do not learn to obey."

One of the five he just wounded had gotten up and was headed to the wood. Gidon said loudly, "If I have to change and follow you into the wood it will not go well with you."

The man turned around and came back. Of the other four, another had died of the arrow shot. He was pierced through and from the amount of blood around him he had bled to death.

Gidon looked at the man who led the group and said, "Herman, you and your boys just will not learn will you?"

The man looked at Gidon and said, "How did you know my name was Herman?"

Gidon almost said it was just a lucky guess, but instead he continued the deception began the day before. "Have you forgotten I am a mighty wizard who can turn into a sabretooth tiger? How many other things do you think so powerful a magician as I might do?"

"We were on our way to the muster, honestly, but we found this path and thought we might refresh ourselves." The big man called Herman was doing all the talking. He seemed to be the only one who could overcome his pain enough to talk.

Gidon spoke to one of the men of Heim. "Could you lead my horses down to water and fill my water-skin? I am also in need of feed for my horses if you have it. Anything you can provide to help us I will pay for."

One of the women said, "We have little use for coin. But if Squire Gidon could see his way to bring us such things as we might need here when next he comes, we should have a crop from which to trade."

The chair from which the Baron had rendered judgment was brought out for Gidon, but of course Princess Loretta assumed it was for her. The women of Heim made it quite clear to her that in this place Squire Gidon was lord and she a person of no consequence. It was a new idea for her to try to get her mind around. The women told Loretta, Gidon was the hero of Heim. He had not only slain dozens in the night but hundreds in the day when Heim was set free, and now he was here to rescue them again. It was of course an exaggeration, but it not only impressed the princess but also the newly punctured varlets sitting on the ground.

Gidon gratefully took the chair. He felt very weary. He looked at this new Herman and his diminishing comrades. The question was, what should he do with them? He was truly sick of the killing but what was the alternative? Was there any alternative?

Lady Dolores insisted on bringing Gidon his food. She told the women, "I am his Lolita by my own swearing. I must serve him as his faithful pet." Belonging to someone was something the women of Heim understood.

The princess asked, "But are you not my Lolita?"

Dolores replied, "No, I was your Lolita by your declaration, but you forgot I am a trueborn lady and a free woman. I asked him to punish me instead of you, but he has made it plain we all must account for our own transgressions. I will fulfill my sworn duty as your chaperone but I will be forever his Lolita."

Gidon, after eating, had to fight sleep. The best way he decided was to render judgment. He asked the women and two men who had been taken captive by them what was their pleasure in the matter? He expected to have to remove four heads this evening.

The oldest woman said, "These men tried to take kisses and feel under our garments, true. Compared to the ones you first saved us from, they were not as bad. We are sick of all the killing. We only wanted to live our lives in peace. The two men who are with us now were out of the hamlet when the last intruders came. They suffered the loss of their families. And now we are trying to go on together.

We do not want bullies or people we have to constantly watch in Heim. If the men say kill them, so say we all."

Gidon said, "We must kill them or patch their wounds. I am reluctant to allow them to travel with us to the king's muster for they are fools and cannot learn from their mistakes. Yet, I will take them from this place when I go if you can sell me a cart, which they shall be tied to and pull. Then, if there is any scheme hatched by one, all will die. In any case Heim will be well rid of them."

The man who had been tending the horses had returned. Gidon spoke to Begleiter. "If any of these men I have shot try anything let me know. If you need to stomp one, go right ahead."

The horse nodded and the varlets all believed he understood perfectly. He handed one of the men his fighting staff and said he should also watch while the women got the arrows out. Gidon told the man if he even suspected one of them was going to do something amiss, he should raise a knot on their head with his staff.

Gidon slipped off to sleep sitting in the chair. The women of Heim who were not trying to get arrows out of the bandits circled around him with hoes and axes in their hands.

One of Herman the robber's men said to him, "He looks like he is in a deep sleep."

Herman answered, "The man is a wizard. They are never fully asleep."

The women of Heim told Princess Loretta and Lady Dolores about all that had happened at Heim, emphasizing Gidon's part in it. Of course, it was not all quite correct. But that is how legends are born and grow.

Chapter 21

Friends and Enemies

It was difficult getting the ramshackle cart down the path along with the few supplies the remaining residents of Heim were able to provide. As soon as Gidon and his entourage were back on the road the people of Heim were busy camouflaging the path so those they did not want to come would have difficulty finding the way. Gidon was determined in the years to come, if it were at all possible, he would make these good people his special project.

Herman, the leader of the diminished gang, reached into his boot and pulled out Gidon's throwing knife. Gidon had left it in the eye of the thoughtful highwayman the day before. "Herman, I am amazed you are returning it to me."

"I want you to trust me and I thought returning this might help me earn that trust," Herman replied earnestly. This did not answer the question of why Herman might want Gidon's trust. But if he was seeking to be approved of Gidon, returning the knife certainly was a step.

Gidon set the order of march with himself in the lead, followed by the cart with now only four malefactors attached to it. The numbers were likely to be diminished further if there was any hint of rebellion. The ladies came last. Their horses were looking better for even the poor feed they had gotten at Heim. The Andorran horse was well known for all the finest attributes of a riding or fighting horse with the exception of being nearly two hands shorter than Begleiter.

By being in the front he could set a pace that pushed the men on foot. He wanted thirty-five miles per day. He could get that out of the men only by alternating the work load between the four of them.

After they had been again underway about the space of an hour, Lady Dolores rode forward to be beside Gidon. He looked her over closely from that vantage, really seeing her for the first time. Like many of the Andosini women of the upper class she had lustrous black hair and an almost alabaster white complexion. She was strikingly beautiful. Of course he had only heard of the women of Andorra from the songs of wandering minstrels. This lady was the first of that type he had ever seen. He was impressed.

After a little time had passed Gidon said, "Pardon me Lady Dolores, but I am captivated by your beauty. You do not seem to be of an age to be a chaperone. In this country it is most common traveling companions for young maidens are much older than you seem and often the nanny of their childhood."

"You are correct, Squire Gidon. It is the same in Andorra. I am but twenty-eight years, yet a widow from my twenty-fifth year. I believe the reason the king, Princes Loretta's father, made me her chaperone is I am one of the few people who have any influence over her at all. He may have also felt some obligation to my dead husband to save me if he could." Dolores paused.

"Lady, I am a young man with little knowledge of the world. But my father tried to teach me to be a keen observer. You are not only beautiful at twenty-eight but I sense you have that regal beauty that will endure even until you are seventy-eight. It is not right such a woman as yourself should not remarry and bless the world with beautiful and intelligent children to make a man's heart glad and the world better."

"It may well be I can hope for no such thing. It is my sadness that I did not appreciate the husband I had until he was lost. The Invisible God does not reward ingratitude," Dolores said.

Gidon was silent for a space of time. "Dear lady, I perceive that you have a most interesting story to tell. You speak of a king who wished to save you and I suppose his daughter as well. Then you mourn the death or loss of a husband you did not appreciate by your declaration. And I believe you a great lady, yet you swore yourself to me after the fashion of your name. You have made me most curious concerning you. I would hear your story."

She began slowly, choosing her words carefully. She wanted to say much in as concise a manner as possible. She wanted to be honest but not extremely self-condemning. "I was betrothed at the age of fourteen to the squire of a noble house. But he would not come to me until he achieved knighthood. My father's house is also a proud one. By the time I was eighteen he became a knight, having already established a record of many noble and daring deeds. It was then he took me for his bride. I was more thrilled to have a good marriage than to have a good man. And he was a good man holding his loyalty to his God, his king, and his wife in that order. Do you follow me thus far?"

Gidon said he did and urged her to go on.

"Because he was a noble man, fearless and brave, he was often gone on the king's business. I came to resent this more and more so finally I would not allow him into my bed. He had many enemies, and being in his chamber all alone one night, an assassin crept in as he put on his nightshirt. Though the assassin failed to stab him to death he did cut him with a blade that had poison on it. Thus it was my husband died alone deserted by his wife." The Lady Dolores paused and bowed her head.

Gidon said to her, "I know this is painful for you. But you have said much to make me think. Please go on."

"After my husband's death I served as a lady in waiting to Princess Loretta's mother until she mysteriously died. It was suspected she had been served poisoned fruit. I was the only lady who did not return to their families. For several years many have been filled with fear, knowing the king's enemies were drawing their circle around him ever tighter. The Princess Loretta, because of her personality, was not only hated by those who hated the king but she had other enemies as well. This was why the king sent her on the journey to King Gregor at the wrong season for traveling. I would not be surprised if soon we will hear of our king being assassinated. Then because the enemies we have encountered have stolen both the dowry and the wealth of our princess I very much doubt she will find the husband she expects."

"Thank you, my lady. That explains a lot. But why should you submit yourself to me?" Gidon asked.

"First of all, I had to stop you from spanking my princess. To do that I would gladly accept your anger on my own body! But there is another reason as well. You impress me as an honorable man not unlike my late husband. I know in my heart I can trust you to treat me well in my submission to you. Once my duty to the princess is fulfilled, I shudder to think what might happen to a woman such as I without anywhere to turn. I do not wish to sound selfish, but I do need a champion as much as Princess Loretta. The difference is, I know it."

Upon this the Lady Dolores was silent and remained so as Princess Loretta rode up to join them. "What is the meaning of leaving me by myself for so long?" she demanded.

Gidon did not wait to hear Dolores answer. He turned Begleiter and rode back to the cart, which was about twenty feet behind. "Herman, what were you called by all your cronies before I met you?"

"What do you mean lord Gidon?" It was obvious Herman did not want to answer that question.

"You know what I mean. Surely you were not satisfied to be called just Herman. You would probably want to be called Herman, prince of thieves or some other superlative." Gidon said the last with a hint of sarcasm. "What did you want to be called and what were you called?

"I never gave much thought to what I wanted to be called." Herman was avoiding the answer.

"Come, come man, you cannot be that slow of mind." Gidon said.

Herman sighed. "Back home I was called Herman Taschendieb."

"So," Gidon said, "you were a pickpocket." Gidon made it sound funny.

Herman sort of grinned and said, "Actually m'lord, I would rather go for the Geldbeutel. You cut the cord on a man's money bag and run. You are more likely to get away with that than trying to see what is in a man's pocket or even if he has one."

"Were you a good purse snatcher Herman?" Herman held up a hand with a finger missing. Had he been caught a second time he would probably have lost the hand.

"That was why I became a Wegelagerer." Herman explained. "I was not really too good at snatching purses and I have done much better as a highwayman. And this way, if you get caught, the Allemande just hang you. It is better than losing yourself in pieces I think."

"Okay." Gidon said, "We will call you Herman Wegelagerer for now and perhaps one day we can find a better purpose for you and you will be a reformed man. We could call you Herman Wegelagerer Reformierte. Or perhaps we would have for you some better name. I have hopes for you." Herman looked grateful, but was he sincere?

"Perhaps all of you men might one day be better than you have been." Gidon concluded.

Two more hours travel brought the little group well into the afternoon. They had lost too much time at Heim. But now they drew abreast a tavern. Raucous noises emerged from the building. Gidon said to Herman. "Would you like a chance to prove yourself?"

Herman appeared eager to do just that, so Gidon told him to get his knife off the cart. Then he gave him a coin. "Tell the proprietor you want two skins of wine. And tell him you want good wine."

Herman happily went into the building. Passing him as he went in was several coarse looking people coming out. They had realized some people were in a cart outside. One of the men walked over to the cart and said to Herman's men, "Let me untie you from the cart. We will do business with your master." He thought their number would keep Gidon from interfering.

Gidon had positioned himself twixt the cart and the women. Another fellow walked in a wide circle of Gidon looking at the women. "How much would you take for the women and their horses?" The man's impertinent attitude rankled. Gidon knew they were not making an honest offer, only taking his measure as a man.

Gidon made no reply. He pulled his sword and charged the man interested in the women. He lay the flat of the sword to the side of the man's head whereupon he dropped immediately like a steer hit between the eyes for the slaughter. Herman's men had grabbed the other fellow even as he tried to untie them. By the time Gidon got to him they had already rendered him unconscious. Gidon ordered them to throw him in the cart.

A very short, fat, and generally dumpy looking woman of indeterminate age had come out with the men. She wore a short thin garment that formed itself around her overly abundant breasts. As she had come out, she was wearing one of the most wicked leers on her face Gidon had ever seen on a human being. Somehow she reminded him of the female Druid Jacklyn. Gidon had literally felt as if she was undressing him with her eyes. She made him feel like he needed a bath. Now her expression turned into an evil snarl. Surely this woman was possessed by demons. She moved surprisingly fast for someone so fat. When she came near to Gidon, she looked as if she was going to leap upon the horse like a savage animal. Gidon had planned to hit her with the flat of the sword but Begleiter again took matters into his own hooves. He whirled and kicked the woman with his rear hooves so fast Gidon was almost unseated. Gidon next saw her lying in a heap unmoving.

Herman came out of the tavern happily carrying two wineskins. "What is going on?"

Gidon commanded that two of his men should be lashed to the front of the cart and Herman should ride in the cart while tying up the prisoner they had taken. He was happy to ride for a bit. Gidon noticed Herman's men were quite pleased with themselves for subduing the prisoner without being told. The women scarce knew what to do, but stayed out in front and did as they were told…

*****

It was getting dusky dark and their new prisoner had regained consciousness. Gidon stopped the group knowing they were going to have to make camp. Herman had been proud of his deal, getting two wineskins and a cup with a few coppers change.

Gidon asked the man, "Is your head hurting?"

The man answered very curtly, "What do you think?"

Gidon said, "I think a cup of this wine would make it feel better."

The man was less disrespectful. He said, "I do not want wine. It hurts my stomach."

Gidon said, "Then why do I smell wine on you?" You either drink the wine or you drink no more."

The man drank the wine and was unconscious in minutes.

Gidon then spoke to Herman's men. "Do you see this varlet? That is what the thieves at the tavern have planned for you. What do you say we turn the tables on them?" The men agreed that was a fine idea.

The men set up camp on the western side of the road arranging bedrolls like all were sleeping. They made a small fire and rigged a tent shelter from some heavy oiled material the women at Heim had donated. Princes Loretta and Lady Dolores were placed, shelter-less, in the woods on the eastern side with strict instruction their lives depended on them being quiet. Gidon went so far as to tie the princess hands and feet as well as put a gag in her mouth. Gidon asked Dolores, "Are you my pet or not?" to which she nodded her head. "Then if she does not sit there quietly you must knock her out." Gidon had toyed with forcing a swallow of the drugged wine down the princess' throat but he was unsure of its potency. Princess Loretta glared at him and gnashed on her gag. She was extremely unhappy.

Gidon took his bow and prepared himself a shooting position. He told the men not to act until he started the reverse ambush going.

The men settled down to wait. One man got too settled and began to snore, until the man beside him punched him in the ribs. There was a startled noise and then the camp got quiet again. Another hour passed and Gidon began to wonder if he had calculated wrong? Then they heard the creak of leather and the sound of wagon wheels. Ten men were converging on the camp. Two were on horseback and appeared to be in charge and another drove the wagon. The seven riding in the wagon jumped to the ground immediately ready to kill men they thought were in a wine-soaked slumber.

Gidon waited till the robbers were nearly on top of Herman's men. He hit the ones closest to them with his first arrows and sent the next two into the leaders. Then he had to pull an arrow from his quiver, which he sent into the wagon driver who was trying to turn the team around. Herman and his men were now engaging five men, but they were too closely locked in fighting for Gidon to shoot another arrow.

Emerging from his shooting point with sword in his right hand and knife in his left, Gidon made the most fearsome yell he could manage. It even unsettled his own men a little, even though they were expecting something. Perhaps a couple had it in the back of their mind that he might actually turn into a tiger. Then as suddenly as it had begun it was all over. Ten men lay dead while only one of Herman's men received any serious wound. They had fought well in spite of the fact they had been so recently wounded with Gidon's arrows at Heim.

The group was richer by one wagon and team, two riding horses with saddles, assorted weapons, and the purses and clothing of the attackers. The men who had come to rob, kill, and enslave were now dead. Gidon told Herman to have his men cut ten poles and plant them in the earth on the western side. Gidon cut off the heads of the malefactors and Herman's men gleefully put them on the posts as a warning to those who would violate the king's law. One of the men told his fellows that if Gidon had led them when they were bandits, they would all be rich now. So Gidon left it to Herman to divide the spoil of their attacker's purses between them. In this way Gidon sought to avoid ill feelings.

In all the activity Gidon had forgotten something. He now remembered the princess and Lady Dolores. He walked across the road to find the place strangely quiet. The princess had fought with her bindings and gag so much she had literally worn herself out and gone to sleep. Lady Dolores was on her knees cradling the sleeping princess in her arms. She looked at Gidon admiringly, "You truly are a great warrior."

"My lady these are but cutthroats and not well-trained fighting men. Up against skilled warriors it might not have gone so well. I have much to learn. Come we have to move." Gidon took the gag from Loretta's mouth. He was sorry to see he had bruised a corner of it just a little. Laying there asleep the mouth looked quite kissable. That thought brought back his longings for Getrudis.

The Lady Dolores said, "Kiss her! Let her awaken to a kiss. Her dignity has been affronted. If she awakens to a stolen kiss, she will feel honored by the admiration of the man who bound her."

Gidon kissed her very gently and continued till she showed some sign of stirring. He traced the outside of her lips with his tongue, always staying in position to look into her eyes. And as she opened her eyes, he held that gentle embrace of lips to lips. Her body started to respond then she realized she was still bound hands and feet. Her eyes flashed and she said, "Sir, you are no gentleman!" He looked back into her eyes and smiled, "Princess you are right!"

Dolores laughed, and Loretta turned her head to look at her. "You have allowed him to do this to me!"

Dolores answered, "My Princess, I suggested it!"

Gidon picked up the princess still bound and carried her to the wagon. He put her unceremoniously over the side. "If you will be a good girl I will untie you. Do I have your word?" It looked like the princess was going to launch a tirade, but she believed Gidon was not kidding. She agreed to be good…for now.

Gidon retrieved his bow and arrows while the men settled the equipment and spoils on the wagon. He regretted he could not burn the bodies but he did not want to take a chance the news of such a fire would get to the tavern. They had to set miles between themselves and any possible enemies.

Gidon asked, "Herman do you know how to ride?"

Herman said, "Not very well."

Gidon said, "It is time for you to learn. Take one of our new horses and get on it. We will harness the other to the cart and tie the ladies' horses to the back of the wagon. You will follow the wagon and make sure of our rear. I will go forward to set the pace. We do not want anything damaged or broken in our night ride, especially us."

The group traveled through the night. Progress was better thanks to the greed of the men who had come to take a spoil. Because of those who would have taken what little they had and put the women and those not slain into bondage, they now had a horse drawn wagon and cart. That meant no one had to walk.

Herman's men had found some wine in the wagon that was not drugged. No doubt it had been purposed for a celebration on the way back from the victory they planned to be at Gidon and his followers' expense. Gidon had Herman force the men to stay out of it, warning them they might have to fight again before the night was over. As a reward and sign he was giving them limited trust, he allowed the former highwaymen to keep their weapons.

One asked his fellows if letting them keep their weapons were an oversight on Gidon's part?

The man answered, "No you fool. He knows he can take us anytime he wishes, so why should he not allow us to stay armed against others?"

The ladies soon wearied of the men in the wagon. They would get no sleep and they did not really trust what the men might do in their exuberance of victory. Even though they had not offered to molest them when once they held them captive, it would be a while before they fully trusted them. When Gidon rode by on his way to check for enemies following, they pleaded to return to their horses.

Gidon acted very stern. "Princess Loretta, if I allow you to return to horse will you obey or shall I need spank you once again?"

The princess retorted, "You are a knave sir. But yes, I will obey." The men in the wagon were much amused by it all, and some heard what Gidon did not, for he was already moving to take care the prisoner was secure when Princess Loretta said under her breath, "For now!"

Gidon rode back to the south some distance till he was out of earshot of his own people. He set Begleiter in the middle of the road and they remained motionless ears seeking to focus on what the dark might conceal. He may have held that position a full ten minutes until certain that if anyone was following, they were far behind.

Then he turned and caught up with his charges and for a while rode between the princess and the lady. He enjoyed the two types of fiery beauty on either side. After Princess Loretta had been studying him for some time she said to him in her sweetest voice, "Squire Gidon, there is something I want to know."

Gidon was immediately on the alert. He knew when she started speaking sweetly, she was up to something. "If it is possible, I will try to enlighten you. If not, I will confess it."

"Herr Gidon, why did you kiss me? Really, why did you kiss me?" Loretta said.

Gidon knew she had already been told the truth. It would be an insult to say her lips were a substitute for the ones he truly desired. He had to think fast. "My princess, you know the Alemanni have been known from the most ancient times as 'the men' do you not?"

She gave one of her little sounds of disbelief. "I know the Alemanni have been known from ancient times to call themselves 'the men,' yes."

Gidon ignored the slight toward the men of Alemanni and continued, "From the most ancient times three things have distinguished the men of the Alemanni as 'the men'."

"Oh, pray tell me Squire Gidon, I am just burning to know what those three things are." She was more than a little sarcastic that time and Gidon thought he might have her, though she did not know it yet.

"The men pride themselves in the understanding of the art of war. They are ever striving to understand the mysteries of true horsemanship. But there is one thing they have always known instinctively…"

"And pray tell Gidon what is that?" You could see she was focusing on the possibilities of how to answer him without even yet hearing what he would say.

"The true men of the Alemanni know the best way to calm a hysterical woman who is not utterly crazy, is with a good sound kiss!"

With that Gidon rode ahead about twenty feet, leaving Princess Loretta speechless and Lady Dolores unable to stop laughing.

The sun was just rising in the sky when they came to a wide expanse of cleared land. Parallel to the roadway, a fence had been erected made of woven limbs as many farmers fenced their land. Gidon's first impression was that he had come to a Hold and was not yet at the Keep. He had been told of Baron Igil's Keep when the Baron von Krieg, Gid-visu, and Herr Brute' had discussed the trip, with him looking on and keeping silent.

The fence at the roadway had armed guards at the gate who seemed not at all concerned Gidon and his men were approaching them. He looked up the way from the King's Highway to see a wood stockade of remarkable size. Perhaps this place did have a tower that was being hidden by clouds so low they seemed to be resting on the top of the stockade.

The planted fields on either side of the path going to the fortifications showed someone was interested in, not only farming greatly, but well. He thought of his father's fields at Eastwatch and hoped they were not going untended for their absence.

Gidon announced himself to the guards on the other side of the gate. "Gidon von Eastwatch, Squire to Baron von Krieg of the King's Riders."

The guard said, "My master's greetings to you, Squire Gidon. This is the Keep of Baron Igil von Suebi. We were expecting you for some days. We did not expect you would have so large a group with you." What the guard was really saying was they had not been told Gidon would be appearing in any other manner than alone.

Gidon said to him, "I seem to have accumulated some companions on the road including two ladies of high station."

As the gate was swung open for him the guard said, "We have heard you specialize in rescuing damsels in distress and slaying dragons."

Gidon said, "It could be we are followed by servants of the Old Dragon."

"Do not worry Squire Gidon. Our master has had quite a bit of experience slaying his servants in the past. Usually these days, we only bother our Baron about them after they have been dispatched to perdition." The guard seemed to relish the idea. He gave a single blast on a huge horn that had a deep penetrating sound.

Gidon led his followers up toward the Keep. Halfway up the way there was a second guard post. Gidon asked, "What is your purpose?"

The guard responded, "If an enemy were to overrun the first position it would be my job to give warning. No matter if the horn did not sound from the first position, the second sounding would be a warning to the castle."

Gidon nodded, "That is very smart. If I ever have occasion to build security on my own Keep, I shall have to do something like that."

When Gidon arrived at the massive wooden gate to the Keep he cried out. "I am Gidon, son of Gid-visu, squire to Baron von Krieg, lately appointed over Eastwatch Keep. May we enter and get refreshed for our journey to Almanya?"

A grizzled head appeared, and then the whole man, as he walked up to stand on the wall. It was then Gidon realized the walls were double, with fill of stone and rubble in between. Over the years such a wall got harder and harder. Around the man's waist was his weapon belt held by the famed Pforzen buckle of hardened silver. This was the great archer Igil, who with his wife Aliruna, had fought with the giants fleeing the land of the Ebiru after they were defeated by King David.

His father had told him the story of the troops of giants who came only to be slain by Igil and his wife Aliruna, when they marched on his Keep in formations. He said there was none braver who ever belonged to the Suebi people and no finer archer in his day.

Gidon was fascinated to see the gate of the Keep swing outward. The gate was made so no amount of forcing the gate could make it go inward, another protective measure for this Keep. Gidon suspected any enemy who managed to pass these walls would have many surprises inside.

Igil called down, "Come inside and we will make food for all your company. Your fighting men may eat with mine. You and your ladies may sup with me and my wife Aliruna."

Soldiers met Herman, and his men. Once they had stacked their weapons, they were led to the soldaten kantina or soldiers' mess hall in the common tongue. Igil had joined them and said, "Squire Gidon, please keep your weapons if you wish. Both your master and your father are brethren of the Long Knives. I know we have nothing to fear from such a man as you. We are honored to have the son of so famous a warrior as Gid-visu with us. And from what we hear you are getting quite a reputation yourself, dragon slayer."

Baron Igil led them into a cozy hall in his home that could not sit as many as could gather at table in Fox Home. Standing near the head of the table was a woman with grey hair that was nearly snow white. She was dressed elegantly in a huntress dress that was beaded with the whitest pearls. To put it mildly, though she must be of very advanced age, probably as old as ninety or more when one considered how long ago they fought the giants, she was still a striking beauty. Gidon could picture Lady Dolores having similar beauty in her good old age, if she managed to live that long.

Igil said, "May I present to you my Lady Aliruna, and the love of my life."

Gidon bowed; Lady Dolores curtsied, and Princess Loretta stood straight. She considered it her due that they should curtsy to her and not the other way around.

"Baron Igil and Lady Aliruna, may I present to you Princess Loretta of Andorra and the Lady Dolores her chaperone. Baron Igil and the Lady Aliruna performed the proper etiquette.

The Lady Aliruna reached out to her and said, "My dear, we are so sorry. We heard by pigeon but two days ago of your father's assassination as he was holding court at La Balma de la Margineda."

Loretta was so weak and tired her legs collapsed under her at the news. Fortunately, the quick reflexed Gidon caught her. A servant brought a wet cloth and Dolores began wiping her face. "She should have been expecting this word, but she is very tired from the trip. We have had many adventures, and until Squire Gidon rescued us, they had all been bad."

The Lady Aliruna nodded appreciatively, "If there is some service we can do for you, we shall."

Gidon picked up the Princess Loretta and sat her at the table on a side, not at an end. The servant brought some warm honey wine for her. Lady Dolores commanded her, "Drink."

Baron Igil motioned Gidon to sit at one end of the table and he sat at the other with the Lady Aliruna by his side. He positioned

Lady Dolores across from the princess so she could not rise easily to serve her. He intended the service of breakfast to be controlled by his staff.

Speaking to Gidon he said, "We were asked by King Gregor to be on the watch for Princess Loretta and her entourage some weeks ago. For a long time, it appeared her location was unknown to all the spies of Almanya and even to Zauberer the seer." He muttered under his breath, "I have never had much faith in wizards. They always make claims they cannot keep."

Gidon said, "He should have consulted our Bishop Elisha." He saw that Baron Igil and his lady wanted to know the princess' story. So Gidon asked Lady Dolores to tell it. She left out nothing giving many details Gidon had not been told when she first informed him of all that had happened.

Baron Igil asked many questions that had not even occurred to Gidon. He began learning more about how to question people from this great man. Finally Igil seemed satisfied he had the information he desired. He looked to his wife and said, "We shall have to send a message to King Gregor that the Princess Loretta has been found and will be escorted to Almanya as quickly as possible. We also need to inform him, if he does not already know, that Goraleck tried to make off with her and probably now has her dowry as well as all other possessions. The King cannot continue to put off bringing this man to account."

Princess Loretta said, "I thank you for your hospitality and kindness this day. I appreciate you saying you would do anything you could to help me. Are you sincere in that?"

Lady Aliruna answered for the two of them. "Of course we are dear."

The princess turned toward Gidon and pointing her finger at him said, "Seize that man!"

Chapter 22

Transitions

Baron Igil leaned back in his chair and laughed. The sound of his laugh rang through the hall. He looked to an old retainer who supervised the serving staff and the old man began to laugh as well. One could see they had shared the comradeship of the warrior when they were young men, and now they had the friendship of the aged.

"Princess Loretta, I apologize. When we first met, I took you for a bratty girl with all the personality of a rock in a mudhole but now I see how wrong I was. That has to be the finest joke I have heard in years. You wanting me to seize the man who saved you! That is wonderful!"

It seemed the Baron could not stop laughing. When it appeared he had quite gotten it under control, a chuckle would work itself up and he would start laughing all over again. The serving staff became infected with his mirth and they broke into peals of laughter. It began to sound as if the mighty heroes of the past had come back to life for a celebration.

'But, but! He spanked me!" Loretta spluttered.

This caused the Baron to start laughing all over again. Even Lady Aliruna and Lady Dolores started laughing. Laughter is infectious. The Baron finally said, "With all that horseback riding the princess has been doing the past couple of months I imagine there is a tight set of buns under that dress." He spoke to Gidon, "How were they son?" His words came out in pieces as he tried to breathe, chuckle, and talk all at the same time.

Gidon caught a bit of the spirit. "To tell you the truth, I had just been busy shooting arrows into men. Things happened so fast I really did not have time to notice. Perhaps I should do it again."

Lady Dolores said, "I had been riding as much as she had. Now I feel I have been left out." So everyone started laughing about that.

Baron Igil said, "Maybe we need have a bun inspection." To which the Lady Aliruna came back and said, "The only buns you need to worry about inspecting are mine old man." So everyone laughed once again.

Things had almost settled down but Princess Loretta, with her characteristic determination said, "But he bound me hand and foot!"

That seemed funny to everyone as well, and it got even the merrier when the Lady Aliruna said to her, "Listen my dear. When my father told Igil he could not have me he went away and got a big pole and rode back into the courtyard on his war steed scattering people everywhere. Then he grabbed me and threw me over his saddle and rode away with me. Getting bound hand and foot sounds a whole lot gentler. It seems these Alemanni men think subduing women is part of their courtship." Everyone but Gidon and Loretta found that humorous as well. Lady Aliruna did not tell them, as he had entered on his war horse, she had held her hands up to Igil and grabbed his arm so he could pull her up.

Stubborn Loretta had to try one more play. "He kissed me!"

The Baron said, "I cannot imagine why anyone would want to kiss a pair of lips like that."

This time the Princess had her own retort. "A lot of men have found my lips quite lovely and wanted to kiss them."

Baron Igil looked at her with fake seriousness, "So why are you complaining when at last you meet a man with the nerve to nibble the luscious fruit below your nose?"

The Princess was dumbfounded and everyone had a last chuckle at her expense. But inside the Princess Loretta something changed in her that day. She began to see the concern Gidon had for her in the midst of their adventures.

*****

A good meal, a bath, and a few hours' sleep in a real bed did wonders for Gidon and the ladies. Gidon was not willing to tarry any longer but longed to catch up to the men from Eastwatch. And the Baron had been busy making preparations while he rested. As they walked across the courtyard, he filled Gidon in on what had been accomplished.

The Baron had decided Gidon's men looked like a bunch of knaves and cutthroats. Gidon informed him that was exactly what they were. The Baron laughed and said, "We would probably do better to put a better face on this pig."

While Gidon slept, the Baron had Gidon's men deloused, bathed, and given a shave plus a haircut. For a couple of the men being barbered, this time was the first such experience of their lives. But Baron Igil had not been finished with them. Aliruna had already called in every seamstress in the Keep for a miracle of wardrobe preparation for the Princes and her Lady. To that Baron Igil commanded the construction of four tunics of basic brown with Gidon's insignia over the left breast. This would give some dignity to Gidon's men, but he was not through. From his own armory stock, the padded armor of the serf with the addition of protective leather, was taken for them.

Only Herman, who now declared himself to the Baron's men as Herman Reformierte, was a problem. He was simply so big no such armor could be found for him. A special woolen undergarment was made and some old chainmail of a long dead hero of large proportion was given him. Even Herman was too small for the giant's armor Baron Igil possessed. But he appeared a changed man once he donned his newly constructed protective gear Baron Igil provided.

It was amazing the difference these new uniforms made in the attitudes of the former cutthroats and thieves. Herman declared he drew power for good from the former knight who possessed the chainmail he now wore, not knowing that knight had been executed for seizing what was not his. Baron Igil, knowing the foibles of men, had moved to make these men of shady past more committed to Gidon than he would ever have been able to do on his own at this point.

As soon as the men had been outfitted with their new clothing, the Master at Arms took them down to the exercise yard to be issued training swords. He introduced them to a weapon they had never handled before. They would be worked hard with the training swords, collecting quite a few bruises in the process. One of the things the Master at Arms kept emphasizing was they should neither cut themselves on their own swords or the friend fighting next to them.

Baron Igil was not through with surprises for Gidon. He said, "My cartwright has been working on a thing unseen in the past. It is a modification of a two-horse farm wagon, but this is something I would never drive off a road. And you have a road all the way to Almanya. The two men stopped at a building with open sides under which were several different types of carriages, many still in the making. "Gidon, I want you to meet Herman Stellwagen, a man who has no peer when it comes to inventing ways to move things around." The two men nodded to each other and Gidon thought to himself, *This may be another Herman I can like.*

"He has invented a wagon in which both people and material may be transported protected from the weather. The only problem is it must be parked in a sheltered place any time you have high winds because it can be turned over easily. With this wagon and good weather, you should easily make seventy miles or more a day. It just depends on the stamina of your horses and the man driving them. I want to give you this wagon, and for its first long trip loan to you Herman Stellwagen. He wants to drive it himself so he can discover ways he can improve the next one he builds. We will be helping each other."

Gidon looked over the wagon which already had his ensign on the side doors. It had large wheels set outside the body for greater stability. The center of the wagon dipped lower than the axles. Gidon opened the door on the right side of the wagon and saw a set of steps that folded inward. Let down, they made getting into the wagon as easy as going up a set of steps. The wagon was designed so passengers rode looking backwards with the seat for the driver on the outside located directly over their heads. On each side, where the people rode, was a window covered with a leather curtain that could be tied down or drawn back to let air in.

The top of the wagon was curved with metal eyelets that were secured through the hardwood frame of the roof structure. To these eyelets were lashed two spare wheels plus jacks. There were sufficient eyelets to add more material but Gidon could see how the more that was put on top, the more top heavy the wagon would become. Piling too much heavy material on top was definitely not a good idea.

The wagon was designed so cargo could be loaded from the rear. The heaviest wood at the back was the part that composed the ramp which folded upwards and seated into the rear of the wagon body very tightly. It was held in place on either side by a locking bolt such as was used to secure doors. Gidon looked at that and thought it a very wise adaptation. Clearly the rear wheels took the bulk of the load so they were made heavier and stronger than the front wheels, which necessitated the two spare wheels on top of the wagon.

Herman Stellwagen explained that by the use of the eyebolts for lashing wagon wheels on top, a single man, if he knew how, could lower a replacement wheel by himself. He also confided that he was trying to come up with a design so the front wheels of the wagon could turn without moving the axle that held the wheels. He said, "I know a hundred ways of doing that which do not work. I will have to find but one way that does work to be a success."

Gidon said he considered what he had done would make him a success that should be remembered down through history. With his thoughts on protecting the women, he had been surprised with the consideration that had been put into that area of the wagon's design. The back walls and sides of that part of the wagon where cargo was stored had been planed very thin. Only the ramp offered any resistance to an arrow passing through. However, any penetrating arrow would then hit the cargo on board and not go through to the individuals. Passengers had protection without added weight. But where the passengers sat, the walls were made as if they had been designed even as a shield was structured. Yet this was invisible to the casual observer outside.

Gidon hoped he would not need the built-in protection, but he was pleased at this marvel of the wagon maker's design. He sought to reward him but Herman Stellwagen said, "My master is a close friend of your father and he has taken quite a liking to you. If it were not so, he would have never chosen to give this to you. To take some reward when my master rewards me well would be to dishonor his gift."

*****

Baron Igil von Suebi may have achieved fame, wealth, and a place in history but it was plain he was most at home among his own men at arms. He and Gidon eventually found a table in the soldaten kantina where two beers promptly appeared before them. There were not many in the hall at this time of the day. The Baron did not believe in anyone just sitting idle, not even himself. So it was plain he was sitting, taking time to be with Gidon, for a purpose.

The Baron began, "Gidon I want to talk to you about the two women under your protection. Since you do not know King Gregor II or the ways of diplomacy, I think there are things you do not understand."

"There is a great deal I do not understand, Baron Igil. I fear that these things are beyond me. The more I see of the world, the less I understand it. I often wish I could go home, not to Eastwatch but to my forests. Just me, my beloved Getrudis, and Snaggle Tooth."

The Baron looked genuinely confused. "Who or what is a Snaggle Tooth?"

"He is the one fanged sabretooth tiger on my ensign." Gidon said. "I thought you knew about my story and my cat."

"No, I thought he was but an expression on your shield, perhaps related to your quick reflexes. But you say he is real. I should like to hear that story one day when we have the time. Right now, I need to get back to the subject of your women."

"The ones who are with me are not really mine you know." Gidon said. "I have my Mistress Getrudis and a girl from Heim who swore herself to me named Frauke. But it is my Getrudis I would have for wife and none other."

Baron Igil said, "Gidon in this life we do not always get what we want. You must acknowledge you do have a third woman, Lady Dolores, who has sworn herself to you according to her name, and you have accepted her, for you called for her obedience to you according to that swearing. What you intended at that time, or the situation you were in, does not matter. The fact is you did it."

Gidon could not do ought but recognize the truth of what he had said. All he could do was merely nod in agreement and wait for the Baron to instruct him.

Princess Loretta is a somewhat different matter. Her father had sent her to King Gregor II according to an agreement made between him and Alemanni diplomats. King Gregor has signed no wedding contracts. He merely agreed to meet the girl. The likelihood of a wedding between our king and the princess of a distant country was always slim. Furthermore, it would make no sense to make an alliance by marriage to a king likely to be overthrown at any moment. All he could possibly do is add to his own enemies with those who conspired to overthrow the princess' father. Would you enter into a marriage that could do nothing to help your kingdom but much to harm it if you were king?"

Gidon had to admit that would be very foolish.

"Finally, you have given King Gregor all the cause he would need for a pretense upon which he could reject the girl. You have exposed her backside to your gaze and spanked her. He could claim you shamed her in both cases. If he was serious about making a great point of it, he could have your head. But there is a reason why he would never do that."

Gidon rested his elbows on the table and laid his forehead into his hands. "So I really made a mess of things in any case."

"For you yes, but not for the King. I imagine he has a plan that includes you. Right now you are responsible for Princess Loretta and

I suspect you will continue to be responsible for her into the distant future, no matter what either of you think of it."

Gidon looked at him ruefully. "Thank you for building me up with all these wonderful benefits before kicking the hanging stool out from under me."

"Cheer up boy. It has been expedient for me to have taken two mistresses in my lifetime. But when I say Lady Aliruna is the love of my life, it is no joke. The love I bear her has never even been approached by my mistresses, even though I care for them and for the children they have given me. You have to deal with life in ways you do not wish to sometimes. But in all of it you can always be an honorable man."

Gidon wondered how he could be faithful to Getrudis and yet have knowledge of other women? That seemed a contradiction. Yet he remembered Bishop Elisha had asked him if he intended to take Frauke? The bishop had taught him much about the great men of the Holy Text who had many wives and concubines, yet the Invisible God blessed them. In spite of this, it did appear obvious having these women caused them all some kind of trouble. It also seemed to him, if he could manage it, being faithful to Getrudis was the better course. He would never want to lose her trust or the sweet relationship that existed between them.

Gidon sought to change the subject to other matters. "You and your lady have been very kind to us, and I do not know how I can repay you."

"Gidon you are the squire of my good friend who is Chief of the Long Knives. And your father is not only my friend and brother in the order, but we have fought before side by side. Do you remember the pearls on my lady's dress when you came to meet her? It was a gift from your father. He must have paid a king's ransom for such a set. He did not ask me to repay. We are friends. The bow I shoot he made especially for me. I know you are aware how long it takes to bring such a bow to life. It was a gift for the love he has for me. We are true friends. And I am your friend as well. I hope you will consider yourself mine."

The Baron grinned with a secret Gidon did not yet know. "Your steed Begleiter may be a little tired today. While you were sleeping and worrying about how to deal with women he was in my pasture, where waited four-year old mares wanting to be bred for the first time. I think he visited every one that was ready. It is a wonder he can get around at all today. I expect this time next year we will have a pasture full of little Begleiter foals romping around. He seems to have his own way of repaying things, and my mares will be sorry to see him go."

The two men laughed together about Begleiter cavorting among the mares.

It was the hour for the noon meal when the Baron and Gidon met again with the ladies. The wagon had been loaded and balanced to Herman Stellwagen's satisfaction. The Baron had provided four of his own horses to replace the two who were pulling the wagon they arrived in. They were geldings and could not intrude into his breeding stock. Herr Stellwagen had observed the wagon horses Gidon had arrived with were so old they were liable to die before they came to Almanya. All was in readiness except for some good food and final words of wisdom between them.

Princess Loretta and Lady Dolores appeared quite stunning in the more travel worthy garments Lady Aliruna and her miracle working seamstresses had provided for them in record time. Aliruna, however, was again dressed in her huntress garb, but in the interim period she had added to it the ensign of her husband over her left breast. Gidon recalled he had mentioned to her that his own Getrudis had made a huntress outfit after he taught her to shoot the bow. She was delighted when he said the men of Eastwatch acted like the garment was scandalous attire. So today she would make her own scandal. She was quite attractive with her white hair contrasting with the ensemble.

Lady Aliruna said she was going to set up a regular post rider between herself and Getrudis. She said it was certain they would be fast friends.

Baron Igil asked Gidon what he thought should be done with the tavern? He said mischief had been hatched there for years, and now seemed a good time to do something about it. The baron was in favor of burning it to the ground and being done with it. Gidon said a well-run tavern at that location could be a blessing to the weary traveler. Why not spy out the place and discover if highwaymen had taken it over. or if all was directed by the tavern owner? If it was not the owner's fault, clean it out for him. If the owner was at the center of the evil, then hang them all and put in an honest man to manage the operation. That seemed to the Baron a fine idea. "It would be good if a village could grow up around the tavern," he said.

When the meal and fellowship finished, all went down to the wagon and men were waiting. Herman and one of his men were seated on the horses that had been captured from the leaders of the group that attacked them. The other two men were on top of the wagon. One was in the seat beside Herman Stellwagen to learn how to drive the team. The other was sitting on top of the rearmost spare wheel where he could watch their rear. The ladies' horses were on long leads behind the wagon. Begleiter was standing beside the wagon horses, looking them over curiously, for they were geldings.

Baron Igil's Master-at-Arms came from the armory with five brand new swords called Spatha. He also had leather and wood scabbards. The particular version he held was approximately thirty inches in length. He handed one to Gidon that had a sabretooth tiger's head upon it, like the broadsword the bishop's swordsmith had made for him in what seemed a lifetime ago. Baron Igil smiled and said, "I think the Spatha makes a pretty good long knife." Gidon's broadsword was attached to his saddle but it appeared the other weapons were inside the wagon. He no longer wished for a pack horse. He had a pack wagon. In days to come Gidon would be surprised at all the thoughtful items Baron Igil and Lady Aliruna had packed into his wagon.

Gidon was anxious to get back on the road again. Still he would miss his new-found friends and benefactors. But sometimes a farewell is just a temporary parting. For Lady Aliruna would be as good as her word when it came to communicating and developing a friendship with Mistress Getrudis.

Gidon played the gentleman, helping the women keep their balance as they entered the wagon. The steps were quite narrow and he thought some kind of railing was needed that folded down with the steps. He saw Herman Stellwagen making notes on a piece of paper which he then tucked away. *He does not miss anything when it comes to his wagon projects,* Gidon thought. Princess Loretta graciously took his hand and favored him with a smile, so he immediately thought she was up to something. But he had a surprise for Lady Dolores. As he took her hand he said, "Watch your step my Lolita." She quickly looked into his eyes with a surprised expression. He favored her with a smile, pleased to see his words affected her for the good.

*****

When the re-equipped group finally got underway, they were a much better appearing party. Inside the wagon Lady Dolores was watching everything passing by outside the wagon with interest. But Loretta sat strangely quiet, seeming not to notice anything going on about her. What no one knew was the Lady Aliruna had paid her a visit in her room even before she was to be woken and dressed. She had given her a direct and blunt description of the way things were, as well as some warnings about how she could truly make her situation in life very bad.

One thing Lady Aliruna laid out with painful honesty was ways she could make her life very difficult with Gidon. She warned Loretta that her perfect features and skin of palest pink alabaster could never get between him and the love of his life, Getrudis. Over her protests of innocence, Aliruna declared to try to do so would earn his hate. She could even be sent away. But if she behaved as an honorable woman in all things and was dutiful and obedient to Gidon, she would likely be rewarded with a very happy life. In other words, Aliruna said, "If you live by your pride you will fail, and you will lose your pride even before you fall!"

Princess Loretta pondered her words. She knew there was a certain charm in her girlishness that Gidon was not oblivious to. But she now knew, for she had learned it the night before, brattiness and hard headedness were not qualities either he or the people he lived among respected. She saw that Lady Dolores had been trying to tell her that and failing because she was not listening. She determined she could act in keeping with her age and at the same time show herself the good sweet woman that endeared people to others. The question was, if Lady Aliruna was correct and she was to be under the authority of Gidon, would he release her if she did find someone suitable to marry? Or perhaps the King would force him to marry her. Could she live with such a circumstance? Would all in his house hate her?

*****

Gidon left it to Herman Stellwagen to set the pace. After all, the vehicle was experimental and top heavy. To overdrive it could end in catastrophe. Their success was dependent on its capabilities and the wise understanding of them. Gidon had shared with the Cartwright inventor his hope to catch up to Baron von Krieg and his father in five days. It would now take six, and that without mishap on the road.

The horses warmed up in the journey down from the Keep to the main road, so when they turned northward it was easy to fall into a smooth gait that let the miles roll by. The road was fairly level and Herman Stellwagen was able to keep a steady pace for four hours that gave the party over twenty miles. The stop came in the fifth hour when the horses got water, then walked the next hour. Then the grade began to rise, but at the pace they were now on it did not slow the animals.

It was during the first stoppage for water Lady Dolores left the wagon and asked to travel alongside Gidon for a way. She told Gidon, "Princess Loretta has not said a word since we began to travel again. I am wondering if she might be ill?"

Gidon answered, "She looked alright when I gave her a hand as she got in the wagon. But you are right. It is not like her not to be talking." They both laughed about that even though the concern for her was real.

Dolores asked Gidon. "How long do you plan to stop for rest tonight?"

"Depending on how tired the horses, but at least the four hours we will be without moonlight. If I had a change of teams, I might chance doing less. I had thought about your horses but do not know if they would accept the harness."

The Lady Dolores said, "Your Lolita does not know. I wish I could help."

It seemed to Gidon she was actively seeking ways to remind him of their sworn relationship and show her intent to keep the commitment she had made. He felt honored even as he was concerned for the future.

Strangely Gidon did feel energized by her commitment. It stimulated him to think this woman, so entrancing in her beauty and personality, had seriously chosen to belong to him, a man twelve years her junior. And there was the stabilizing influence of her realistic maturity when so much seemed to pose a challenge to his own presuppositions.

When he finally called a halt for the night, Gidon was surprised to see the princess emerge with a pot and ladle she had found among the provisions. She asked Gidon if one of the men could build them a fire and set up a tripod for her pot.

Gidon said, "Princess, I appreciate your desire for a hot meal but I am planning on precooked food for supper so we can get right to sleep."

Princess Loretta responded, "I thought we might cook some stew overnight so your men could start out with warm food to give them strength on the morrow."

Gidon gave the order for what she required.

By the time her pot was fixed only one man was ready to begin his watch. The remainder was in bed. The coriander and parsley along with the stewing goat pieces made an odor that was sure to cause men to wake up hungry. Princess Loretta consulted with Lady Dolores on the right amount of spices for she had never learned to cook. That night, as she sat alone by the fire keeping the pot stirred, she prayed the food would not be rejected.

The fire worked its chemistry on the ingredients and the whole was cooked down to a savory stew in four hours of stirring and simmering. Men gathered around and dipped portions into their own bowls, sopping the now hardening bread they had into the mixture. None complimented her on her culinary skills but no one poured their bowl out either. As the wagon began to roll Loretta lay prone in the hammock designed for a weary traveler.

Gidon was asked by Herman Reformierte if this was the same Loretta they had known? Gidon replied, “People, especially women, are like faceted jewels. They have many sides.” He thought that so sufficiently insightful that perhaps even Herman might be impressed.

*****

A young man rode toward Eastwatch on a tall, long-legged horse. He led an equally leggy animal so much like the first they may have been twins. Though he sat his horse like a military man his clothing was devoid of armor, with only a thick cloak which also served to wrap him when he rested, and a broad brimmed hat such as was favored by Herr Brute’ to ward off the rain and sun. His only weapons were a short version of a Spatha and a dagger. Even his saddle was trimmed down to the minimum required for his need and the horses’ comfort. One had the feeling he could ride as well without a saddle at all as with one. But saddles do more than help a man sit a horse. It held his water bag and his pouch of dried meat in place as he rode as fast as the terrain allowed.

He had been told that when the road forked, he was to bear left down a roadway overgrown and treacherous. He was surprised to discover the entire distance was mowed of grass and cleared of rock. When he came to the work crews along the way he found the first were laying out a reasonably straight path for a new road. The next crew was digging down the sides of the path laid out to make a smooth base against which a road could be made with reasonably shallow grades. He saw someone was in charge of this, a one-handed man who knew a bit about how to build a road.

He also took stock of the fact those who were doing the actual work were being guarded, but not harshly. This meant some kind of pledge of honor had probably been made by the prisoners so the guards were but a token gesture. Everywhere the men worked there were carts laden with water so laborers would not suffer from thirst. The whole operation appeared far more humane than prisoners were usually treated to.

The rider rode his horse into the middle of the village where he found the local tavern. He long ago learned the quickest way to find a person in a small village or town was to inquire at the tavern. And he was dry from the dust on the last twenty miles of road under construction. He left his horses standing after warning some urchins to not get near their back hooves for these were high spirited animals quick to kick and bite.

As he walked into the tavern, he was already speaking to Fat Max even as he walked up to the counter. "Good man, will you direct me to Fox Home?"

Fat Max gestured at the corner favored by the long knives. It was now occupied by the three women of Fox Home plus Lady Brigitta and Durchgefüweg. "There is the Mistress of Fox Home, speak to her."

The young man swept off his hat and bowed with a flourish. He was caught up in the aura of so much feminine loveliness in one place. He saw they were being guarded by one guard in a blue cloak and two fighting priests. "According to what I have been told about the women I could expect to meet," he said, "you must be the Mistress Brunhild," pointing at the woman sitting in the corner.

Brunhild nodded and smiled.

"That means you are the Lady Brigitta, wife of Brute' von Alemanni."

Brigitta bent her elbow to raise her hand about level with her face and wiggled her fingers at him.

Beside her was the Lady Gwynedd and he got her right as well. Then he spoke to Getrudis saying, "You must be Mistress Getrudis to whom my Lady Aliruna has written the message I now carry, though she sends greetings to you all."

It was then he looked at Durchgefüweg. Something happened to the young man at that moment. For several seconds he tried to speak and could not. Gone were his smooth charming manners. He could but stare and drink in her beauty. Finally he blurted out, "My lady…apologies… I know not your name."

"My name is Durchgefüweg, and I am but a tavern serving girl and no lady."

The fellow caught some of his old charm back and said, "My lady, I beg to differ. No woman can touch a cup and move it with the grace you have that is not to the manor born. I care not what you do to make your way but you are a lady, if only in my heart!"

Brunhild clapped her hands and cried, "Well said. Durchgefüweg, you have been found out." All the women laughed and the young man blushed red. He thought himself the butt of the joke, not knowing the secret held between them.

Getrudis guided the conversation to the necessities of the moment. "Durchgefüweg, you should show this man how to get his mount to the stables. I am afraid he is so taken with you he might not be able to follow directions.

The man said, "I have two mounts, Mistress." As if that was important.

Brunhild said, "I think we can accommodate two as easily as one. After you get through at the stables and bring our Durchgefüweg back, she will see you get cleaned up and bring you to Fox Home for supper." Durchgefüweg grinned at her. She had no intention of being his wash girl this day. She liked being seen as a lady again. It seemed a long time.

Chapter 23

Mysteries Revealed

The transition that took place in Princess Loretta was met with surprising response from the men who once held her captive. Though they were far from praising her culinary skills, they were appreciative of her efforts as well as her change in demeanor. It would lead to some interesting situations as the men became more comfortable with the maturing princess.

In her exploration of the content of the wagon, she made a surprising and unique discovery. It was the four recesses into the water tank that spanned from one side of the wagon to the other, located at the lowest point on the vehicle. Herman Stellwagen had shown remarkable insight into the ability of water to help stabilize the wagon by placing such a tank in a position where it could act as ballast does on a ship, instead of mounting water barrels on the sides. The storage recesses reduced the tendency of the water to slosh from one side to the other because they acted as bafflers.

The benefit the princess recognized was the recessed containers also held beer and wine at a somewhat cooler temperature. She could use these to gain favor with the men. Thereafter when a stop was made to water the horses, Loretta gave each of the men a small portion of beer as well.

Gidon started to protest, when she first distributed the drink, but when he saw the men's response to what she did, he kept mum, even though he knew that the alcohol in the beer would make the men desire more water than usual. He could smell water in the air and knew a sizable stream lay not far ahead. They could again water the animals and refill the tanks, when they came to it. They would, after all, eventually run out of beer, and the spaces left when the beer was removed would increase their water supply.

Princess Loretta approached Gidon with his own portion and he thanked her. She said, “I am pleased to be able to do some little thing to help my lord.”

Gidon did not completely trust her but he did appreciate the way her efforts appeared on the surface. The girl he originally met would have scarcely been willing to stay up while others slept stirring the savory stew as she had done. He decided complimenting her would encourage good behavior, “I am appreciative that your efforts have increased the happiness of our men.”

Loretta at first felt the impulse to retort phooey concerning the happiness of the men and demand how her actions affected his happiness with her? But then it dawned on her Gidon had said it influenced the happiness of our men, not his men. He had included her, saying the men were at least in part hers too. She held the little keg to her breasts and twisted her body back and forth giving Gidon a sweet smile that made her naturally red lips seem awfully appealing. Then she turned and went back to the wagon. Gidon noticed she was not walking with her princess walk. She absolutely seemed to be bouncing with each step.

Lady Dolores came up beside Gidon. He asked, “What do you think is going on with the princess?”

Her response was surprising. “Dolores is pleased and hopeful, Lolita is surprised and careful.”

Gidon looked at her and wondered if she was trying to give some mysterious answer like some mystic seer? He decided that she was too honest a woman for that and had not yet decided exactly what was going on. Dolores returned her horse to the back of the wagon and climbed inside. Gidon was confident his Lolita was going to try to learn more about what was going on in the mind of the princess for him.

Gidon sent Herman Reformierte and his mounted companion ahead to scout the water he could smell. Herman returned saying, "It is a wide stream yet fordable even though the water will come up to the wheel hubs. The bed in the stream is gravel and the current is not swift." Gidon asked him what had happened to his man. Herman answered, "There is a spot just up from the ford where animals came to drink. He is an excellent man with a sling so he hoped to have fresh meat by the time they got to the stream."

Gidon then spoke to Herman Stellwagen. "I presume you have some long ropes we can use to secure the wagon either to trees or horses to insure a safe portage?"

Herman the Cartwright said, "We know of this stream at our Keep. The water level is not constant and the current changes often. I have ropes, pulleys, and turnbuckles in a compartment under my feet. I think those will be adequate. There are eyebolts we can use on the frame fore and aft on both sides. I will take care of it when we get there."

Gidon was satisfied, if they were careful, they would be safe.

*****

Durchgefüweg thought this young man, who traveled on two horses with no protection, very interesting. He must be a brave man to venture out on his master's business this way. He was slightly older than her, possibly even in his mid-twenties, and he was lightly built for his height. Not at all like Gidon and the Baron, who seemed encased with bulging muscles. But clearly this man's duty was to carry messages, not engage in pitched battles.

She was keenly aware that since they had gotten the horses in front of the tavern, he was hardly taking his eyes off her to see where he was walking. After he stumbled the third time she said, "Sir, I think it would be wise if you watched where you are stepping. You are liable to stumble once too often and put a knot on your head. Or perhaps you will soil your boots. We are getting near to the stables."

Durchgefüweg thought to herself that he must not be the only person losing their mind. She had walked with this man all the way from the tavern to the stable and had never asked his name. "Sir, I am going to be embarrassed before Herman the Schmeid and his family if I cannot tell them your name. How are you called?"

"My name is Johannes Reisende. My birth name is Johannes. My father was very religious and he liked that Apostle best. The Baron Igil gave me the name Reisende when he gave me the duty of carrying messages and documents on his behalf. It is a good name for a man who travels on his Baron and Lady's business, which is why I am here."

"Did you grow up at the Baron Igil's Keep?" Durchgefüweg asked out of curiosity.

"No my lady. My father had been badly injured in war so he leased some land from a Hold Master maybe four days ride from here. After he died my father thought it for the best we go to Baron Igil. The man who married the Hold master's widow did not seem to like the followers of the Invisible God. It was at that place I grew up. I saw a very pretty and sweet little girl who looked a little bit like you. I think in my boyishness I loved her, but I could never hope to grow up with her and tell her so, for she was to the manor born."

"You know it is not the way to reach a woman's heart, telling her she looks like someone you used to love." Durchgefüweg wanted it planted in his head she was not the girl he was speaking of.

"No, my lady, but I did look forward to seeing her, even though she was so much younger than I. We went to the Chapel on the Hold every month till the true owner died." He laughed, "It was there people started calling me Johannes Taufer because one Sontag I threw one of my playmates into the river. Everyone said I was trying to baptize him!"

Durchgefüweg laughed and said, "Yes, I remember."

Johannes said, "What?" dragging the word out slightly.

"Oh, I only meant I remember something like that happened near where I grew up. The boy said he was only trying to baptize a sinner." Durchgefüweg hoped her twisting of the truth would be accepted. She did not want anyone to know where she was from.

Durchgefüweg pursued the illusion and asked, "So what happened to the little girl that you loved?"

"Nobody seems to know. I heard she had just disappeared and her protector had been murdered. Some think she may have been carried off, and I kind of hope she had."

"Why is that?" Durchgefüweg asked.

"We heard just days ago Herr Bruno, the new Hold master, had not been seen for some time. People went into his house looking for him. He was found in his basement torture chamber badly beaten. There were dead people down there as well. He was saying that he had been beaten up by demons, but he had all sort of Druid symbols on the walls. We do not know who beat him but we think he got what he deserved. He is now in chains and on his way to Almanya to await the King's Justice. When they unsealed the Chapel, where we used to worship… Forgive me my lady. I have said too much and do not need to speak of what was found in the Chapel. I am ashamed I have spoken of this to you. But you are easy to talk to. I shall never forget the day I met you."

Durchgefüweg started crying and Johannes put his long arms around her, quite forgetting his horses' reins. He was holding the tearful girl when Herman the Schmeid came out. "What is this?" he exclaimed. "You make our sweet Durchgefüweg cry and lord or no I will knock your head off!"

Durchgefüweg had to rush to explain to Herman he was comforting her, not causing her to cry. She begged him to please not knock his head off. She well knew that the Schmeid was such a powerful man that, failing Johannes hurting him with his dagger, he could literally do it.

Johannes Reisende made a courtly gesture with an arm saying, "I am gratified sir that this lady has such faithful friends as you. I have an engagement tonight, but on the morrow I would be honored if you would join me at the tavern for the famous Mead of Eastwatch. He walked into the stable with Herman and saw a war horse already in a stall. It was just then Herr Brute' rode in on his own mount, so Johannes commented, "It looks like my own steeds will be in good company this night."

Herr Brute' gave Herman the Schmeid the reins to his horse. Almost immediately the older woman of the three appeared and took them from his hand. "Thank you Adela," the schmeid said gratefully.

The older daughter made her appearance before the group. She was quite shy, which was perfectly understandable considering all that had happened to her at Heim. She curtsied before Johannes Reisende and said, "Would the lord wish me to take his horses?" To her everyone who had fine horseflesh was a lord. Johannes handed her the reins and said, "Give them your best."

"You need not worry sir. Adelina is most painstaking with the animals. She loves them as much as I do." Adelina looked at Herman adoringly, basking in the warmth of his praise. She had come to almost worship this gentle powerhouse of a man who she thought was very much like the war horses he loved to care for best of all.

Brute' said, "I had not known the women's names Herman. Tell me, does your little girl's name also begin with an 'A'?"

The little one looked at Brute' and smiled. She was not afraid of Brute' in spite of his scars. For the man she most admired, even before Herman the Schmeid, also had scars on his face, and that was Gidon who had rescued her as well as her mother and sister from the bad men who came to Heim.

"Yes Master Brute'. She is called Adeline. All are named for Saint Adèle. This has been the practice in her parent's family for three generations because of the esteem the family held the saint in. Why I do not know. But every night I thank the Invisible God for bringing them into my life."

"And to which of the two older women are you married? The mother or the daughter?" Brute' asked.

Herman the Schmeid grinned sheepishly. "To be honest I do not know. It has not seemed to matter. We all work together quite well."

Brute' turned to the messenger. "Johannes Reisende, I remember you from when I last visited Baron Igil. I suppose you have business here and have not come just for the pleasure of staring at our Durchgefüweg?" That was the Baron's way of telling him not too subtly he had noticed the young man could not keep his eyes off the maiden.

"Yes, Master Brute', I remember your visit well, along with the fine stallion upon which you were mounted at the time. I do not see him in the stalls."

"No, I lost him trying to ride by night on the road we are now making anew. It was a shame. The horse I now have is steady but I have yet to try him in battle, save at the monastery and I was dismounted for much of that fight."

"I imagine this one will do fine. He has the look of some of Herr Tweitman's stock." Johannes said.

"You know your horseflesh. Since you have already had a close look at the road we are building, I want to take you to inspect my men who compose the first guard of Eastwatch Keep. You can send Durchgefüweg on her way. I would not have you distracted, so that you give Baron Igil a description of curves when we are talking about making narrow ways straight." Herr Brute' gave one of his laughs that usually seemed as if they came from the grave.

There was no doubt Johannes Reisende was reluctant to bid Durchgefüweg adieu. My lady, can I hope to see you at Fox Home tonight?" He gave her one of his courtly bows.

"You forget sir, it is my duty to escort you so you do not get lost." she replied.

Brute' was feeling a bit impish so he said, "You do not have to bother about that girl, I will be happy to show him the way."

Durchgefüweg gave him a frown that said she did not appreciate the humor. "He has a bath reserved for him at the tavern before he goes to Fox Home."

Brute' thought he might say he could get a bath at the Burgomeister's home but thought, having had fun, it would not be good to provoke the woman.

*****

Gidon was amazed at how complex the process of moving the wagon across the stream really was. But Herman Stellwagen, moved about placing ropes and equipment as if this was a task performed every day. He had thought the matter out and was now intent on teaching Gidon's men as he worked. The team of horses was unhooked from the wagon while he instructed a man on the other side just how to choose a beam and cut it to be hooked to the traces once the horses were across.

Ropes were hooked to the frame eyebolts at the bottom of the wagon and the framework eyebolts at the top of the wagon. The lower ropes were to be used to keep the wagon from turning in the current and the upper were to keep it from tilting from the pushing of the water. He personally secured the ropes to trees and rigged the roping so they could belay the wagon and hold it secure without much effort on the part of the men. Gidon did his best to remember what he saw the cartwright do in case he needed to do such a thing again when he was without an expert.

Gidon stripped his chainmail and his weapons so neither he nor the horse would be cumbered as they crossed and re-crossed the stream. He felt very vulnerable.

Lady Dolores rode her horse across the stream giving it enough time to be sure of its footing with each step. When he offered to saddle the horse of Princess Loretta, she told him she would feel much safer if he would carry her across on his horse. Gidon knew that was not really the safest way, but her expressed dependency was not a thing he was taking for granted. They did make it across safely but both women had clothing, damp from spray, that needed to dry.

After they had successfully accomplished the crossing and pulled the ropes and equipment from the other side Herman Stellwagen confided to Gidon he saw sign the stream was rising from melting snows in the mountains. By tomorrow he thought it would have been impassable for several days.

The ropes were draped and the metal parts dried and rubbed with oil. The roping would not be completely dry by the next morning but that could not be helped. The men all could strip down to under breeches but the women had a more serious problem, for they were concerned with womanly modesty.

Princess Loretta was a bit disturbed when one of the men of Herman Reformierte walked up to her clad only in his under breeches. He had been the one who first came to scout the stream with Herman and stayed to hunt with his sling. In all of the work that had to be done he quite forgot to give her his present. He had gotten three fat conies for her to practice her culinary skills upon. No one thought to tell him it was not part of princess education to learn how to gut and skin rabbits.

But the princess was determined to prove herself in all things. Gidon saw she was about to make a mess of the project and came to help her. He was wearing only under breeches and the tunic he had stored in the wagon with his chainmail before the crossing. His only other accoutrement was the weapons belt. Loretta found herself enjoying the muscle that showed in his arms dressed as he was. She had to force herself to pay attention to his instruction. After showing her how to do it, he did not volunteer to do the other two but rather told her to try while he was there to watch.

As she worked on the project, she came to realize Gidon's move of putting the gutting and skinning of the creatures back in her hands had been intentional. He had gotten some amusement from watching her trying. And it had been a kind of test. *Well, I showed him*, she thought. *I am just as good as any serf girl he will find!*

The men had rigged a spit so the rabbits could be cooked over the fire. After the difficult chore of moving the wagon across the stream, all agreed they tasted extra fine. And to honor the critters not a scrap was left but some of the internal organs which baited set-hooks hoping for a morning breakfast of fish before moving on.

After the meal Loretta and Dolores had a curtain put up using tent material; they had their own fire and line intending to get their clothing completely dry. Dolores informed Gidon he must come on their side of the curtain as their protector. They wrapped themselves in mantles for modesty and he complied. But Dolores had a surprise for him. After everything was hanging and drying nicely Dolores turned her back to Gidon raising the mantle above her hips. "See there my lord. Are not the buns of your Lolita every bit as firm as the princess?"

All three of them laughed and there were a few pokes in the ribs and winks on the other side of the curtain. The hardened men who were once forced to follow Gidon had now become quite fond of him and protective of the women as well. The ladies settled down and watched the fire, one on each side of Gidon who leaned against the front wagon wheel. It was cozy.

One of the men sang an old song with his high tenor voice and the others joined the chorus. A measure of wine had made all drowsy. It was a very good thing no enemies lurked about that night.

*****

When Durchgefüweg left Johannes, she headed straight to Fox Home. With every step the enormity of the error she had made grew in her mind. She was frightened her secret might get out and she was also unsettled because she really liked the man, the boy she had once known, had become. Could there be any hope that the girlish daydreams she had harbored about this young man when she was but a child actually could really come to pass? Her life had been filled with so much pain she was afraid to hope, but able to fear disappointment.

She found the three women of Fox Home gathered around the long table busy with needle and thread. Brunhild looked up at Durchgefüweg and smiled, "We are glad you are here. We are just putting the finishing touches on some garments for the messenger from Baron Igil and Lady Aliruna. We did not want him to feel ill at ease because of his dress at supper tonight."

Brunhild, always the quickest to read people said, "My dear, what is worrying you?"

Durchgefüweg sank down in a chair. "All this work you have done to help me hide my identity. I may have given it away a few minutes ago. For he knew me when I was but a child. He is from my real father's Hold. He recounted an incident when his father and he would come to Chapel on our Hold. He had thrown a rude playmate in the river, and all the children called him Johannes Taufer. I said I remembered, and then I had to make up a story that something like that had happened at my home and the children called that boy John the Baptist because he was trying to baptize sinners."

"Do you think he believed your story?" asked Gwynedd.

"You mean my lie. Oh, I hated lying to him. I just did not know what to do."

"Men are often quick to believe lies when they are captivated by beauty." Gwynedd observed. "But sometimes they only pretend to believe a lie because of their feelings for the woman. Does he have real feelings for you?"

"When I was a little girl I thought so. I know I would daydream about him. But those are childish fantasies. I know today he as much as told me that when he was a lad he was sweet on the daughter of the manor. That was me." Durchgefüweg found herself clinging onto a strand of hope once more.

Brunhild, so seldom shaken, said, "Tonight I am sure all will be revealed. And I am confident the outcome will at the least not be too bad. I think we have finished his garments, so after he gets clean, present these to him."

Getrudis said, "One thing I would advise is that you do not act as his wash girl. He does not need to see too much of you before he comes to dinner. And let us be frank. Those breasts of yours could be a real distraction for a man."

Gwynedd said to Getrudis, "You should know about the trouble you can get into by letting certain men, like one named Gidon, see too much of his wash girl." And all the women laughed.

*****

As predicted, the stream was swollen when Gidon and the men arose. In the middle of the night the women had collected their now dry clothing and slipped into the wagon to take advantage of hammocks, which to say the least were more comfortable than the gravelly damp ground. It took no debate for the men to have a consensus of opinion on being quiet and allowing them to sleep till breakfast was ready.

The swollen stream proved a difficulty when it came to retrieving the set hooks laden with fish. The men had been wise to choose places where water was calm and formed pools outside the now fast-moving channel. Had they put them into the main body of the swift flowing stream there would have been no fish for breakfast. But the big fish chose the quiet pools to feed on the little fish which did not care to fight the stream. The little fish fed on what the stream washed in, then the big fish fed on the little fish, and the men fed on them.

There is a convenient way to eat a breakfast of fish cooked over an open fire. The fish is gutted but otherwise left intact. A piece of hardwood with a point is inserted through the mouth and pushed so it comes out beside the tail. Then, when the fish is cooked, the head is removed and it is opened from the bottom, where it was previously gutted. When spread open, the skin and scales make the plate from which the cooked fish is consumed. Whatever remains is then tossed into the water where it goes to feed the life in the stream. There is nothing to clean up.

A single fish caught that morning was more than enough to satisfy most appetites, with the exception of Herman Reformierte. It was not till after breakfast the portage ropes were placed on top of the wagon to dry in the sun as they traveled. The group started out with light hearts and full stomachs. They were catching up to the company from Eastwatch. Gidon could see the sign of their passage on the roadway. And he was glad he saw no sign of other travelers between them.

*****

One of the young women from Heim who had been employed at the tavern served as the wash girl for Johannes Reisende. Of the four women and two girls Oma had selected, none had yet had the experience of caring for a traveler in this way. They were again instructed on the proper manner in which to conduct both the washing and themselves. Oma had hastened to remind them this was simply a service and they should not put a sexual meaning to it. There was always a fear that, considering what they had endured when Heim was invaded, a sense of panic might rise up to haunt them.

Durchgefüweg had told Oma what had happened during the conversation at the stable. It was Oma who decided only a fully mature woman would be used in this first experience for the sake of avoiding an issue and for an example to the others. But she also chose the one who most resembled Durchgefüweg. In this way she hoped to confuse Johannes' mind. An allusion helped by the fact the women had started copying her hair style. But Oma as much as told Durchgefüweg that since they had both been attracted to one another when they were young, and that attraction had been quickly reborn, it seemed to her he would soon realize who she really was. And then she would have to explain why she lied to him.

Johannes Reisende felt very ill at ease with so many women passing through and watching him as he enjoyed his hot tub bath. Oma explained the women and girls were in training which was why they were all in his room and she was supervising them. She said, "I thought a gentleman such as yourself would be patient with us. We will not charge you for the bath because you are helping me teach these girls." She neglected to mention he was not being charged at all because he was the guest of Fox Home.

Durchgefüweg made a point of not entering the washroom because she wanted him to focus on Benedicta, the woman who had been selected to wash Johannes because she looked the most like her. When he was dried and his hair combed out, he returned to his room to find Durchgefüweg waiting with the clothes made for him by the women of Fox Home. He asked, "Does the Mistress of Fox Home see that all her supper guests receive new sets of clothing?"

Durchgefüweg was suddenly embarrassed, fearing he might have been offended. "No. But you see that even though their men have been gone but a short time they miss them desperately, and tonight is a special night because they believe Lady Aliruna will have included news of them in her letter to Mistress Getrudis. So that makes you very special to them."

Johannes Reisende looked her directly in the eyes and spoke with great sincerity. "My lady, I would wish to be very special in your eyes!"

Durchgefüweg blushed deeply. "I think it fair to say I do find you special. But more than that I could not, would not say, until I know more about you." She paused. Then she said, "I must go and change for supper while you are getting dressed. I will return shortly." She left the room feeling deeply disturbed, feeling she again had spoken and behaved foolishly. She admitted to herself that something about this man, she knew when they were younger, made her lose her self-control.

She purposely chose the very plain dress and not the fine one Brunhild had given her for special occasions. How to handle the situation was still not settled in her mind. So until she felt it was safe or even right to reveal herself to him, she was determined to be cautious. But it was plain to her that he was somewhat ill at ease, being dressed more finely than she, when they started out for Fox Home. But one thing he did see in making the short walk was the respect Durchgefüweg had earned in the village from the people who lived there. He thought this spoke well for her character.

When the couple arrived, they found they were not the first of the guests for supper to already be at Fox Home. Herr Brute' was seated at one end of the table with Brigitta by his side. Bishop Elisha had been asked by Brunhild to sit at the other end and officiate over the meal. Mistress Brunhild placed herself in the middle of the table with seats on either side of her for Gwynedd and Getrudis. Snaggle Tooth had invited himself to the meal. Frauke had chosen to work with the serving staff to make sure things went on satisfactorily during the meal. She had already become a real asset to all of the household.

The table had been set so Baron Igil's rider would be directly across from the ladies. And Durchgefüweg would be by his side. At the last minute the Burgomeister and his wife sent their apologies saying one of their grandchildren was not feeling well and they could not come. It was well known they doted more and more on the children and were reluctant to leave them solely in the care of the nanny. Their absence made Johannes Reisende feel more like he was the focus because their side of the table was reduced from four to two.

As they waited for the first course to be served, Johannes Reisende expressed his appreciation for the clothing. He said, "My job is to move as quickly as possible to deliver the messages in my care. I do not carry any extra weight including clothing. In truth, I usually deliver the messages or documents and wait for a reply. It is seldom I am treated so royally and particularly by such a group as impressive as yourselves."

The bishop said, "In the Land of Eire there is a stone that is very hard to get to. But they say that anyone who can reach the stone and kiss it is given the gift of eloquent speech. It could be our friend has kissed such a stone." That evoked laughter and helped to set everyone at ease.

A meal at Fox Home is always a superb affair since Brunhild became the Mistress. Two hours of pleasurable eating and talking made more delightful by the companionship passed. Johannes had been fascinated with Snaggle Tooth and he returned the compliment. Johannes told the story how Baron Igil had presumed the great cat's appearance on Gidon's ensign figurative until he was told the animal was quite real. He and his lady were both anxious to come and meet the remarkable sabretooth.

Johannes Reisende began by telling the ladies of the greetings sent by the Lady Aliruna. He conveyed a general letter to the Mistress Getrudis that could be read before the whole, and there was another separately sealed letter that was for her eyes only. He said that he did not know the contents of the private letter. He offered his help if there were any questions concerning either, saying he would try to answer them honestly.

It was then he got quite serious. He said, "It is not my intent to insult any of you. I hold you all in the highest esteem. However, I think there is a matter where all have not been completely honest with me, and I do not know why. When I was a boy there was a girl much younger than I and above my station in life. I was for all of that, hopelessly in love with her in my boyish way. To this day some of those emotions remain. Should she yet live I expect her age would be about the same as Durchgefüweg, who looks very much like I should expect her to look. Today, if she was yet unwed, she would be called the Baroness Odilia. I am suspicious that Durchgefüweg might be that woman, especially since everyone has worked so hard to turn me away from the idea including the lady herself. All I know is Durchgefüweg makes me feel very much as I did so long ago, except this love I feel for her is deeper and stronger than anything that might lurk in the heart of a child. What do you say to my confession?"

The silence in the room was like a weight. Who would answer this young man first?

Chapter 24

GID-VISU

Herman Stellwagen appreciated the urgency Gidon felt to catch up with Baron von Krieg and his father Gid-visu. The Baron and Gid-visu were also concerned about Gidon. They had been moving ahead of the reports concerning his adventures and by this time felt concern he had not rejoined the company. Herman Stellwagen had gotten everything his wagon horses had to give and now they were at the point where they could not continue moving as rapidly as before.

The mounts used by Herman Reformierte and his man were failing fast. They were not of the quality of Begleiter or the Andorran white horses rode by the women. And even Begleiter, Gidon's great mount, had lost weight and was showing strain. Begleiter had been making more miles than the other horses because Gidon was always watching his back as well as keeping an eye to the front. The young squire tried using Princess Loretta's horse to give Begleiter some rest time where he was not carrying his weight. But the horse objected very strenuously. Gidon had heard stories of horses who would run themselves to death in response to the need of their riders and he counted his steed one who would do just that.

On the morning of the sixth day since leaving Baron Igil, they spotted the company moving ahead of them in the distance. Gidon considered staying on the move instead of stopping for water and feed when those ahead of him paused for midday, but the condition of the horses argued against it. Gidon took a full stop and even walked the riding animals for the first hour after restarting their march. The women walked with him instead of using the wagon. They wanted to lighten the load there as well. Even Herman Stellwagen came to the front of his horses and led them. Baron von Krieg, being informed by scouts of Gidon's nearness, called an early stop in their day so his party could rejoin the group.

When the Baron got a closeup look, he saw the need for Gidon's horses to have a day of rest. He proclaimed the following day a Sontag or Lord's Day so everyone could rest. The round knight's pavilion tent Lady Aliruna provided came out of the wagon for the first time. Inside it was about twelve feet in diameter. It allowed considerable space for people to rest in some measure of comfort, though the sides were only about five feet tall. The one drawback to such a tent was that it was not designed for a cooking or heating fire. But well-trimmed wicks allowed for light and a little warmth to dispel the night chill.

It was quite a meeting when Princess Loretta and Lady Dolores were introduced to the Baron and Gid-visu. The fighting priests were present as their stories were told, but Herman Stellwagen chose to seek rest early after caring for the horses. He saw no need to hear it all twice. The King's Rider caused Herman and his men some discomfort when he questioned them about their past activities and he took notice they were wearing Gidon's ensign and carrying fine swords courtesy of Baron Igil. So he finally said, "I suppose if my squire and my friend in arms find some merit in you we should at least give you a chance."

Gidon thought he might tease Loretta and give her another test at the same time. He announced to the group the princess was learning to skin animals and cook so she should be allowed to help with the food preparation. The princess was not going to be outdone. She said, "Oh yes. I want the lessons and the practice. I might need the experience when Squire Gidon reduces me to a scullery girl."

They all laughed at her quick wit and saucy retort, but Gidon was not through with her.

"Baron, I believe Princess Loretta might wish to lodge a complaint with you about my shameful treatment of her after rescuing her. She might want you to have me whipped or something. After all, my crimes are spanking her, tying her up, and then when she was in a helpless condition, I did kiss her."

The Baron bowed to the princess. "It is entirely my fault Princess Loretta. I should have sent him away for the mandatory seven years as a Page where he could have learned knightly behavior. But that is supposed to start in our country when a lad is seven years old. He started rather late so there may be little hope for him."

The princess suddenly got very serious. She said, "I did give him a rather difficult time so I think his actions were not inappropriate. In truth he did not spank me very hard, And as for the other, it was because he could not be sure of me. If he spanks me again, I shall scream and yell but I will always believe he has my best interest at heart."

"Well spoken, princess. All women could scarce say that about every man but I think you are safe trusting your backside to this one. Indeed, I have trusted him with my very life and he has proven true," responded the Baron.

Lady Dolores spoke up. "Indeed sir. If what we hear is correct it may well be the princess will be trusting his judgment for some time. As for me, I have sworn myself to him. Which oath, I will fulfill without any reservations, as soon as my duties to Princess Loretta are complete." She felt better for having made public declaration before these men.

When the meal was finished and some wine passed around, the group was lounging contentedly within the tent. Baron von Krieg said, "My friend Gid-visu has been promising to tell the story of how he came to be over three hundred years old. I know him for an honest man so I believe his claim to be true even before I hear the account. However, he has promised and I have eagerly awaited the day to know all. If the women will indulge us in silence, this is the night the matter needs to be told."

The Baron seated himself beside the fighting priests and the women took places near Gidon, the princess was sitting beside him with the lady prone at his feet. Gid-visu rose and stood at the center of the tent so he could be fully erect. Gid-visu said, "The only way I know how to tell this is from the beginning:

"At the time my story begins, my name was Gidon as my father and his father before him. I lived with my wife and family in the stone and thatch house which is now at the perimeter of the village as you travel from Giant's Gap to Eastwatch. At that time my home lay completely outside the village so I could come and go without neighbors knowing what I was about. Even then I was a forester like my father before me. But I as yet had no reputation for building bows. That would come three hundred years later after my return.

"It took quite a bit of effort to provide for a wife and six children. We had been married nine years and six of those years she presented me with the total of three sons and three daughters. On the day the beggar came I was getting my things together to go to the forests to see what it would provide with the early spring. This beggar was quite unlike most beggars we see, even beggar priests. He was dressed in a dirty yellow robe that looked as if he had come a long way. It was soiled and stained but the fabric was like nothing I had ever seen in my life. He knew my name and I immediately believed he had chosen my house on purpose.

"After we fed this beggar, he said he had come with a message. But he never said who this message was from. His exact words were, 'I have come to tell you that it has been seen you are not a man who respects religion. You must pray and seek truth, otherwise some terrible calamity could befall you and your family.'

"I laughed at him and said, 'To whom must I pray? I do not believe in the gods of the trees and those in animals. I do not believe in the gods of wood and stone made with men's hands. How should I know that any god at all really exists?'

"The beggar said, 'There is a God to be sure, and demons are real. If you pray that the True God would reveal Himself, with all sincerity, He would do so. And you would be safe from the demons as well.'

"I laughed at him and sent him on his way. As he walked away, he seemed to be swallowed by the early spring fog. It was eerie how he just seemed to vanish in the fog."

One of the fighting priests interrupted. "Pardon me lord Gid-visu, but your account of the fog being of an eerie nature does not make sense to me. Is not the early spring fogs a natural thing sent to us by the True God to remind how the earth was watered before The Flood? We need to know more concerning this."

Gid-visu nodded his head. "Pardon me if I should be lacking in details. They have been ever present before me for many years, so I tend to picture them when I do not say them. The first reason the fog seemed eerie and unnatural to me was the way the beggar disappeared. When a person walks away from you in fog it often seems they disappear from the top down. In this fog the beggar disappeared from the bottom up. It became more unnatural because as the day progressed the fog did not dissipate in the sun but seemed to grow stronger. I had to set out in a fog so thick I did not see the trees around me at times. I have seen nights in the forest when I could see better than I could that day.

"It was the next thing that happened when I had gotten deep in the wood that heightened the strangeness of it all"

The people leaned forward in expectation of what he would say. The princess drew close to Gidon's arm and Dolores set up and rested against his legs.

"I saw a rare silver fox. Its fur seemed so lustrous and soft looking I thought how wonderful it would be to bring it to my wife. She was so much in my heart, not just because of her beauty but because of her wonderful spirit. For her to have such a fur would be a thing unlike that owned by even the wealthiest in Eastwatch. It was like the fog had opened between me and the animal but it was yet too far for a shot at a fox who was watching me. They are so quick. I knew I had to get closer. But each time I began to get close enough to shoot the wily animal would move away again.

"The trailing of the fox continued for hours. It was the same thing over and over as if the animal was toying with me. A few times I thought to give up. It would be an interesting thing to tell around a fire with some warm mead in my hands on a winter's day. But each time I thought to give up it seemed right at that moment the animal would approach. Only just a bit, but enough to make me think he would come too close one of these times and I would have him. I lost all track of time. Neither did I any longer know where I was in the forest.

"At last it seemed as if the fox was moving through a greenish yellow mist. I had gone too far and too long to give up now. I was determined to have that fox!"

This time the other fighting priest stood up. "We have heard of such a green and yellow fog surrounding events when something supernatural is about to occur. People who have told of such a thing have been recorded in the Scriptorium. Often they have reported time seems to change. But you said you had already lost track of time so you would not know if time had changed or not would you?"

"That is right," Gid-visu replied. "I believe time had changed. I even believe I had traversed seas, though my feet never left the ground or stepped into a boat. What was going on was beyond a feeling of eeriness. This thing I was experiencing seemed both very real and very strange."

Gid-visu continued. "After following the fox through the greenish yellow mist, with fog like a cloud over its head, I could not say how long it had been. We came to a place where all these phenomena disappeared and I was looking at the fox and feeling very tired. I had managed to wear out my shoes on the trip but I still did not know how far I had traveled. My feet were very sore.

"The fox ran around a great stone and I was so exhausted all I wanted to do was sit down and lean into that stone to maybe sleep a little bit. I had despaired of ever getting that fox. It was then one of the most beautiful maidens I have ever seen in my life walked round the stone to where I sat.

"She said to me 'If you linger there you will die.'

"Then she posed a riddle in a poem that I remember to this day;

In stones there are spirits,
In the waters a voice is heard:
Wind of hell sweeps the earth!

"She wore a dress that was most strange. Such a garment I had never seen the like of before. But it was very fine material with rich stitching all over it and it flowed down to almost touch the ground. She was not very tall but from what I could make out it seemed her figure was as perfectly proportioned as her face.

"I think I had said it when I first saw her, but if so I said it again. 'Who are you and where am I?'

"She seemed both amused and serious at the same time. When she spoke it was like the tinkling of small bells. 'In our tongue my name would be difficult for a man from your land to pronounce. A translation into your tongue would call my name something like Jewel Maiden. I was…I am the favorite concubine of the Mikado Toba.'

"It was not that I wanted to be impolite but I was getting more and more confused and I still really did not have any answers. I asked her, as politely as I could what or who was a Mikado Toba?

"She said, 'Mikado is his title. It is like emperor. I believe you have such a person in your world?'

"'Yes, we have a man called the Holy Roman Emperor who has great authority.'

"The Jewel Maiden said, 'Yes, this is the way it is in our land. He has authority of life and death over all his subjects. Many there are who hate the Mikado, and many hate me for my influence on him. Especially the aristocratic women called Nyokan hate me. This is why they plotted an attempt on his life and tried to make it look like I was behind it. Because of all that has happened I am in these woods to meet you as part of my labors to bring order back to the land.'

"I told her I did not understand how meeting me at this place would do these things.

"Again, the Jewel Maiden smiled and it seemed it was as if she knew some great secret she was about to impart. 'They would have never dared to attack the Mikado or seek to bring down my person if they had not been influenced by a demon.'

"I asked her how she knew all this to be true? At times I wondered if she might not be more than she appeared.

"'We know this demon well,' the Jewel Maiden responded. 'He likes to inhabit brothels where he enters into the poor women, many of whom were sold by their families into prostitution. Then he lures the worst of men into committing acts that are outrageous and often end in their execution. Sometimes the men being influenced by the demon inside the girls insanely kill them as well.'

"'It was this very demon who in Cathay entered into Hojii consort to the Emperor Iuwao. It is not limited by boundaries of distance or time. His purpose is to inhabit women closest to emperors and kings in all lands to bring the leaders of men to destruction whenever possible.'

"Again I told her the story seemed rather hard to believe. She told me that I should think about it a little while. What is it that can influence a man who has a good and loving wife at home to risk all in a brothel?

"The Jewel Maiden continued her story. 'There was a holy man at the Summer Palace when all this occurred. He chased the demon and forced it to go into this stone. But he did not have the power that comes from the God of gods. So all he could do was cause the demon to go into this large stone. We call it the Death Stone because he has the power to kill many of those who touch it, and especially if they lean against it.'

"I told the Jewel Maiden that it did not make sense to me that I should be lured here. She said, 'You have many things to learn here and something to give. We must have this from you to accomplish the plan to ultimately defeat the demon, even though he is confined for now. And I need for you to do these things so I can resume my position with the Mikado who loves me above all other women.'

"Once again I told her that I did not understand my value in all this. She did not answer me directly but said, 'It was because this mission was so important that Inari, the chief of all demons who appear as foxes, agreed to lure you here and help us in our purpose. You will be rewarded greatly but I warn you that anytime Inari helps humans there is always a price to pay. You cannot do anything about it for you are already being assessed that price.'

"I feared what that price might be," Gid-visu told the group. "But I knew not how to escape.

"She then led me some distance into her land far away from the Death Stone. It is difficult to describe the place she took me to. It had a roof but all the sides were open. And when she closed a side the shutters came down from the top and were made of some kind of wood. Even the floors were of a wood I did not know. There was a pallet on the floor and for a pillow a block on which one was supposed to rest his head. It was all very strange but not at all uncomfortable. She bathed me and fed me some food I did not recognize, then she gave me a drink of some strange wine. I slept very soundly and when I awoke birds were singing their morning songs, and I found new clothing laid out for me with beautiful soft slippers for my feet."

Baron von Krieg stood and stretched his legs. "It seems to me this woman is either a witch or demon herself. Did you ever have any indication she might not be all she claimed?"

"Yes," Gid-visu replied. "When I was reclining drowsily on the mat, she let her hair down. It went well below her hips to the back of her knees. For a moment I thought her hair might be a tail attached to her head and not her spine. But as she changed her robe, I could see she was completely a woman and her beauty never shifted. I admit she stirred me but I knew she was totally given to the man she called Toba."

Gid-visu continued with his account. "It was yet early when we set out for a place she called the Amadera Temple. She told me a story about true love that was supposed to have taken place at this temple, but for the life of me I can no longer recall it. When we got there we did not go inside the temple but instead we went to a pond which had a tablet beside it, which she told me was inscribed with the words Birth Water. She invited me to drink. I said I did not wish to drink the water that comes from a woman when she gives birth. It was then she told me this was not the water from women but the water that gives women the ability to conceive. Then I drank and it tasted very sweet.

"It was then I saw a pavilion floating in the water on the far side of the pond. On the pavilion, a woman who was wearing a dress not unlike the one Jewel Maiden wore, but it was far more exquisite. She was playing a musical instrument that looked like a long narrow table with many strings running the length thereof. I did not know this instrument but was told its name was called Koto. The Jewel Maiden said the woman who was playing it was a master, hence she played the seventeen-string variety which was often played at the court of the Mikado.

"I asked the Jewel Maiden who this woman was because I believed it was to her I had been brought. She said she was Hito-koto-Kwannon and I had the honor of looking upon the living embodiment of the goddess of love and wisdom. I smiled because I plainly did not believe this. She said to me, 'Do not mock! Do you see her smile? She smiles with eternal youth and infinite tenderness.'

"Once more she gave me a riddle in the form of a poem;

The flowers fade.
Touched by frost, leaves float to earth.
In the bosom of the sea,
Flowers hidden neath waves give birth,
Petals fade not, like on the land.
Nor feel the chill of winter's hand.

"You wonder how I can remember these poems so well? Well, so do I! But I have turned them over and over in my mind for many years. This is the first time I have told the whole of the story to anyone."

Once again a fighting priest rose to his feet. "You say the Jewel Woman proclaimed this other woman the goddess of love and wisdom. There have been many such declarations down through history beginning with Semiramis also known as Astarte. Why even Jezebel is a good example of what I am saying. Almost all of these women have been shown to be in league with the devil, and none I know of has not been an adulteress also."

Gid-visu replied, "Worthy priest I dispute nothing you are saying. I am only telling what occurred. Be patient till my story is finished and then you may judge it how you will. There is something in what you say that is related to all the other accounts of goddesses of love and wisdom. She said the divine feminine is best revealed in the infinite beauty of conception, and this is the way the demon would be defeated. I did not know what she meant by that at the time but I later learned."

The priest said, "Go on with your account. I am fascinated how it will all end."

Once again Gid-visu picked up his narrative. "Jewel Woman led me to the water's edge nearest the pavilion. She said she could not stay but I should go out to meet the goddess. I took off my clothes and attached them on my head. When I started to go into the water to swim out to her, tentacles came up out of the water trying to grab me and pull me under. If it had not been for some young maidens swimming in the water unmolested, I would have been surely drowned. I barely made it back upon the shore.

"Then the maidens brought together some floating boards that I could walk across even though I felt terrified for fear of falling in the water. It was then I saw the maidens I took to be but young girls were fully grown women. They were smaller in every way but they were, all twenty-eight of them, adult women. They looked very much alike but later I would be able to identify each one of them separately. Every time I looked they would be swimming around the pavilion always keeping the same order. When I asked the love goddess about this, she said they were her followers and representative of certain constellations seen in the night sky.

"I was with her for thirty days, which I calculate was ten years back home for each day I was with her. During that time she would play for me and bring incredible sounds out of her instrument that sometimes made me think it was speaking to me.

"Each day masters would come and teach me. One master taught me a form of fighting called Open Hand. Another taught me a form where the weight of the opponent is used against him. I was taught about making bows with incredible strength. Others came and taught the use of swords and many other cutting instruments. Some were masters at using farm implements as weapons and others were expert with the use of staffs. Some came to talk to me about seeing beauty in all things. It seemed each master used only one day to impart his discipline but I now realize they were investing many years into me.

"And every night…Well every night one of the followers of the love goddess would come out of the water after I had eaten and had drink. I would lie there helpless as they overshadowed me and on the following morning I would feel so weak I could hardly move. Then the goddess would give me some of the Birth Water and I would be completely restored. Oh, I forgot to mention, each one of the water maidens left me a bag filled with some kind of riches. I got many pearls, gold, and gemstones, as well as beautiful bags of jade.

"On the twenty-ninth day I was told my lessons were complete. But on the bank of the pond two beautiful women were seated playing a board game, instead of the masters I was used to seeing waiting on me. I watched for a little bit and then asked the love goddess what they were playing with the black and white stones? She told me the name of the game was Go. Its object was to encircle an opponent. Then I asked her if I might go to the shore and watch them play for a little while?

"She told me, 'To you they look like beautiful women but they are evil demons whose goal is to encircle you. If they trapped you, three hundred years would easily go by while you were under their spell. And this would mean what you came here for would not be accomplished. You have already been here longer than you know.'

"I wondered at her words but I did not wish to be entrapped by demons so I stayed with the love goddess while she played her instrument, and on this day for the first time she sang to me in the tongue of the land where we were at. I was surprised to be understanding so much when I thought I had been there but a short time.

"In the evening after we had eaten together, she did a ceremony where she prepared me a drink then read the leaves at the bottom of the cup. She pronounced everything as being most auspicious. She did not render me unable to move as had the maidens but held me on the strength of her kindness and beauty. It seemed the feast of love went on through all the night.

"In the morning she told me that she was with child. His name would be Yoshitsuni. He would be in his lifetime the greatest swordsman in the land and set all things right. 'All the knowledge the masters have imparted to you will be shared with him through your seed,' she said. Then she told me I would not be remembered as Gidon and the great thing I had done would not be known. 'Instead the people will believe your son, Yoshitsuni, learned his great knowledge of swordsmanship from King Tengu the goblin. But do not be dismayed; you will yet do many things to help men before the whole of your tale is told.'

"I saw Jewel Maiden waiting for me on the shore. Hito-koto-Kwannon bowed low before me. She said, 'I am grateful for the great sacrifice you have made to set part of the world back in order. Our small gifts are poor repayment. Jewel Maiden has a further gift for you. That is, in the future when you or your sons have need of wealth, they will be able to find precious stones and gold in the mountains wherever they might be.'

"The swimming nymphs, who followed the love goddess, in their constellation's turn assembled my walkway one last time. They, like her, were now heavy with child as well. I walked over with all my bags of riches and the Jewel Maiden bowed also before me. She opened up a bag and inside there were clothes that seemed very much like the ones I came in. But they were more richly made and softer to the touch.

"I could see Inari, the demon fox, waiting just ahead. It is not an exaggeration to say that now I knew what it was I felt very wary of it. Then it spoke to me and said, 'Human kind, you have nothing to fear from me. What is done, is done. There remains only to take you home.'

"And it seemed that we had no more started out than we were on the edge of my forest and I could barely see my house in the distance. But something was not right. I turned back to look at the fox, and behind me was a naked woman of great beauty. She said, 'Silly mortal, the price has been exacted. Now go forth. Which do you want? The illusion, or the real thing?' With that she turned and even as she was walking away, she also faded away even as the priest had done before my journey began.

"The first thing I noticed was how the village was much closer to my home than when I left. As I got nearer, I was amazed at how much the place had deteriorated in the short time I had been gone. I opened the door to my home only to find an old-woman who looked about starved standing in the room. She started to scream. I said, 'Please do not scream. Tell me what is going on here.'

"The old woman said, 'I know you not and you enter my house. I was, I am frighted. I was about to go and lay down to starve in my poverty. Take what you want if you can find anything.'

"I then said, 'Come with me, and we will go to the tavern where I will buy food.' So she led me to a tavern far different than the one I had known. That was when I met Fat Max and Oma for the first time. While the woman ate, I asked Max about the family of Gidon the Forester. At first they could not figure out who I was talking about. Then he remembered a woodsman named Gidon had disappeared about three hundred years earlier leaving his family in an awful state. He thought all descended from that family died in a plague about two hundred years ago.

"It was then I went insane for a little while. Max and Oma put me up in a room in the Inn portion of the tavern. They safeguarded my wealth so I would not be robbed and Oma came up to feed me every meal. She cared for me as if I were a baby. It was while I was in this mournful state I refused any more to be called Gidon and changed my name to Gid-visu using the name I had been called in the other world."

Gid-visu looked at Gidon. He was surprised to see water flowing down his father's cheeks. "It was through Max and Oma that I met your mother. If it had not been for her I do not think I would have ever recovered my right mind. Bishop Elisha married us within a fortnight of our meeting. Apparently that Birth Water was still working in me, for it was not long till you were conceived."

Gid-visu appeared quite exhausted and sat down. Apparently reliving the events took much out of him. Gidon could see he still mourned the loss of his first wife and children. He wondered what they had thought when he disappeared? Probably that their husband and father had been killed by some wild animal.

The fighting priests talked among themselves. They could see the bishop knew more about the whole thing than he had ever let on to them. What kinds of people was it that Gid-visu had been communicating with? Were they people at all or demon spirits? It was hard to say.

As the group began to break up and each sought the spot where they would rest for the night, they were consumed with their own thoughts concerning the story they had just heard. Gidon was wondering if his aptitude for weapons might come from the mystical forces at work that caused his father so much sorrow?

Princess Loretta moved behind the curtain separating the tent. Beds had been made for them so they could stretch their limbs instead of being in the confines of a hammock. After Gidon and whoever else was sleeping in the front settled into deep sleep, the princes whispered, "Dolores are you awake?"

Dolores mumbled back, "I am now."

Loretta let the remark pass over her head. "I was thinking about what the Jewel Maiden said about the aristocratic women being jealous of her and the relationship she had with the emperor."

"What about it?" Dolores asked.

"In our home there were people who were jealous of me and some wanted to kill me."

"What are you saying my Princess?"

"If they should manage to kill me it would not make them one bit more a princess, would it?"

"Go on," Dolores was now more finely attuned to what she was saying.

"Well if someone was jealous of Gidon's mistress, and that person sought to destroy the relationship, that would not make them one bit more likely to be able to take her place would it?"

Dolores said, "Princess you are becoming wise. Many people live their whole lives grasping for what they cannot have without learning what you have understood this night."

A long pause took place and then Loretta said, "Good night Dolores. You have been a great friend to me and I am sorry for all the grief I ever caused you. I really love and appreciate you. I hope we both will serve Gidon well."

"Good night Loretta," Dolores said. Loretta smiled. She had spoken to her familiarly as a friend.

Chapter 25

Haki's Scars

Johannes Reisende stood before the prominent women of Eastwatch waiting expectantly. The fact the group did not break into laughter, and in particular Durchgefüweg, made him even more confident of his deduction she was truly the Baroness Odilia, the love of his life. He had harbored a secret fantasy that one day she would be passing by in her carriage, complete with all manner of people serving so beautiful a lady, guarded by gallant men at arms on fine horses. In his fantasy she would see him in the crowd of adoring onlookers and stop the carriage. Putting all dignity aside she would run to him and fling herself into his arms, proclaiming she had searched and searched for many years hoping to find him. He never imagined himself in the situation he was now in, risking the ridicule of these people, declaring his belief a simple tavern girl was the girl he adored from afar when but a boy.

It was the bishop who broke the silence. "Supposing Durchgefüweg was the woman you seem to think she is, what would be the possible reason we might have for hiding her identity?"

Johannes had not really thought about that part. "I suppose it would be to protect her from something, or probably someone." His mind went to her stepfather now on his way to Almanya in chains. "If it was her stepfather she was being protected from, there is no further need for worry because he is under arrest and enroute to receive the king's justice."

"Those that serve the Evil One are a slippery lot. So many things can happen to circumvent what should be a simple matter of dealing with a devil worshipper. Till the matter is concluded and the Baroness Odilia is not only safe from her stepfather but also safe from his fellow vengeful toadies. It is better she stays hidden wherever she is." The bishop's words opened up a new way of seeing the situation for the young man.

"Now, I have a question for you." Brunhild was ever the one who could make things plain, and this was no exception. "Since you have been here in Eastwatch you have scarcely been able to keep your eyes off Durchgefüweg. Is what you are expressing a love for this girl, or for the one you admired as a boy?"

Johannes was quiet for some time thinking on the question. "I think Durchgefüweg and Odilia are one and the same. But when I saw Durchgefüweg for the first time my heart went out to her. I fell in love with a woman, not with an ideal I had in a child, when I was but a boy. It is her I want to know all about and be with till my last day on this earth."

The Bishop looked satisfied. "You have spoken well young sir. I think Odilia will remain missing for now. If this woman is willing you may court her. I think that would be acceptable behavior. But there will be no mention of the other name or what you once suspected. Do I make myself clear? Not to anyone including your master."

Johannes Reisende drew himself up to his full height, "On my honor, whether my lady will accept my courtship or not I will keep mum. May I ask Durchgefüweg in the presence of you all whether she will accept my courtship? I will find as many excuses as I can to come this way."

Herr Brute' said, "If I know anything at all about these women, they will help you to find excuses."

The group laughingly agreed to that certainty and the meeting proceeded somewhat merrily. It was only later that one among them had cause for tears.

The open message from Lady Aliruna was read to the group by the bishop since he was the most highly educated of the group.

Though all read fairly well, which was no small thing in a land that put no emphasis on such kinds of education for women, he was still the man of letters amongst them.

When the part of the message was read recounting how Gidon had rescued the Andorran Princes Loretta and Lady Dolores who were traveling to meet King Gregor. Brigitta commented that it was so like Gidon to find adventure and maidens to rescue wherever he went. Herr Brute' said, "Well I am glad he found one maiden to rescue."

The conversation was kept light. No one wanted to bring up the terrible danger he had been in acting all alone. They saw no cause to heighten Getrudis concern for Gidon.

When they read the part about him stopping with the women at Heim to find some had stayed in the old hamlet, and the highwaymen he had put on their honor had gotten there before them, all felt the tenseness of the situation Gidon had been in. Having women in his charge and others needing rescue changes the perspective. Lady Aliruna, famed for her use of the bow many years earlier, went into some detail how he shot each one of the highwaymen intending only to wound and not kill.

To that Herr Brute' had gruffly remarked that Gidon was entirely too gentle hearted and he should have killed them all. Johannes Reisende contributed to the written account by volunteering the information that shooting as fast as he did, he actually did kill one of the men by accident.

Herr Brute' remarked, "Good, when you kill an enemy, he causes you no more trouble!"

Johannes said, "He actually turned those men into his followers but I am sure the Lady will write of that in some detail."

Bishop Elisha went on to read how the princess had not obeyed Gidon and stayed out of danger, so he grabbed her and lifted her skirts so she would feel the full force of the spanking he administered. And later when there was another incident, he bound her and gagged her so she would not give away the ambush he had set for some other bad people. The lady wrote nothing about him kissing her for the sake of Getrudis. She missed no opportunity to put both incidences in as humorous a light as possible.

Getrudis remarked, "He has never spanked me. He would never have to worry about me disobeying him in such a situation."

Brunhild remarked, "He could never spank you. He might enjoy it too much." Everybody laughed at that and Getrudis got a little embarrassed remembering intimate moments they had shared, particularly when she sat on his back and in his hands. Deep inside she was already yearning for those times to return.

Lady Aliruna wrote about the princess losing her dowry and her family fortune along with the wealth Lady Dolores brought with her, while her men at arms fought their way through the land Goraleck claimed. Bishop Elisha declared that was a most serious matter. He doubted King Gregor II had ever seriously considered her as his potential queen, because the land of Andorra was so very far away and in jeopardy as well. No matter how beautiful the princess, kings must marry for reasons of state and for siring progeny with good connections. A young woman without dowry or personal wealth was in a most difficult situation among royalty. Not many young women get to marry for love in this world.

Brunhild nodded her head wisely, "Among woman kind we are most fortunate."

Getrudis spoke, "I do not see much value in a dowry. It seems a way to enrich the husband. Most of the people in a station in life where valuable dowries are given do not seem to need more wealth than what they already have."

"In the land from which I come," said the bishop, "the wife often wears her dowry price underneath her clothes. To lose a piece of it is like saying she no longer cares for the marriage and they can be divorced."

"And what if she lost a piece by accident, or what if she was assaulted and robbed?" asked Getrudis.

"Well then she could have a problem." The bishop continued, "In the land of the Alemanni the dowry is supposed to insure the husband's kindly treatment of the wife. He may use the dowry as a guarantee on business deals. And that requires him to be most careful. But if the wife considers herself poorly used, she may return to her father's house and the dowry demanded to be returned. But as for the Princess Loretta, unless she is tied to a great house in this land, there would be little value in her dowry except for its costliness."

"Yes, and even more so, since her father has been deposed and murdered." Johannes Reisende added. "We got word of that just before she arrived under Squire Gidon's protection."

"The poor girl," Getrudis said, to be followed by similar sentiments from the other women. They could sympathize with her loss even though their fathers had not dealt with them as kindly as they might.

The rest of Lady Aliruna's general letter was read and in spite of much encouragement Getrudis refused to read her private letter. She wanted to make sure she knew the reason for Lady Aliruna sending her a private communication before she agreed to make it public. And it was the reason for the private letter that brought forth tears. Even though the lady reassured Getrudis most strongly of Gidon's undying love for her, in the midst of the difficult situation he was in, the problem remained. Lady Aliruna had faced the reality of Baron Igil being forced by circumstance to take two women in her younger days. And, even though those women had given the Baron many sons and daughters, it had not diminished his love for her. She wanted Getrudis to understand that even though we might be ruled by others, our hearts are always ours to keep, even if the king should command Gidon retain the women.

*****

Baron von Krieg had proclaimed the day a Lord's Day, whether it was actually Sontag on the calendar or not. The priests would prove they were as adept at conducting worship services as they were at wielding weapons. A gathering of the Church Army was declared and the men assembled on a smooth area where sound could carry well. The young priests proved they had fine voices for the singing of the psalms found in the holy text. And the exhortation to put aside the cares of the world so each man might please the Invisible God, who through the king calls men to be soldiers, was delivered with such oratorical brilliance every man in the troop felt inspired to be more diligent.

The afternoon was spent walking horses so they would not stiffen up. This gave people opportunities to engage in conversation. Gidon and the women made a point of moving through the encampment speaking with all who desired to address them. Lady Dolores was soon much admired by all for her approachability and wit. Many of the men spoke with the forthrightness the Allemande were known for and expressed their appreciation for being able to meet so grand and beautiful a lady. Princess Loretta proved a quick learner and soon the two became the secret ideals of womanhood in each man's imagination.

But a day of such respite always seems to pass by so quickly and it came time once again for the meeting to take place in the knight's tent for the purpose of hearing the Baron explain how he had gotten the grotesque scars, especially those on his back. This night even Herman Stellwagen had joined the group. Like Gid-visu the night before, the Baron stood before the men who were leaders. Reliving the experience seemed to make an energy in the body that would not allow the painful past to be recalled while sitting.

"Like my friend Gid-visu I need to find a beginning that puts all I have to say into context. I am glad to see Herman here tonight for he was busy in the conflict we had with Goraleck that year. We were younger men then, though Herman was not so young as I."

Herman Stellwagen nodded appreciably as if to say those days were not ever far in the recesses of his mind. "There were many dangers that year as I recall. Many good men were lost over the summer. The battles continued right up through the first snows."

The Baron picked up on his narrative and said, "To understand my story correctly we would have to go back to when I was seven years of age. We lived in the fortress outside of Eastwatch at the Rising of the Little Dan, the very same place my friend Gid-visu and Gidon call home. It is now the monastery whence these good priests have come. I say this all for the benefit of you ladies in particular since you are from a far country."

The women had placed themselves near Gidon as the night before.

"It was in my seventh year I was sent to Almanya to serve as a Page. During those times it was the custom for the noble ladies to rule over much of the time a young Page had, teaching him things like the chivalric code. One of the reasons I wound up with the souvenir of that year of war on my back was I took their teaching too much to heart. Women do not normally fight the wars. We do not see many shield maidens on the battlefield.

Most of the time young lads spend seven years as a Page before being made a knight's squire. It was my good fortune, or so I thought, to become a Squire at age twelve. I was at that time as big and powerful as most men and yet had some growing to do. For a time I was squire to King Gregor I. He was much involved with his religious studies. He did not even take to the field for tourneys, and his knights made a point of keeping him as safe as possible in the all to frequent wars. Most of my time as his squire was spent in taking care of equipment and trying to find opportunities to train.

All this was happening while your father was away on his adventure Gidon, and took place a long time before you were born. When I had the opportunity to receive my knighthood, I turned it down because I frankly did not feel qualified to assume knightly duties. However I did accept a position in the army with twenty men in my company. I was little older than Gidon is now. True it was a small company but I was to learn later the reason it was so small was because of the mission planned for us.

We were supposed to go into the western lands dominated by Goraleck and spy out all encampments that were not permanent. And then we should endeavor to listen to conversations to find out what was being said about the reasons they were in those places. I knew we were not the only such unit ordered to do this because we were only given the area around Goraleck's castle for about the space of twenty furlongs in every direction."

"That was still a sizable area for one small group to cover in a very short time," Gid-visu said. "How many such groups were out doing the work you were doing?"

The Baron responded, “I cannot say. We were not told anything about other groups. Not even the purpose for which we were supposed to be gathering the information. What I did know was I did not like the assignment. In my youthful ignorance I thought it was not the proper thing for a man of honor to be doing. Something about spying just did not sit well with me. It did not fit all the foolishness my head had been filled with.”

“And yet for many years now you have been a King’s Rider whose duty it is to know what goes on in the land.” Gid-visu said. “Do you ever feel like you are caught in a web of fate?”

The Baron paused and thought about what he had said. “You know we can never say for sure what we are going to do in life. It is only what the Invisible God wills or allows.”

The Baron continued his account: “We had been working, gathering information for about a month. I had noticed patrols were increasing and people seemed more and more suspicious of those they did not know. In retrospect it seems likely that perhaps some others doing what we were had been caught. We began to avoid contact instead of joining men at their fires and listening to the gossip.

When I had begun the mission, it seemed to me having two woodsmen among my men would be an asset. I soon learned I was mistaken, especially as it became more and more important to move surreptitiously. Woodsmen are not concerned with moving soundlessly or not leaving evidence of their presence like foresters. It was the carelessness of a woodsman that put Goraleck’s men on our trail and it was the noise he made that told them where we were. As a result of his actions we found ourselves surrounded by more than a hundred men.

Princess Loretta had been following the story intently, especially since she recently had very unpleasant experiences in the land of Goraleck. She asked, “Forgive me Baron von Krieg, but what sort of evidences of their presence should the woodsmen have concealed?”

“My lady, the bear does not bother to conceal the evidence of his presence in the wood because in his mind he owns the wood, therefore it is his privilege to do his business in whatever spot it suits him. But a man does not own the wood. He must conceal the evidence of natural functions lest his enemies know his presence." The Baron had put it as gently as possible.

"Oh, I see," said the princess, slightly embarrassed.

The Baron returned to his account: "As I said we were surrounded by a hundred or more regular fighting men. It was then I made my great mistake. They called out to us to throw down our arms and surrender and we would be treated honorably as prisoners. I knew that if I chose to fight all my men would likely die as well as me. I surrendered to save my men as well as my own life. I trusted evil men to keep their word.

"As soon as we surrendered, they tied us up securely. It was then the leader of the hundred took off the head of each of my men before my eyes. I protested that we had been told that if we would lay down our arms in surrender we would be treated honorably as prisoners. The leader said to me words I will never forget. He said, 'Spies are usually hung or quartered. I promised to treat you and your men honorably as prisoners. I have granted them the honorable beheading. And you will go as our prisoner to the dungeons of Goraleck where you will answer all questions put to you.' From that day forward I always have tried to carefully consider the content of men's words.

"The trip to the dungeons of Goraleck's castle was not all that far, but my captor tried to make every inch of that a misery. They put a noose around my neck so each time I stumbled it would nearly strangle me. It was on this journey that I received my first beating. It was done with knotted ropes. I had fallen and they beat me all over till I was able to get up. If I had merely laid there waiting for them to quit, I am convinced they would have beaten me to death. This beating left my body bruised all over so what came later was even more agonizing from the first.

"When I entered the dungeon at Goraleck's castle I was immediately taken down to the torture chamber. The man who committed suicide when we rescued Heim was the first torturer I met. He asked me no questions. I was stripped completely naked and tied face down over a shipping barrel that had been cut especially for that purpose. He had a whip that cut into the skin and laid the back bare in five long strips with each blow. He hit me exactly two times because his orders were to administer ten lashes. My back was ripped open in ten long stripes from shoulders to buttocks. The agony was awful. I must have passed out but was brought back awake when briny water was thrown across my back.

"I was left stretched out across the barrel for some hours. I could not tell how long, but I felt I would die of thirst before I died of pain. I must have eventually passed out again for I was brought back awake when someone poured water over my head. I tried to lick the water as it ran down the barrel, I was so thirsty. This water pouring over the head occurred again and again. Each time the person observing me thought I was passed out they poured water over my head. So I would fake being unconscious so I could get a little more water."

No one said anything. They all sat quietly in shocked horror; the two women had to work holding back tears.

"It had been quite some time that I had spent strapped over the barrel when a man came in. I could not see what instrument of torture he had in his hand but when he popped it the sound was very much like what you hear when a bullwhip is popped over the heads of oxen. He said, 'Can you hear me, you piece of meat for my grill?' All I could do was nod my head. I was afraid not to. 'I am here to ask you one question. If you answer it the torture will stop. Do you understand me?' Again I nodded my head.

"He laid the whip across my back making the first cut you see from side to side. 'I did not hear you,' he said. My throat was quite dry but I managed to say yes. I was thinking in my mind, please do not hit me again and I will tell you anything you want to know.

"'How many teams like yours are out spying in King Goraleck's kingdom?'

"I shook my head. I did not know.

"He laid the whip across my back again. I found my voice. I screamed! Oh, how I screamed! The sound seemed to encourage him, for you can see he did it to my back six times. But it did not bother me as I was unconscious.

"Sometime, I do not know when, my legs from hip to knee were beaten with a smaller strap. Do not think the pain was lessened because of the smaller whip. If anything, it was intensified as it cut into the meat and muscle below. I screamed and screamed from pain. I reached a point where I said, 'I do not know the answer to your question. Kill me and be done with it. I would not help you if I could!'

"I woke lying on the stones of a prison cell. My cloak had been thrown in the cell for me to use. It was the one spark of humanity I ever saw out of the dungeon keepers. I lay there for some time sleeping as an escape from pain, wakening only when my head was raised by a fellow prisoner to force a few drops of water down my throat. There was never enough.

"After some time passed my head was raised and some cold soup was forced down my throat. In a short while I had gained enough strength to look around. Sharing my cell was a man who appeared very old. There was nothing to him but skin, bones, and very long hair and beard. I asked him, 'Who are you?' He said to me, 'I am no one. I used to be someone but now I am like the dead. I am no one.' I did not have the energy to reply.

"I woke when he forced what passed for food down my throat. The water was awful, but I learned to appreciate the moisture, never mind the taste. After a little while I got strong enough to realize he was feeding me my soup ration and half of his. All the little pieces of maggot ridden bread he gave to me. He was slowly starving himself to death to save my life.

"When I tried to move the skin on my back pulled terribly. The man explained that he had sewn my back up when I was unconscious. Since he had no proper needles and thread, he had used a piece of bone from a previous occupant who had died. My captors had allowed that man to rot and be eaten by rats in the cell. Then he had made the string to pull my skin together by plaiting his own hair. He said it would never be pretty but perhaps the skin could knit itself back together."

Gidon said, "So that is why the sutures look so large. It was no small needle that put the holes in your back to pull the skin back together."

Baron von Krieg nodded. “Even the old man’s hair was dirty, so from the beginning my body had to fight all manner of infection.

“I must have lain in that cell for at least a month when the old man died. I banged on the door and told the guard he was dead. They said so what was that to them? I told them they would not mind then if I ate him. This brought two of them rather quickly. I had made a sword of sorts by wearing down the leg bone of the previous tenant of the cell to where it had a sharp point. When they threw open the door and came in, I stabbed the second one with the bone and, using his eating knife, stabbed the first man also. I locked them in the cell leaving them wounded and bleeding. Several times I nearly passed out from the effort. I ate the guards’ supper and it was almost too much for my stomach. Their wine, poor as it was, aided my digestion.

“Move by careful move I managed to work my way out of the dungeon and up to the battlements. It was often one move at a time and then waiting for the next opportunity to move unseen. When I jumped from the battlements it was like falling into sewage. Fortunately, some of King Gregor’s men were in the wood not far from the castle and they saw me go into the moat. They cleaned me up and took me to Zauberer the Wise, who was nearby to consider siege plans. He treated me and fought the sores in my body for months till at last my strength returned. I have many to thank that you see me here today.”

Gidon said, “You have said nothing about how you went south and fought the Italian Band or became Chief of the Long Knives.”

The Baron responded. “I was asked to tell the story about how I got my scars. And I have done so. The things you now ask about are for another day.”

So, as was done the night before, everyone retired to where they would sleep. For come the morning they would have to be up early and again making their way to Almanya. But rest did not come easily for all. An hour or so after the women retired behind the curtain Dolores came out clothed in a nightgown and carrying a blanket. She knelt by Gidon’s head and said, “Can your Lolita lie at your feet? I have been having a terrible nightmare about the Baron’s suffering.”

Gidon nodded his head, so she spread her blanket and he sat up to cover her with his cloak. Then he remembered he was in his nightshirt. If the garment rose up during the night she could wake looking up at his manhood. Gidon said, "I think it will be better if you lay by my side."

They had just rearranged things and settled down when Loretta came out from behind the curtain. She spoke very pitifully, "I am having very bad dreams. Can I stay beside you for protection?"

So Gidon, trying to be the protector of the women, wound up with a very beautiful woman on either side beneath his spread cloak. He thought of his Getrudis and how it would seem to her if she ever heard of it. But the more he thought of her the more his mind filled with the thoughts of the wonderful times they had shared. The consequence was his manhood became filled with the desire for her that was ever present in him. He groaned inwardly and thought that if either of the women should wake, they would naturally conclude they were the cause of the rise under his nightgown. Worse yet, what if it broke free? He struggled manfully to get his mind off Getrudis, but the harder he tried the more insistent his mind became till finally he fell asleep watching Getrudis dancing naked in the forest once more.

*****

Brunhild came to the door of Gidon and Getrudis chambers. She heard the girl sobbing even though a hall separated her from the bedroom shared with Gid-visu. Brunhild entered to find Frauke was beside Getrudis holding her hand and Snaggle Tooth also was on the bed trying to pull at a bit of hair on her head above her eyes as if she was a kitten. That was a very unusual thing for a male cat to do.

Brunhild spoke to Getrudis, "What is troubling our little flower?"

Getrudis stood and hugged Brunhild. "The content of Lady Aliruna's personal letter to me is most unsettling. She has even implied my Gidon might have to copulate with that, that Princess! And I guess her chaperone too! What shall I do? How shall I bear it?"

She handed Brunhild the letter and tearfully waited while she read it. After a space of time Brunhild said, "I see the Lady Aliruna is quite convinced of Gidon's love for you. Whatever should happen, no one can unseat you from Gidon's love except yourself. You will grow ever closer by enduring trials together, whatever they might be. Bitter recriminations for what cannot be helped could build a wall of separation you would not want. Be patient and understanding. You might be worrying over nothing, and if trouble does come you will keep him with your understanding and love."

Frauke said, "Mistress Getrudis, when Squire Gidon accepted me into his house you knew he had the right to take me. But still you were for me becoming a part of the household. He never asserted his right over me. And I am told I am fair to look upon. Why should he take these women even if he does come to have that right?"

Getrudis said, "Frauke you are more than fair, you are a ravishing beauty. I think Gidon wants more for you than the station in life you now have. I think he would have you married with a loving husband and children of your own."

Brunhild said, "From what we read this night it would seem Lady Dolores bound herself willingly to Gidon in a manner not unlike what Frauke did. She followed the custom of her people and her name. From what Lady Aliruna said it seems her husband thinks Gidon sees a potential counselor in her, not a lover."

"Well, she could be both," Getrudis said. "And does he not already have much counsel in you and Oma?"

"Remember what the bishop says," Brunhild replied, "There is wisdom in a multitude of counsel."

Brunhild pointed out the obvious, "None of us is where Gidon is. But Lady Dolores is there. I suspect one of the reasons the King of Andorra might have sent her with his daughter is because she is a wise woman."

Getrudis sniffed, "I do not know if you are encouraging me or offering solace to me, or some other thing. But I am glad for your friendship. How long can Gidon be gone anyway? I have heard that those who responded at the first call have finished their training and are returning home."

Frauke said, "I have heard that Goraleck is marshaling troops and hiring mercenaries in response to what King Gregor is doing."

"Where did you hear that Frauke?" asked Brunhild.

"Some of the workmen newly arrived to work on the Keep were saying it."

Gwynedd entered the room in time to hear their conversation. "We are going to have to do what women have always done. Be patient. Watch. And, wait.

"Have any of you heard about Herman One Eye's woman coming to town?" Gwynedd was trying to change the subject.

"No, what happened?" asked Brunhild.

"It seems she has gone over the women from Heim yet unattached most thoroughly. She picked one as a candidate for her son Wolfgang. She said that the other women had suffered enough and did not need to be afflicted with the kind of men Herman's other sons were."

"Gwynedd, what sort of woman did she choose for Wolfgang?" Of the women present Getrudis was the only one who actually knew him, so her curiosity lured her away from her own problems for a time.

"She chose a rather plain girl, not ugly, but plain. She has brown hair the color of a dried leaf. She is tall and leggy but appears quite strong. And I have heard it said she is very smart." Gwynedd went on to say that in her opinion Wolfgang's mother had probably made a very good choice.

They talked long into the night before the women bid one another a good night and retired to their beds. Getrudis was not happy but she was determined her beloved Gidon would never see anything but support coming from her lips and actions.

She fell asleep dreaming of being in Gidon's arms and stealing a kiss each time he stirred in the night.

CHAPTER 26

DAMSELS IN DISTRESS

Lady Dolores was first to wake among the cuddling group of three. The tectonic upper-thrust was not misread by the widow of a great knight. She recognized the natural functioning of the male body. But it did invigorate her to realize once again, even though she was of twenty-eight years, she was privileged to be near a man who seemed to have greatness thrust upon him. It seemed to her an opportunity to relive the past and in some way make up for past mistakes. God help her, she was determined to meet the challenge. But it was one that must be prepared for in small and careful steps.

Herman Reformierte was already up and about. He seemed to be striving very hard to prove himself worthy of his new position in life. He had not only saddled all the horses in Gidon's group, but also the Baron's Schlachtross. He now had his men committed to their several duties, though still under his watchful eye. Also, the man who rode with him on the captured horses was doing some last minute preparation, for nothing would be in the way when it came time to bring down the knight's tent. And the men who rode with the wagon were helping Herman Stellwagen get the things pertaining to it properly loaded once more.

There had been some discussion about where the massive wagon should be positioned in the company during the march. It was decided that it should not be near the front because it was no longer the pace setter. Toward the rear it gave Herman's man the opportunity to continue as lookout lest they be overtaken by unwelcome persons. This still seemed a potentially useful exercise even though their numbers were now great enough to discourage the average adversary. They had already had enough adventure with more than average enemies on this trip.

The baron had pretended to be asleep until the princess arose and began to get things together to go back in the wagon. Then he sat up and looked at Gidon. "Boy I know not the cause of this strange attraction you have on women. If I had two women sleeping on either side of me we would have had a two legged cat fight before morning. You think the four-legged kind can bite, scratch, and squeal when they get into it, but they cannot touch the twin legged variety."

Gidon said a little playfully, "I am surprised you are thinking such things. I thought you utterly committed to Gwynedd."

"I am indeed. But seeing you reclining over there trying to figure out what to do with the situation does get the imagination stirring. It is a sign I am getting old that the biggest thing on my mind is getting to Almanya and seeing Zauberer the Wise for a refill on my potion."

They laughed together.

Gidon said, "Tell me sir how old do you have to get before the pressures of the flesh quit driving you crazy?"

The baron laughed. "You do not ever get that old I believe. An old man once told me that when you get so old you could not do anything with a woman if you had one, the imagination will still drive you crazy!"

"Then there is no truth in the saying that a man is not truly old till he stops looking at women?" Gidon said grinning.

The baron replied, "There is likely more truth in the saying that a man who has stopped looking is dead. But enough of this, we need to get started on the day, not heat our minds thinking about women."

Gidon said, "Yes, I have been dreaming all night about Getrudis."

"Me too." said the baron, meaning he was dreaming of Gwynedd, but that was not what he said.

"What?" said Gidon, "What have you been doing dreaming about my woman?"

The Baron threw his blanket at him. They were laughing when Dolores came in wearing traveling clothes with Gidon's ensign over her left breast, freshly done in fine needlework.

Gidon looked at her sternly. "Who told you that you could do that?"

Lady Dolores was crestfallen. She had expected to be praised, and perhaps questioned about how she could have found the time to do so intricate work. And now the words that rang in her ears sounded very much like a rebuke.

"I am sorry my lord, but Lady Aliruna had put the ensign of her Baron on her huntress dress. I thought you would be honored if I showed my devotion by placing your ensign on my travel dress so everyone who saw it would know I am yours. I will go and remove it immediately."

Baron von Krieg growled, "Gidon if you need some help with the spanking of your women to keep them in line just let me know."

Lady Dolores looked at the Baron and caught the glint in his eye. She now knew that meant he was enjoying the situation. She then looked back at Gidon and caught the slight hint of a smile. She stomped her foot and said, "Oh you men. You are making sport of me!"

Gidon and the Baron laughed out loud. Gidon stepped to her and saw where a little tear had formed in the corner of her eye and kissed it, tasting its saltiness. "Your pardon dear lady. You caught us making humor over other matters and I fear we just continued at your expense. It is very fine work and you do me honor. I thank you."

Herman Reformierte and his man came in the tent. "Your pardon sirs, we are ready to strike the tent and fold it once you vacate. I have but one question. Should we keep the tent poles we cut to pitch this camp?"

Gidon said, "No, there is no shortage of wood so we do not need to haul the weight. Just leave them beside the road so the next traveler can use them if he wishes."

It is one of the amazing things about setting up and tearing down a military encampment that the more days the unit stays in one place the more complex the process of getting under way again becomes. It is a thing that has been true in every army of mankind since the beginning of this world. But with the encouragement of its leaders every unit slowly begins to get under way with a speed opposite to the manner in which it came to a halt.

As Herman Reformierte and his man expected, the women were reluctant to renew their travel from inside the wagon. They mounted the horses with the fullest expectations of being in Gidon's company through the day. But the Baron had work for his squire, which demanded he move up and down the line encouraging people to move at a steady pace, instead of forever expanding and contracting the distance between elements. Should an enemy attack at a point where the line was not even it would be very easy to drive a wedge and split the command.

Baron von Krieg rode out ahead of the column by the space of half a mile and the ladies rode at the head of the column escorted by Herman Reformierte and his man, keeping out of the dust of the column. They were followed closely by Gid-visu and his wagon of bows and arrows. As they approached a little road, little more than a path, going off to the West, it seemed so quiet they scarce paid it much attention.

Then suddenly what appeared to be a scouting party of about ten rode out onto the roadway. The scouts were as surprised to find the advancing column as the column was to encounter them. It was as if they came out of nowhere. Herman and his man had not as yet been trained to fight from horseback and the suddenness of the encounter gave them no opportunity for any kind of preparation. They were quickly unhorsed, and on their backs, wounded in the road. Two of the scouts grabbed the horses of the men and two more took the women. Another two turned their attention toward Gid-visu hoping to kill him and seize his wagon leaving four more trying to decide what to do next as they saw the fighting priests running to engage them.

The initial focus of attention being on the women and Herman Reformierte had given Gid-visu enough time to string his bow and begin shooting arrows. His first two arrows killed the two scouts who were coming toward him and his third arrow went toward one of the four who were conversing. He hit the one that seemed to be the leader of the scouting party. When he fell that convinced the remaining three to make a hasty retreat back up the road where four had already gone with women and horses. It had happened very fast and then it was over. Three of their new enemy lay dead and two of their own were wounded.

One of the priests gave three blasts on his horn which signaled the presence of enemy forces. This would recall Baron von Krieg and summon Gidon who was at the rear of the column.

Gidon came up from the rear at a full gallop. It seemed the horse had all four feet in the air all the time. As he approached the front his eyes took in the three bodies and saw the missing women. He reached across the saddle and his double-edged sword fairly leaped into his hand. Sometimes the weapon seemed to sing in the air when set free. His blood was up and he intended to kill any enemy he could catch up with, when cutting through the red haze of his anger came the words, "No son! No!"

No other voice than that of his own father could have stopped him. Begleiter responded almost without being told. He turned and trotted up to Gid-visu scarcely breathing heavy with the sudden exertion he had made.

"I think I killed the leader of the scouting party, but if his second in command is any kind of a tactician, he will have an ambush set for those who follow too quickly. You need to organize your pursuit forces and I will trail them and see what I can learn." Gid-visu called out to Herman, "Are you wounded and dying or can you and your man take charge of my cart?"

Herman growled back, "We are not dead yet. We just had the breath knocked out of us more than anything. But I intend to make some of them dead before this is over." He was walking toward the cart, dripping blood with every step, but he considered his worst injury having the wind knocked out of him. One of the priests moved to care for the wounds of Herman and his man. But first the priest had to calm Herman down so he would be still and let him work. Herman was embarrassed and mad for he considered himself to have failed Gidon.

Gid-visu, along with his bow and arrows, took with him some water. Thus equipped, he began tracking the scouting party that had attacked them. He moved parallel to the path they had come down keeping to the trees. In the space of an hour he caught up to the place where four men from the scouting party lay in concealment to ambush anyone who moved up the trail after them. Gid-visu saw his assessment had been correct. One man would be all was needed to manage the women after they were bound and another could hold onto the captured horses. Unless he missed his guess, these scouts would have their mounts secured not far away. Once they struck against anyone following, they would run to their mounts and move down the path to try one more attack before they sought to flee to the main body. Any more ambushes experienced fighters would know to be folly in this circumstance.

Gid-visu quietly circled where they lay in wait and found the horses tied, just as he expected. He went to the horses with some treats and petted the animals so they would not get alarmed. Then he led them southerly over a small rise and tied them where they could have water and graze, guaranteeing they would be content till he returned.

He then moved stealthily back to a point where he could see the ambushers. He saw they were getting restive and fidgety. If he did not do something they would soon head for their horses and discover they were missing. He set three arrows beside him and laid a fourth in place on the bow. His first shot went into the man who seemed to dominate the group. Only then Gid-visu yelled, "Lay down your weapons and surrender."

One man rose up to run and Gid-visu sent an arrow straight through his heart, shooting him through from back to front. He dropped immediately, dead before he hit the ground. "You have a choice. Surrender to me and my men or die where you are." The men dropped their weapons and held up their hands to show they were now unarmed. The man he had shot first had stopped wiggling on the ground. He certainly looked dead.

Again Gid-visu spoke. "You: the ugly one. Tie the dead men's hands behind their back." Both men started to respond prompting him to laugh.

*****

The Baron had returned to the column. It did not need much explanation for him to understand what had occurred. He looked at the three bodies intently. "From their clothing and weapons, I would think these might be the Sea Peoples who raid mostly in the Aegean Sea. The question is, what are they doing this far to the north and west and so far inland?"

Gidon had retrieved his bow and arrows from his wagon and had the men separated out so the wagon and carts were brought together. He was planning to have a small crew of about fifteen guarding the stuff while the main body would go in pursuit of the lost women.

The Baron spoke to Gidon saying, "Well I will say this much for you. You made a good swap in horseflesh. Any one of the horses your attackers lost to you was better than the two you lost to them."

Gidon grinned, "I must be honest with you. My father was responsible for that trade. He took all three of the men himself."

The Baron looked at Herman and said, "What were you doing? Do not tell me. You were so busy looking at the women and day-dreaming about them, you forgot your job was to protect them. And you nearly got yourself killed for your inattention. I swear, if any of our people had been killed you would have joined them."

Herman thought it best to say nothing because he believed the Baron might yet do him in for his stupidity.

"Gidon, are you not taking too many men and leaving our equipment in danger of being captured?" the Baron asked.

"Sir, I do not know about these things and would be grateful for your instruction. But I thought it best we take as many as possible since we have no idea what forces we will be facing." Gidon was totally unsure if he was doing the right thing or not. "I think it unlikely they would come back around and attack us because they had not expected to run into us. Also, from where our column was positioned, it seems unlikely they could see the extent of our force, neither did they have the time to really make an assessment."

Then Baron von Krieg asked a harder question. "Why should we go after these women to rescue them at all? Our mission was to bring men to Almanya for training. Taking after these women is not part of that mission so why should we waste valuable time trying to rescue them again?"

"Sir, I had rescued them before, which put them under my protection. Since I am your squire, they are under your protection as well. Rescuing the people at Heim was not part of our mission to bring men to Almanya for training, but we stopped to do so because it was the right thing to do. And as one of the King's Riders it is part of your job to set things right in the Kingdom. Not only that, two of our men were wounded by these people and they tried to kill my father, who as I understand it, is not only your friend but also a member of the Long Knives. That is another debt of honor we need to repay them. As far as the women are concerned directly, we but need to recognize they were taken in the land of the Allemande. So that alone is an insult to our king. And indirectly this is an insult made worse because these women were on their way to see the king in an official capacity. Such insults cannot go unanswered."

"Well spoke Gidon. And though that is not all the reason we must rescue them it is sufficient for now. So how do you think we should proceed?"

"Let me go in the advance with Herman Reformierte and my two other able-bodied men. We can use the three newly captured horses to hopefully meet up with my father. You lead the column and when we rejoin, we can set the next stage of our plan based on what my father might tell us."

"Head on out Gidon and we should catch up with you before too much time has passed." The Baron was secretly pleased with all Gidon had laid out even though he knew quite well the young man was affected emotionally by the loss of the women and his fears for them.

Gidon had his men together and they were headed down the trail in less than five minutes. He kept the men moving at a steady and reasonably fast pace even though he continued to warn them to keep a sharp eye both ahead and to the sides. He was not surprised to find four men tied face down in the middle of the trail, prisoners of his father. One of whom was dead and another who had been only pretending to be dead. Gidon sent one of his men back to the column to let them know what lay immediately ahead and to take them three more mounts, Gid-visu keeping one for future use.

Gid-visu told how the man giving the orders had lain pretending to be dead while his own men tied him up. He had forgotten dead men do not continue bleeding, so whether he was initially unconscious or always trying to make him careless, his ruse did not work. He told Gidon that he had asked the men who they were, and one of the men had answered they were the Peleset raiders of the Sea Peoples. The leader rebuked and threatened the man who spoke. So after that he could get no more information. Gid-visu said he probably should have gone ahead and killed him when he first saw the man was faking.

Gid-visu also said he did not think they would find any more ambushes. Their next fight should not happen until they caught up with the total force. He believed these people had encountered them by accident, since the entire purpose of their raiding would be to take a spoil, not fight battles.

Gidon decided to move on ahead with Herman and his other remaining man. He told his father that hopefully he might have some information on how they could deal with the forces ahead. It seemed to him essential they soon have some idea of the numbers they were dealing with, though he was very sure they were superior in size to their own force.

Once again Gidon started out at a demanding pace letting the few miles slip away much faster than the Baron would be able to follow. Thus it was they came upon a hamlet that had been despoiled by these people called Peleset raiders, not once but twice. Once when they came through headed eastward and then to a lesser extent when they were retreating. Gidon talked with the headman who told him they had not been interested in killing people, only in taking captives for slaves, for there was not much wealth in the little area where the major endeavor was breeding sheep and goats and farming the scattered open areas of the forest.

The village headman produced a young lad the Peleset had left behind. "What is your name and why did your people leave you behind?" Gidon asked.

"My name is Walid. I was left behind because I was sick three days. I am one of the people of Mizraim. In fact, I am a descendant of Casluhim, a son of Mizraim. Most of these people in this force are from the city state of Ekron. Even the giants with us are mostly Ekronites, though some are Anakim. They did not have much regard for me since I am from those far to the south of their home. My master was called Anak for he was one of the Anakim. My master is among those who eat human flesh. He would have eaten me, when I could not serve, but was fearful because he knew not why I was sick."

"Walid, why were you so sick?" Gidon asked, curiously afraid the young man would say he got sick on human flesh.

His answer was a little better, though not one to endear him to Gidon. "The Peleset worship their gods by drinking large amounts of beer and wine among other things. I had gotten very sick from being forced to drink over much, but they did not know that. I had hoped to use my illness to get free of Anak and save my life."

"What do you propose to do to save your life now?" Gidon asked.

Walid said, "I had not thought about it. I suppose I had thought the Aleman people kindlier disposed than my own."

"Your people have my women. They have wounded my men and taken my horses. Do you think I would feel kindly disposed to any of your people? And more the less so, because we Alemanni have fought the Nephilim giants before." Gidon looked at Walid with such fierceness the scars on either side of his face took on a reddish-purple hue. The boy began literally shaking before Gidon.

The headman of the hamlet then spoke and said, "Are you Gidon the Dragon Slayer?"

"I am."

"The woman who says she is a princess was threatening the Peleset when they brought her through here. She said they were women who belonged to Gidon the Dragon Slayer. She kept saying how much danger the Peleset were in for taking them, and when she saw the giants, she started telling them one of your great ambitions was to become known as Gidon the Giant Killer. She really made them angry, for they began biting things with their teeth. Did you know they have two rows of teeth? They also have six fingers and six toes instead of the five humans have. But there was something in the way she said things that really did make them angry."

Gidon laughed and said, "That is Princess Loretta of Andorra alright. She is really good at making people angry, but in this case I really do not mind. Angry people are easier to kill."

Gidon turned his attention back to Walid. "I want to know some things and if you answer me true you will live. If you do not, Herman here will tear your arms off for me." It was the first time Herman laughed since the Baron had threatened to kill him. It only added to Walid's terror because he judged Herman was saying he would enjoy it.

"I want to know how many men are in your group of raiders? Are they all mounted? And how are they armed?"

Walid answered the total force was about three hundred men. A few had been killed since they first began the raiding of the Allemande. The only ones who were not mounted upon horses were those driving wagons. The preferred weapons were swords and spears, though bows and arrows were sometimes used. Gidon had the sense he was telling the truth but he approached the opinion with caution knowing lives would ultimately depend on being right.

Gidon turned to the headman of the hamlet and asked, "Did either of my women say anything about me being a shapeshifter or a skinwalker?"

"Yes, the woman wearing your ensign over her heart said you were a 'formwandler oder gestaltenwandler' and could turn into a sabretooth tiger whenever it pleased you." The headman answered a little nervously, plainly indicating he partially believed the old myths and legends.

"And how did they react to that information?" Gidon looked at him intently trying to discern what would represent the man's opinion and those of the sea raiders.

"They said they did not believe in such things but I heard two of them talking in the common tongue and realized it was part of their ancient religious beliefs. They have not discounted it as being impossible I think." From the way the man answered Gidon saw that neither had this man.

Gidon had a plan. "I saw you had a smithy. Is your schmeid good at his work?"

"Yes, I think he is quite good. People come from round about to have him make tools and such instead of using their own schmeid when they have one."

"Fine; go get your schmeid and bring me your leather worker right away. We have no time to lose." The man departed from Gidon at a trot. Gidon was sure at his age he did not run much. He supposed it was the idea that perhaps this man he had been talking to could really turn into a sabretooth that energized his feet.

The schmeid got to Gidon first which went well with what he had in mind. He had drawn out on a piece of wood what he wished to have made. He told the man he wanted two made just alike to fit the left hand. The other man's hand, Gidon said, would be almost the same as his own. The schmeid suggested that instead of using leather belts he use cord to attach the weapons so they could be better adjusted to hold firm, since he would obviously be very active and putting stress on the contraption.

Gidon was impressed with the man and gave him a coin of great value. The schmeid said, "This is far more than such a job is worth m'lord. I would gladly do it for nothing to strike a blow at these men who have disrupted our home and made off with our wives and daughters."

Gidon said, "Our bishop has said the workman is worthy of his hire. And I am paying you with coin taken from thieves and robbers. There may come a day when I will need your help and not be able to pay, but with the help of what you are making me and the Invisible God, we will bring home your wives and daughters."

The schmeid said, "I understand that you are no shapeshifter of any sort else you would not appeal to the Invisible God. I will get busy and together we will make these pagans think you are one before you baptize them in their own blood." He hurried to his forge for the matter was urgent.

The leather workman took in the last part of the conversation. So Gidon explained he would need two pouches and it would have to be constructed to safely carry the implements without cutting through. The man said he would go watch the schmeid lay out the weapons so he would get the size just right. He also recommended that the pouches should have shoulder straps. Gidon could see the wisdom in that idea and agreed. He gave the leather worker a coin of equal value to the one he gave the schmeid. He too did not wish to take money, for he also had a wife and daughter among those carried away.

Gidon calculated he had several hours till Gid-visu caught up with him and still more time must pass for his allies to gather here, and still they would have to move on up to make contact with the enemy of three hundred. Gidon would have far less men than they, so things would have to be done to change the odds in their favor. He calculated that fear cultivated in an enemy was a great weapon.

Gidon sent the hamlet's head man on a mission to gather as many horns as he could find. It turned out one of the people had a thriving trade going manufacturing hunting horns for trade from horns of goats. He purchased the dozen the horn maker had on hand. Everyone wanted to give to the enterprise of defeating the sea pirates in order to free wives and children.

Gidon asked Herman Reformierte, "Do you remember what I sounded like the night I made a tiger's roar?" Herman said he did, but his first attempts at imitating the sound were rather poor.

Walid spoke up. "If you would allow me, I can imitate the challenging sound of a male sabretooth. Those among my people who have heard them would be fooled by how well I do it."

Gidon said he wanted to hear him make that roar. When Walid made the roar it was nothing like what he had ever heard Snaggle Tooth make and Gidon told Walid so.

Walid answered by explaining that sound he made was what a male sabretooth often used to challenge other sabretooth tigers in the land he came from. The royal descendants of Mizraim hunted the sabretooth, so they could wear their skins. They early learned to imitate the sound so they could lure them into traps. The male tigers would get very angry that another male would be intruding into their territory and act instinctively instead of thoughtfully. He said many men died when sabretooth tigers did think things through, for they were not unintelligent.

The schmeid had finished his work and presented the new weapons to Gidon before Gid-visu arrived. And the leather worker had done his work as well. He had gone so far as to assist the schmeid in making special straps to retain it in place instead of just any old cord. Everyone in the hamlet hoped Gidon would be successful.

Gid-visu arrived hours ahead of the column of fighting men and Gidon presented him with his special version of the weapon. His father was uncomfortable with the idea of using Walid as part of the ruse he intended to use on the enemy, but was finally won over after having his circumstance explained and getting to talk with the young man.

Gidon wrote out his plan for throwing the enemy forces into confusion and left it with his remaining man, along with the horns, save three, which he planned to take with him.

He had Walid mount the man's horse and gave Herman strict instruction concerning watching him. Then the four of them began their trip forward to find where the enemy had encamped for the night. As they were leaving, the schmeid brought up a cumbersome bag with four iron poles sticking from it. He said, "This is something you might use to complete your ruse. I barely finished it in time."

Walid was sure they would use a place they had passed in the middle of the day when they had been traveling eastward. It had water and a place that would only have to be secured on two sides to keep the animals from wandering during the night. It also had the advantage of being defensible from ordinary troops. But Gidon had no plan to make them think they were facing ordinary men at arms.

Gidon was still trying to make sure he could trust Walid not to betray them when he had opportunity. As they rode, he began to question him concerning his religious thinking. He might learn more about whether he was trustworthy or not by learning about his god.

"Tell me Walid. Do you not worship idols of stone, wood, and brass?"

"Yes, and they are sometimes also made of silver and gold if one has enough money."

"I am confused concerning why you would think something made with the hands of men could help you?" Gidon tried to sound sincere.

"Did your ancestors not worship gods of animals and trees before you turned to the Invisible God?" Gidon saw Walid would be difficult to get in a corner in a debate over which kinds of the pagan gods were better.

"Today our major god is the fish god. He is worshipped among those who follow the Peleset way. The word 'Peleset' means we are wanderers. Hence we are sea pirates. But we did not always worship gods made by men's hands. In the beginning we worshipped the One you call the Invisible God. Often He was known as Yah or El." Walid was trying to make it plain to Gidon.

"My forefather founded the land of Misr. But he did not wholly trust God when He said there would never again be a worldwide flood. He saw the great river that nourished our land flood every year. So he had a mighty ship placed in his burial chamber and turned away from the True God. In time his children came to proclaim they were living gods among the people and demand worship. This was something the real God would not tolerate so he allowed men's minds to become blinded. No less so than those among his descendants called Peleset."

"If you know all this, why do you not turn to the True God?" Gidon asked.

Walid said, "I intend to, now that I am free of these people. But the reason most will not turn is because demons live in the idols and they like being worshipped. So men do things for these demons hoping they will in turn help them. But you cannot always trust demons not to eventually turn on you and destroy you."

Gidon spoke somberly. "I have heard that before. We are not perfect in this land but it is a good land. I think you will be very happy among the Alemanni."

Chapter 27

Superstitions and Realities

The fact Walid had been correct in his guess concerning where the Peleset would pitch camp was audible before they came in sight. Once the location was certain they withdrew a goodly distance and found a place where the horses could be secured without discovery. Horses, who were not trained as Begleiter, needed to be placed far enough from the trail they would not call out to any horses traveling the path. To assure this they had to be placed where they would not be able to pick up on activity on the pathway.

The next project was to scout out what defense the Peleset raiders would throw up against anyone following them. When they worked their way forward the cause of a knocking sound they heard, along with men's voices, became plain. The Peleset were constructing a barricade with sharpened stakes across the pathway to discourage an onslaught of horsemen, and behind that a breastwork was being fashioned from which men could defend with bow and arrow. It would be an effective defense should the Baron be so foolish as to follow the enemy's plan for what should occur. As had many enemies in the past, they underestimated the resourcefulness of the Alemanni.

The decision was then made to circle north. This would allow them to check out the area Walid said they would likely place the animals. There they could have their needs met and yet be contained.

Again they found things just as he had predicted. Animals were still being moved into the area, but the intent was plain. Moving such a large number of animals was difficult, especially for people who most often fought from the seas. Gidon thought it likely they wanted to be finished before dark. Just as importantly, the time to strike and remove the herd needed to be carried out early in the morning when guards become relaxed and sleepy. The difficulty was in the number of men assigned to guard the animals. It looked as if they were planning for not less than six guard points where at least two footmen per station would be placed.

The last bag the hamlet's schmeid had given them was hidden away where they planned to meet after finishing the work on the western side. There they hoped the road would be less well guarded. The expectation would prove correct. No enemies were known to be pursuing from that direction. The Peleset plan to meet a heavy force making a frontal assault was an error. One they would have been less likely to make had they known how small the size of Baron von Krieg's forces were in relation to their own.

Gid-visu had admired the pair of appliances Gidon had the schmeid construct. Those were claws designed to fool the Peleset into thinking a shape shifter had taken the form of a sabretooth and attacked during the night. They would capitalize on the story Dolores had told. It would work on their minds if it was carried out successfully. This ruse would require all enemy attacked be killed, and injury by any other weapon covered by the tearing of the claws. It was a risky undertaking that could easily fail. Success would only be possible through the use of all their skills and the blessing of the God of Hosts.

When they got to the western side of the camp, it was a welcome discovery that the guard position was set right in the middle of the road, and a large bonfire was being stoked for the comfort of the guards. This would mean those gathered around the fire would be effectively night-blind making it easier for the four of them to move undetected. The only drawback would be that after they had taken their prey and moved into the camp to make the attack look like a tiger's, they would have to spend some valuable time recovering from the exposure to the intense light of the fire themselves. But it was a problem they would just have to accept and deal with.

In a few minutes watching, someone, evidently the man in charge of the guards, came around. He chewed them out for having so large a fire. But Walid interpreted the man's words and said he had only told them to let the fire die down, so in the scheme of things the man's instruction neither helped nor hindered their plan. It was supervision they hoped had come too late, without requiring immediate action.

It looked that in the end only five men were assigned to the western watch. One, who by virtue of his size seemed to consider himself the chief among his fellows, lay down and soon appeared for all intent asleep. Music began to come from the encampment and Walid explained it was part of the entertaining of their gods and it would only end when the dancing priestess/prostitutes were carried off into orgiastic groups where they would be used until all the men in their group was exhausted. If one of the priestesses passed out, they would just continue to use her until they were finished or she was dead. Such was their sexual excess under the influence of perverted lust.

The men of Allemande were disgusted with what they heard and it hardened their hearts toward the men they were about to kill. Gidon was fearful for his women. He was afraid that these pagans in their excesses might try and attack them. He was determined that such practices should end in this land, even as the first King Gregor had commanded when he had assumed the throne.

Gid-visu and Gidon each chose their targets and coordinated firing so arrows were in the air in unison. Four men fell, and the fifth roused, chose to stand up. He took two arrows in the chest. Herman did his part by retrieving the spent arrows, as Gidon and his father did the grisly work of clawing the men so no other weapons but the claws were readily apparent. They made it into a very grizzly scene in the hope of putting great fear into the Peleset.

Gid-visu made very sure that Herman and Walid understood how to get to the rendezvous point. He understood that such forests were not the kind of terrain these men were familiar with. He told

Herman he was not to blow his horn unless their plot was discovered. The purpose of the horn would change as their plan progressed.

When Gidon and Gid-visu got back to the north where the enemy horses were held, they made a significant discovery. In addition to the guard posts there were now at least three mounted riders moving among the horses to keep them calm. In spite of this some of the animals were exhibiting tension and occasional disputes between horses would occur. It was obvious that the original plan of taking the horses further north and back to the east could not be handled in a timely manner. There were just too many animals. An alternative plan had to be put in place.

The two men pulled back where they could speak in low whispers without fear of being given away. Gidon said, "It is plain we cannot successfully make off with the horses. Even if we managed to kill all the guards, which is really iffy, we could not drive that many horses and still carry out the rest of the plan."

Gid-visu said, "It seems to me that if we cannot take away their means of escape or attack, the next best thing we could do with them is disrupt their camp. We can just drive the animals through it."

"But what about the women and other captives they have within? We go running a bunch of animals through there and someone is liable to get hurt." Gidon was not at all happy with the situation, but felt that he should have foreseen the problem. But for someone who had never seen so big a herd of horses, the immensity of the numbers needed to mount three hundred men is difficult to visualize.

Gid-visu said, "Anything we do has some element of chance and danger while doing nothing is guaranteed to result in more people dying, and many of them will be our own. We have got to disrupt the camp and keep it on edge until the Baron gets here."

Gidon was not happy but he nodded his agreement. "I suppose the first thing we should take out is the northern most guard post where we originally intended to drive the animals through the rift in the little vale's wall."

Gid-visu said, "Go and retrieve the tiger's mouth the schmeid gave you. We might well use it yet."

When Gidon was going about the recovery of the device he heard some commotion at the western watch. Walid had done his tiger imitation and the dead men had been discovered. He hastened to the meeting point to bring them down to assist in the new plan. Events would have to progress in an orderly way from their perspective, while it appeared calamitous to the enemy.

Herman and Walid got to the gathering point very quickly. Herman was grinning broadly. He breathlessly told how the bodies were discovered and no one wanted to take up the watch position. They all now believed the story Lady Dolores told about Gidon being a shapeshifter and no one wanted to stay there. One of the giants had come to the scene and said, "Shapeshifter or no, he will die like all other men."

The man in charge of the guard told him he should take up the watch in place of the fallen men since he was unafraid. But in spite of his big words he would not do so. He made some threats and then walked away. The officer of the guard could do nothing, for who wants to challenge a giant? All three of the men shared grim smiles at Herman's report. They could not laugh out loud or even chuckle for fear the sound would carry.

During the time Gidon was gone for the tiger's mouth and to gather his men, Gid-visu slipped down to the guard post near the north valley exit and killed the two men there with his knife in a blazing move that took out the most alert man first, He was so quick and so quiet that none of the other guards were aware of what had taken place. He moved back up the path a little pace and met his son and his men as they came down.

Gid-visu said to Herman, "I have a job for you with those steel teeth. There is an old mare down in the herd who was about to foal but it turned wrong and she is laying down there dying with the foal half out and already dead. When we start the herd moving, I want you to use those iron tiger's teeth to bite a chunk out of her neck and flank.

Walid spat in disgust, "In Misr we would have helped the mare deliver, and neither animal would have been lost. But these sea pirates know nothing of taking care of horses like their land-based brethren.

And they do not care to learn. That is why we have lost many horses on this raid."

When they slipped on down to the guard post, and the two men Gid-visu had already killed, an unexpected thing occurred. The two Andorran horses belonging to the ladies walked right up to where Gidon was crouching, being followed by the horses they had gotten from would be robbers that originally came from the tavern on the roadway. "Horses are not dumb," Gidon whispered. "They know who treats them well." Fortunately, the men riding to calm the herd were not very attentive to what individual horses were doing.

Gid-visu said, "This puts another wrinkle in our plan. Gidon, you must take these horses around to where we have our others hidden before we start the stampede. We do not want the women to see these horses and try to catch them. It would increase the likelihood of them getting hurt."

Gidon had to agree but thought just perhaps his father was going to do something so dangerous he wanted to keep him out of it.

Gidon rigged makeshift halters and reins for Herman to use in holding the horses while he and Gid-visu left to work their way down opposite sides of the herd. With each guard post, depending on the level of watchfulness, they took out the men. In most cases arrows could be used, since they seemed to be mostly sleeping in turns. They continued their bloody work until meeting at the last guard station which was between the horses and the camp.

One of the men on horseback approached this guard position and when he dismounted was killed before he could even turn around. Gid-visu put the man's cloak around his shoulders and slowly worked his way toward the farthest night rider. When he was in position and attacked him, Gidon took the other rider down with a well-placed arrow.

Altogether they had killed not less than fifteen men guarding the horses without being discovered. Those who would hear the story in years to come would say it was nothing less than a miracle. Gidon went to Herman who was still holding the Andorran mounts and those horses taken from the thieves from the inn. Taking the leads from Herman, he set out northward. To get these horses to Begleiter and the other mounts he would move around toward them in a wide arc.

Herman then went to the downed mare which was by this time quite dead. As Gid-visu steered his captive mount to the back of the herd to begin driving them into the enemy camp, the smell of the blood released by the iron jaws began to put the horses into a panic. Already unsettled, when Walid again sounded his tiger roar, they broke into a run which Gid-visu helped along by blowing his horn. Herman gave his own a blast, blowing so hard the veins stood out on his neck.

Just as Gidon suspected, Gid-visu did not stop with just stampeding the horses. He continued to run them all the way through the enemy camp. He snatched a spear from the hands of one man, standing with a confused and drunken look on his face, and promptly thrust it into a man with a long sword. The man was not dressed as the Peleset so Gid-visu assumed he had probably been sent with them by Goraleck. He grabbed the sword from the man's hand even as he began to fall and continued through the camp slashing men on either side until he rode clear of the camp on the southern side. After riding some distance into the wood his horse collapsed under him. It had been hit with an arrow and had literally run itself to death responding to his command.

Gid-visu left the horse and headed for the preset meeting spot in the eastside of the camp. Behind him he could hear all sorts of noise, much of which was sounds of panic. They had accomplished their purposes it seemed.

Herman and Walid had followed the path Gidon had taken, stopping only to bury the pieces of horse flesh. It would spoil the illusion if those things were found by the enemy.

*****

The morning sun was beginning to lighten the sky by the time the men managed to get back together. Gidon, who had gotten into position on the eastern side first, managed to send an arrow through the temple of a giant. It dropped him immediately. Another he hit as he was looking over the hastily constructed breastworks catching him on the bridge of the nose and driving through to the brain. He flailed around so violently he managed to hurt a number of the sea peoples he was with.

There was not much desire by the Peleset to venture beyond the breastwork because most of the camp was either sodden drunk, or hungover and exhausted from the night's orgy as well as the horse stampede. There was also a great fear of being caught alone by the shape shifting dragon slayer. But the best part was because of their fears no one wanted to take out their anger on any of the captives, particularly the princess or her lady in waiting.

Herman and Walid got some sleep while they waited for orders. The confidence they felt made them inclined to be careless but Gid-visu now had his blood singing and would not tolerate anything that would put the goal in jeopardy.

It was hard to get Gidon to lay down in a concealed spot from which he could waken and immediately respond to any possible threat. Gid-visu told him the ride through the camp had gotten his blood flowing, so he would need Gidon to be ready to go when his energy gave out. But when he finally got Gidon to rest, Gid-visu began repositioning himself, looking for enough targets of opportunity to keep the raiders from being able to rest at all.

Their morning efforts had already had some good impact. Hung over men, stinking of illicit sex, got on one another's nerves and fights began to break out. Whoever was supposed to be in charge was rapidly losing all semblance of command as the situation appeared more and more dire to their sodden minds. It was the sort of situation a man capable of pulling a bow of tremendous power could capitalize on, as his arrows would seemingly appear out of nowhere to hit what seemed impossible targets.

Gid-visu called on the reserve of strength known only to older men. It is the hardness of muscle and sinew built only by years of work that young muscle, however powerful, knows nothing of. He was determined to let Gidon rest and keep him from the danger as long as possible. When the Baron and his forces arrived, there would be time enough to sleep.

It was after the noon hour that the first mounted element of the Baron's force made contact with them. They were mounted upon the horses Gidon had sent back. The footmen were coming along behind at the quick step used by Roman soldiers and taught them by Herr Brute'. Because of days spent on the road they would arrive in fine shape and able to do battle when called upon.

When Gidon awoke he was surprised to find Bishop Elisha resting not too far from him. "I did not expect to see you here," he said.

"I was at my prayers and realized you would have need of me," the bishop answered simply.

Gidon did not ask him on what day he was at prayer, suspecting it might even have been this morning. He had a way of covering a great deal of territory when the Invisible God said "Go."

*****

When the women had been suddenly assaulted on the road to Almanya they were completely taken by surprise. Initially they thought perhaps Herman Reformierte and his man had been killed as they saw them unhorsed by the enemy. But at the last, even as they were being led up to the seldom used roadway the scouts had originally came from, Dolores, looking back over her shoulder, saw them move.

She spoke to Princess Loretta in the Andorran tongue saying, "Be of good cheer. You know Gidon will soon be coming for us."

One of the scouts growled something unintelligible in the common tongue.

"They will soon bind us," Dolores said. "Let us be quiet for now so perhaps they will not gag us. Then we can use our tongues to work on their minds a little and make things easier for Gidon."

The scout growled again and this time his words were very understandable, "If you speak again in that foreign tongue, I will smash your mouth!"

When the scouts stopped to form back up, they were unsettled by the loss of the three men. They contented themselves with binding the hands of the women and tying their feet together beneath the underbellies of the horses, while making rude remarks. They attempted no more because they wanted to move quickly.

It was when they got back underway Princess Loretta spoke, telling them they were in great trouble for not only had they taken a princess on her way to see King Gregor, but they had also taken women belonging to Gidon the Dragon Slayer. It was not until they separated to set up an ambush that Lady Dolores warned them of the trouble they were in, telling them the Dragon Slayer was able to also turn himself into a sabretooth tiger at will, as the ensign depicted. She even went so far as to tell them that if they would surrender to her right then, she would ask her great lord to spare their lives!

The suggestion they should surrender to a woman caused them to mock Dolores, but her words spoken with such boldness caused them discomfort. When they met up with the vanguard the men reported what the women had been saying about the man they belonged to being a dragon slayer and a shapeshifter.

The leader of the point said, "I do not believe in shapeshifters. Those are old wives' tales invented to frighten little children and the gullible."

One of the men closest to him spoke. "I do not know about that. Is not Dagon our great god shown to be half man and half fish? Is he not a shape shifter since it is told he appears in different forms? And what of those gods in Misr who have bird heads and dog heads and more? Are not they shape shifters? And what about the Fallen Ones who came down to seduce women, from whom the giants and titans came? Did they not appear to the women in altered form?"

"You sound like a scribe. When we get back to the hamlet let us ask and see if they have any stories of shape shifters here about." The leader of the vanguard was quite sure they would be told no such things were known of in the land. Nevertheless, all who had heard the speech of Lady Dolores and the comments of the leader and his friend eyed the woods uneasily as they made their way back. Dolores saw this and knew she had accomplished her purpose.

The leader of the vanguard met with the chieftain of the raiding party on the eastern side of the hamlet. Since getting into pitched battles with Alemanni forces was not the purpose they were sent out for, the little army retreated westward. He was sure that he would not be pursued far, even if they were outnumbered. They had been told the king of the Alemanni was only training men this year against the possibility of future war. The king who had recruited them took this training quite seriously because this was not the way kings normally used their serfs. Most of the time they went forth with little instruction, after all they were most useful absorbing the shock of attacks and could be replaced with more peasantry if they were killed.

The point leader discussed with the chief of the sea peoples those things the princess and lady had said concerning a man they claimed to be a dragon slayer wanting to kill giants. The chief was not wholly certain of the idea about asking in the hamlet about shapeshifters but decided they must ask since the promise had been made before too many witnesses. It is not usually wise to ask questions in public when unsure of the answers.

The chief of the sea peoples asked the headman of the hamlet about shapeshifters when they reentered the hamlet. The headman had heard the women, as they continued to talk about their shape-shifting hero when carried into the hamlet a few minutes earlier. He said, "We have not had so much a problem with shapeshifters in recent times. But there are those who turn into badgers and wolves as you no doubt know. What we really fear is when another creature begins to stalk this time of year. But I do not know its name in the common tongue. In our ancient language we call it das groß Vielfrass."

The sea people chieftain was impatient with the leader of the small hamlet using words he did not understand. He was about to strike the man when a man assigned to accompany the sea raiders by Goraleck spoke up. "The thing he is speaking of is the Great Wolverine. I was not aware any existed here in many years."

"What is the Great Wolverine and how is it different from any other of the nasty beasts?" the chieftain asked.

Goraleck's man responded, "The Great Wolverine hibernates like the badger, and unlike normal wolverines. Many of the creatures died when the far north turned to ice, because they went to sleep and never woke up, for summer did not come. They are even more bad tempered and voracious than the average wolverine, and it is said they can be inhabited by shapeshifter spirits like the badger."

The sea raider chief looked at the village headman, "So you see those beasts about here?"

"Not this year, so far." He was not going to say the Great Wolverine would generally avoid men unless provoked or starving. "We do not know of anyone being a shapeshifter in our region. But that is not to say they are not out there."

"So you know nothing about shape shifting sabretooth tiger men then?" Challenged the sea raider chief; he wanted the matter to appear more doubtful to his men.

The hamlet headman said, "Those things are from farther south. Whether such a man has brought these ladies north I can say neither yay or nay." He bowed and walked away satisfied he had done nothing to make the people who were carrying away their wives and children any more comfortable.

Thus the stage was set because of the boldness of Princess Loretta and Lady Dolores abetted by a quick-witted hamlet leader. The fear of the shapeshifter would make for much discomfort among the sea raiders.

*****

When the camp was set and defenses began to be set up, the ladies horses were taken from them. They were placed with other captives that had been taken in the sea raiders' foray into Alemanni territory. Around the captives were placed four wagons of booty. The sea raiders made a distinction in their tongue between riches taken on land and plunder taken on the sea. But the wagons formed the basis of the barrier the sea raiders used to keep the captives under control. It was the same barrier that would serve for their protection when the horse herd stampeded through the camp causing injury to many of the raiders.

As soon as the captives had realized they had great ladies thrust among them they turned to Princess Loretta and Lady Dolores for instruction and encouragement. It was their nature to assume these women knew more about what was going on than those taken from hamlets and villages.

Loretta turned to Dolores and asked, "What shall we do? And, how shall we encourage them?"

Dolores said, "We should get them busy doing something useful and get their minds off the problem." She saw one of the giants standing by the fence and said, "You, giant, what is your name?"

The giant pointed at his chest. "Yes, you." Dolores said, "It makes no sense just calling you giant if I know your name."

"My name is Oog son of Gog," said the giant, not knowing how to deal with the strange experience of so bold a woman addressing him. After all, most human women would cower in fear. This was what he expected and this beautiful woman appeared totally unafraid.

"Okay, Oog son of Gog, you need to help me and go get me a shovel." Dolores commanded.

Oog stood there a few minutes, so long Dolores began to wonder if he had gone to sleep. Then he said, "Why do I need to help you?"

She looked at him and put her hands on her hips. "I am the woman who counsels Gidon the Dragon Slayer. I speak in his ear. You will want me to save your life when he comes for me and the princess."

Oog said, "What makes you think he can kill me?"

Dolores quickly responded. "You have never seen him fight. What makes you think a man who is friends with Baron Igil, the giant slayer, cannot kill you?"

Oog walked off without saying a word. Dolores began to think she had failed and wondered what trouble he would bring back? But then she saw him coming with two shovels and a ground breaking spade clutched in his massive hands. "If you require anything else lady let me know."

Dolores said, "If you will bring me firewood, a goat, and salt it would be appreciated. If you will bring me two goats, we will also cook food for you."

Oog bowed and walked away. But he soon returned with two goats already skinned as well as firewood and more. He lay down outside the fence and growled at anyone, man or giant who approached the enclosure. Later, after he had eaten his goat the captives cooked with their own, he fell so hard asleep he did not even wake for the stampede. And after one of the fleeing horses smashed his head, he would never waken again.

Princess Loretta sought to entertain the younger children most of all. She found that it pleased her to have them gather round like little chicks gathering around a mother hen. But to her surprise she found the women and older girls who had been carried away were interested in her stories. First she told them about their own capture and how Gidon, the Dragon Slayer had single handedly rescued them from dozens of highwaymen. She told them what a noble and brave man he was. She emphasized he was so great the highwaymen he did not kill bound themselves willingly to his service.

Then she told the captives about Lady Dolores, and how she was the widow of the First Knight of Andorra. She told them he was so brave and noble that the enemies of the king, her father, could not best him in combat so they sent an assassin to kill him most foully with poison.

Then she told them of the Baron Igil and his wife Lady Aliruna. She recounted how they had fought together to kill a massive number of giants. This was a story all knew well and they even joined in singing some songs and reciting poems about their daring deeds.

It was the princess' story telling that helped the mothers among the women comfort all the children when the ungodly worship of their pagan gods began. All were afraid, for they knew these people practiced human sacrifice. And they particularly liked sacrificing children, some said. But stories about how such evil had been overcome in the past by the Invisible God helped immensely.

And so it went far into the night, until the camp was disrupted. First the camp was thrown into a panic when it was reported a sabretooth tiger attacked the western watch killing all the guards. As soon as they found out what had happened the children began to cry out and say "Gidon is coming!" Their excitement actually added to the turmoil of the camp.

Then, a few hours later, the horses stampeded through the camp. The Lady Dolores saw Gid-visu ride through the camp and she thought Gidon might appear at any minute. It was then they heard the sabretooth tiger had attacked the horses and killed many of them along with all the guards. Not only that, they were told the shapeshifter had many thousands of soldiers with him. Of course, the women knew the unit going to Almanya did not have so many as they were saying had attacked, but they held their peace allowing fear to increase.

But then they heard word of a thing they did not know whether to believe or not. It was said that when some of the Peleset raiders tried to move up through the vale where the horses had been, they encountered a huge wolverine of extremely bad temper. Before they could escape the creature, it was rumored he had torn open at least a dozen of the sea raiders and killed many. No one was willing to venture back into the valley, even to recover the bodies of the fallen.

The ladies were pleased with the fear that went through the camp. It was plain that their captors were much distracted. Just disposing of the bodies would be a chore and the flesh of dead giants rot quickly, especially those who eat human flesh.

Their captors completely forgot the care of their captives. Before things got too bad the last of the food was distributed among the children. They were cuddled together under and against the wagons, each one of the women trying to embrace or have close to them as many as possible.

The camp was astir and establishing order was a great difficulty for the Peleset commander. Turmoil swirled all about. So many hung over and sick from the excesses of the night before were useless. The chief of the sea raiders knew he would have to keep all who could work busy, lest all discipline fall apart. And they now saw the necessity of putting in defenses against any attack coming from the western side as well as the northern valley. They began to feel very vulnerable and stranded because of the loss of the horses.

All the work was being done by men uncertain when the next arrow would come from the sky. They hit their marks with such uncanny accuracy some began to claim they had seen a man in a flying chariot shooting flaming arrows down upon them. Such was the fear, all manner of tales and rumors were being told. It took all of their leaders' influence to keep his company from falling into utter chaos.

A sense of impending doom hung heavy over the camp of the Peleset. It seemed that just at the height of worshipping their gods the night before those gods had abandoned them.

Chapter 28

Battling the Invaders

The point of the Baron's forces arrived after the noon hour. It consisted of Gidon's man, who had taken back the three mounts, and other men who were gold cloaks. They were now mounted on newly captured horses. Gid-visu went out to meet them. He had the men sit their horses just out of bowshot. His instruction was simple. They were to call out challenges to the Peleset to come out and fight.

One of the men looked at Gid-visu and said, "What if they do come out to fight?" He was very concerned with provoking the enemy when they were so outnumbered.

Gid-visu's reply was simple as the original instruction. "They will not."

The men looked at each other doubting. "They will see your small number and immediately believe your challenges are a trap. But just to keep them unhappy we will endeavor to put an arrow into every man who looks over the bulwark."

Gidon and the bishop came out of concealment to greet the men. Just the casual manner in which they moved, seemingly taking no notice of the enemy forces, added more evidence in the sea raiders minds a large concealed force was hidden out of sight. Herman came out with a fabricated bucket of waterproofed canvas brimming with fresh water for the horses. He spoke to Gidon in a low voice, "Walid has an idea he would like to share with you. He is staying out of sight in the hope none of the Peleset will see and recognize him."

Gidon nodded and went along with the bishop to where Walid was hidden. Walid spoke to him from his concealment and Gidon said to him, "Walid, this is Bishop Elisha, who will be able to instruct you in the Way of Truth. He has worked very hard on me for many years."

Walid said, "Let us move back to where our horses are so we may be better able to talk."

When they got to the horses Bishop Elisha cupped his hands and took water from the stream and blessed it. They all had a drink savoring the sweetness of water that had been purified in its travel over many stones. Gidon saw a small piece of gold in the stream and retrieved it, handing it to the bishop, upon which the bishop blessed the Lord God who could even put gold coins in fishes' mouths.

Gidon said to the bishop, "Walid wishes to become a follower of the Invisible God."

Bishop Elisha said, "That is very good. I shall take him with me when I depart. Where are you from my son?"

"Holy Bishop, I am Walid from Misr, descended from Casluhim, a son of Mizraim. Do you know of this land?"

"Yes, I am from just north of your home. I come from a little place known in the common tongue as the House of Bread. It was down to the land of Misr the Son of the Invisible God went when the Idumaean king, who was a false king like Goraleck, wanted to kill Him.

Gidon interrupted, "Herman Reformierte, the man you saw watering the horses, Bishop, is one of my men. He said Walid had an idea that might help us win this conflict. I am sorry to change the subject but time is not our friend. Could you now tell us what is your idea Walid?" Gidon waited expectantly, for all Walid had suggested had been good thus far.

Walid began his explanation calling upon the bishop to confirm what he was saying to be true. "Bishop Elisha, you being familiar with the land of Misr know very well that we have used huge war drums to encourage our men and cause fear in our enemies for centuries. In the vale, from which we stampeded the Peleset horses, there is a rift. I am thinking that if we could construct a great war drum and set it in the rift aimed at the encampment, so the sound was increased down through the vale, we might cause the Peleset to become even more unsettled.

The bishop said, "If you could find a hollow tree nearby you might have a natural drum. If the terrain permits, you could then sling it between two horses and you might be able to move it to the rift. I have a great stag skin I brought with me to sleep upon that could be made into a drumhead."

Gidon said, "Then all we need is a hollow tree that is not rotten on the outside."

The bishop said, "I will pray for it. Perhaps our Lord will also tell us where such a tree is." He then immediately went over to the side of the stream and got on his knees to pray."

Gidon spoke to Walid saying, "You stay here and I will send Herman and his man to help you."

Gidon went back to where the gold cloaks were still mounted in the roadway. He told his man to join with Herman and go to where the horses were kept. The man was happy to leave his conspicuous position until Gidon said, "You are going to be a hero and help us win the battle." The man seemed very ill at ease with the idea of being a hero till Gidon told him it was less dangerous than being a highwayman. Armed with that small reassurance he set out to find Herman and get on about the business of being a hero.

Three hours after the point men arrived, the footmen came. Gidon thought Brute' would have been pleased with how well his men had performed moving down the road. What was surprising was an hour and a half later the citizens of the hamlet they had passed through began to arrive. They lost no time setting cooking fires and starting the preparation of warm food for all the fighting men.

The Baron asked their help in building a spike barricade, not telling them he did not expect to need it. It was after this the Baron called a counsel of war with Bishop Elisha, Gid-visu, Gidon, and the hamlet headman.

The bishop reported first that a hollow tree had been found and was even as he spoke being moved into position in the rift by Walid and Gidon's two men.

Baron von Krieg said, "As you all know we are greatly outnumbered even though Gid-visu and Gidon have decreased the numbers significantly. We know that among the slain of the enemy at least two giants and a man who probably belonged to Goraleck can be counted. I expect from what our friend from the hamlet has said there probably is no more than six giants in the group. I want them all dead."

Bishop Elisha interjected, "Pardon me Baron, but the issue lies not only with the giants but the Peleset themselves. The Invisible God wants all of them including their priestesses to be slain. They carry a stain in their very souls and He so ordered this many hundreds of years ago. Because of the failures to obey God in this matter many great kings and noble men and women have fallen."

"But what about Walid? He wishes to follow the Way of Truth." Gidon said.

The bishop looked at him tenderly. "My son, do you not yet know when a man embraces our God and humbles himself before Him, he becomes a new man?"

"Okay, they will all be slain," the Baron said. "It is for a certainty their crimes in our land have been great enough to be worthy of death."

"Now we have the matter of how we are going to slay them. I have a plan but it will require the help of you people," said the Baron looking at the headman of the hamlet. "From the hills we can see into the enemy camp. So if we are in a place where we can see their fires they will also be able to see ours."

Everyone nodded, agreeing with the Baron's observation.

"I would like for your villagers to gather enough kindling for each man to light at least five fires on the hills round about. Each one of your people will be accompanied by one of my soldiers to defend them. I want them to start campfires and keep them going to make them look surrounded by a vastly superior army."

The Baron was not through. "Gid-visu, how are you and Gidon's arrow supply holding up.?"

Gid-visu replied, "By the time we are through with this night we will have about used up what we brought up with us."

The headman spoke up. “I have brought with me two men who are good huntsmen. They have a goodly number of arrows between them.”

Gid-visu said, “Our bows have tremendous power. They could shatter normal arrow shafts and cause us injury.”

The headman responded, “Take our huntsmen with you and get them in position where they can shoot their bows. In this way you will save your arrows. I think you will find my people will prove themselves to you.”

Gid-visu agreed even though he knew that hunting men and hunting animals were two different things. But they would have to accept the added liability men not trained for this kind of war might pose. They needed the help. At least they were huntsmen.

Once everything was set the men began taking care of the different elements of the Baron’s instruction seeking to make sure they got the right men to the correct place. But they began their work with fresh bread with butter and still warm pieces of goat and lamb in the mix.

The bishop walked with Gidon as he headed for the rift with a huntsman following along behind. “How is Getrudis?” Gidon asked.

“I was wondering when you would get around to her,” the bishop said. “She has heard about the two new women you have from the Lady Aliruna, though I daresay she was not told the whole of the matter. She knows for instance that you spanked the princess.”

“Does she know I kissed her?” Gidon asked.

“No, she does not know about that. Why did you do it?” The bishop had stopped walking and was looking at him intently.

“I am not quite sure. I could use as an excuse Lady Dolores told me to do so. But it comes down to the fact it was my choice whether to do so or not.” Gidon had asked himself the same question many times.

“What about Lady Dolores? We heard she had sworn herself to you.” The bishop began walking again. He was leading up the path and guiding the conversation as well.

“She has so sworn. She is a very smart woman, though a tragic figure in a sense. It seems she did not appreciate the husband that was hers. I think she is trying to make up for that in her loyalties." Gidon still did not fully understand her but had he been pressed he would have admitted that he did not really completely understand any woman.

"Bishop, I really love Getrudis in every way a man can love a woman. I am fearful that I may be required to do things that could hurt that love and that is one thing I truly do not wish to do." Gidon felt as if he wanted the bishop to work one of his miracles.

"Gidon, Getrudis is truly committed to you. When I return, I will reassure her of your love. No matter what you may be forced to do she will not forsake your love. She is truly a wonderful woman. You need to communicate with her as much as possible though, however hard it is."

Gidon nodded, determined to follow the bishop's counsel.

When they got to the rift everything was in readiness. They gave the men the food and wine they brought, and while they ate Gidon took the first turn on the drum. He beat out a consistent and slow cadence. The drum would sound and travel out toward the camp. When the echo came back from the far hills, he would strike the drum again. The huntsman had taken a position to the side ready in case anyone dared come up to investigate. Bishop Elisha returned to the main camp passing men working their way upwards to start their fires from that side.

When the men had finished eating and taking care of their necessities Gidon turned the drum over to them and with the huntsman worked his way to the western side of the camp. He could already see a large number of twinkling campfires from all sides. Surely their enemies must feel themselves surrounded.

Gidon asked the huntsman to follow him to the western side where likely they would pick off their first targets. He asked the huntsman his name to which he replied, "My name is Wuotis and the other huntsman with me is my brother Wuodan." To which Gidon said, "With names like that your father must have intended you be huntsmen."

Wuotis said, "My father was a huntsman as was his father. Is not your father a great warrior?"

Gidon replied, "I think my father would rather be known as a great bowman and bow maker."

Wuotis replied, "Yes, among those who use the bow, Gid-visu's skill is known far and wide. Many would sell everything they have to own one of his bows. I make my own and they are good enough bows. They have to be because with them many are fed."

When they got to the western side, Gidon observed the building of the spiked defense like the one on the east side, but they had not managed to build the breastworks on this side. Even though this was Gidon's first experience of such an operation, he considered the decline in efficiency in erecting defensive fortifications evidence in the breakdown of the sea raiders' discipline.

Once again, they had built their fires too high, so over the course of a couple of hours Wuotis was able to pick off three Peleset with well-placed bow shots.

Gidon suggested they swing to the southern side of the camp and seek to get in some more targets of opportunity, particularly focusing on the guards.

At the first position they came to there were three guards. There was an argument going on between two of them and they were not as attentive as they should be. One man was standing a little farther away from his two compatriots at the guard post trying to stay out of their argument. It seemed the incessant drumming coming down the valley to the north had put their nerves in a ragged state. Gidon was able to bring a knife under his ribcage into the heart while Wuotis, exhibiting fine skill, was able to kill one and wound another. Gidon went to the wounded man and finished the job. Wuotis asked, "Why did you not take him prisoner?"

For some reason Gidon did not see fit to tell him the bishop had ordered they all be killed. He simply told Wuotis that having a wounded man making noise would increase the likelihood of their being caught. This was true and probably a better answer under the circumstances than the other. Gidon thought it foolish to second guess the instruction of the Invisible God.

Completing the southern circle yielded five more kills. They decided to go back to the main camp as the night was far along.

Probably Gid-visu and Wuodan would have already started their work of unsettling the camp. It would not be good if by some mistake they got in one another's way. And Gidon hoped to find something to write on so he could send a note to Getrudis by way of the bishop. He would later learn that both his father and the Baron had composed missives to their women for the bishop to take back.

In the early morning hours, the hamlet's headman sent some of his people up to relieve Walid and Gidon's men on the big drum. Within the Peleset camp the constant beating through the night had reduced some of the people to quivering balls of humanity with massive headaches or overwhelming depression. Even though the captives were heartened by its beat, they too began to feel the impact of the drumming, becoming listless.

At sunup the Baron walked out on a small promontory to the left of the road as it faced the enemy camp. He placed his horn to his lips and blew. Its sound echoed over the hills and men in equidistance distribution raised their own horns to their lips and blew as well. The desired effect was accomplished. The Peleset reached for their weapons and tried to take up positions against attacks they expected from all directions. But nothing happened. After the space of about fifteen minutes the big drum to the north began its steady drumming once more. Three men in the Peleset camp fell on their swords. The impact on morale was awful. No one was paying any attention to camp discipline any longer.

Three giants, the last three among the Peleset headed to the north determined to stop the big drum once and for all. But Gid-visu and Wuodan had positioned themselves there after the sun rose. Gid-visu, using his heavier bow and armor piercing arrow points, dropped the first giant almost as soon as he appeared. It took three arrows to the chest. The next giant was also his, but they had locked their minds on the objective and were coming fast. As soon as the third giant was in range of Wuodan's bow he started firing arrows. In an amazing display of speed and accuracy the man hit the giant again and again. He kept coming forward, ignoring his wounds, to finally fall at the feet of the huntsman. Wuodan looked at Gid-visu and grinned but then he wiped his brow. His body was reacting to the stress.

Wuodan went to get some of his neighbors, sending them back to Gid-visu. They used the two horses that had brought the hollow tree drum into position to pull the giants together in a pile. This was difficult at first because the horses disliked the smell of the giants very much. Then they covered them with a huge mound of pine wood that was full of resin. Once this was lit, it burned very hot and the noxious smell of burning giants floated down into the camp making everyone sick to the stomach. And still the drum continued its incessant beating. All in the camp waited for what they thought a mighty force to attack them but it never came. At the evening hour the drumming ceased. The silence worked on Peleset nerves as heavily as the drumming had. The fear of what was to come was heavy upon them all through the evening hours leaving them all exhausted.

*****

It was just past the noon hour the bishop called a holy convocation. It took several hours to bring all the men in from their places in the hills. Those manning the great drum were the last to leave their post. Bishop Elisha had directed none should be omitted, promising the enemy camp in their fear would never be aware of the absence of troops surrounding them.

One of the fighting priests had built an altar from natural rock by the stream near where it widened out into a pool. A man from the hamlet approached the priest and said, "Would it not be easier to shape the stones just a bit instead of always searching for the right stone to go in a place?"

The priest looked at him and said, "To cut a stone for this altar would be to profane it for these stones represent the Son of the Invisible God."

The man said, "Forgive me holy man. In the years to come I will visit this altar often and keep it in good condition."

When the people were formed out in the open on the western side of the road, the Bishop stood on a cart brought by the villagers and spoke to all assembled saying, "We are now gathered before our enemies as the Church Army of the Lord of Hosts. Since you have been faithful to Him in these things, He will honor you as He did others many a time in the past. I bid you all to wash yourselves in the place where the stream makes a pool and make supplication for a great victory from the Lord. If you will sanctify yourselves, men at arms and men of the hamlet alike; repent and turn away from any wickedness, then God will heal your land of this blight upon it."

People went down to the pool, soldier and serf, man and boy, alike; setting up a partition so women and girls could bathe modestly. Even though there was a joyful spirit in the bathing the people never lost sight of the holy purpose they were about.

The Baron had considered a complete defeat of the Peleset and the saving of the prisoners a virtual impossibility. Then he heard the noises coming from the camp of the sea raiders as they started calling on their gods once again. He considered that an encouraging omen. With an enemy at their gates they turned to ritual gluttony and debauchery in the hopes their god would save them. The commander of the camp had completely lost control over his men.

He turned to the bishop and said, "Death will truly walk through the camp of the Peleset this night."

He called for the headman of the hamlet asking him to send men into the wood to cut thin straight growths of hardwood trees that could be easily made into pikes. He ordered fires made in preparation for hardening as many wooden points as practical in a very short period of time. Suitable trees began to come in even before the fires were ready, for these people had a mind to work.

Most of the night would be used in cleansing bodies, praying, stripping poles, and hardening wood tips of the trees. They would not be the best weapons in the world but the Baron felt more and more confidence in what these people would do. After all, many of the people held prisoner were friends and neighbors, which usually meant in a small hamlet many were also relatives.

It fell to the fighting priests to lead the mass of pike men made up of people from the hamlet and the Baron's troop in a foray that would come from the woods to the south of the Peleset and drive through to the vale where the horses had been lodged.

The Baron, Gid-visu and Gidon were joined by the two hunters, Wuotis and Wuodan, who insisted they should also be allowed to stalk the drunken camp when the time came. Asked what they thought qualified them they simply replied, "Though we are huntsmen, never have we been part of the Wildes Heer or as it is known in the common tongue, the wild host. Every huntsman should have at least one in his lifetime."

Once the Baron accepted them, Herman Reformierte said he must go forth with Gidon. He was told by Gidon that his feet were far too clumsy, but he declared, if Gidon would take him along, no cause for regret would he know. This was how it came about Herman, armed with the sword given by Baron Igil, would be part of the shadow of death to first move through the camp.

Bishop Elisha said, "Then with me the number will be seven. A perfect number to defeat those uncircumcised heathen."

Gidon said, "But bishop, most of the men here are uncircumcised."

"Yes, but Gidon they are not heathen! That makes all the difference." The bishop spoke under his breath, "We shall endeavor to take care of the other matter with time."

The Baron asked, "Bishop Elisha, why must you go into the camp with us? Why not wait till after the battle?"

The bishop answered simply, "The captives need me. I will get them ready and bring them out at the right time."

It was only a couple of hours before dawn when the camp of the Peleset grew quiet. Gidon had positioned himself where he would make his walk down the relative center of the camp for Gid-visu had noted the position of the holding area for the captives. The bishop walked without weapon to his right, with Herman stationing himself beside him. Several times men roused up. When they did so with the bishop, he would but touch them with his hand and they would lay back down to be touched by Herman with a stroke Gidon taught him.

No one, from the time they first entered the camp till they reached the prisoners rose up to offer serious resistance. Afterwards men would say the Peleset had succumbed to a sleep that was even beyond drunken slumber.

The Baron walked the eastern side accompanied by Wuodan and Gid-visu worked the western side accompanied by Wuotis. Gid-visu had become fast friends with both men. When asked why, he would only say he liked their spirit. In years to come that friendship would deepen. The men were like death angels passing through the camp, which seemed to be encompassed in an eerie haze.

When Gidon got to the prisoner holding area both the princess and Dolores were standing by the rail looking for him. Dolores said, "You see Loretta, I told you he would come for us tonight."

The bishop followed Gidon over the rail, and while Gidon was smothered with kisses from the two women, the man of God went to the huddled masses of people who were yet fearful something would go wrong. They were eager to get out of the place and be free. And the camp was filled with the most appalling stench. The Baron would later say the place smelled worse than any battlefield he had ever been on.

Gidon took each woman gently in his arms and gave them separately a firm kiss beginning with each cheek and finally on the mouth. He said, "I must go and finish my business but I will return for you shortly. I thank God for protecting you and keeping you well. But now I must do my part."

And so, in moving forward it was Gidon who would find the priestesses of Dagon. With Herman by his side they looked upon one of the most gruesome sights he would ever know in his life. When all else had been done, these women had been sacrificed to the gods with many cuts and much pain. He could only imagine the type of demonic inspiration that had infected the men who had done this thing.

Gidon also discovered the commander of the Peleset in his tent. He was drunken but aware of all that was happening. Gidon sent Herman for the Baron who came very quickly.

The Peleset chief said to him, "Who are you?"

The Baron answered, "I am the Baron von Krieg, King's Rider for King Gregor II, and Chief of the Long Knives, come to give you justice for invading our land and despoiling our people."

The man looked at the Baron and laughed a very empty sounding laugh. "You must have brought a mighty force with you to defeat me so handily."

"No, we are a small force mostly made up of conscripts and Alemanni you have wronged. We do not waste great efforts on the likes of you."

"Well, I am sure you will not grant me death by combat so will you at least give me death that is honorable and an honorable burial?"

"No, I will grant you a quick death, not an honorable one. Your head will adorn a stake not long from now." With that the Baron slipped his long knife down by the neck into the man's heart and when he removed the blade the fellow fell backwards off the stool, but the Baron had removed his head in one stroke before he completed the fall.

The Baron looked at Gidon and said, "Come my friend, we have work to do," and he walked out of the tent. Gidon stood there wordlessly for a moment. The Baron had called him his friend. Not squire or boy, or any other term he had used in the past. The Baron considered him his friend. That was an honor greater than all the titles that could possibly be bestowed!

When they reached the northern end of the camp a torch was lit and held up on high. This was the signal for all the other forces to begin their march with the homemade pikes. They came with a fury abandoning all semblance of quietness. A fever of revenge seemed to inhabit the people for all the evil they had done.

Gidon made his way back to the women with the ever-faithful Herman Reformierte by his side. They had to be on guard lest some villager in his zeal should mistakenly impale them with his weapon. No need for a command to leave no survivors. Gidon had never seen such fury as was with these people now their anger was unleashed.

When Gidon arrived where the former prisoners were, he saw the bishop had already organized the group and was preparing to lead them out. He had not realized how many captives the Peleset had.

There were people, not only from the local hamlet but three others as well. Some women grabbed on to Gidon by either arm ignoring his blood-spattered clothes. It was for sure that he was going to be of little help to the bishop guiding the people. But then he saw Gid-visu had come with the hunters.

Gidon got his hands free from the women's grasp and established a grasp of his own about both his charges' waists. Dolores established their place as his women subservient to Getrudis by saying, "We look forward to writing Mistress Getrudis and telling her how gallantly you rescued us, not once, but twice. We envy you the love you two share. And are thankful you have a little love for us!" Gidon held them tighter in gratitude.

When they had cleared the camp and made the relatively short walk around to the eastern side Gidon was beginning to feel the letdown that comes after a battle. He did not know how men like his father and the Baron kept going. He was almost staggering with exhaustion and spent nerves. He guided the women to the spot where he had last rested and rolled out his skin that he had left there, saying, "Ladies I am tired." He lay down upon the skin.

One of the old women from the hamlet brought them fresh goat's milk, chilled in the stream. With that she also had some bread and cheese. The women roused Gidon to eat and drink with them but he was fast asleep again before he finished his portion.

Lady Dolores said, "He is so tired,"

Herman spoke and said, "He has scarcely rested since the two of you were carried away."

Dolores asked Herman to get some water and the two women stripped Gidon's body while he was gone. He slept right through it. But he did rouse some when they began to clean his body and check for wounds. They saw more of his body in this sleeping state than ever when he was awake. The princess said, "Look at his muscles. He is really powerful."

Lady Dolores replied with but one word, "Everywhere!"

The women did the best they could to clean his clothes and they slipped his under breeches back on him and covered him with a fur while he slept through it all. For a little while the sleep of exhaustion made his mind deep and dreamless. He rested away from the ghosts of dead men and butchered priestesses. But those dreams would return. They always do.

The Baron set a guard of his gold cloaks on the treasure wagons and instructed the headman to take such tents and clothes and other accoutrements of the Peleset for the village. All weapons except for knives were to be stacked for the use of his little army.

He instructed the bodies should be burnt and failed to mention the chief, whose head was to be impaled on a pike, was excluded from the order. Whether this was intentional or not, none could say.

Gid-visu asked that the horse which had died under him might also be burnt and the gear from the animal brought to him. He did not want so noble a steed to be meals for vultures and scavengers. He also promised the headman of the village that if they captured any horses that were still roaming free, he would purchase them. He told him they should be taken to Herman the Schmeid at Eastwatch by the Rising of the Little Dan. Herman would take the horses and escort those that brought them to his mistress Brunhild where she would pay what they were worth.

This seemed satisfying to the leader of the hamlet for they had little use for horses who consume quite a bit of hay and feed as well as having other needs.

The leaders settled down to rest as the other requirements were worked out, Some of the captives would wish to return to their homes. Others would find a new home in the hamlet that rescued them, and others still would attach themselves to the Baron's army, as they called it.

Tomorrow would be soon enough to sort most matters out.

Chapter 29

Planning Ahead

Gidon had slept the sleep likened unto that of the dead for a number of hours. Whenever he stirred or cried out from some unwelcome dream the women cuddled beside him soothing his mind with their feminine softness. Twice he had cried out "Getrudis!" and Loretta and Dolores would look at each other. As the Lady Dolores had already stated, they knew there was no hope of supplanting the love he had for his Mistress, but were thankful for the godly love and concern for them they could share. Finally Gidon awoke and immediately realized the services the women had performed for him while in his state of exhaustion. He felt no shame at being before them naked, but was thankful, after all they had endured, they could reach into the resources of that strength bound in the tender reaches of a woman's heart to do him sweet service.

He thanked the ladies for working to clean his clothing then asked for the dress the Baron's squire should appear in. They rolled up one dried garment and unrolled the other, dutifully assisting his still tired and sore body in donning the heavy woolen undergarment, chainmail and tunic. The old hamlet woman, who had brought him food before he slept, now brought him beer and a bowl of stew with good common Landesbrot to dip in it. In this manner he was refreshed somewhat.

Gidon said to his women, "Should I not call Herman and have him set up a partition down at the pond where you two may bathe?"

Lady Dolores responded, "We had Herman set a partition around us when we were washing your garments so we could sponge away the worst of our filth from that awful camp."

Princess Loretta began to show more of her developing personality when she said, "Yes, we stripped completely naked before you while you lay there sleeping on the ground. What a treat you missed!" All had a good laugh.

Much had happened while Gidon slept. The wagons of the Peleset had been brought out of the camp and lined up with the treasure wagons still being kept together under guard. There had been enough horses recovered to pull the wagons and mount all the men of the Eastwatch force. All would now ride the rest of the way to Almanya. The extra saddles and bridles would go with them to be presented to King Gregor for his military use. A wagon, filled with weaponry, would go to Herr Brute' von Alemanni, the King's Master at Arms for Eastwatch Keep, and so the king would be informed. King Gregor II would be able to count them part of his spoil but they would already be where they could do the most good.

The headman of the hamlet announced they were changing the name of their home to Riesenbano, which being interpreted in the common tongue meant Giant's Bane. He proudly announced they could boast their very own giant killer in Wuodan. Someone would later comment, Gidon had killed two giants and Gid-visu two as well while Wuodan had killed only one. But Gidon said Wuodan had killed his giant and this gave his hamlet a claim to fame, a warning to enemies, and the kind of pride that might draw others to want to live amongst brave people.

Baron von Krieg had decreed the spoiling of the Peleset mercenaries was to belong to the people of Giant's Bane. It was to include tenting, clothing, coin, and conveniences. Only the swords, crossbows and such were to be surrendered to the Eastwatch armory. The Long Knives did not think such weapons should be held in common hands, and the Keep needed weapons.

The first order of business was an inventory of the four treasure wagons for the purpose of division. Gidon was asked if he would like to observe this undertaking since he was trained in numbers and assessments by both the bishop and his father. But he begged to be excused, saying he needed to compose a letter to Mistress Getrudis for the Bishop to take back to Eastwatch. The Bishop sent him parchment and ink and he set down on a knoll with Princess Loretta and Lady Dolores just higher than the activity at the wagons.

Just as he began struggling over the words he needed to say, for he was less interested in writing an account of his adventures than expressing his devotion to Getrudis, Walid came to bring the women down to the treasure wagons. Gidon was not paying those things much attention, so fixated was he on expressing his undying and unwavering love to his beloved. He knew the bishop would tell all that was fit to tell about the adventures that had taken place.

For a very long time he just stared at the parchment, but words failed to appear on their own. Then he remembered a love poem written by someone across the narrow sea. The words did not quite fit the situation between him and Getrudis but remembering the flow and sentiment he began to write. From the time he started writing till the end he did not pause. It flowed out with all his passion and commitment.

Princess Loretta came running up the hill followed more slowly by Dolores. "Gidon, guess what!"

Gidon looked up at her, his mind awash with the thought that had so dominated his writing. He could not speak, but only wait. "They found a trunk with my dowry and store of wealth among the treasure in the wagons; the Lady Dolores wealth as well!"

"Good, good, now you do not have to be dependent. You can make your own choices free from feeling compelled to go a certain way." Gidon said. He did not know whether he was happy or sad.

The ladies knelt on either side of Gidon so he could only look at them one at a time. Princess Loretta said, "Gidon, do you not realize we have already made our choices. I would rather be your serving wench than the greatest queen in the world."

The Lady Dolores chimed in, "Gidon, I am committed to being your Lolita. Whatever you require of me; that will I do. Please do not send us away."

Gidon knew he should be happy. He had the devotion of some very fine women and the respect of some very noble men, not even to mention the commitments of men who had once been varlets but now willingly obeyed when he commanded. But he was not at all happy.

Dolores asked, "Why is my lord so crestfallen? Have we displeased you?"

"No, it is not that. I am honored by you. But you know the one who occupies the center of my being is Getrudis. I have written something to her but now I fear my mind too ignoble to express all that is in my heart and soul. It is no offense intended to you ladies. However much I appreciate your devotion, I am afraid. I am fearful of saying the wrong thing to her. Was not this parchment so precious, I would have already torn up the pale product of my stumbling thought.

The Lady Dolores became the model of efficiency dedicated to her master's pleasure. "Let me see what you have written."

Gidon handed her the parchment and she read it aloud:

> "You Have I Chosen—Steadfast In That Love Twill Be.
>
> I will never repent my love for you in word, or thought, or deed.
> You are godly good in thought and action alway.
> To speak of your beauty is injustice to your more comely attraction.
> I am bound by oaths of service to God, king, and lord;
> Whatsoever oaths demand of bodily service they cannot sway my heart;
> It is yours woven forever in the holy knot of all-encompassing love.
> Our love we sealed in the presence of the Invisible God forever.

That which you deserve none other can demand;
This I hold in remembrance night and day.
In this world my strength and might may one day fail;
But the bond of holy love will hold into eternity.
By promise made with holy assurance,
Ever you to love wholly and without variance.
You have I chosen, steadfast in that love twill be."

The women sat in silence. Tears fell silently. They came abundantly from Loretta and fell over her pale pink alabaster skin. When Dolores tried to speak it first came out as a sob. When she tried again, she said, "Were the man I loved so to write me I would adore him forever. If she is not moved by your words, and understand fully what is in your heart, she is not the woman I think she is."

The women hugged Gidon and fetched a candle where the parchment could be rolled and sealed with wax. Gidon could not seal it with his own signet for he did not as yet have a ring. It would have to do.

The Baron walked up the hill, watching the ladies hug Gidon as he came. "It seems whatever you have it never quits working for you. I can imagine Goraleck would be in a fine state if he knew the Peleset he hired to raid on land had also helped themselves to the treasure his men had taken at great loss from these ladies."

Gidon smiled at the Baron, but after such a night's labor it had a hard edge. "You know how much pain I feel that Goraleck should be so disappointed in all his endeavors. I hope we can one day give him the permanent disappointment he has earned."

"Well Gidon, I know you prefer these fine ladies' company to my own, but it is time you stopped lingering with them. I have need of you, and also you must be present when the bishop speaks and leads the people in a prayer of thanks giving."

Gidon stood up straight and said, "Yes, my lord Baron." And the four of them walked off the knoll together.

*****

It took some time for all of the common people to assemble. The people of the newly named Giant's Bane had not only been happily involved in family reunions as their loved ones were returned to them alive, they were busily packing up for transport back to the hamlet all the newly acquired materials that would enrich them greatly as a hamlet. Already an agreement had been made with the bishop to send them priests to teach the people The Way of Truth in service to the Invisible God. But other agreements had been made for a future relationship with their new friends to the south by way of the Baron of Eastwatch Keep. As relations were cemented, the Baron von Krieg and Gid-visu thought things would be mutually beneficial between the village of Eastwatch and hamlet of Giant's Bane in spite of the long distance between them.

The many captives that were rescued had a tendency to cling together. Slowly some had become attached to the local community. Others committed to travel to Almanya with the trainees, and others became attached to the men from Eastwatch in personal relationships. One very large woman, who had a young son, already of huge proportion, had separated herself from the group and begun following Herman Reformierte as he carried out his duty. He had tried a number of times to shoo her away but she just looked at him and smiled. He had approached Gidon about her, but Gidon looked at her and noted she was plain but not ugly, and strong like Herman. He told Herman she was breaking no rule and could walk where she would. Herman, the former cutthroat who once would risk all for a purse, began to be afflicted with an extreme case of nerves.

On one occasion, when the bishop was near, the woman approached him. She said to him, "Holy man of the Invisible God may I ask you a question?"

The bishop countered with his own questions. "What is your name daughter, and what is your status?"

"My name is Brynhild, named for the Valkyrie shieldmaiden because, as the fates would have it, my father's name was Budli. I was widowed when the Peleset raided our farm and took away me and my son captive."

The bishop nodded and said, "And what is your question?"

"Since I have lost both home and husband, I need to take a spoil that will provide for me and the boy. May I take a spoil?" Brynhild asked.

The bishop looked at her seriously but his eyes held just a twinkle of humor, "It is not the fates that determined your name or your experiences but the Invisible God. I perceive the spoil you want is not a thing but a person. Am I not right?"

"You are correct sir. I wish to take that big lout Herman Reformierte as my spoil. He needs a shield-woman for his own good." Brynhild was a very direct woman.

"Daughter, a man is not like an ox or a goat which might be taken as a spoil with no thought to its opinion. Men should go to women because they love the woman chosen." The bishop now spoke patiently and gently but the twinkle in his eye remained.

"He loves me alright. I just have not told him yet!" Brynhild declared.

And so it was, the first marriage occurred between the former captives and their rescuers.

*****

At long last, Bishop Elisha was ready to speak to the people. As always his first words were addressed to the Invisible God thanking Him for the miraculous victory He had given them where some three hundred of the Peleset had all perished with no loss of life to the Alemanni. He said, "I adjure you all not to forget to be thankful upon every remembrance of this occasion when God worked wonders on your behalf. Remember that those who forget to be thankful begin to believe they have done great things solely in their own power. And when we forget to give God the glory, we miss out on the blessings He would give us in this world." When the bishop let off speaking these and many other memorable words, he blessed the people.

However, as is often the case with mankind, greed reared its ugly head among the men at arms going to Almanya. They declared that, even though after the wealth of the captives was returned and there remained a considerable fortune, it should not be shared among those who remained behind on the main road guarding the material going to Almanya.

No one seemed to know who started the discord. And overlooked was the fact that not only the general equipment was being guarded by the orders of both Gidon and the Baron, the things of value belonging to those who made the march up the path to the battle were also watched over by the men left behind. Even with an equal and fair distribution among all, each man would be far wealthier than he had ever been in his life.

The Baron settled it all by declaring that all men either stayed or went by his orders and since all had done their duty, they would all share equally as prescribed by the chivalric code, which meant each leader would get a double portion of the distribution. He further declared that since they had argued about it the bishop would take all the portions back to Eastwatch to be locked in the Burgomeister's dungeon until their return. That way no man would lose his wealth in Almanya.

One person asked what would be done if through circumstance they did not return home? The Baron in answer decreed that any man who did not return home would see his portion given to his family so they would be benefited by his service to his people. This solution might not have satisfied all but it could not be disputed since the Baron was in authority.

Dolores came to Gidon and asked, "Since my lord is going to be busy here, should not Princess Loretta and I travel down with the bishop to our wagon and await you?" Gidon suspected she had more on her mind but readily assented. The next day promised to be tedious and simply waiting would be a hardship on the women.

In what seemed a lengthy duration, the bishop's new wagon was ready, laden with the tithe of the spoils to be driven by Walid. The four treasure wagons, now reduced to three, were next in his little convoy, followed by a wagon laden with swords and such.

The wagons that were destined for the King and Almanya would travel down with the Baron along with sufficient horses to ensure that all his forces would ride. It would be an interesting spectacle when men who had never ridden a horse had to learn. They could not pick the soft places to land as Herr Brute' had once humorously recommended to Ohtrad.

The last night Gidon had with the two women, before they headed out with the bishop was a somber affair. It seemed they all dreaded the morning when they would have to separate for a day or two. But there was pleasure in the warmth of the fire and the exchanging of pleasantries between the ladies, Gid-visu, Baron von Krieg, and Gidon. The women had come to hold all these men in great admiration and enjoyed their company.

In the morning when they said their goodbyes the women were plainly tearful. You would have thought they were parting forever instead of but a short while. But in the women's minds was the uncertainty of knowing their futures were commanded by a king they had never met, in a foreign land where in all likelihood they would spend the rest of their lives. They had made their preferences known to Gidon but even the Baron was subject to the desires of King Gregor. And in that respect, they were no different.

When the wagons began to roll, with the bishop's wagon in the lead, the ladies chose to ride together on their Andorran steeds. The fresh air of freedom, away even from the confines of a stuffy wagon, was a blessing. It was not until they stopped in late morning to water horses and take care of human needs the bishop got a chance to approach Lady Dolores. He said to her, "I have been wondering. What is the true purpose of your leaving Gidon to travel back ahead of him?"

Dolores said, "I imagine you already know."

The bishop smiled, "I am thinking you intend to send a letter back with me to Mistress Getrudis."

"Will you carry it for us Reverend Bishop? It is most important the good woman knows the nobility of her master." Dolores favored the wise man with her smile.

"Of course I will. I trust your wisdom to write complementary to his own missive without ever letting on that you have seen it," said the bishop.

Gidon was sorry to see the wagons roll out for he was already missing the companionship of the women. He had allowed Herman to go with his men as escort for the wagon train because he considered the man useless at the present away from his Brynhild. Whatever had happened between them, he could only guess. But under the stars the character of the man was more transformed by the woman than all the time Gidon had spent on him.

Gid-visu came to Gidon saying, "Son, you and I need to talk with the Baron about future plans." So, after making sure all things were proceeding orderly, they met together on the spot now called Gidon's Knoll.

Gid-visu said to the other two, "I think we should make some future plans now because what I have in mind will require King Gregor's authorization and commission."

The Baron said, "Now I am intrigued. I am wondering if our minds might be working together." Gidon felt a bit lost in the conversation.

"I am thinking we should work together to turn both Riesenbano, or Giant's Bane and Heim into fortified Holds. We could not only organize these areas to be more productive but use them to establish way stations where at the very least messengers could safely rest and get a change of horse between Almanya and Eastwatch. Together, with Baron Igil's Keep, we would be on our way toward making this part of the kingdom more connected and secure." Gid-visu had clearly been thinking on the subject in great detail. Within his mind were more complex plans than could be immediately laid out.

Baron von Krieg said, "Gidon has already made promises to the people who remain at Heim and I have noticed that you, Gid-visu, have been using the now free ranging horses as a basis for future relation with the people of Riesenbano. If the king would approve it, I do not see why it would not only work to the king's good but our profit as well."

Gidon asked, "When should we approach the king with the idea? Surely he is being consumed with this muster and I doubt he is all that easily approachable."

The Baron then said, "Gidon you forget that I am a King's Rider as well as being Chief of the Long Knives. In those capacities I have the king's ear. And your father, well, he is the king's friend even as he is the friend of the king's father. I am sure he will find it easier to speak with the king than even I."

Gidon asked a question that had been in his thoughts for years. "I know my father is the king's friend but one thing I have never been told is how he became the king's friend?"

The Baron said, "I will tell you because I know your father well and he will not tell the whole of it:

"Your father first met King Gregor I when the king was on a hunt. Gid-visu was in the same wood resting and seeking to recover his mind and body after going on a very hazardous mission for the Long Knives.

"This happened before I became Chief of the Long Knives. He had defeated a man in bare handed combat who was a spy from another land and an assassin. In the course of the fight he had suffered a terrible blow to the midsection that bothers him to this very day. It would have disabled a less fit man but it took even him some time to regain most of his vigor.

"He heard the commotion of the hunt and positioned himself on a high point to watch when the hunting party rode by in the valley, intending they should never know of his presence. They had been pursuing a great white stag because of the belief pursuing such stags brings happiness even when it is not to be caught. On this occasion the white stag, well ahead of the hunt, hid itself in a clump of bush, waiting for the hunting party to appear. Gid-visu watched this happen, noting it as strange behavior indeed.

"When the hunting party appeared, the mighty stag bounded through a bed of rosemary in an attack that first impaled the king's horse, and then wounded King Gregor I in the leg. As you should know a white stag in a bed of rosemary is the sign of remembrance and sorrow. The stag had pulled his antlers out and was about to attack again when Gid-visu stood up and from his place made a tremendous shot that went through the stag's neck. At that point the stag ran away and later they could not find any trace of blood from the neck wound.

"The white stag as you know is ever the symbol of huntsmen and foresters, as well as a symbol of the Invisible God. For Gid-visu, the encounter with the stag meant he should spring forward and upward ever going onward to overcome difficulties. His quest should ever be the pursuit of the higher aims of his craft and not to be enslaved by his sorrows.

"With King Gregor I was a seer named Hubertus who was a servant of the Invisible God. He said the stag was a messenger to the king telling him he should undertake the role of kingship with piety and assert his divine authority for the benefit of both highborn and serf alike. The king saw, intertwining his and Gid-visu's understandings of the messenger from the Invisible God, a further indication they should be dear friends in this life. The king considered all he had been told concerning the omen and determined it was time for noble men to appear and work to unite Aleman and time has shown this to be the case."

"So how did my father become friends with King Gregor II?"

Gid-visu said, "I knew King Gregor II when he was but a young prince, before his royal father turned the throne over to him."

Gidon said, "I do not mean to be rude dear father, but just knowing someone and even knowing about a man saving your father's life does not necessarily make him more than an acquaintance. How did you actually become friends?"

"Sometimes those kinds of things are hard to say. Some men meet and become friends immediately. Others become friends over a period of association. Some even become friends after they have fought one another." Gid-visu said philosophically.

"You mean like what happened between me and Herman One Eye or the Baron and Brute'. I can understand that." Gidon said.

Baron von Krieg spoke. "Sometimes war can make one friends. But that is not a guarantee even when one saves another's life. In the case of King Gregor II your father has saved his life on the field of battle not once but twice. But after all we have just gone through, I would think you have had quite enough talk of war and killing."

"It is not that I relish talk of war and killing. What we have just done turns my stomach even though it was necessary. But for all the years of my life, since I had first begun to think on these things, I have wanted to know the truth of what I only knew of from afar. It is something to know your father is friend of the king without knowing the reason why. After all, we are not highborn people." Gidon explained.

It was then Gid-visu stated something profound that has been true of people of high station throughout all the fallen history of man. "Just because people are highborn does not mean they are high in the standards they bring to their world. A king cannot trust others to be his friend because they have a prominent place in the kingdom. Right now, I would dare to say some of those complicit in the attacks on key people in the kingdom are among the very people closest to our king today, which is why we must unearth and expose them."

"Back to the point. What did you do in battle that made King Gregor II your friend?" Gidon was impatient to know the answer after so many years of waiting.

The Baron said, "Once more I will answer because I know the modesty of my friend. It was in the war of unification against Queen Gimbutas, who as you may remember led the people known in the common tongue as the Battle Axe People. King Gregor had laid siege to her castle which was built mainly of timber, but was hard to assault because of the mounds they had made to elevate the structures."

"Yes, I remember studying that at the monastery. The walls were made to fall by tunneling through the mounds and under the walls causing them to collapse." Gidon said.

"Yes, but it was not just the tunneling but the fact fires were set in the tunnels under the walls, weakening even the fill stones between walls." Gid-visu said.

"If you two do not quit talking I shall never finish telling of it," the Baron said. Both apologized and bid him go on.

"Though her people were known for their stone battle axes, the sling men in the army were beyond compare. One of the slingers put a stone over the great distance between the wall and struck the head of King Gregor II's horse. The animal dropped and was immediately dead, trapping the king's leg under him. When those in the castle saw what had happened the gate was opened and a large number of men wielding battle axes sallied forth intent on taking the king prisoner if they could. Otherwise they would simply kill him.

"Your father rode to where the king lay trapped under his horse and pulled the king's large twohanded sword from under the dead animal. Then he stood over the king and began to cut men to pieces with that sword making wide swings all around until others could free his trapped leg. Then he gathered such men who had come to the fight and drove the queen's men back into the castle. Men lay cut and chopped to pieces everywhere." The Baron was getting expressive with the telling of the thing but Gid-visu was grimacing more and more with the memory.

"King Gregor II had a ceremony on the battlefield where he named him Master of the Two-Handed Sword and presented to him the weapon with which he had defended the king's life." The Baron ceased speaking.

"Then that is the two-handed sword which hangs in the reception hall at Fox Home?" asked Gidon.

"It is the very same," answered Gid-visu. "I treasure it not because of the day but because of the fact it was a gift of the king."

"So, when was the second time you saved King Gregor II's life in battle?" Gidon asked.

"My god boy, do you not ever let up?" The Baron exclaimed.

Gid-visu offered his opinion that the second instance could hardly be called a battle. It was more like a covert strike of archers while the army was on the move.

"I have said before and I say again that I have long awaited answer to the question of your relation with the king. Who knows if I will ever get this chance again? It sometimes seems to me everyone knows more about my father than I do." Gidon was determined this chance to learn about his greatly loved and admired poppa would not pass.

Gid-visu chose to answer the question instead of allowing the Baron to tell it. He said, "We were on a march to engage Goraleck. We were coming down on a broad field with forest on either side. King Gregor II intended to engage Goraleck in battle on that field but there was no sign yet of his forces. The king led us out onto the eastern edge of the field trying to decide if he should go further since Goraleck had not appeared.

"Just as the king made the decision to proceed, dozens of arrows flew out from the forest on the side closest to the king. His horse was struck and began to pitch and buck wildly. The horses' pain was probably keeping the bowmen from finding their mark. It seemed quite plain that if something were not done they would eventually find their target. It was then I rode my horse between the king and the bowmen in the trees. That was about it."

The Baron said, "You see how this man does? He only gives you part of the story and calls it all there is. What he did not tell you was that he not only rode his horse between the bowmen and the king, he got hit with two arrows. The first got him in the big muscle of his upper leg and the second cut through his armor and traveled along-side his ribs."

Gidon now knew the source of two prominent scars his father carried. He had seen them often when in the sauna or bathing room. He also vaguely remembered the year his father came home in the Fall walking with a limp. He was quite little then.

But what of the other scars on his father's body? They were stories yet untold. Remains of battles he did not care to relive. Gidon could understand that since he already had gained three scars, two on his face and one on his side this summer. None of them evoked pleasant memories or spoke of the glorious feelings of battle he had heard minstrels sing of. Wars were deadly, dirty, bloody work no matter how righteous the cause.

*****

When the women arrived at the campsite, made when the little force had set out on the rescue mission, they found an ugly one-eyed man who wore a wrap around his forehead at an angle to cover the bad eye. They had not met him but had certainly heard enough of him. When he learned these women also belonged to Squire Gidon he sought to ingratiate himself with them offering to do anything they might require because of his good friend Gidon. The friction between Herman One Eye and Herman Reformierte was both palpable and instantaneous. Brynhild stopped the initial confrontation by warning her man he better not get into any trouble that would keep them from keeping their appointment come the night. That settled that.

The valuables of Princess Loretta and Lady Dolores were transferred to Gidon's wagon, along with one of Gidon's shares of the spoil. This was done with the help of Herman Stellwagen and a couple of able-bodied men. Once that was done the Lady Dolores began to work her thoughts toward the composition of a letter to Gidon's Mistress Getrudis. She was keenly aware that doing her job well could impact all their relationships for years to come.

She knew that it was to her shame that she was not dedicated as she ought to be to the worship of the Invisible God and thus did not pray as she should. So this time when she bowed her head in prayer and sought His help in these matters it seemed right to be completely honest and acknowledge to Him her shortcomings. Within her heart she knew He heard.

Chapter 30

The King Cometh

There was a unique unity and bonded purity in the women the Invisible God allowed to come into Gidon of Eastwatch's life. For instance, at the very same time Lady Dolores was in prayer for guidance in communicating with Getrudis, the Mistress of Gidon had gone to prayer with the ladies of Fox Home for the safety of not only their men but the relationships with those they had been blessed with.

An observer might have noted a very strange thing in the actions of one sabretooth tiger who had bonded his association with Gidon in front of the monastery many days before. As the women gathered and kneeled in prayer, using the bed of Gidon and Getrudis for a prayer bench, the old cat had set on his haunches placing his forefeet on the bed in imitation of the women. At least we would call it imitation. For while animals do possess a spirit, it is well recognized humanity is singular among earthly creations in possessing a soul. It was the uniqueness of the soul in man that conformed him in Creation to the image of the Invisible God. Or so the Bishop Elisha had tried to explain to students such as Gidon and young priests alike.

Lady Dolores, continuing in an attitude of prayer, composed the letter to be sent representative of the Princess Loretta and herself. The message was short yet spoke volumes concerning their attitude toward the man they owed their very lives to.

"To: Mistress Getrudis, ruler of the heart of Squire Gidon von Eastwatch by the Rising of the Little Dan.

And, to Lady Gwynedd of Eastwatch Keep, beloved wife of Baron von Krieg, King's Rider and most gallant servant of the Invisible God.

And, also to Mistress Brunhild, Mistress of Fox Home, and our lord Gid-visu, who longs to overcome all obstacles barring his return to your noble person.

From: The Princess Loretta of Andorra, now in exile to your fair shores, and The Lady Dolores, chaperone to Princess Loretta,

Greetings to you, in the Name of the Invisible God, who rules over all.

It is with great joy we write to you in respect to those men you hold dear to tell you of the valor and honor of these men. In all the time we have known them they have behaved with the utmost gallantry, valor, and honor in all things. It is with a firm hope we desire to continue our association with them and become fast friends and allies with the women they hold dear.

We specially wish to mention to you, Mistress Getrudis, the great debt we owe Squire Gidon, who has accomplished our rescue not once but twice at great peril to himself.

In the first instance he accomplished our rescue singlehanded against many highwaymen.

In the second he rescued us at great peril with the help of Baron von Krieg and lord Gid-visu from a force of hundreds of the Peleset who have invaded your fatherland and our adopted land. Bishop Elisha can tell you more of the particulars.

We wish to mention to you in particular, Mistress Getrudis, how Squire Gidon had our persons totally dependent on him many days, and in all that time behaved himself with the highest standards of chivalry so that we came to admire him greatly and commit ourselves to his authority. We know so fine a man could have nothing less but the most noble and amazing Mistress, so we look forward to being your friend and more than a friend. Perhaps you would honor us by considering us sisters.

Master Gidon has spoken of you often and has great longing after you. No woman could be more finely blessed than to have such a noble heart joined with hers.

We send you our love and admiration, for we have seen with what esteem he holds you. And we understand you to be among the very finest of women upon this earth, and whose friendship we greatly desire.

Sealed with both the seals of Princess Loretta and Lady Dolores of the Andorrans.

*****

Outside the wagon in which the message was being composed the assembly of persons, wagons, and carts going to Eastwatch was being placed in order on one side of the roadway and the increased body of people, wagons, carts, and supplies going to Almanya was being organized facing in the opposite direction.

Beginning with the Baron, a number of people had expressed concern about the bishop having to pass by the den of thieves called a tavern on the way. Again and again, Bishop Elisha had reassured people that the den of thieves was no more, having been transformed by Baron Igil into a true place of refuge to the weary traveler. As usual, no one thought to question the source of the bishop's knowledge, everyone assuming he was being informed by the Invisible God.

When the entourage under the Baron von Krieg's command arrived and was again sorting itself out to proceed to Almanya, Herman One Eye was very eager to present himself to the Baron in the presence of Gid-visu and Gidon. He turned over what he called the King's Commission to the Baron with a very happy smile. In actuality what he bore was an order from the king that Herman One Eye should enter into service under the Baron for whatever purpose the Baron might desire.

This "commission" did not really change Herman One Eye's status from what it was when he was sent to escort the men to Almanya other than to guarantee him steady work. But since it pleased the one-eyed mountain of a man so much the Baron decided to play along with his ideas. He ordered the man that, as soon as he arrived at Eastwatch, he was to visit his wife at their hovel and then don a tunic with the king and Baron's ensigns upon it. It would be his job to visit each hovel and cottage where men had left their women and mothers to go to the muster. The Baron warned him, since he would bear on his person the insignia of both King Gregor II and the Baron of Eastwatch Keep, he should diligently be ever respectful of the king's subjects he was sent to assist.

The Baron gave Herman One Eye a pouch of coppers to fund his expenses, which he placed in his Geldbeutel intact in the separate pouch so he could keep up what he spent on the Baron's business. Anywhere he found a need, because of the absence of the men, he was to correct the problem, be it something in need of repair or some wrong needing to be righted. In the fulfillment of that duty, he was to give a full accounting by informing the Lady Gwynedd and Herr Brute' all he had done. The Baron remarked, after Herman One Eye had happily gone to supper, if he did what he had been instructed it would keep him busy for the bulk of the summer, meaning he should complete the work just in time to help his son, Wolfgang, with his own harvest. The men saw Herman's "commission" as both humorous yet capable of yielding some genuine benefit to the community.

Because of this "commission" Herman One Eye would emerge at the end of the summer a better man. He would have real friends in the Eastwatch region and gain respect from his wife he had never possessed before. It would have been possible for some scribe to write an accounting of the development of the relationship between Herman One Eye and his wife and the blessings that flowed from it in the few short years of their lives. But such things are generally lost to man and known only in the eternal records of the Invisible God.

*****

While things were getting organized, Brynhild, the new wife of Herman Reformierte came to call on Gidon's ladies at his wagon. She tried to observe the niceties of highborn etiquette but was so large a woman she could not help being a little clumsy even if she had known how to curtsy and phrase all the words deemed proper. And, because of her extremely isolated life before this, she did not. Princess Loretta received her, treating her attempt at doing things correctly as if she did not come short in any way. Once she would not have been at all tolerant of a so-called unrefined person in such a situation. She had become more accepting of individuals since her many trials and humbling experiences also made her infinitely more likable.

Ostensibly she had come to beg Squire Gidon's forgiveness. She had not considered her new husband was under the authority of Gidon and as such could not marry without his permission. It seemed, she said, the bishop had overlooked the matter also. Brynhild was also deeply concerned when one of the people told her, as she was coming down from the battlefield to this camp, Gidon would likely have wanted to exercise the Rechts des Herrn and he might be angry he was cheated out of it.

Princess Loretta said, "What is that?"

Lady Dolores said, "You know. We call it the *droit du seigneur* in Andorra but in the common tongue it is the lord's right to the first night."

For a brief moment Loretta was inclined to tease the poor woman. But since she had been genuinely disturbed about the matter, she told the woman, "I think that practice only applies when the bride is a virgin. You were a widow, am I not correct?"

The woman smiled and said, "Yes." For once she was glad for her widowhood. Even though, after observing Gidon's behavior toward people she did not think such an ordeal would be so difficult.

Lady Dolores said, "I do not think the right to the first night has been practiced in this country since before slavery was abolished. Whoever told you such a thing was having fun at your expense."

Princess Loretta then told her Gidon was a very good man and would never keep one of his retainers from marrying whom they would, seeing how much of a problem the subject of marriage could cause him with the king. "He will just want you and Herman to be happy."

Brynhild had but one more question, a very personal one. "I know neither of you are married to Gidon and both of you are high-born. Yet I have observed you serving and caring for him as if you two were his servants or perhaps even concubines. Is he going to marry one of you?"

Both women laughed. "No, he has a mistress, made his under the laws of heredity, so their children would not be bastards. We serve him because he is very good, and if he were to ask, we would willingly be his concubines. But he does not ask. We have pledged ourselves to him and now his mistress as well. That is a done thing, subject only to be changed by the king."

Brynhild said, "Since my new husband is one of his retainers and leader of some of the others, I suppose I will see you often. I hope you will not mind if I say that it would be pleasant if we are friendly."

Lady Dolores smiled and said, "We will be more than friendly. We shall be friends."

*****

One of the men left to guard the equipage beside the main road had killed a wild sow with six newborn piglets in the early morning of the same day Bishop Elisha and his caravan arrived in late afternoon. She had been drawn by the food the men were preparing. The hunter and some friends had hung the sow to drain and put the various portions of the internal organs and intestines into pots. But then they had been distracted from processing the food by their duty.

When the bishop arrived with Brynhild she had taken notice of the meat badly needing attention. After her visit to Gidon's Princess and Lady, she approached the hunter who had gotten the meat with an offer. She told him she was very good at both cooking and preparing the other parts of porkers so she would take care of everything if allowed to have the piglets. To this the man readily agreed. Being village bred he did not relish the business of working on the animal. In Eastwatch this was generally entrusted to the butcher as part of his trade.

She put her new husband to work building two makeshift ovens to her specifications. One was to cook the sow and the other was for the piglets. To other men she gave orders, demanding every time they were not to linger, for it was getting darker. She made inquiries concerning what seasoning was on hand and most of it came from Herman Stellwagen who knew everything that was on board Gidon's wagon. As soon as the sow's oven was at proper temperature the ribs were split and put inside after being basted with apple vinegar.

Brynhild would let no one else do the work of cleaning the intestines, insisting they must be absolutely clean. From somewhere she procured a bit of goat and put a man to grinding it and selected portions of the sow into one common mound of course ground meat. She expressed great pleasure at the discovery of coriander, marjoram, and salt among the supplies from the wagon to which she added a measure of wine and a wild onion that grew in the region. She then had the same man who had been working the meat start working the ingredients together until they were thoroughly mixed. When all was in readiness the ingredients were stuffed into the now clean intestines. Brynhild said, "It will not be the best bratwurst I ever made but I daresay no one will refuse their portion."

The hams, turning on a spit soon began to be carved to go with pieces of Landesbrot and cheese. Still later that night the ribs, which had been cooked slowly with its vinegar basting, also satisfied the many appetites. Princess Loretta and her Lady feasted on a piglet while Brynhild and her Herman enjoyed another. Brynhild even made peace between her Herman and Herman One Eye by presenting him with his own piglet. And yet there was bratwurst, enough for all to have a bit, at breakfast. Brynhild was a woman who knew how to multiply the food at hand.

When all had been fed Brynhild reminded Herman Reformierte they had an appointment to keep, but first she must go to the creek and cleanse herself of the consequences of processing the sow and piglets. Herman Reformierte picked up a groundsheet and dutifully, and even a little bit happily, followed her to the creek where she stripped off her clothes to wash them and herself.

Herman stared at her in awe, amazed such a woman would be his wife. She appeared in the moonlight fully as tall as his self. On their wedding night he had not seen her unclothed as she now appeared. Even though she had already given birth to one child, now sleeping under the princess' wagon, she had none of the softness of abdomen or breast such events normally produce. Her entire body seemed a large curvaceous perfection. She was not only named for a shieldmaiden but appeared the very essence of what shieldmaidens were imagined to be. He blessed God for the day he met Gidon, even if he did later shoot him with an arrow! It had proven worth it!

*****

When the three leaders of what had been the battle alliance arrived, the men having resumed the roles of Baron and squire, along with the Master of Fox Home, found a treat waiting in the form of piglets prepared by Brynhild. The Baron remarked to Gid-visu that if she could prepare so good a piglet under these conditions, she should certainly make a good cook in the new projects proposed. Gidon thought to himself that this would mean he would lose Herman Reformierte as well when that day came. And just when he was on his way to being a very useful asset.

It was not so difficult preparing each group to travel in the appropriate direction as it was organizing that travel. Placement of peoples and vehicles would affect how smoothly and compactly each convoy, called a geleit in the ancient tongue, would travel. And as the name implied, the purpose of that organization was the protection and intactness of the whole so the escorts would have less trouble keeping thieves along the way from slipping among the vehicles, not to mention organized bands of robbers.

Even as things were, there would be a painful and completely unnecessary lesson taught the travelers of the group heading to Eastwatch. In the hurry to load a wagon with military equipment armor and swords, these things had been deposited in the bottom of a wagon by a lad wanting the job of driving the vehicle on the journey. He thought the duty as driver would make his travel easier so he claimed skill he did not possess.

Then when spears were brought to him to load on the cart, instead of taking the armor out and placing the spears on the bottom he just piled them into the cart with the spear tips facing in the direction of the journey. He put a couple of ropes over the load so nothing would fall off the sides and considered the job done. His error of lading was missed in the inspection before wheels began to roll.

The group had not traveled far till his inexperience as a driver caught up with him. He sunk a wheel into a hole in the ground tilting the load forward toward the driver's bench and the young driver. Then the load of spears shifted forward sliding easily across metal armor. The fellow was simultaneously impaled by a number of spears painfully extinguishing his short life. Because of his folly a lot of time was lost. While some buried him in an unmarked grave on the side of the road, his wagon was unloaded and re-laded properly. Then his duty as a driver was given to a man not only more capable but also more modest. And even the young man's name was forgotten even as his folly became a hard joke.

Bishop Elisha brought his group out on the roadway and headed south before those bound for Almanya resumed their journey. It would turn out that by the time, several days later, they reached the Y intersection whose left fork would take them to Eastwatch, they would find a cobbled road had been constructed taking them all the way home. The men who had come there to make war and stayed to build had displayed a mind to work. In the irony of events, the bishop they once were sent to kill conducted holy worship for them and rested among them that night before going on down to Eastwatch.

*****

When the journey to Almanya was resumed the air was very somber. No doubt the men going to the muster were thinking on the days of hard training ahead. Even Gidon had concerns he might not measure up to the expectations so many had of him, beginning with those of his father and the Baron. He certainly did not want to come home in some disgrace to be diminished in Getrudis eyes. You might well think after so many varied adventures compacted into such a short period of time, he would have no doubts in himself. But blind assurance has never been the case with men who achieve great things, no matter what façade they show the world.

Princess Loretta and Lady Dolores were very much afraid. The princess had been sent as a potential candidate for marriage to King Gregor II. But it had been a very slim possibility from the outset. The problem was that even if the king rejected her, he still had power over her person, for she could not return to her own land and live. Both women had hoped for a measure of security in swearing themselves to Gidon for whom they had strong affection that was more than just tender attachment. Though by Andorran royal standards he was a bit uncouth, they had learned he possessed true nobility in thought and deed. But the bond they had with him the king could take away with but a word.

Baron von Krieg had already seen more of this world than he wanted or desired. Even so he had expanding goals, the greatest of which was to get back to his sweet Gwynedd. He had no illusions that she would not be greatly challenged by her increased status and responsibilities as the Lady of Eastwatch Keep. The Baron did not want her worn down by these things so he was anxious to get back to her and turn the responsibility into the joy of creating something new and good. Also, the idea of spending time working with his friend Brute' was something he looked forward to. Once they had tried to kill each other on the field of battle and now they were joined in an endeavor to protect not only king and country but also the faith in the Invisible God.

Gid-visu longed for nothing so much as Brunhild. He could imagine her ruling Fox Home with the wisdom that seemed so inherent in her. She acted so people did not know they were being commanded but only thought of themselves as being guided. She would become more motherly toward all as her body swelled with the child she would bring into the world as her gift of love to Gid-visu. To him it would not matter if that child was boy or girl. In either case it would bear the signature of both of the lovers woven together in the love knot that was a wonderful child. He wanted to speak and sing to it even as it lay in the womb, a pleasure he had been denied when Gidon was forming, and one he took too lightly three hundred years earlier. He had to get home!

Brynhild, of all the people going to Almanya, was not filled with heavy concern, for she had achieved her greatest goal. She had a man that seemed to be walking in what the hill people called der Weg des Segens, known in the common tongue as the path of blessing. Through him she hoped her son might have a better life than any he might have known living very remotely as they had. And it seemed that his master was also pleased with her and that could not hurt future prospects. The sun shone bright above, and the future appeared to shine equally so.

It was the last night the little group expected to spend on the road that proved so hard for the Princess, the Lady, and Gidon. Gid-visu, noticing the somber mood, especially in his son Gidon, ordered the tent from the wagon erected. He told the group this was the night they would be entertained by ghost stories and the like. Gidon was very interested in this because he had never heard his father tell such tales or even show any desire to listen to them.

So, a fire was kindled outside the tent and a number of people gathered around to hear the ghost stories.

Gid-visu told the story of the wild huntsman who haunted a particular stretch of road. People walking down this road at night would hear a voice from out of nowhere saying, "Stay in the middle of the road." One night a local man who knew the stories of the wild huntsman, but cared for nothing when he was drunk, was walking down the road staggering from side to side. He heard the voice from nowhere saying, "Stay in the middle of the road." The man replied to the voice with great sarcasm, "How can a man stay in the middle of the road when it is not steady in one place under drunken feet?" In the early hours of the morning the drunken man's wife heard a clump sound at the door to their hovel. She said to herself, "My husband is drunk again. I will let him sleep it off outside the house." In the morning she opened the door expecting to find her drunken husband but all she found was his feet and a pouch of gold with enough coin to have her home fixed where she could live comfortably the rest of her life without a drunken husband.

The Baron told another story of a wild huntsman ghost who was known to inhabit a certain region. One day a poor old woman took her produce to a nearby town. Her practice was to sell what she had and use the proceeds to get fine pieces of pottery she then sold in her village. In this way she supported herself. On this particular trip she had done well at her business, but the sales came later in the day than usual. It was already quite late when she was able to buy the pottery for selling back home. Since the business left her no extra money for sleeping in an inn, and she feared sleeping on the street, she started home even though it was already dark. Her first awareness that the wild huntsman was riding that night was when she heard a hunting horn and the baying of hounds that sounded like they came from out of the deep. The old woman began to hurry along the road, walking at a very fast pace.

Then she heard the sound of galloping horses' hooves coming up behind and she began to run as fast as she could. She had just come to the fork in the road where people said many strange things were seen at night when she stumbled and fell. From the sound when her bag hit the ground, she knew all her pottery was broken. Then two strong hands took hold of her shoulders and lifted her into a sitting position.

A voice said, "Old woman, why are you running so fast?"

She replied, "I feared the wild huntsman was hunting me, and now I have broken my pottery and shall starve this winter."

The man whose figure she could barely make out picked up her bag saying, "Your pottery is still intact. Walk home carefully for there are many dangers."

She took her bag of pottery, thanking the man but not believing her pottery unbroken. When she got to her hovel, she laid the bag on the table and the sound she heard convinced her again that pottery was broken, so she fell on her cot and cried herself to sleep. In the morning when she awoke, she looked into her bag to see if a single piece had survived. All her pottery was intact and scattered in the bag were so many gold coins she never had to make the long journey to the town again.

Then one of the fighting priests stood to tell the story of the lazy and ungodly monk consigned to haunt his monastery. It seemed there was once a monk who was not only lazy but also very ungodly. His father had gotten him into the holy orders because he was too lazy to work. He was even so lazy he would not find a rich woman to woo so that his future might be secured through an advantageous marriage. He was content to let each day pass, not caring about tomorrow. He continued his lazy practices even after becoming a monk. He would not even make his bed or clean his cell. It was observed that when the other monks were at prayer, he was even too lazy to move his lips in pretense of prayer. One night it was his job to keep candles burning before the altar through the night, but he was so lazy he fell asleep on the church floor. When he awoke, he found that he had become stuck to the floor and could not rise up from it. Anywhere his bare skin had touched the floor he was not able to remove himself.

So he was stuck to the floor by cheek, hand, and ankle. Many proclaimed it a judgment on his laziness and a warning to others. The priests discussed whether to cut off the hand and ankle but that would not solve the problem of his face being attached to the floor as well. Finally, after many days of discomfort, the lazy monk died and immediately became unstuck from the floor. Forever after in that monastery any monk who left his cell with cot unmade or floor dirty would return to find his blanket in the floor lying on human waste. And any time a candle would be low before the altar at night the person assigned to care for the altar would get a hard jab to the ribs from out of nowhere.

Lady Dolores was not to be outdone when it came to ghost stories. She told the story of the cowardly Andorran knight who haunts the forests bordering her country. It occurred when Hannibal crossed the Pyrenees after landing troops at the Port of Empuries and crossing north Catalonia, going up the Segre River to invade Andorra. The king of the Andorrans said he could not cross for he had not asked permission. In truth they feared so mighty a foreign army in their land. For that reason, the king sent all his army out to oppose Hannibal. But one knight, in an act of cowardice, fled with his men into the forests south of Andorra expecting the kingdom would be overthrown by Hannibal. So great was his flight he became separated from his men and even lost his helm. This knight had kept his hair very long and was vain about his appearance but in the flight his face was cut and badly disfigured by all the branches and thorns he encountered till finally his long hair became entangled in the trees. His horse ran out from under him and he was suspended with his armor pulling the hair so tightly he could not move to free himself. After many days some of his men found him and in the hopes of being reconciled to the king, they set him on fire. They burned the knight even as he still hung from the tree. Since then the cowardly knight had often appeared to men at arms when they were most afraid, still burning with an eerie fire and warning against fleeing in the face of the enemy.

Gidon was asked to tell a ghost story as well but he begged off saying he did not know any. The truth was his heart was so full he could not focus on getting a story together where he could tell it. Brynhild began to realize there was not much emphasis put on one's social class among these people. She did not know people like the Baron, Gid-visu, and Gidon had all climbed higher than the place in society to which they were born. But seeing an opportunity to entertain the group and fit in she declared she had a story to tell but was not sure it fit in as a ghost story. The group told her that anything that amused the group fit in and begged she tell her story.

Brynhild said the story was one told up in the mountains from where she came. It seems that up there were many trolls who live in caves and often men gained access to them through hollow trees. While the natural form of a troll was ugly and misshapen, they could appear just like other people and were only identified by their actions. Many years ago, some people near her home were going to build a chapel but things kept happening so each attempt was destroyed before it was finished.

Finally a chapel bell arrived, but there was no belfry in which to hang it. As a temporary remedy, the people constructed a frame on which they hung the bell and began to ring it continuously to drive out trolls. It was commonly known trolls hate church bells. A man named Rolf saw a woman hurrying away into the deep forest, where normal women do not go, so he followed her. He observed her flee into a hollow tree and he went to the tree and began to cut it down with his axe. The woman came out from someplace behind him and began to beg him not to cut down the entrance to her home.

He said, "What will you give me if I do not cut it down?"

She said that he could possess her body.

Then he told her, "I know you, that you are a troll. If I were to seek to possess you, then you would eat me."

She then offered him a great pouch of gold but only on the condition he told no one of her and her home and would not come again for more. But Rolf was careless with his money and with his tongue. Because he did not keep his word his crops failed, his animals died, and all manner of evil befell his property. It was then he took his axe, deciding to go extort more gold from the female troll. When he got there, she did not respond to his call and when he went to chop down the tree a great big ugly troll appeared.

It said, "You have betrayed my daughter," and then it ate him. You should never make a bargain with a troll. You will always lose.

With that the party broke up and three people, two women and a man, clung together inside the tent, each filled with their own fear for tomorrow. Morning light came all too soon.

Gid-visu ordered that this time when the tent was struck the poles were bundled and tied down on top of the wagon driven by

Herman Stellwagen. Near the castle there would not be enough wood to be searching out poles for a tent.

After they started out, what Gid-visu had said became easily seen as correct. The land first became farms and hovels. Then as the tops of the castle began to appear in the distance, farms and forests gave way to wide fields on which armies could train and maneuver. The farther they progressed the more they saw of various groups such as lancers drilling and pike men marching and falling into various battle formations. It was a stirring sight to watch the banners and pennants flying in the breeze while below them men went through the paces of many kinds of maneuver. Most men from Eastwatch expected they would be joining in such groups within the next day.

Coming down the road toward them they could barely make out at first the flag and pennants that were testimony to the presence of the one responsible for the muster. Gid-visu dismounted his cart and walked forward to join Baron von Krieg and his son Squire Gidon, where they stood holding their horses. Behind them were Princess Loretta and Lady Dolores flanked by the fighting priests. The pike men of Eastwatch had run forward in their gold cloaks to stand behind them.

The men drew their swords and set the points into the ground before them. The group could now make out the figure of King Gregor II on his war steed with a strange man in a chariot beside him. He was followed by many men in shining armor.

The Baron said, "That will be Zauberer the Wise in the chariot. All down through the Baron's column went the word, "The King is Coming! The King is Coming!"

The Baron, Gid-visu and Gidon knelt behind their swords. The ladies went into deep curtsies and as one the gold cloaks of Eastwatch took a knee. They were all thrilled the king had come out to meet them and receive them unto himself.

I enjoyed your book. The wisdom of the father and friends was beyond their years. It was awesome how the characters worked together to accomplish their goals. The women were strong, supportive and worked well together. It was a good read. Looking forward to the next book!

—Lanelle Horton

ABOUT THE AUTHOR

Michael Lendon Ford was born when the joke between his father and mother was the advertisement of the Ford Motor Company, "There's a Ford in your future." His was a family that valued hard work, honesty, and dedication. But the heritage of those ideals had been hidden and eventually forgotten over the centuries.

The child, Michael, came under conviction concerning sin, and desperately asked Jesus to save him at the age of five. It was at that church in the Peach Orchard community of Macon, Georgia where he first met the prophecy preacher Ed Vallowe, and learned to play baseball.

When the family moved to a newly built community outside Robins Air Force Base, the young Michael became part of the Royal Ambassadors and was taught to box by men who had originally been part of the Army Air Corps. There he first heard the call to preach at the age of ten and met the famous oratorical preacher R. G. Lee. Dr. Lee gave him a booklet titled, "If I Were a Jew."

Deciding that being a preacher, with the Spirit's promise most he preached to would not hear was not a pleasant idea, he fled the call and prepared for the life of a soldier.

At Bremen High School, he discovered in their library a set of books detailing the major battles of the Civil War. And, after his expulsion for fighting, he discovered in the Buchanan High School library, a collection of old books with detailed information on the Crusades. Thus began a lifetime interest in history and Archaeology, as well as the usage of weapons throughout time.

As a young man he walked battlefields in Africa, Japan, and Europe, as well as the United States, wherever he was stationed, all in the study of the Art of War. He also had the privilege of learning from men knowledgeable in battlefield tactics.

In 1967, the Six-Day War was the cause of Michael's great awakening to where mankind was on God's timeline of human history. In 1969, he married the woman who is the love of his life, and in 1975, he began to preach.

He has often said, thinking he was fleeing from God, he was unknowingly, heading where God would have him serve. But as Jonah found out before him, rebellion extracts a high price.

It was as a member of the Messianic Association he learned about his family heritage from one of its past presidents, whose hobby was Onomatology. What he learned explained a lot of things about his life.

Perhaps you read this section expecting to read of awards, decorations, honors, and accomplishments. You could have been given boring lists of those things, which with the price of a cup of coffee, will buy you one. But I have written about the author of this book, who will one day kneel before his Maker as one who must give account. As soldiers who have gone before him, he will have no excuse, but will simply rely on the Salvation and Mercy of his LORD.